Billionaires: The Royal

MAISEY YATES

ABBY GREEN

OLIVIA GATES

MILLS & BOON

First Published in Great Britain 2019
By Mills & Boon, an imprint of HarperCollins *Publishers*
1 London Bridge Street, London, SE1 9GF

BILLIONAIRES: THE ROYAL © 2019 Harlequin Books S.A.

The Queen's New Year Secret © 2016 Maisey Yates
Awakened by Her Desert Captor © 2016 Abby Green
Twin Heirs to His Throne© 2016 Olivia Gate

ISBN: 978-0-263-27558-2

9-0519

MIX
Paper from
responsible sources
FSC® C007454

This book is produced from independently certified FSC™ paper to ensure responsible forest management.

For more information visit: www.harpercollins.co.uk/green

Printed and bound in Spain
by CPI, Barcelona

About the Authors

Maisey Yates is a *USA TODAY* bestselling author of more than thirty romance novels. She has a coffee habit she has no interest in kicking, and a slight Pinterest addiction. She lives with her husband and children in the Pacific Northwest. When Maisey isn't writing she can be found singing in the grocery store, shopping for shoes online and probably not doing dishes.

Che~~ck out her websi~~

I~~n~~ ~~her~~ ~~threw~~ in a very glamorous care~~er in fil~~m and TV—which really consisted of a lot of standing in the rain outside actors' trailers—to pursue her love of romance. After she'd bombarded Mills & Boon with manuscripts they kindly accepted one, and an author was born. She lives in Dublin, Ireland, and loves any excuse for distraction. Visit www.abby-green.com or e-mail abbygreenauthor@gmail.com

Olivia Gates has always pursued creative passions such as singing and handicrafts. She still does, but only one of her passions grew gratifying enough, consuming enough, to become an ongoing career—writing.

She is most fulfilled when she is creating worlds and conflicts for her characters, then exploring and untangling them bit by bit, sharing her protagonists' every heart-wrenching heartache and hope, their every heart-pounding doubt and trial, until she leads them to an indisputably earned and gloriously satisfying happy ending.

When she's not writing, she is a doctor, a wife to her ~~...~~ nt girl ~~...~~ at ww~~...~~

Billonaires
COLLECTION

January 2019

February 2019

March 2019

April 2019

May 2019

June 2019

THE QUEEN'S
NEW YEAR
SECRET

MAISEY YATES

To my husband.
This has been the best ten years of my life,
and I know the next ten will be even better

CHAPTER ONE

KAIROS LOOKED ACROSS the bar at the redheaded woman sitting there, her delicate fingertips stroking the stem of her glass, her eyes fixed on him. Her crimson lips were turned up into a smile, the invitation, silent but clear, ringing in the space between them.

She was beautiful. All lush curves and heat. She exuded desire, sexuality. It shimmered over her skin. There was nothing subtle or refined about her. Nothing coy or demure.

He could have her if he wanted. This was the most exclusive and private New Year's Eve party in Petras, and all of the guests would have been vetted carefully. There was no press in attendance. No secret gold diggers looking for a payout. He could have her, with no consequences.

She wouldn't care about the wedding ring on his finger.

He wasn't entirely certain why *he* cared about it anymore. He had no real relationship with his wife. She hadn't even touched him in weeks. Had barely spoken to him in months. Since Christmas she had been particularly cold. It was partly his fault, as she had overheard him saying unflattering things about the state of their

union to his younger brother. But it hadn't been anything that wasn't true. Hadn't been anything she didn't
already know.

Life would be simpler if he could have the redhead
for a night, and just forget about reality. But he didn't
want her. The simple, stark truth was as clear as it was
inconvenient.

His body wanted nothing to do with voluptuous red-
heads sitting in bars. It wanted nothing but the cool, blond
beauty of his wife, Tabitha. She was the only thing that
stoked his fantasies, the one who ignited his imagination.

Too bad the feeling wasn't mutual.

The redhead stood, abandoning her drink, crossing
the room and sauntering over to where he sat. The corner of her mouth quirked upward. "You're alone tonight,
King Kairos?"

Every night. "The queen wasn't in the mood to go out."

Those lips pursed into a pout. "Is that right?"

"Yes." A lie. He hadn't told Tabitha where he was
going tonight. In part, he supposed, to needle her. There
was a time when they would have been sure to put in
a public appearance during every holiday. When they
would have put on a show for the press, and possibly for
each other.

Tonight, he hadn't bothered to pretend.

The redhead leaned in, the cloud of perfume breaking
through his thoughts and drawing him back to the moment, her lips brushing against his ear, his shirt collar.
"I happen to know that our host has a room reserved for
guests who would like a bit more...*privacy.*"

There was no ambiguity in that statement.

"You are very bold," he said. "You know I'm married."

"True. But there are rumors about that. As I'm sure you know."

Her words stuck deep into his gut. If the cracks were evident to the public now...

"I have better things to do than read tabloid reports about my life." He *lived* his tragic marriage. He didn't want to read about it.

She laughed, a husky sound. "I don't. If you want a break from reality, I'm available for a few hours. We can bring in the New Year right."

A break from reality. He was tempted. Not physically. But in a strange, dark way that made his stomach twist, made him feel sick. It was down deep in the part of him that wanted to shake Tabitha's foundation. To make her see him differently. Not as a fixture in her life she could ignore if she wished. But as a man. A man who did not always behave. Who did not always keep his promises. Who would, perhaps, not always be there.

To see if she would react at all. If she cared.

Or if their relationship had well and truly died.

But he did nothing. Nothing but stand, moving away from the woman, and the temptation she represented. "Not tonight, I'm afraid."

She lifted her shoulder. "It could've been fun."

Fun. He wasn't sure he had any idea what that was. There was certainly nothing fun about his line of thinking. "I don't have fun. I have duty."

It wasn't even midnight, and he was ready to leave. Normally, his brother, Andres, would be here, more than willing to swoop in and collect the dejected woman, or any other women who might be hanging around eagerly searching for a *royally* good time.

But now, Andres was married. More than that, Andres

was in love. Something Kairos had never thought he'd see. His younger brother completely and totally bound to *one* woman.

Kairos's stomach burned as though there was acid resting in it. He walked out of the club, down the stairs and onto the street where his car was waiting. He got inside and ordered the driver to take him back to the palace. The car wound through the narrow streets, heading out of the city and back toward his home.

Another year come and gone. Another year with no heir. That was why he had commanded Andres to get married in the first place. He was facing the very real possibility that he and Tabitha would not be the ones producing the successor to the throne of Petras.

The duty might well fall to Andres and his wife, Zara.

Five years and he still had no child. Five years and all he had was a wife who might as well be standing on the other side of a chasm, even when they were in the same room.

The car pulled through the massive gates that stood before the palace, then slowly toward the main entrance. Kairos got out without waiting for the driver to assist him, storming inside and up the stairs. He could go to Tabitha's room. Could tell her it was time they tried again for a child. But he wasn't certain he could take her icy reception one more time.

When he was inside her body, pressed against her, skin to skin, it still felt as if she was a thousand miles away from him.

No, he had no desire to engage in that farce, even if it would end in an orgasm. For him.

He didn't want to go to bed yet either.

He made his way up the curved staircase and headed

down the hall toward his office. He would have a drink. Alone.

He pushed open the door and paused. The lights were off, and there was a fire going, casting an orange glow on the surroundings. Sitting in the wingback chair opposite his desk was his wife, her long, slender legs bared by her rather demure dress, her hands folded neatly in her lap. Her expression was neutral, unchanging even as he walked deeper into the room. She didn't smile. She gave almost no indication that she noticed his presence at all. Nothing beyond a slight flicker in her blue eyes, the vague arch of her brow.

The feeling that had been missing when the other woman had approached him tonight licked along his veins like a flame in the hearth. As though it had escaped, wrapping fiery tendrils around him.

He gritted his teeth against the sensation. Against the desire that burned out of his control.

"Were you out?" she asked, her tone as brittle as glass. Cold. Chilling the ardor that had momentarily overtaken him.

He moved toward the bar that was on the far wall. "Was I here, Tabitha?"

"I hardly scoured the castle for you. You may well have been holed up in one of the many stony nooks."

"If I was not here, or in my room, then it is safe to say that I was out." He picked up the bottle of scotch—already used this evening by his lovely intruder, clearly—and tipped it to the side, measuring a generous amount of liquid into his glass.

"Is that dry tone really necessary? If you were out, just say that you were out, Kairos." She paused then, her keen eyes landing at his neck. "What exactly were you *doing*?" Her tone had morphed from glass to iron in a matter of syllables.

"I was at a party. It is New Year's Eve. That is what people customarily do on the holiday."

"Since when do you go to parties?"

"All too frequently, and you typically accompany me."

"I meant, when do you go to parties for recreational reasons?" She looked down, her jaw clenched tight. "You didn't invite me."

"This wasn't official palace business."

"That is apparent," she said, standing suddenly, reaching out toward his desk and taking hold of the stack of papers that had been resting there, unnoticed by him until that moment.

"Are you angry because you wanted to come?" He had well and truly given up trying to figure his wife out.

"No," she said, "but I am slightly perturbed by the red smudge on your collar."

Were it not for years of practice controlling his responses to things, he might have cursed. He had not thought about the crimson lipstick being left behind after that brief contact. Instead, he stood, keeping his expression blank. "It's nothing."

"I'm sure it is," she said, her words steady, even. "Even if it *isn't* nothing it makes no difference to me."

He was surprised by the impact of that statement. By how hard it hit. He had known she felt that way, he had. It was evident in her every interaction with him. In the way she turned away when he tried to kiss her. In the way she shrank back when he approached her. She was indifferent to him at best, disgusted by him at worst. Of course she wouldn't care if he found solace in the arms of another woman. So long as he wasn't finding it with her. He imagined the only reason she had put up with his touch for so long was out of the hope for children. A hope that faded with each and every day.

She must have given up completely now. A fact he should have realized when she hadn't come to his bed at all in months.

He decided against defending himself. If she didn't care, there was no point discussing it.

"What exactly are you doing here?" he asked. "Drinking my scotch?"

"I have had a bit," she said, wobbling slightly. A break in her composure. Witnessing such a thing was a rarity. Tabitha was a study in control. She always had been. Even back all those years ago when she'd been nothing more than his PA.

"All you have to do is ask the servants and you can have alcohol sent to your own room."

"My own room." She laughed, an unsteady sound. "Sure. Next time I'll do that. But I was actually waiting for you."

"You could have called me."

"Would you have answered the phone?"

The only honest answer to that question wasn't a good one. The truth was, he often ignored phone calls from her when he was busy. They didn't have personal conversations. She never called just to hear his voice, or anything like that. As a result, ignoring her didn't seem all that personal. "I don't know."

She forced a small smile. "You probably wouldn't have."

"Well, I'm here now. What was so important that we had to deal with it near midnight?"

She thrust the papers out, in his direction. For the first

time in months, he saw emotion burning from his wife's eyes. "Legal documents."

He looked down at the stack of papers she was holding out, then back at her, unable to process why the hell she would be handing him paper at midnight on New Year's Eve. "Why?"

"Because. I want a divorce."

CHAPTER TWO

TABITHA FELT AS if she was speaking to Kairos from somewhere deep underwater. She imagined the alcohol had helped dull the sensation of the entire evening. From the moment she'd first walked into his empty office with papers in hand, everything had felt slightly surreal. After an hour of waiting for her husband to appear, she had opened a bottle of his favorite scotch and decided to help herself. That had continued as the hours passed.

Then, he had finally shown up, near midnight, an obvious lipstick stain on his collar.

In that moment, the alcohol had been necessary. Without it the impact of that particular blow might have been fatal. She wasn't a fool. She was, after all, in her husband's office, demanding a divorce. She knew their marriage was broken. Irrevocably. He had wanted one thing from her, one thing only, and she had failed to accomplish that task.

The farce was over. There was no point in continuing on.

But she had not expected this. Evidence that her ice block of a husband—dutiful, solicitous and never passionate—had been with someone else. *Recreationally*. For pleasure.

Do you honestly think he waits around when you re-fuse to admit him into your bed?

Her running inner monologue had teeth tonight. It was also right. She *had* thought that. She had imagined that he was as cold to everyone as he was to her. She had thought that he was—at the very least—a man of honor. She had been prepared to liberate him from her, to liberate them *both*. She hadn't truly believed that he was off playing the part of a single man while still bonded to her by matrimony.

As if your marriage is anything like a real one. As if those vows apply.

"You want a divorce?" The sharpness in his tone penetrated the softness surrounding her and brought her sharply into the moment.

"You heard me the first time."

"I do not understand," he said, his jaw clenched tight, his dark eyes blazing with the kind of emotion she had never seen before.

"You're not a stupid man, Kairos," she said, alcohol making her bold. "I think you know exactly what the words *I want a divorce* mean."

"I do not understand what they mean coming from your lips, Tabitha," he said, his tone uncompromising. "You are my wife. You made promises to me. We have an agreement."

"Yes," she said, "we do. It is not to love, honor and cherish, but rather to present a united front for the country and to produce children. I have been unable to conceive a child, as you are well aware. Why continue on? We aren't happy."

"Since when does happiness come into it?"

Her heart squeezed tight, as though he had grabbed

it in his large palm and wrapped his fingers around it. "Some people would say happiness has quite a bit to do with life."

"Those people are not the king and queen of a country. You have no right to leave me," he said, his teeth locked together, his dark eyes burning.

In that moment, it was as though the flame in his eyes met the alcohol in her system. And she exploded.

She reached down, grabbed the tumbler of scotch she'd been drinking from, picked it up and threw it as hard as she could. It missed Kairos neatly, smashing against the wall behind him and leaving a splatter of alcohol and glass behind.

He moved to the side, his expression fierce. "What the hell are you doing?"

She didn't know. She had never done anything like this in her life. She despised this kind of behavior. This emotional, passionate, *ridiculous* behavior. She prized control. That was one of the many reasons she had agreed to marry Kairos. To avoid things like this. She respected him, and—once upon a time—had even enjoyed his company. Their connection had been based on mutual respect, and yes, on his need to find a wife quickly. This kind of thing, shouting and throwing things, had never come into play.

But it was out of her control now. *She* was out of control.

"Oh," she said, feigning surprise, "you noticed me."

Before she could react, he closed the distance between them, wrapping his hand around her wrists and propelling them both backward until her butt connected with the edge of his desk. Rage radiated from him, his face, normally schooled into stone, telegraphing more emotion than she'd seen from him in the past five years.

"You have my attention. So, if that is the aim of this temper tantrum, consider it accomplished."

"This is not a tantrum," she said, her voice vibrating with anger. "This is the result of preparation, careful planning and no small amount of subterfuge. I went to a lawyer. These papers are real. These are not empty threats. This is my decision and it is made."

He reached up, grabbing hold of her chin, holding her face steady and forcing her to meet his gaze. "I was not aware that you had the authority to make decisions concerning both of us."

"That's the beauty of divorce, Kairos. It is an uncoupling. That means I'm free to make independent decisions now."

He reached behind her, gripping her hair, drawing her head back. "Forgive me, my queen, I was not aware that your position in this country superseded my own."

He had never spoken to her this way, had never before touched her like this. She should be angry. Enraged. What she experienced was a different kind of heat altogether. In the very beginning, the promise of this kind of flame had shimmered between them, but over the years it had cooled. To the point that she had been convinced that it had died out. Whatever potential there was had been doused entirely by years of indifference and distance. She had been wrong.

"I was not aware that you had become a dictator."

"Is it not my home? Are you not my wife?"

"Am I? In any meaningful way?" She reached up, grabbing hold of his shirt collar, her thumb resting against the red smudge that marred the white fabric. "This says differently." She pulled hard, the action popping the top button on the shirt, loosening the knot on his gray tie.

His lip curled, his hold on her tightening. "Is that what you think of me? You think that I was with another woman?"

"The evidence suggests her lips touched your shirt. I would assume they touched other places on your body."

"You think I am a man who would break his vows?" he asked, his voice a growl.

"How would I know? I don't even know you."

"You don't *know* me?" His voice was soft, and all the deadlier for it. "I am your husband."

"Are you? Forgive me. I thought you were simply my stud horse."

He released his hold on her hair, wrapping his arm around her waist and drawing her tightly against his body. He was hot. Hard. Everywhere. The realization caused her heart rate to go into overdrive, her eyes flying wide as she searched his gaze. He was aroused by this. By her. Her circumspect husband who barely made a ripple in the bedspread when he made love to her was aroused by *this*.

"And how can that be, *agape*? When you have not let me near you in almost three months?"

"Was it I who didn't let you near me, or was it you who didn't bother to come to me?"

"A man gets tired of bedding a martyr."

"A woman begins to feel the same," she said, clinging to her anger, trying to ensure that it outstripped the desire that was wrapping itself around her throat, choking her, taking control of her.

He rolled his hips forward, pressing his hardened length against her hip. "Do I feel like a martyr to you?"

"I've always imagined it's the bright future of Petras

glowing in your mind's eye that allows you to get it up when you're with me."

He curled the hand pressed onto her back into a fist, taking a handful of material into his grasp and tugging hard. She heard the fabric tear as cool air blew across her now bare back. "Yes," he said, the word dripping with poison. "I am so put upon. Clearly, the sight of your naked body does nothing for me." He pulled her dress down, baring her breasts, covered only by the thin, transparent lace of her bra. "Such a hardship."

He leaned in, tilting his head, pressing a hot, open-mouthed kiss to her neck, the contact so shocking, so unlike anything that had ever passed between them before, she couldn't hold back the sharp cry of shock and pleasure.

She planted her hands on his shoulders, pushing him away. "Who else have you done this with tonight? The woman with the red lipstick? Did you have her like this too? Am I benefiting from the education that she gave you?" He said nothing, he only looked at her, his dark eyes glittering. Her stomach twisted, pain, anger overtaking her. She grabbed hold of the knot on his tie, pulling hard until it came free. She tossed the scrap of silk onto the ground before grabbing hold of his shirt, wrenching it open, buttons scattering over the marble floor.

She stopped, looking at him, her breath coming in short, hard bursts. He was beautiful. He always had been. She'd been struck by his sheer masculine perfection from the moment she'd first seen him. So young, so foolish. Nineteen years old, away from home for the first time, and utterly taken with her new boss.

Of course, she had never imagined that a young American girl who had come to Petras on a study-abroad program would have a chance with the king of the nation.

Oddly, he was almost more compelling now, in this moment, than he'd been at the first. She had slept with this man for five years. Had seen him naked countless times. The mystery should have been gone. She knew they didn't light the sheets on fire, they never had. It was her, at least she imagined it was. He was her only lover, so she had no one else to compare it with.

Apparently, *he* went out and found women with red lipstick, and things were different. *He* was different.

Rage mingled with the sexual heat rioting through her.

She ran her hands over his chest, the heat of his muscle and skin burning her palms. She should be disgusted by him. She shouldn't want to touch him. Instead, she was insatiable for him. If he had been with another woman, then she would wipe her from his mind. Would erase her touch from his body with her own. She would do what she had not managed to do over the course of five years of marriage. She would make him crave her. Make him desire her.

And then she would leave him.

She leaned forward, parting her lips, scraping her teeth over his chin. He growled, pressing her up against the desk again, pushing her dress the rest of the way down her hips, allowing it to pool on the floor. She didn't recognize him in this moment, didn't recognize herself.

"Did you have someone else?" She asked the question through clenched teeth, as she worked the buckle on his belt, then set about to opening the closure on his dress pants.

He leaned in, claiming her mouth with his, the kiss violent, hard. Bruising. He forced her lips apart, his tongue sliding against hers as he claimed her, deep and uncompromising. She let the rage of the unanswered question simmer between them, stoking the flame of her desire.

He took hold of the front of her bra, pulling it down, revealing her breasts. He bent his head, taking one tightened bud into his mouth and sucking hard. She gasped, threading her fingers through his hair, holding him tightly against her. She wanted to punish him, for tonight, for the past five years. She didn't know what else to do but to punish him with her desire. Desire she had kept long hidden. Until tonight, they had never so much as yelled at one another. This was more passion than either of them had ever shown.

Perhaps it was the same for him. An outlet for his anger. A punishment. But it was one she would gladly allow herself to be subjected to. Because for all that she knew she would walk away from this damaged, destroyed, she knew that he would not walk away from it unscathed either.

He shifted, blazing a path between her breasts with the flat of his tongue, his teeth grazing her neck, her jaw, before he finally claimed her mouth again. He reached between them, freeing his erection, so hot and hard against her skin.

She planted her hands on his shoulders, pushing them beneath the fabric of his shirt, scraping her fingernails along his flesh, relishing the harsh sound that he made in response. He tightened his hold on her, setting her up on the surface of his desk, moving to stand between her spread thighs. He pressed his arousal against her slick, sensitive skin, still covered by her flimsy panties, rolling his hips, sending a shock wave of pleasure through her body.

"Answer me," she said, digging her fingernails more deeply into his shoulders.

He shifted, sliding his hands down beneath the fabric of her underwear, his fingertips grazing the sensitized bundle of nerves there. "You want to know if I did this to another woman?" His words were rough, jagged. He hooked his finger around the edge of her panties, drawing them to the side, pressing the head of his shaft to the entrance of her body. "You want to know if I did *this* with another woman?"

"Just answer the question," she hissed.

"I think you would have me either way."

Her face heated, humiliation pouring through her. He was right. In this moment, she would be hard-pressed to deny him or her body anything. "Is that why you won't tell me? For fear I'll turn you away?"

"I'm used to you turning me away, Tabitha. Why should I waste a moment of regret over it now?"

She slid her hands down his well-muscled back, cupping his ass. "You would regret this." She rolled her hips forward, taking him deeper inside her body, just another inch. "You would regret not finishing this."

"No," he said, and for a moment, her heart sank. For a moment, she thought he meant he would not regret losing out on this moment between them. For a moment, she thought that yet again, she was alone in what she was experiencing. "I was not with anyone else. I did not touch another woman. She propositioned me. She whispered in my ear. I said no."

Then he kissed her before driving deep into her body. She gasped, and he took advantage, tasting her deeply as he flexed his hips again, withdrawing slightly before seating himself fully inside her again.

A rough groan escaped her lips, white-hot pleasure streaking through her. She clung more tightly to him, wrapping her legs around his back, urging him on. Urging him to take it harder, faster. She had no patience. Had no more desire in her to cultivate an effort to take things slow, to practice restraint. There was nothing but him, nothing but this. Nothing but years of anger, frustration, being uncovered as their inhibitions were stripped away layer by layer, with each thrust of his body into hers.

A shudder wracked his large frame, pleasure stealing his control. She relished that. Took pride in it. But it wasn't enough. She wanted to give him pleasure, she absolutely did. Wanted him to think of this later, to regret all of the years when they didn't have this. To look back on this one moment and ache forever. For the rest of his days, no matter whom he married down the road. Whoever came after her, whether she bore children for him or not, Tabitha wanted him to always think of her.

But pleasure wasn't enough. She wanted to punish him too. She dug her fingernails deep into his skin and he growled, angling his head and biting her neck, the action not gentle at all, painful. He flexed his hips, his body making contact with that sensitive bundle of nerves, and she knew that he was trying to do the same to her that she was doing to him. As if she deserved his wrath. As if she deserved his belated, angry gift of pleasure. *He* was the one who had done this to them. This was his fault.

She tightened her grip on him, met his every thrust with a push from her own body, met his each and every growl with one of her own. She had been passive for too long. The perfect wife who could never be perfect enough. So why bother? Why not just break it all?

She closed her eyes tightly, fusing her lips to his, kissing him with all of the rage, desire and regret that she had inside of her, the action pushing them both over the edge. It had been so long. So very long. Not just since she had been with him, but since she had found pleasure in his arms. So many months of coming together when she was at the optimum place in her cycle, perfunctory couplings that meant nothing and felt like less than nothing.

This was different than anything that had come before it. He'd given her orgasms before, but nothing like this. Nothing this all-consuming. Nothing this altering. This devastating. This was like a completely different experience. She was falling in the dark with no way of knowing when she would hit the bottom. All she knew was that she would. And when she did, it would be painful beyond anything she had ever known before. But for now, she was simply falling, with him.

The last time. The last moment they would ever be together.

She wanted to weep. With the devastation of it. With the triumph of it. This was it for them. The final nail in the coffin of their marriage. How she desperately needed it. How she resented it. She wanted to transport herself somewhere in the future. Years from now, maybe. To a time when she'd already healed from the wounds that would be left behind after they separated. A moment in time when she would have already learned to be Just Tabitha again, and not Tabitha, Queen of Petras, wife of Kairos. But Tabitha, on her own.

At the same time, she wanted to stay in this moment. Forever. She wanted to hold on to him forever and never let go.

Which was why she needed to let go. She so badly needed to let go.

The pleasure stretched on, an onslaught of waves that never ceased and she couldn't catch her breath. Couldn't think beyond what he made her feel. It wasn't fair. It just wasn't fair. Why was this happening now? She had always believed this was there between them, that it could be unlocked, somehow, but they had never found it. Not until this moment. This very last moment.

Finally the storm subsided, leaving her spent, exhausted. Smashed against the rock. She was wrung out. She had nothing left in her to give. No more rage. No more desire. Nothing but an endless sadness for what her life had become. She looked at the man still holding her tightly. The man still inside her body. The man she had made vows to.

A man who was a stranger, half a decade after she'd first made love to him.

"I hate you," she said, the words a hoarse whisper that shocked even herself. A tear slid down her cheek and she didn't bother to wipe it away. "For every one of the past five years you have wasted, I hate you. For being my husband but never really being my husband. I hate you for that too. For not giving me a baby. For making me want you even when I hate you."

He pushed away from her, his gaze dark. "Let me guess, you hate me for that too."

"I do. But the good thing is, that after today, we won't have to see each other."

"Oh, I think not, *agape*. I think we will have to see each other a great many times after today. A royal divorce is going to be complicated. There will be press. There will be many days in court—"

"We signed a prenuptial agreement. I remember the

terms well. I don't get anything. That's fine. I've had quite enough from you."

He made no move to dress, made no move to collect her clothes. And he didn't look away as she bent to gather them, pulling them on as quickly as possible, internally shrinking away from his gaze. Finally, she was dressed. It was done. It was over.

She made her way toward the door on unsteady legs, everything inside her unsteady, rolling like the sea.

"Tabitha," he said, his voice rough, "I want you to know that I don't hate you."

"You don't?" She turned to face him, her eyes meeting with his unreadable face. As immovable as stone.

He shook his head slowly, his eyes never leaving hers. "No. I feel…" He paused for a moment. "I feel nothing."

She felt as though he had stabbed her directly in the heart. Anguish replaced any of the pleasure, any of the satisfaction that had been there before. He felt *nothing*. Even in this moment he felt nothing.

The rage was back then, spurring her on, keeping her from falling over. "You just screwed me on your desk," she said, "I would have thought that might have made you feel something."

She was all false bravado. It was either that or burst into tears.

His expression remained bland. "You're hardly the first woman I've had on a desk."

She swallowed hard, blinking back more tears. She had made the right choice. She knew she had. Had he yelled at her, had he screamed, had he said that he hated her too, she might have wondered. But those black, flat, soulless eyes didn't lie. He felt nothing. He was indifferent, even in this moment.

Tabitha had heard it said that hate was like murder. But she knew differently. It was indifference that killed. And with his, Kairos had left her mortally wounded.

"I wish you luck in your search for a more suitable wife, Your Highness," she said.

Then she walked out of the door, out of his life.

CHAPTER THREE

"WHERE IS YOUR WIFE, Kairos?"

Prince Andres, Kairos's younger reformed rake of a brother, walked into Kairos's office. There was still glass on the floor from where Tabitha had shattered it two days ago. Still a dark stain where the scotch had splashed itself over the wallpaper.

All of it shouted the story of what had happened the night Tabitha had left. At least, it shouted at Kairos. Every time he walked in.

It was nearly as loud as his damned conscience.

I feel nothing.

A lie. Of course it was a lie. She had stripped him down. Reduced him to nothing more than need, desperate, clawing need.

Another woman walking away from him. Threatening to leave him there alone. Empty. While his pride bled out of him, leaving him with nothing.

He couldn't allow that, not again. So he'd said he felt nothing. And now she was gone.

"Why? What have you heard?" Kairos asked, not bothering to explain the glass, even when Andres's eyes connected with the mess.

"Nothing much. Zara tells me Tabitha called to see if

I could find out if you were using your penthouse any-time soon. I wondered why on earth my brother's wife would be stooping to subterfuge to find out the actions of her own husband."

Kairos ground his teeth together, his eyes on the shards of glass.

I feel nothing for you.

If only that were true. He was…he didn't even know what to call the emotions rioting through him. Emotions were…weak and soft in his estimation, and that was not what he felt.

He was beyond rage. Beyond betrayal. She was his wife. He had brought her up from the lowest of positions, made her a queen, and she had the audacity to betray him.

"No explanation, Kairos?"

Kairos looked up at his brother. "She probably wants to go shopping without fear of retribution."

"Right. Are the coffers of Petras so empty she has to worry about your wrath? Or is her shoe closet merely so full."

Kairos had no idea what her closet looked like. He never looked farther than her bed when he was in her room. "She left me," he said, his tone hard, the words like acid on his tongue.

Andres had the decency to look shocked. Surprising, because Andres was rarely shocked and he was never decent. "Tabitha *left* you?"

"Yes," he ground out.

"Tabitha, who barely frowns in public for fear it might ignite a scandal?"

Kairos dragged his hand over his face. "That is the only Tabitha I know of."

"I don't believe it."

"Neither do I," Kairos said, his voice a growl.

He paced across the office, to the place where the remains of that glass of scotch rested. It reminded him of the remnants left behind after an accident on the highway. One of the many similarities the past few days bore to a car crash.

I hate you.

He closed his eyes against the pain that lashed at him. What had he done to make his wife hate him? Had he not given her everything?

A baby. She wanted a baby.

Yes, he had failed her there. But dammit all, he'd given her a *palace.* Some women couldn't be pleased.

"What the hell did you do?"

"I was perhaps too generous," Kairos said, his tone hard. "I gave her too much freedom. Perhaps the weight of her diamond-encrusted crown was a bit heavy."

"You don't know," Andres said, his tone incredulous.

"Of course I bloody don't. I had no idea she was unhappy." The lie was heavy on his chest.

You knew. You didn't know how to fix it.

"I know I haven't been married very long…"

"A week, Andres. If you begin handing out marital advice before the ink is dry on your license, I will reopen the dungeons just for you."

"Perhaps if you'd opened the dungeons for Tabitha she wouldn't have left you."

"I am not going to keep my own wife prisoner." But dear God, it was tempting.

Andres arched a brow. "That isn't what I meant."

Heat streaked along Kairos's veins, and he thought again of that last night here in his office. Of the way she'd felt in his arms. His cool ice queen suddenly transformed into a living flame...

I hate you.

"We do not have that sort of relationship," Kairos said, his voice stiff.

Andres chuckled, the sound grating against Kairos's nerves. "Maybe that's your problem."

"Everything is not about sex."

Andres shrugged. "It absolutely is. But you may cling to your illusions if you must."

"What do you want, Andres?"

"To see if you're okay."

He spread his arms wide. "Am I dead and buried?"

His brother arched a brow. "No. But your wife is gone."

Kairos gritted his teeth. "And?"

"Do you intend to get a new one?"

He would have to. There was no other alternative. Though the prospect filled him with nothing but dread. Still, even now, he wanted no one else. No one but Tabitha.

And now that he'd tasted the heat that had always shimmered between them as a tantalizing promise, never before fulfilled...

Forgetting her would not be so easy.

"I do not want a new one," he said.

"Then you have to go and claim the old one, I suppose."

Kairos offered his brother a glare. "Worry about your life, I'll worry about mine." He paused for a moment, staring again at that pile of broken glass. The only thing that remained of his marriage. "I will not hold her prisoner. If Tabitha wants a divorce, she can have her damn divorce."

* * *

Tabitha hadn't seen Kairos in four weeks. Four weeks of staring at blank spaces, eyes dry, unable to find any tears. She hadn't cried. Not since that single tear had fallen in his office. Not since she'd told him how much she hated him—and meant it—with every piece of herself. She had not cried.

Why would you cry for a husband that you hated? Why would you cry for a husband who felt nothing for you?

It made no sense. And so, she hadn't cried. Tabitha was nothing if not sensible. Even when she came to divorce, it seemed.

She was slightly less sensible when it came to other things. Which was why it had taken her a full week of being late for her to make her way to the doctor. She had no choice but to use the doctor she had always used. She didn't want to, didn't want to be at risk by going to a doctor who was employed by the royal family. But her only other alternative was going to one she had no relationship with. One she had no trust in at all. News of her and Kairos's divorce had already hit the papers, and it was headline news. If she went to an ob-gyn now, everything would explode. She couldn't risk it. So she was risking this. She swallowed hard, her hands shaking as she sat on the exam table. Her blood had already been drawn, and now she was just waiting for the results.

She had waited so long to come to the doctor because she was often late. Her period never started on time. For years upon years every time she had been late she'd held out hope. Hope that this time it wasn't just her cycle being fickle. Hope that it might actually be a baby.

It was never a baby. *Never.*

But it had been a full week, and still nothing. And she

couldn't overlook the fact that she and Kairos had had unprotected sex.

Nothing unusual there, though. They always had. For five years they'd had unprotected sex, and there had been no baby. The universe was not that cruel. How could God ignore her prayers for five long years, and answer them at the worst possible moment?

It couldn't be. It *couldn't* be.

For the first time, when the doctor walked back into the room, her expression unreadable, Tabitha hoped for the *no*. She needed it. Needed to hear that the test was negative.

She knew now that she couldn't live with Kairos. It was confirmed. She couldn't make it work with him. He didn't care for her. And she…she felt far too much for him. She could not live like that. She simply couldn't.

"Queen Tabitha," Dr. Anderson said, her words slow. "I had hoped that King Kairos might have accompanied you today."

"If you read the paper at all, then you know that he and I are going through a divorce. I saw no reason to include him in this visit." The doctor looked down and Tabitha's stomach sank. A *no* was an easy answer to give. A *no* certainly didn't require Kairos's presence.

"Yes, I do know about the divorce," the doctor said. "All members of royal staff had been briefed, of course."

"Then you know why he isn't here."

"Forgive me for asking, my queen," the doctor said. "But if you are in fact carrying a child, is it his?"

"If I am? You've seen the test results. Don't play this game with me. Do not play games with me. I've had enough."

"It's just that…"

"This is *my* test. It has nothing to do with him. My entire life does not revolve around *him*." Tabitha knew she was beginning to get a bit hysterical. "I left him. I left him so that he wasn't at the center of everything I did. We don't need to bring him into this."

"The test is positive, my queen. I feel that under other circumstances congratulations would be in order," Dr. Anderson said, her tone void of expression.

Before this, before the divorce proceedings, Dr. Anderson had always been friendly, warm. She was decidedly cool now.

A King Kairos loyalist, clearly. But Dr. Anderson didn't have to live with him.

"Oh." Tabitha felt light-headed. She felt like she was going to collapse. She was thankful for the table she was seated on. Had she been standing, she would have slipped from consciousness immediately.

"Based on the dates you have given me I would estimate that you are…"

"I know exactly how far along I am," Tabitha said.

Flashes of that night burst into her mind's eye. Kairos putting her up on the desk, thrusting into her hard and fast. Spilling himself inside of her as they both lost themselves to their pleasure. Yes, there was no doubt in her mind as to when she had conceived. January 1.

The beginning of the New Year. What was supposed to be the start of her new beginning.

And all she had was a chain shackling her to Kairos now that she had finally decided to walk out the door and take her freedom.

Of course this was happening now. When she'd released hold of her control. Her inhibitions. There were reasons she'd kept herself on a short leash for so many years. She'd always suspected she couldn't be trusted. That she would break things if she was ever allowed to act without careful thought and consideration.

She'd been right to distrust herself.

She balled her hands into fists and pressed them against her eyes.

"Are you all right?" Dr. Anderson asked.

"Does it look like I'm all right?" Tabitha asked.

"It's only that…*is* it the king's baby?"

Rage fired through Tabitha then. "It is *my* baby. That's about all I can process at the moment."

Dr. Anderson hesitated. "It's only that I want to be certain that I didn't overstep."

As those words left the doctor's mouth, the door to the exam room burst open. Tabitha looked up, her heart slamming hard against her sternum. There was Kairos. Standing in the doorway, looking like a fallen angel, rage emanating from him.

"Leave us," he said to the doctor.

"Of course, Your Highness."

The doctor scurried out of the room, eagerly doing Kairos's bidding. Tabitha could only sit there, dazed. She supposed that there was no such thing as doctor-patient confidentiality when the king was involved.

She turned to face her nearly ex-husband—who was looking at her as though she were the lowest and vilest of creatures. As if he had any right. As if he had the right to judge her. After what he had said. After what he had done.

"What's the matter, Kairos?" she asked, schooling her expression into one of absolute calm and stillness. It was her specialty. After years of hiding her true feelings behind a mask for public consumption, she went about it with as much ease as breathing.

"It seems I'm about to be a father." He moved nearer to her, his dark eyes blazing. Any blankness, any calm he had presented the night she had left him standing in his office was gone now. He was all emotion now. He was vibrating with it.

"You're making an awfully big assumption."

He slammed his hands down on the counter by the exam table. "Do not toy with me, Tabitha. We both know it's my child."

"Except that *you* don't. Because you can't know that. You haven't seen me in weeks. I didn't go to your bed for months before our last time together." Heartbreak made her cruel. She'd had no idea. She'd never been heartbroken before him.

"I am the only man you have ever been with. You and I both know that. You were a virgin when I had you the first time. I sincerely doubt you went out and found the first lover available to you just after leaving my arms."

She swallowed hard, her hands trembling. "You say that as though you know me. We both know that you don't. We both know that you feel nothing for me."

"In this moment, I find I feel quite a lot."

"I've only just found out. It isn't as though I was keeping a secret from you. Where exactly do you get off coming in here, playing the part of caveman?"

"You were going to keep it from me. The doctor called me. If you knew you were coming to the doctor to get a pregnancy test, why didn't you include me?"

"Because," she said, looking at the wall beyond him, "that's the beauty of divorce. I don't have to include you in my life. I get to go on as an individual. Not as one half of the world's most dysfunctional couple. I would have told you. I was hardly going to keep this from you. If for no other reason than that the press would never let me."

"How very honorable of you. You would let me in on my impending fatherhood based on what the media would allow you to keep secret. Tell me, would you allow them to announce it to me via headline?"

"That sounds about right considering the level of communication we've always had. Honestly, I haven't much noticed the absence of you in the past four weeks. It was pretty much standard to our entire marriage. Sex once a month with no talking in between."

"Still your poisonous tongue for a moment, my queen. We have a serious issue to deal with here."

"There is no *issue*," she said, her hand going protectively to her stomach. "And there is no *dealing* with it. What's done is done."

"What exactly did you think I was suggesting?" His dark features contorted with horror. With anger. "You cannot seriously think I would suggest you get rid of our child. Just because you and I are experiencing difficult circumstances at the moment—"

"No. That isn't what I thought you meant. And what do you mean difficult circumstances? We are not undergoing difficult circumstances. If anything, we're experiencing some of the best circumstances we've had in years. We aren't together anymore, Kairos. That's what we both need."

"Not now. There will be no discussion of it."

She stood up, feeling dizzy. "The hell there won't be. I am not your property. I can divorce you if I choose, discussion or not."

"Can you? I am king of Petras."

"And I am an American citizen."

"In addition to being a citizen of Petras."

"I will happily chuck my Petran passport into the river. As long as it will get you off my back."

"We are not having this discussion here," he said through clenched teeth. "Get dressed. We're leaving."

"I have a car."

"Oh, yes, my driver that you're still using. From the house that I own that you are currently living in."

"I will sort things out later," she said, stinging heat lashing her cheekbones. It was humiliating to have him bring up the fact she was dependent on him to not be homeless at the moment. Particularly since she had made such a big deal out of knowing she would get nothing from him after the divorce. But still, he wasn't using his apartment in town, nor was he using the car and driver that were headquartered there. So he could hardly deny her the use of them. Well, he *could*. But he wasn't, so she was taking advantage.

"Oh, I sent your driver home. The only driver currently here is mine. You are leaving with me. Now."

He stood there, his arms folded across his broad chest, his dark eyes glued to her.

"Don't look at me. I have to get dressed."

"It is nothing I haven't seen, *agape*."

She treated him to her iciest glare. "Rarely."

The biting word hung between them and she felt some guilt over it. Truly, the state of their sex life was partly her fault. If not mostly her fault. But having him touch her out of duty… It had certainly started to wear on her.

Eventually, it was just easier to lie back and think of Petras. To close her eyes and think of other things. Hope that it would be over quickly. To not allow herself to feel a connection with him. To shut walls around her heart, and around her body. The less she felt during sex, the less pain she felt when it was over. The less disappointment each time he got up and left immediately after, each time the pregnancy test was negative. The less distress she felt over the fact that any intimacy between them was all for the purpose of producing a child. That it was completely void of any kind of emotion between the two of them.

Yes, the fast, disappointing sex in the dark was mainly her fault.

"As you wish, my queen." He turned away from her, his broad back filling her vision. And, damn him, she felt bad. Guilty. He did *not* deserve her guilt.

She kept her eyes on him as she stripped off the hospital gown she was wearing. On the way the perfectly cut lines of his suit molded to his physique. He was a handsome man. There was no denying it. He was also a bastard.

She finished dressing, then cleared her throat.

Kairos turned, the fierceness in his expression wavering for a moment. An emotion there that she couldn't quite put a name to.

"Let's go," he said.

"Where are you taking me?"

"To the palace." He hesitated. "We have some things to discuss."

"I don't want to discuss this right now. I've only just found out I'm pregnant. I believe you had to know before I did."

"You at least had a suspicion."

"You think that makes it easier? Do you think that makes any of this…?" Her voice broke, her entire body shaking. "I should not be devastated in this moment. I hate you for this too. I was supposed to be happy when I finally conceived. You've stolen that for me."

"Who stole it, Tabitha? I was not the one who asked for a divorce."

"Maybe not. But you made your feelings for me perfectly clear. It's poison now, already working its way through my system. You can't fix it."

He said nothing as they walked out of the exam room and continued down the long vacant hallway toward a back entrance. His car was waiting there, not one driven by a chauffeur. One of his sports cars that he got great enjoyment out of driving.

He was a low-key man, her husband. Responsible, levelheaded. Serious.

But he liked cars. And he very much enjoyed driving them. Much too fast for her taste. But he never asked her opinion.

"I'm not especially in the mood to deal with your Formula 1 fantasies," she said, crossing her arms and tapping her foot, giving him her best withering expression.

"Funny. I'm not particularly in the mood to put up with your attitude, and yet, here we are."

"You have earned every bit of my attitude, Your Highness."

"So angry with me, Tabitha, when you spent so many years with so little to say."

"What *have* I said, my lord?"

He made a scoffing sound in the back of his throat. "My lord. As if you are ever so deferential."

She arched her brow. "As if you ever deserved it." She breezed past him and got inside the car, slamming the door shut behind her and setting about to buckling her seat belt while he got in and started the engine.

"What happened, Tabitha? *What happened?*"

"There was nothing. Like you said. Nothing. And I can't live that way anymore."

"You're having my baby. I don't see you have an option now. Clearly the divorce is off."

He revved the engine, pressing the gas and pulling the car away from the curb.

"The divorce is no such thing," she said, panic clawing at her insides. "The divorce is absolutely on. You might be royalty, but you can't pull endless weight with me. I am not simply another subject in your country. I have rights."

"Oh, really? And with what money will you hire a lawyer to defend those rights? Everything you have is mine, Tabitha, and we both know it."

"I will find a way." She didn't know if she would. He wasn't wrong. She was nothing. Nothing from nowhere. She had climbed her way up from the bottom. From a poor household on the wrong side of the tracks with parents who would spend every night screaming at each other, throwing things. Her mother hurling heavy objects at her stepfather's head whenever the mood struck her.

And that was before everything had gone horribly wrong.

There had been no money in her household. Not enough food. All there had been was anger. And that was an endless well. One that her parents drew from at every possible opportunity. That was her legacy. It was all she had. It was why she had vowed to find something different for herself. Something better.

What she had found was that sometimes everything that filled the quiet spaces, everything that went unsaid, was more cutting, more painful than a dinner plate being hurled at your head.

Kairos said nothing but simply kept driving. It took a while for her to realize they weren't heading back to the palace, but when she did, a cold sense of dread filled her. She realized then that she honestly couldn't predict what he might be doing. Because she didn't know him. Five years she had been married to this man and she knew even less about him today than she had on the day they had married. Impossible, seemingly.

She'd spent three years as his PA prior to them getting engaged and married. Three years where she had cultivated a silly, childish crush on him. He had smiled easier then, laughed with her sometimes.

But that was before his father had died. Before the weight of the nation had fallen on his shoulders. Before his arranged engagement was destroyed by his impetuous younger brother. Before he had been forced to take on a replacement wife that he had never wanted, much less loved.

Those years spent as his PA had been like standing on the outside of a forest. She had looked on him and thought, *I recognize him. He's a forest.* Being his wife was like walking through it. Discovering new dangers, discovering that it was so dark, she could barely see in front of her. Discovering she had no idea where the trees might end, and where she might find her freedom. Yes, the deeper she walked, the less she knew.

"You aren't planning on driving your car into a river or something dramatic, are you?" she asked, only half joking.

"Don't be silly. We spent years trying for an heir, I'm not going to compromise anything now that we have one on the way."

"Oh, but otherwise you would be aiming for a cliff. Good to know."

"And leave Andres to rule? Don't be ridiculous."

It occurred to her suddenly, exactly where they were heading. Unease stole over her, her scalp prickling. "What are you planning?"

"Me? Perhaps I'm not planning anything. Perhaps I'm being spontaneous."

"I don't believe that."

"You're so convinced that I don't know you, and yet, you think you know me, *agape*? How fair is that?"

She didn't think she knew him. But she wasn't about to admit that now. "You're a man, Kairos. Moreover, you're a distinctly predictable one."

"If I cared about your opinion at all I would be tempted to feel wounded. Alas, I don't."

He turned onto the private airfield used by the royal family and her heart sank. Her suspicions were very much confirmed. "What is it you think you're doing?"

"Oh, I don't think I'm doing anything. This is the situation, my darling bride, either you come with me now or we do this here in Petras."

"Do what, exactly?"

"Come to an agreement on exactly what we will do now that we are to be parents. And by come to an agreement, I mean what I will decide. Do not forget that I am the king. Whatever laws might govern the rest of the people do not apply to me."

Rage filled her, flooded her. "Since when? You've never been the most flexible of men, but you've never been a dictator."

"I've never been a father before either. Neither have

I ever been in the position of having my wife threaten to leave me."

"I didn't threaten to leave you, Kairos. I left you. There is a difference."

"Regardless. Come with me, and we will have a discussion. If you refuse, then I will ensure that I get full custody of our child, and you will never see him. I give you my word on that. And unlike you, when I make a vow, I keep it."

CHAPTER FOUR

KAIROS LOOKED AT his wife, who was seated across the cabin from him on his private plane. He had a feeling she was plotting his death. Fortunately, Tabitha was quite petite or he might harbor some concern over her having access to any cutlery. At this point, he doubted she would hesitate to attempt to take him out with her fork. In many ways, he couldn't blame her. But he had to guard his own self-interest, and guard it he would.

There was no room to be soft in this.

She was having his baby. An heir. *Finally.*

At any other time this would have been a cause for celebration. The completion of his duty in many ways. A fulfillment of deathbed promises made to a father he'd never quite pleased during his life.

The moment he'd found out, the only thought he had was how he could capture her. Keep her with him. He had no idea what he was going to do beyond that. But he had managed to get her on the plane, even though it had taken threats. Now, they were en route to his private island off the coast of Greece. The villa there had always been used by the royal family of Petras for vacations. Kairos had never taken Tabitha there. He had not been on a vacation since he had taken her as his wife.

Of course, this was no vacation. Some might call it a kidnapping. But he was king. So he imagined he could classify it as some kind of political detention. She was, after all, carrying the heir to the throne of Petras. If she were to leave, it would be kidnapping on her end.

At least, that's how he was justifying things. And he was king. The amount of people he had to justify his actions to was limited to one. Himself.

She didn't look angry. She looked as smooth and unruffled as ever. Her hands were folded in her lap, her legs crossed at the ankles, her lovely neck craned as she looked out the window. She managed to appear both neutral and haughty, a feat he had only ever seen managed by Tabitha.

Years of routine. A marriage so mundane he could go days without looking at her. Even if they were in the same room. He would look in her direction, but, he realized, never truly look at her. It was easy sometimes to go a full week without words passing directly between them. Communication with a phone or servant as the go-between.

And in the space of the past four weeks everything had changed. She had asked for a divorce. Then he'd torn her clothes off and taken her like a rutting animal. Now there was a baby.

The past four weeks contained more than the past half decade they'd spent as husband and wife. He was having a difficult time wrapping his head around it. Around who he had become in her arms in those moments in his office. He was angry. Enraged that she would walk away from him after all he had done for her. Enraged that half-formed fantasies he had barely let himself dream would never come to be.

He had imagined they would be married all of their lives. He had never imagined she would end it.

"Are you quite comfortable?" he asked, because he could think of nothing else to say and he had grown quite uncomfortable with his role as uncivilized beast and the little play they were currently acting out.

He was the responsible one. He'd never acted out, not once in his life. His father had impressed the weight of the crown upon him at an early age, and Kairos had always taken it seriously. He had seen the consequences of what happened when one did not. Had had it ingrained in him.

Control was everything. Duty. Honor. Sacrifice.

He was surprised how easily he had cast it off the moment his wife had handed him divorce papers.

And so, he was attempting to reclaim it.

As you kidnap her. Brilliant.

"Yes," she said, her tone brittle. "Very. But then, I don't have to tell you your private plane is luxurious. You already know."

"Indeed."

"How long had I been working for you the first time we flew on this plane?"

"A couple of months, surely," he said, as though he didn't remember it clearly. He did. There was something so charming and guileless about her reaction to the private aircraft. It had stood in stark contrast to the response of his fiancée at the time, Francesca.

He had noticed it then, as he compared the two women unfavorably. Francesca was, of course, eminently suitable to be a royal bride. That was why he had selected her. Love had never come into play. She had been raised in an aristocratic family, trained to be the wife of a political leader from an early age.

Of course, it had all blown up in his face when she had slept with his brother. That might not have bothered him so much, had she not done it quite so publicly. Not that she had intended for it to go public. Ruining her chances of becoming the queen of Petras had not been the plan. That much he knew. Still, a video had surfaced of the two of them together, and that did it for their wedding.

He needed to find a wife to fill in for the royal wedding that was already planned, and quickly. And so, he had selected Tabitha to be his bride. A logical decision. An acceptable flesh-and-blood woman.

Perhaps all women were destined to go crazy at some point in their lives. His mother certainly had. Walking out on her husband and children in the dead of night, never resurfacing again. Francesca most certainly had when she'd compromised her position as queen simply so she could experience some pleasure with Andres. Obviously, Tabitha was the newest victim of the craze.

Or maybe it's you.

He gritted his teeth.

"I was impressed with it then," she said. "I remain impressed. I am less impressed with the fact that you hijacked my person."

"It was a hard-line negotiation, not a hijacking. Surely you see the difference."

"The end result is the same to me, so why should I care about semantics?"

"You were quite impressed with the plane," he said, his voice hard, "as I recall."

"Don't tell me you remember."

"Of course I remember. You were very young. Wide-eyed about everything you encountered here in Petras. Especially everything concerning the royal family and the palace. I had a fair idea about your background, because of course I screened you before hiring you. I knew you came from a modest upbringing."

"That's a generous way of putting it."

"Impoverished, then. Yes, I knew. But you were bright, and you were certainly the best person for the job. You were motivated, in part because of your past. I thought, possibly more driven than any of the other candidates to succeed."

"Are these the same thoughts you had when you selected me to be your wife?"

He could sense the layers hidden beneath the question, but couldn't guess what they were. "I also knew you," he said.

She made a scoffing sound, uncrossed her legs, then recrossed them the opposite direction, annoyance emanating from her in a wave. "Oh. You *knew* me. As in, were acquainted with me. How very romantic."

"Did I ever promise you romance, Tabitha?" She said nothing, her glare glacial now. "No. I did not. I told you that I would stay faithful to you, and I have. I told you that I would be loyal to you, which I have also done. That I would do my duty to God, country and to you. I have done all of that, to a satisfactory degree, many would say. You were the one who decided it wasn't enough."

Righteous anger burned through him. He had not lied to her. He had not told her he would give hearts, flowers or any frilly symbol of weak emotion. He had pledged commitment.

She seemed to have no concept of that at all. He would never have taken her for being so faithless. He had thought she was like him. Had thought she was logical. Had thought that she understood sacrifice. That duty and honor superseded emotion.

"A theoretical marriage is a lot different than actual marriage. I can hardly be held to assumptions I made before I had ever had a…a relationship."

"Certainly you can. Everyone makes vows before they marry. For the most part, they have never made such vows before."

"And sometimes marriages end. Because in spite of the best intentions of everyone involved, things don't work out the way you thought they would."

"As I am also not a fortune-teller, I fail to see how I can be held accountable for not fulfilling needs you did not voice to me. In addition to not being able to see the future, I cannot read your mind."

"Even if you could, I can only imagine that you would find it unworthy of listening to."

"When exactly did you become such a pain?" he asked, not bothering to temper his anger. "You were not like this before we were married."

"That's because before we were married, you paid me to be your assistant. An assistant is not a wife."

"I was very clear when I proposed to you that this would not be a typical marriage. That it would in fact reflect some of the duties that you took on as an assistant."

"Well, maybe nothing changed, then. Nothing but me." She crossed her arms, closing herself off from conversation, and turned away from him.

He gritted his teeth, and determined that he would not speak to her again until they landed. Once they were on the island… He didn't know. But she wouldn't be able to escape him. Not until he allowed it.

If that was kidnapping, then so be it.

But he was not going to take the end of his marriage lying down. The sooner she realized that, the better.

CHAPTER FIVE

IT WAS STRANGE, landing on what you knew was your husband's private island, an island you had never been to before. He'd never brought her here, to this place, to this villa. It was incredible, like every property the Demetriou family owned. Just like the penthouse downtown that she was staying in while she avoided the reality of her life, just like the palace.

This was different. White walls, a red roof, placed on white sand in the middle of the blue, glittering bright sea. Like a beautiful piece of jewelry, perhaps part of the crown jewels. It was isolated, nothing like the palace, so filled with staff, tour groups and political leaders. Nothing like the penthouse, enveloped in the busy motion of the city.

She blinked against the sun, pale light washing over everything around them.

"Why don't you come in?"

She looked at Kairos, suddenly overcome by a sense of déjà vu. Of being in a new place with him, for the first time. That day she'd first walked into his office as his assistant.

"Come in. Sit down."

Tabitha shifted where she was standing, unable to de-

cide what exactly she should be staring at. At the most beautiful, opulent surroundings she had ever seen, or at the most blindingly handsome man she had ever laid eyes on.

She crossed the room, taking a seat across from him at his desk.

Tabitha was suddenly brought straight back into the present as she imagined that desk. The one they had conceived their baby on. Walking into his office that day, she never could have imagined that eight years later she would end up screwing him on it after asking him for a divorce.

She blinked against the stinging sensation in her eyes. They weren't tears. She was not going to cry any tears for him. For the man who didn't feel anything for her.

She followed him into the villa, unable to remain entirely unimpressed with her surroundings. She was used to opulence. She had spent years working with him in the palace prior to their marriage, and had had a good dose of exposure to it even before she herself was royalty. After nearly a decade in these kinds of settings she should be used to them.

But a small part of her was still very much that girl from the single-wide trailer, utterly unable to believe that she now rated entry into these sorts of places.

This—this small weakness for luxury—was the flaw in her armor. At least, the entry point by which to reach many of the others.

Everything in the room was white, large windows looking out over a lush garden, an infinity pool and beyond that the sea provided the only color. That was one of the first things she had noticed when she came to live in the palace. Even when she was simply in the apartments provided for her as an employee, the decor had been simple, but the quality unsurpassed.

It made her feel small and gauche to think of her observations now. The linens had been pure white, no pattern, or ornate embroidery to draw the eye. It was all in the feel of it. So soft it was like touching a cloud. Everything was like that. The tissues and the toilet paper even. Tiny pieces of luxury that added up to the kind of comfort she had never even imagined existed.

"My room is upstairs, at the end of the hall, feel free to choose whichever quarters suit you best."

She looked over at him, reminded yet again of that first meeting.

She had never seen an office quite like this. And she had never seen a man quite like him. When she entered the prestigious university that was currently facilitating this study-abroad program she'd been exposed to a higher class of people, a higher class of living than ever before. But this was somewhere far beyond that.

For one thing, he was a prince. No matter how blue the blood, that placed him several rungs higher on the social ladder than any of the old-money Americans she'd encountered. For another, he was unlike any of the other men she interacted with at university. He was a man, a real man, for a start, not a boy barely edging into his twenties.

In his perfectly cut custom suit he was daunting to say the least. Add the fact that his face was objectively the most beautiful masculine work of art she'd ever seen, and she found herself unable to speak. That never happened. She'd learned early on that if she wanted to im-

prove her position in life she would have to attack her goals with single-mindedness. She could never afford to look like she didn't belong, because people would be all too willing to believe her. So she had cultivated confidence from the beginning.

It deserted her then. All her words drying up completely.

"It's nice to meet you," he said, not offering her his hand, but rather a simple incline of his head. "I have read your file, and taken the recommendation of my advisor into consideration. However, I did not follow the advice. I merely took it under consideration."

She frowned, not entirely sure what to make of the comment. "Really?"

"Yes. A fact you should be grateful for, as he felt you were a bit too pretty to serve my needs."

Her face burned. But it wasn't with anger, as it should have been. Well, there was a bit of anger, but also a wave of excitement that had no business being there. "I was not aware my looks had anything to do with whether or not I would be a qualified assistant."

"They don't. Not to me. Though, I imagine his concerns center squarely around my younger brother, Andres, not me."

She was well educated on the royal family. Applying for a job at the palace without proper knowledge would be foolish. She was well familiar with Prince Andres and his reputation with women. She was also immune to such things. She was focused. She'd been accused of having tunnel vision by people who were nice, and of being frigid by people who weren't. None of it bothered her. She had goals. And once she reached those goals she could ex-

pand her horizons. Until then, she would move on with a single-minded focus and make apologies to no one.

No, Prince Andres didn't concern her.

The fact that some of her focus had splintered the moment she'd seen Prince Kairos concerned her a little bit. But that was an anomaly. Nothing to be concerned about. She would be back to normal as soon as she became accustomed to him, to the surroundings. Assuming she had a chance to do so.

"There's no need to be concerned," she said.

"You haven't met him yet."

"I don't need to meet him. I have not gotten as far as I have in my life by being silly, or easily seduced by princes. I'm here because this is not the kind of work experience that can be matched. I'm here because of what this will do for my résumé in the future. I'm not here to become the subject of tabloid gossip."

He smiled and the expression echoed in her stomach. "Then congratulations. I would like to hire you." And there he stood, extending his hand.

She stood as well, wrapping her fingers firmly around his, ignoring the zip of heat that passed between them. She had just told him that she had no desire to become tabloid fodder, and she would not be undermined by betraying the fact that his touch affected her.

She buried it. Buried it down as deep as it would go.

"Excellent."

"Very. If you're ready, I can show you to your quarters."

"Do you need me to escort you?"

Tabitha blinked, coming back to the present sharply. "No. You can send my things up later. I'm assuming you had my things packed."

"No," he said. "However, your room should be stocked with all the amenities you might require."

"Translated into direct English, please, rather than your particular brand of doublespeak."

"I called ahead. Clothing, makeup and other toiletries should be delivered shortly. To the room of your choosing. There are no servants in residence at this house, that's part of the attraction to it."

"I wouldn't know, as this is the first time I've ever been here."

"I haven't been here since we were married, as you well know. I've been busy running the country."

"You're right. I am well aware."

She turned away from him then and walked up the stairs, acutely aware of his dark gaze following her every move. She didn't know why he should watch her with such attention now, when he had certainly never done so before.

She stiffened her posture and continued on, as though she were completely unaware of his attentions. She'd spent a very long time pretending she didn't notice how little he saw her. This should be no different.

She scoffed when she reached the landing and looked down the expansive corridor. There were a dozen rooms on this floor, at least. He had made it sound different somehow. Talking about his room being at the end of the hall, saying there were no servants in residence. Still, she should have known that his family owned nothing modest.

She selected the first door, if only because it would be the farthest away from him.

It was white like the rest of the rooms in the house. A four-poster bed was at the center, with gauzy, pale fabric draped over the carved wooden spires. The floor was marble with a plush rug at the center. The only color was provided by a jade vase positioned on a table set against the far wall, with bright cheery crimson flowers bursting from it. She wanted to take the vase, and the flowers, and hurl it to the ground.

Its very existence made her angry. As though it were trying to tell her she should be happy to be here. As though it were trying to prove that this was a wonderful, beautiful place.

Most of all, it made her furious because she had to wonder if this was the only room that contained flowers. If her husband had known she would choose this one because of its proximity, or lack thereof, to his room.

If he knew her so well, while not knowing her at all.

Suddenly, a wave of exhaustion washed over her. She was pregnant. Kairos had all but kidnapped her and brought her to an island. He wanted to negotiate, or terminate her parental rights.

She stumbled over to the plush bed, sinking down onto the covers. She felt weighted down by despair, as though her clothing were woven together with thread fashioned from lead. She closed her eyes, letting the bed pull her in as her clothing pushed her down. Her head was swimming with thoughts, confused, present and distant. Mainly, though, as she drifted off, she thought of Kairos. Of the day he asked her to be more than his assistant.

"Two weeks, Tabitha. The wedding was to be in two weeks' time. Now there is a video all over the internet of Francesca and Andres having my wedding night without me." Kairos's hands shook as he relayed the story, a

glass of scotch in his hand, his normally completely cool demeanor fractured.

His dark hair was disheveled as though he had been running his hands through it, his tie loosened. She had so rarely seen her enigmatic boss appearing to be anything beyond perfectly composed that Tabitha's resolve, built over the past three years of working for him, was tested. And was failing.

She had become accustomed to the taciturn man who walked into his office in the morning, barking orders, setting about the workday with efficiency that was swift, brutal and beautiful to behold.

This man, this man who seemed tested beyond his limits, was a stranger to her. Brought her right back to square one.

"What are you going to do?" she asked.

"You're my personal assistant, I thought you might assist me."

She laughed, her stomach tightening. "Well, cheating fiancées and doomed royal weddings aren't really my forte."

"I thought everything was your forte," he said, treating her to a look that burned her down to her toes.

"After the wedding I'm leaving. You're going to have another assistant. You're going to have to get a little bit more self-sufficient." It was probably the wrong time to bring that up, but she felt somewhat desolate about it. But she was done with university now, she had a business degree and had achieved most of it remotely while acting as Kairos's assistant, a special privilege given to her since she'd been selected for the job.

She should be excited. Looking forward to the change this would bring. To the advantage she would have with a degree from a prestigious school and three years of work experience for the royal family of Petras.

Instead, she felt as though she was being ripped away from her home. Felt as though she would be leaving a part of herself behind.

"I don't want another assistant," he said, his voice rough.

"That's just the alcohol and the emotional distress talking," she said.

"Perhaps. But nothing says that alcohol and emotional distress aren't honest."

"Probably more honest than the general state of things."

"Probably." He studied her hard. "I like you," he said, "I want you to know that."

Her stomach tightened further, her breath rushing from her lungs in a gust. "Well, that's flattering."

"You have been the perfect assistant, Tabitha. You have more poise than many women who were raised by kings. You are smart, diplomatic, and most importantly, you have not slept with my brother. Or, if you have, it wasn't captured on video."

She thought of the devastatingly handsome Prince Andres, and felt nothing. Kairos was the only man who had ever tested her resolve. And he never even tried. "I can honestly tell you that Andres has never so much as tempted me."

"Is there anything you do not excel at? Any skeletons in your closet?"

"I... You read my résumé."

"Yes. If you recall, I read yours and that of several hundred other hopefuls. You were indeed the most suitable. Beyond that which I could have ever anticipated."

He set his glass of scotch down on his desk. "I don't know why I didn't see it before."

She couldn't breathe. God help her, she couldn't breathe. "See what?"

"Tabitha. I think you should marry me."

"Tabitha, are you well?"

Tabitha started at the sound of Kairos's voice. It was rare for her to be woken up by him. In fact, she couldn't recall if she ever had been. He didn't spend the night with her. He never had.

She opened her eyes, bright afternoon light filtering into her vision. She suddenly remembered where she was. Remembered that it was not that day when he first proposed, or any of the days in between that she'd spent as his wife. No, it was now. She was carrying his baby. They were divorcing.

The hopeful little ember that burned in her stomach, thanks to that dream, that memory, cooled.

"Not especially," she said, pushing into a sitting position and scrubbing her hands over her eyes.

Suddenly, she felt self-conscious, childish because of the gesture. She was not in the habit of waking up in front of him. For all that they had a physical relationship, they had very little intimacy.

She dropped her hands to her sides, balling them into fists.

"I brought your clothing up. And everything else."

"Did you…" She looked around the room. "Did you put it all away?"

"Yes. I was hardly going to ask you to do it. And as I said before, there are no servants in residence here."

"You don't have any service at all?"

"I occasionally employ the services of a chef. But for the purposes of this trip, some preprepared meals were brought along with your things."

"It's just you and me, then?"

He nodded, his dark gaze unreadable. "Yes."

"On the whole island?"

"On the whole island," he confirmed.

"Oh."

"What?"

"I don't think we've ever…really been alone before."

"We are very often alone," he said, frowning.

"In a palace filled with hundreds, in a building other people live in."

"I have never kidnapped you before either. You've also never been pregnant with my baby. Oh, yes, and we have never been on the brink of divorce. So, a season of firsts. How nice to add this to the list."

She stood up, stretching out her stiff muscles. "Where exactly do you get off being angry at me? We are here because of you."

"I'm angry with you because this divorce is happening at your demand."

"Had I not demanded we divorce, I wouldn't be pregnant."

"Had you not frozen me out of your bed perhaps you would have been pregnant a couple of months sooner."

She gritted her teeth, reckless heat pouring through her veins. "How dare you?" She advanced on him, and he wrapped his arm around her waist, pulling her close. "Don't."

Her protest was cut off by the press of his mouth against hers, hot and uncompromising, his tongue staking a claim as he took her deep, hard. She had no idea where these kinds of kisses had come from. Who this man was. This man who would spirit her away to a private island. Who kissed her like he was dying and her lips held his salvation.

It stood out in such sharp contrast to that kiss on their wedding night. The first time they had been alone in a bedroom like this. His kiss had been gentle then. Cool. She had waited for this moment. For heat to explode between them. Because she felt it. She had always felt it. It had been there from the moment she first walked into his office, no matter how hard she might try to deny it.

But everything he'd done had been so maddeningly measured, so unreasonably controlled. She had been shaking, from the inside out. With nerves, with desire. He had been gentle. Circumspect.

He left the lights off. That surprised her, because she had imagined that he would prefer to see her. At least, she had imagined that men preferred such things. She had no experience with them, and suddenly she regretted it. She hadn't. Never. Until now. Now, she was married to Kairos. She was his princess. She was his wife. And she had no idea how to please him.

They had two weeks to adjust to the idea of marrying each other, and during that two weeks he hadn't touched her. He had waited, because he'd said there was no point in doing anything differently. Not when it was so close. Not when he had the chance to do right by her.

She had told him, of course, that she was a virgin. In case he found the idea appalling in some way. In case he disliked the idea of being with a woman who had no practical experience. He had not been appalled. But it was then he'd insisted they wait.

So here she was, a bride dressed in white, and all that it symbolized, married to a man she didn't love. A man who did not love her, about to find out what all the fuss was about.

She might not love Kairos, but she was attracted to him. In her mind, this was ideal in many ways. She didn't love him. But she respected him. She cared for him. She was attracted to him. They had everything pleasant going for them, and nothing outrageous or unpleasant. Nothing that would turn them into the kinds of screaming monsters her parents had become under the influence of love and passion.

And so she waited. Waited for him to close the distance between them. But he was in no hurry. Finally, he crossed the room, a dark silhouette. She could see him working his tie, removing his jacket, his shirt. She could see nothing of his body, but she could tell that he was naked by the time he reached her. It was then that he kissed her. Cool, slow. Different to how she had imagined.

His skin was hot, but his movements were chilled and deliberate. He divested her of her gown quickly, making no ceremony of it. His touch was skilled, easily calling out a response in her as he teased her between her thighs, stroked his thumb over her nipples. But it was happening quickly, and she didn't know what she was supposed to do. Didn't understand her part in it. And he gave her no hints. He had her on her back quickly, testing her readiness with his fingers. Sliding one inside her first, then another, stretching her. He did this for a while, as though he were counting the time. As though he had read a textbook on how to make a woman's first time hurt as little as possible.

Then he settled between her thighs and pushed into

her quickly. She gritted her teeth against the pain, bit-
ing her lip to keep from digging her fingernails into his
skin. She didn't have an orgasm.

He did. Of course he did.

He withdrew quickly after that, moving into the bath-
room and starting a bath for her. Then he returned, ush-
ering her in, waiting until she was submerged in the
water before meeting her gaze. "I imagine you want some
time alone."

No. She absolutely did not want time alone. She
wanted him to hold her because she was pretty sure she
was going to break apart. He had changed something
deep inside of her. And he hadn't finished. She was shat-
tered, but she wasn't remade.

"Yes," she heard herself saying, not sure where the
response had come from.

"I'll see you in the morning."

She snapped back to the present, to this moment. To this
kiss that bore no resemblance to anything that had occurred on that night. He had accused her of changing,
but he wasn't the same either.

He kissed her neck, down to her collarbone, retracing
that same path with the tip of his tongue. She found herself tearing at his shirt, her heart thundering hard, every
fiber of her being desperate to have him. Desperate to
have him inside her again. Like that night in his office.
That night when the promise that had been broken on
their wedding night was finally fulfilled.

I feel nothing.

His words from that night reached between them, hit
her with the impact of a slap.

She pushed away from him, breathing hard. "Don't."

"You want to," he said, his words cutting and far too true.

"So? We don't have to do everything we want." She, of all people, truly shouldn't. "Anyway, I know from experience that sex with you produces a host of regrets."

"Do you regret being pregnant?"

"How can you not regret it? You're going to find a new wife." She disentangled herself from his hold, moving away from him, over to the window, turning her focus out to the view. Out to the sea below. "Having your heir belong to the wrong woman must be an upsetting prospect."

"Not especially. Because I do not intend to divorce you."

"Why?"

"You are having my child. There is no reason for me to marry another. None at all."

"So, you're suggesting we simply...*ignore* our marriage?"

"If you prefer. I should like to reach some kind of agreement with you, but you have been very unreasonable lately."

"And you have been a cold fish for the last five years."

She found herself being tugged back up against him, his lips crashing down on hers. He gripped her chin with his thumb and forefinger, his dark eyes blazing into hers. "Did that feel cold to you?" he ground out after they separated.

"You contrary man. Why do you only want something once it's been taken from you?"

He drew back as though she had slapped him. "I..."

"You can't deny it. And you don't have an answer."

His expression went blank. "If you regret the pregnancy, perhaps you should simply turn custody of the child over to me."

Everything inside of her screamed at the thought. "You misunderstand me," she bit out. "I don't regret having a child. I regret having *your* child. It would have been better for me to wait to get pregnant until I could find a man that I actually wanted to spend my life with."

He took a step back, his eyes filled with rage. His face, normally so controlled, normally schooled into such a careful, neutral expression, telegraphed every bit of his anger. "Such a pity then that it is my child you carry. Dinner is served in an hour. If you do not join me you can starve."

"Are you going to lock the kitchen?"

"I may yet. Do not test me, Tabitha, for you will not like the result." He turned, walking out of the room, slamming the door hard behind him.

He had commanded that she not test him. And so that was exactly what she intended to do.

CHAPTER SIX

Kairos could not fathom his own behavior. But then, he could not understand Tabitha's either. He had given her more credit than this. Had chosen her to be his wife because she was smart, faithful, levelheaded. Because she had served him as his assistant for years and never given him reason to distrust her. During his engagement to Francesca he had thought he might forge something of an emotional connection with her. His trust had been misplaced. Francesca had betrayed him with Andres.

He owed Andres a fair amount of anger for that. Both of them, really. And yet, he had never been able to muster much of it up. He was only grateful he had discovered Francesca's duplicity prior to making vows to her. And it had given him a chance to find someone better. To re-evaluate what he expected out of marriage.

Women, it turned out, betrayed you eventually.

Well, you, specifically.

He took in a sharp breath, looking out through the living room at the terrace, at the table that was set with dinner for both of them. If she didn't come down…

He was seized with an image of himself storming back upstairs, flinging the door open, throwing her over his shoulder and carrying her down to the dinner table. Failing that, perhaps he would just throw her on the bed and finish what they had started earlier.

He gritted his teeth, battling against the erotic images that were battering against his mind's eye. Threatening to shatter his control. He had already behaved appallingly where she was concerned, and he would not compound his sins.

Why not? She left you. The one thing she promised she would not do.

He hated this. This feeling of helplessness. She inspired it in him more often than any other human being on the planet. From the first day they had married. He had never felt any hint of awkwardness around her when she was his PA. And he'd been determined to hang on to that relationship. That meeting of the minds, the mutual understanding, that felt so right. It had made her the best assistant he'd ever had. By all rights, a nineteen-year-old from Middle America should never have been able to serve him the way that she had. And yet, for three years, she had been by far the most efficient and hard-working PA he'd ever had.

She'd transcended her circumstances and risen to the occasion. He imagined she would do that as a wife as well.

Though, it was disingenuous to pretend that all of the unforeseen issues fell on her shoulders. Their disastrous wedding night had been his fault.

He hadn't satisfied her. He had hurt her. And with his actions, it felt as though he had built a wall between them. Yes, a certain amount of distance was desirable. He didn't want to become emotionally entangled with her. Not with feelings that went beyond cordial affection.

But when they had entered her suite, and his lips had touched hers for the first time without an audience, something had shifted inside of him. The rock wall he had built up around his control was cracking, crumbling. He had felt...a deep ache that had transcended anything he could remember feeling in recent years. A desire for something that he couldn't put a name to. Like seeing something familiar, shrouded in fog. Something that called to him, echoed inside of him, but that he couldn't identify.

Frustrating. Terrifying.

He went into the bathroom, running some hot water. She would probably be sore. He had done his best to make it as painless as possible, since he had known it was her first time, but he knew he had failed, on more than one level.

She didn't seem happy with him, when he ushered her into the bathroom.

He stood there, watching her as she submerged herself. It was a strange thing, seeing her naked now after so many years of looking at her as nothing more than an employee. Now she was exposed. Uncovered. He had been inside of her body...

He felt his own body stir in response to that memory. He had to go. Until he could get a handle on his response to her, he had to leave.

Unless she asked him to stay.

But he would not force that issue. Not after he had handled their first time so badly.

"I suppose you want some time alone?" he asked.

She shifted beneath the water, drawing her knees up to her chest and looking down. "Yes."

Her words rebuilt some of the wall inside of him. It

was good. It reminded him of why distance was impera-
tive. Why control mattered.

"I'll see you in the morning."

He walked out of the bathroom and dressed quickly in
her room, before leaving and heading to his own quar-
ters. Once he was inside, he stripped his clothing off
again, heading straight for the shower. He turned the
cold knob as far as it would go, stepping beneath the icy
spray, gritting his teeth.

He would not repeat the same mistakes again.

He would not.

"I'm here." Tabitha's voice drew his attention to the top
of the stairs. She was there, looking more beautiful than
he could ever remember. Was this change happening inside of her beginning to affect her appearance? Her blond
hair was loose, bouncing around her shoulders. So different to the usual restrained bun she often chose to wear.

Her dress was also completely unlike anything she
would've worn back at the palace. But then, the instructions he'd left for the personal shopper tasked with amass-
ing a small wardrobe for her here in the island hadn't
been any more explicit than her size.

The dress had skinny straps and a deep V that made
the whole gown appear to be resting precariously over
her full breasts. It looked as if the slightest tug would
snap those straps and see the dress falling down around
her waist, settling on her voluptuous hips. She had applied a bare minimum of makeup, a light pink gloss to
her lips, a bit of gold on her eyes. It was a more relaxed
look than he was accustomed to seeing.

His body responded with a hunger that was becoming predictable.

"I'm glad you decided to join me."

"Well, now you won't need to put a lock on the pantry."

She began her descent, her delicate hand resting on the banister. His eyes were drawn to her fingers, to her long, elegant fingernails, painted a delicate coral that matched her dress.

"I'm pleased to hear that, *agape*."

"Don't call me that," she said, her tone sharp.

"What?"

"*Love*. It's always been a little bit of a farcical endearment, but it just stings all the more at the moment."

She breezed past him, heading outside to where the table was set for them. He followed after her, trying not to allow that helpless sensation to overtake him again. How did she do this to him? He ruled an entire nation. He was the master of his, and every domain, within its borders. Somehow she made him feel as inept as a schoolboy who didn't even have dominion over his own bedtime.

"I am sorry, I shall try to endeavor not to call you nice things," he said through clenched teeth.

She paused, looking over her shoulder, one pale eyebrow raised. "Just don't call me things you don't mean."

It was hard to think of a political response to that. Of course he didn't love her.

He cared for her, certainly. There was nothing duplicitous about his lack of emotion. He had made that clear when he proposed to her that afternoon in his office after his engagement to Francesca had blown all to hell. He had outlined exactly what the relationship between Tabitha and himself would be. Had told her he intended to base it upon the mutual respect they had for each other.

That thought, of just how honest he'd been, of how she had known fully, and agreed to this, reignited his anger.

And he forgot to search for the political response.

"Actually, my queen," he said, "I could instead call you exactly what you are. Not a queen. Simply a woman that I elevated far beyond her station. Far beyond what she was equipped to handle."

"Are you going to malign my blood now you've mixed your royal lineage with it? Perhaps you should have thought of that before you used my body as the vessel for your sacred heir."

She continued to walk ahead of him, her shoulders stiff. She took her place at the table, without waiting for him to come and hold her chair out for her. For some reason, the lack of ceremony annoyed him. Perhaps because it was yet more evidence of this transformation from his perfect, biddable wife, into this *creature*.

It wasn't perfect. And you know it.

He didn't like that thought. It only damaged the narrative he was constructing in his mind about the truth of his marriage. The one that absolved him from any wrongdoing.

The one that said he had told her how their marriage would work, and now she had an issue with it. That, the fact she had been warned, meant that now the fault rested on her alone.

It allowed him to open up all sorts of boxes inside of him, boxes he normally kept closed, locked tight, and pull out all the hurt and anger kept there, examining it, turning it over, holding it close to his chest.

He took his seat across from her, lifting his water to his lips. For a moment, he regretted not serving alcohol out of deference to her condition. She didn't deserve his deference.

"How is it you expected we might discuss things with more success cut off from civilization?"

"For a start," he said, leaning back in his chair, "I very much appreciate having you somewhat captive."

"I'm not sure how I'm supposed to feel about that."

"Oh, don't concern yourself. I'm not worried about how you feel."

"No, of course you aren't. Why start now?"

He set his water glass down hard enough that some of the clear liquid sloshed over the side. "I'm sorry, have I done something recently that conflicted with our initial marriage agreement?"

"You are…" She looked up, as though the clear Mediterranean sky might have some answers. "You're distant. You're cold."

"A great many people might say that about you, *agape*."

"Don't call me that," she said, blue eyes flashing.

"I don't recall agreeing to your edict, Tabitha."

"You want a list? I'm working on a list," she said, ignoring his words. "The only time in five years you ever bothered to get angry with me was when I told you I was going to leave you."

"You *want* me to get angry with you?"

"I want you to feel *something*. Anger would be a start."

"You have your wish. I am exceedingly angry with you."

"You barely speak to me. You only touch me when attempting to conceive. I am essentially part of the furniture to you. If you could have had an heir with a bureau in possession of childbearing hips, I've no doubt you would have done so."

"The same can be said of the way you treat me. Moreover, I never promised you anything different. What vow have I broken?"

A slash of color bled out over her pale cheekbones. "A woman expects her husband to treat her a certain way."

"Does she? Even when the husband told her exactly how things would be? If your expectations differ from the reality I lined out for you early on, I fail to see how that's my fault."

"Nobody imagines their marriage is going to be a frozen wasteland."

"A frozen wasteland is exactly what I promised you," he said, his tone biting. "If I had promised to love and cherish you, then I suppose you would have every right to feel cheated. To feel lied to. But I promised you respect, and I promised you fidelity, I promised that I would treat you as an equal. If I have failed on that score then it has only been in the days since you violated the promises *you* made to *me*."

"I know what you said. What *we* said, but… Five years on things feel different. Or they feel like they *should* be."

"I see. Were you ever going to tell me that? Or were you simply going to freeze me out until I was the one who asked for an end to the marriage?"

She curled her fingers into fists, and looked away from him. "That isn't…"

"Do you not enjoy being held accountable for the breakdown of our union, Tabitha? Because if I recall, you spent the past five years doing much the same thing you accuse me of. If an honest word has ever passed between us, I would be surprised. Did you think I didn't notice that you have grown increasingly distant? Did you think it didn't bother me?"

"Yes, Kairos, I imagined that it didn't bother you. Why

would I ever assume that you cared about there being any closeness between us?"

"Because there was a time when I at least called you a friend."

Her golden brows shot upward. "Did you? Do you consider me a friend?"

"You know that I did. I assume you remember the day that I proposed to you."

"Oh, you mean the day that you watched a video of the woman you had chosen to marry having dirtier sex with your brother than I imagine you ever had with her? The day that you—drunkenly—told me you thought I would be a better choice to be your queen? I find it difficult to put much stock into anything you said that day."

"Then that's your mistake. Because I was sincere. I told you that we could build a stronger foundation than Francesca and I ever could. I told you that I had been having doubts about her even before her betrayal."

"Yes, that's right, you did. And why were you having doubts, exactly?"

"The way you behaved…it was such a stark contrast to Francesca, even on her best of days. I found myself wishing that it was you. When we traveled together, when I went to you to discuss affairs of the state…I found myself wishing that you were the one I was going to marry. I respected your opinion. And I felt like I could ask you questions, when with everyone else I had to simply know the answers."

He felt stripped bare saying these things now, without the buffer of alcohol, five years older and a lot more jaded than he had been then. But she needed to hear them. She needed to hear them again, clearly.

"And while it is a very nice sentiment, it isn't exactly

the proposal every girl dreams of," she said, her tone brittle.

"It seems very much that you are angry with yourself for accepting a proposal you now deem beneath you. How high you have risen. That the proposal of a king is no longer good enough for you."

"Maybe I am the one who changed. But people do change."

"Only because they forget. You forget that you are going to have to leave my palace, leave Petras, search for a job. Struggle financially. Perhaps even face the life that you were so eager to leave behind. Marriage to me offered you instant elevation. The kind of status that you craved."

"Don't," she said, "you make me sound like I was nothing more than a gold digger."

"Oh, you would have done all right finding gold on your own. But validation? Status? For a piece of white trash from Nowhere, USA, that is a great deal more difficult to come by."

She stood, shoving her plate toward the center of the table. "I don't have to listen to you insulting me."

"You want me to call you something honest. Though, I hasten to remind you that I learned these words from you. This is what you think of yourself. You told me."

"Because I trusted you. Clearly, my own fault."

"No, I think I was the one who was foolish to trust you."

"We could go back and forth for days. But it doesn't solve anything. It doesn't erase the fact that I think we're better off apart. We should never have been a couple, Kairos, and you know it. As you said, I'm little more than a piece of white trash from a tiny town. You're the king of an entire nation. You wanted to marry someone else."

"You might be right. But it's too late for regrets. We are married to each other. And more than that, you're carrying my child."

"Plenty of people work out custody arrangements."

He stood, knocking his chair backward and not caring when it hit the ground with a very loud thump. "And do those people still want each other? Do they exist constantly on the verge of tearing each other's clothes off and having each other on the nearest surface?"

The pink in her cheeks intensified. "You can only speak for yourself on that score."

"Really? I don't think that's true." He was suddenly gripped by lust, lust that mingled with the ever-present anger in his chest. He wasn't sure whether he wanted to yell at her, or press her against the wall and claim her body again. Both. He wanted both. Even though neither made sense. "You want me."

"Go to hell." They were the harshest words he'd ever heard on her lips. So much sweeter than the sophisticated chill had ever been.

"There. There at least, some honesty. Perhaps you should try it more often."

"I gave you honesty."

"Your version of honesty was a list of complaints that you could have, and should have voiced years ago. Ideally, before you accepted my proposal. What changed? What changed that you can no longer stand what you agreed would be enough to make a marriage?"

His words hit her with the force of the slap. And she just stood there, reeling. Tears prickled her eyes, her tongue was frozen. He was making too much sense. Making too good a case for how aggrieved he was by her request for divorce. He was right. She had not spoken an honest word to him. She hadn't asked him for what she wanted. Hadn't told him she was unhappy.

But she didn't know how to do it without opening herself up, and reviewing bits and pieces of pain that were best left hidden. Didn't know how to do it without confronting her fears. And anyway, she hadn't imagined that he would care.

She hadn't trusted herself enough to voice them. To deal with them.

She wasn't sure she trusted herself now.

"It isn't what I wanted," she said, her voice hollow.

"You just said what you wanted changed."

"Yes. No. It isn't that simple," she said, panic gripping her neck, making it impossible for her to breathe.

"It seems fairly straightforward to me, *agape*, but then, I do not know much about the inner workings of the female mind. Throughout my life I have seen women act in ways that are inexplicable to me. My mother walking away from her position at the palace, Francesca compromising our union for a bit of stolen pleasure. You divorcing me. So, it comes as no surprise to me that I do not understand what you're trying to tell me now."

"You don't know everything about my past," she said.

It was for the best that he didn't. Best that he never did. She looked back on the Tabitha she'd been, before university, before she'd put distance between herself and her family, and saw a stranger.

But he didn't seem to know the Tabitha she was now. And she didn't know how to make him. Didn't know how to make him understand who she was. *Why* she was.

She didn't even know if it would change anything.

If nothing else, it would show him. Why he should let her go. Why she wasn't suitable. And it would remind her too.

"Do I not know you?"

"No. I know you did some cursory searching, as far as I was concerned. My name. But you don't know everything. In part because I don't have the same last name as my mother, nor is her name the same as the one listed on my birth certificate, not anymore. I don't share a name with my stepfather either. Not having those names excludes quite a lot from a cursory search. Of course, you found nothing objectionable about me. Nothing but good marks in school, no criminal record, no scandal."

"Because that's all that mattered," he said, something odd glittering in his black eyes.

"Yes. It is all that mattered. You were only looking for what might cause problems with my reputation, for you, as far as the public eye was concerned. You weren't actually looking for anything real or meaningful about me."

"Come off your high horse, Tabitha. Obviously you didn't care whether or not I found anything meaningful out about you, because you deliberately concealed it from me."

She lifted her shoulder, her stomach sinking. "I can't argue with that. I can't argue with a great many of the accusations leveled at me today. I wasn't honest with you. I didn't tell you. I preferred to run away, rather than telling you what I wanted. But a lot of it is because… I don't actually know what I want. I started feeling dissatisfied with our relationship, and wanting more. And that confused me."

"Well, hell, if you're confused, what chance do I have?"

"I can't answer that question," she said, sounding defeated. Feeling defeated. "I don't know the answer. All I know is that I never thought I would marry. Then I met you, and I can't deny that I felt…attraction. It confused me. I had spent years getting through college, school of every kind, really, with a single-minded focus. I wanted to be better than my birth. I knew that education was the only way to accomplish that. I set about to get good grades, high test scores, so that I could earn scholarships. And I did that. I knew that if I split my focus, I wouldn't be able to. Then the internship at the palace came up, and I knew I had to seize it. I didn't have connections, I didn't have a pedigree. I knew that I needed a leg up in order to get the kind of job that I wanted."

"I imagine, ultimately, the chance to become queen of the nation was too great a temptation to pass up?"

She laughed, hardly able to process the surreal quality of it all even now. "I guess so. It was a lot of things. A chance to have you, physically, which I wanted. A chance to achieve a status that I'd never even imagined in my wildest dreams. I'm from nothing. Nothing and nowhere, and I wanted something more. And that… How could I refuse? Especially because your criteria suited mine so well. You see, Kairos, I didn't want love either. I didn't want passion."

"You said you were attracted to me."

"I was. I am. I suppose that's something I can't deny now. But I thought perhaps I could just touch the flames without being consumed by them. Then I realized that holding your fingertips over a blaze for five years is nothing more than a maddening exercise in torture. You're better off plunging yourself in or disengaging."

"And you chose to disengage?"

"Yes. I know that I can't afford to throw myself in."

"Why is that?"

"Reasons I haven't told you. Things you don't know."

"I'm not playing twenty questions with you, Tabitha, either tell me your secrets, or put them away. Pretend they don't matter as you did all those years. Jump into the fire, or back away."

Her throat tightened, her palms sweating. She hadn't thought about that day in years. She had turned it into a lesson, an object, a cautionary tale. But the images of the day, the way that it had smelled, the weather. The sounds her stepfather had made as he bled out on the floor, the screams of her mother when she realized what had been done... Those things she had blocked out. The entire incident had been carefully formed into a morality tale. Something that served to teach, but something she couldn't feel.

Not anymore.

Use what you need, discard the rest.

"I never wanted passion. Or love. Because...I shouldn't. I'm afraid of what I might be. What I might become. I think I've proven I have the capacity to act recklessly when I'm overtaken by strong emotion," she said, realizing that to him, the admission must seem ridiculous. For years all he had ever seen was the carefully cultivated cool reserve she had spent the better part of her teenage years crafting from blood and other people's consequences.

"Tell me," he said.

She was going to. Her heart was thundering in her ears, a sickening beat that echoed through her body, made her feel weak.

But maybe if she said it, he would understand. Maybe if she said it he would get why what he'd offered had seemed amazing. Why it had felt insufficient. Why she'd chosen to end it instead of asking for more.

"I was walking home from school. I was seventeen at the time. It was a beautiful day. And when I approached the trailer I could already hear them fighting. Not unusual. They fought all the time. My mother was screaming, which she always did. My stepfather was ignoring her. He was drunk, which he very often was."

She didn't let herself go back to that house. Not even in her mind. It was gritty and dirty and full of mold. But more than that. The air was heavy. The ghost of faded love lingering and oppressive, a malevolent spirit that choked the life out of everything it touched.

"I didn't know," Kairos said.

"I know," she said. "I didn't want you to." It stung her pride, to admit how low she'd started. To admit that she had no idea who her biological father was to a man for whom genetics was everything.

She was a bastard, having a royal baby. It seemed wrong somehow.

You always knew it would be this way. Why are you panicking now that it's too late?

Because the idea of it was one thing, the reality of it— all of it—her marriage, her past, her life, was different.

She'd spent the past year growing increasingly unhappy. And then Andres had married Zara. Watching the two of them physically hurt. It twisted her stomach to see the way they smiled at each other. Put a bitter, horrible taste in her mouth.

Made her feel a kind of heaviness she hadn't felt since she'd stood in that grimy little trailer.

"Tell me," he said, an order, because Kairos didn't know how to ask for things any other way.

"She kept screaming at him to listen. But he never did. She was so angry. She left the room. I thought she was going to pack, she did that a lot, even though she never left. Or that maybe she'd given up. Gone to take a nap. She did that sometimes too depending on how much she'd had to drink. But she came back. And she had a gun."

CHAPTER SEVEN

A COCKTAIL OF cold dread slithered down into Kairos's stomach. He could hardly credit the words that were coming out of his wife's mouth. Could hardly picture the gentle, sophisticated creature in front of him witnessing anything like this, much less being so tightly connected to it. Tabitha was strong. She possessed a backbone of steel, one he had witnessed on more than one occasion. When it came to handling foreign dignitaries, or members of the government and Petras, she was cool, calm and poised. When it came to organizing his schedule, and defending her position on hot-button issues, she never backed down.

But for all that she possessed that strength, there was something so smooth and fragile about her too. As though she were a porcelain doll, one that he was afraid to play with too roughly. For fear he might break her.

If she were that breakable, you would have shattered her on your desk.

Yes, that was true. He had not thought about her fertility then. Had not taken care with her, as he had always done in the past.

But still, he hadn't thought in that moment. He simply

acted. This revelation challenged perceptions that he had never examined. Not deeply.

"What happened?" he asked, trying to keep his voice level.

"She shot him," Tabitha said, the words distant and matter-of-fact. Her expression stayed placid, as though she were discussing the contents of the menu for a dinner at the palace. "She was very sorry that she did it. Because he didn't get back up. He died. And she was sent to jail. I don't visit her."

She spoke the last item on the list as though it were the gravest sin of all. As though the worst thing of all was that she had distanced herself from her mother, not that her mother was a murderer.

"You *saw* all this," he said, that same shell he had accused her of having wrapping itself around his own veins now, hardening them completely.

"Yes. It was a long time ago," she said, her voice sounding as if it was coming straight out of that distant past. "Eleven…twelve years ago now? I'm not sure."

"It doesn't matter how long ago it was, you still saw it."

"I don't like to think about it," she said, her blue eyes locking with his, looking at him for the first time since she had started telling her gruesome story. "I don't think you can blame me for that."

"No, not at all," he said.

"It wasn't relevant to our union. Not relevant to whether or not I would be good for the position."

"Except it clearly was, as I think it is probably related to the action you have taken now."

She looked down. "I can't argue with that. I was growing frustrated in our relationship, and I don't like to give those feelings any foothold on my life. I don't like to allow them free rein."

"Surely you don't think you're going to find a gun and shoot me?"

"I'm sure my mother didn't think she would do that either," Tabitha said, starting to pace, her hands clasped in front of her. She was picking at the polish on her fingernails, something he had never seen her do before. It was then he noticed that she wasn't wearing her ring. How had he missed it before?

Perhaps you were too wrapped up in imagining those fingers wrapped around your member to notice.

He gritted his teeth. Yes, that was the problem. Whatever had exploded between them was stealing his ability to think clearly.

"Where is your ring?"

She stopped thinking and looked at her fingernails. "I took it off."

"It was very expensive," he said, though that was not his concern at all, and he wasn't sure why he was pretending that it was.

"I know. But it is also mine. That was part of our prenuptial agreement if you recall."

"I don't need the money, I was just concerned something might have happened to it."

"It's in a safe. In a bank. It's fine. But there is no point in me wearing it when I'm not your wife. I would hate to start gossip in the press."

"We already have."

"Imagine the gossip if they knew my past as well."

"Enough. No one is going to find out. Because I will not tell. Anyway, it is not a reflection on you."

"Isn't it? My genetics. Our child's genetics."

"If blood determined everything I would be a tyrant or absent." He didn't like to speak of his parents. Talking about his father, and his rages, was much simpler than talking about his mother, who was not there at all. But either way, it was a topic he preferred not to broach.

"Well, you're neither of those things," she said, "but Andres isn't exactly well-adjusted."

Kairos laughed, thinking of his brother and the large swath of destruction Andres had spent the first thirty years of his life cutting through the kingdom, through Kairos's own life. "He has settled, don't you think?"

Tabitha laughed. "I suppose he has. I'm not quite sure how they managed. A real marriage. Especially out of their circumstances. If any marriage came about in a stranger way than ours, it's theirs."

"Zara is not exactly conventional. Or suitable," Kairos said.

Tabitha looked up at him, deep, fathomless emotion radiating from her blue eyes. "Perhaps I should have been more unsuitable?"

Her words made his heart twist, made his stomach tighten. "Tabitha, I cannot imagine the things you have seen," he said. He wasn't sure why he said it. But then, he didn't know what else to say.

"I'm the same person."

The same person from before she had told him about her experience, he knew that was what she meant. But for him it only highlighted the fact that he didn't truly know her at all. She was right. The Tabitha who had witnessed the murder of her stepfather was the same woman he had been married to for the past five years. The same woman he had known for nearly a decade.

But he didn't *know* her. Not really. How could he? She

was all things soft, beautiful and contained, and he had imagined she had grown that way, like a plant that had only ever experienced life in a hothouse.

It turned out she had been forged in the elements. An orchid put to the test in a blizzard. And she had come out of it alive. Beautiful. Seemingly untouched.

It humbled him in a strange way.

"We do not know each other," he said.

"I've been saying that," she said.

"Yes, you have been. But I didn't realize how true it was until now. You know *my* life, so I did not imagine there were such secrets between us."

"We don't talk about your life," she said, "not beyond what you had for dinner last night."

He couldn't argue with the truth of that statement. "There is nothing to tell. The evidence of my life is before you. You have seen who I am by my actions. I don't see the point in rehashing how I felt when my mother left."

"You felt something," she said, her voice muted.

"Of course I did," he said. The very thought opened up a pit of despair inside of him. Helplessness. And a dark, black rage he would rather not acknowledge lived within him. "We are strangers."

"Strangers who have sex," Tabitha added.

"Yes," he said, "certainly. And yet, I'm not even entirely certain I know your body."

Her cheeks turned pink. "You did all right with it last month."

"And the times before that?" This line of questioning was not pleasant for him. What man liked calling his own prowess into question? But it wasn't so simple as prowess. He had the ability, but he'd always held back with her. Always.

That was the very beginning of where he had gone wrong. He had imagined that he needed to go slowly, that he needed to mitigate the passion between them.

The truth of it was he had been attracted to her from the moment she walked into his office. Even during his engagement to Francesca. And while he had never acted on it, it had been there, shimmering beneath the surface like waves of heat over the sand. He wanted her. He had always wanted her.

He had kept a part of himself closed off because it was so strong. Because, like her, he rejected strong emotion, strong desire.

But perhaps it would be possible to open up the physical, to have that, while keeping the rest of it safe. Perhaps it might give her what she craved. Or at the very least thaw some of the chill that was between them.

"Yes, I did then. Or, maybe my clumsiness was simply covered by the explosion between us," he said.

"There was nothing clumsy about it," she said, the color in her cheeks intensifying.

"I have held back every time we've been together," he said. "Except then."

"Why have you held back?"

"Why have you?"

"I think I explained that." She swallowed visibly. "Anyway, it doesn't matter. We don't work. We've established that."

"Have we?" Desperation clawed at him like a wild beast. "I'm not sure that's true. We've both admitted to holding back. And I think it's safe to say that we're both liars."

"I never lied to you."

"There is one very specific word I can think of in response to that. It has to do with the excrement of a bull."

"Crassness does not suit you, Kairos."

"Or, perhaps it does," he said. "How would you know?"

"I wouldn't. And it isn't my job to know. The function of ex-wives is just to walk off into the distance and spend all of your money. It isn't to know you."

"All right," he said, an idea pushing its way into the forefront of his mind even as the words exited his mouth. "You will be free to do so. But I have conditions."

She frowned. "What are you talking about? We both know I don't actually get any of your money."

"It doesn't have to be that way. The prenuptial agreement is very rigid. And I am a man of means. It is unreasonable of me to withhold a portion of that from you after all you have…suffered at my hands. Moreover, you are the mother of my child and therefore a consistent lifestyle will need to be kept whichever household he is staying in at a given time, don't you agree?"

"I don't…I don't understand."

"As I said, there will be conditions to this agreement."

"What do you want?"

What he wanted was for everything to go back as it had been. What he wanted was the wife she had been all those years ago. The wife he had imagined she would be forever. The perfect complement to the man he presented to her, the man he presented to the world. Yes, they were liars, but they had told such compatible lies. Such quiet lies.

This explosion of truth wasn't compatible, and it wasn't quiet. It had left rubble and shrapnel everywhere, the shattered pieces of the life they once had littering the ground in front of them. There was no ignoring it. There would be no putting it back together as it was. But he wouldn't leave it. Wouldn't give up.

They were having a child together. He would not be an absentee father. He would not allow her to be a distant mother. There would be no echoes of his childhood. Not if he had anything to do about it.

And he *did*. He was king, after all.

"Two weeks. I want fourteen days of honesty. I want your body, I want your secrets. I want everything. And if, at the end of that time, you feel like you still don't know me, if then, you feel like you cannot make a life with me, then I will give you your divorce. And with it, much more favorable terms than we originally agreed upon. Money. Housing. Shared custody."

"Why?" She looked stricken, as though he had told her she had to spend two weeks in the dungeon, rather than two weeks with her husband.

"It doesn't matter why. I am your king, and I have commanded it. Now," he took a deep breath, trying to cool the flame that was roaring through his veins. One of triumph. One of arousal. "Either take off your dress, or tell me another secret."

CHAPTER EIGHT

TABITHA'S HEART WAS pounding so hard, she thought she might pass out. She wasn't entirely certain whether she was living in a nightmare, or a fantasy. Kairos did not ask her to take her clothes off. He just didn't. He didn't make demands of her like this at all. And yet, there was no denying that now, her normally cool and controlled husband was looking at her with molten fire in his dark eyes, his gaze intense, uncompromising.

"I'm certain that you did not command me to take my dress off here on the balcony." Retreating into her icy facade was the most comfortable response she could find. After all, the cold didn't bother her. It was this heat, this searing, uncompromising heat that arched between them.

"I am certain that I did." The sun had lowered in the sky some since they had first come outside, and now the rays cut through the palm trees, illuminating his face, throwing his high cheekbones and strong jaw into sharp relief. He looked like a stranger. Not at all like the man she had married. A man who would never have made such a command of her. She was shaking. Shaking from the inside out. Because she had no choice. Had no choice but to accept his devil's bargain. She would be a fool not to. He was offering her a chance to raise her child without struggle, without fighting for custody, without fighting for the bare necessities.

But deeper than that, more shamefully than that, she simply wanted to obey. Even though she could hardly imagine it. Slipping her dress off her body, out here, in the open air, the breeze blowing over her skin. To just let go of everything. Of her control. Of her fear.

"We're the only ones here." His words jolted her out of her fantasy.

He was right, of course, there was no one else here. There was no one to see. But that wasn't what concerned her. The fact that there was no one around only frightened her more. There would be no consequences here. No one to stop them. No perfectly planned and well-ordered events on their calendar to interrupt. No rules, no society, no sense of propriety. There was nothing to stop her from stripping off her clothes, from closing the space between them and wrapping herself around his body, giving herself over to this desperate, gnawing ache that had taken her over completely.

She turned away from him, heading toward the entrance to the villa. She felt the firm hand on her shoulder, and found herself being turned around, pressed against the wall. Her eyes clashed with his, electricity skittering along her veins, collecting in her stomach. "Where do you think you're going?"

"Away from you. Away from here. Because you're crazy."

"Your king gave you an order," he said, his tone shot through with steel. It should make her angry. It should not make her feel restless. Shouldn't make her breasts ache. Shouldn't make her feel slick and ready between her thighs. But he did. *He* did.

His anger, his arrogance—never directed at her before, not like this—was a fresh and heady drug she'd never tried before.

"I see." She swallowed hard. "And will he punish me if I don't comply?"

"I would have to set an example," he said, his tone soft, steady and no less strong.

"For who? As you have already stated, there is no one here."

"For you. For the future. I cannot have you thinking you can simply defy me. Not if this is to work."

"I haven't agreed to—"

He reached up, gripped her chin and held her tight. "You may not have agreed to stay with me forever, *agape*. But you have no choice other than to agree to this two weeks. I do not wish to spend any of that time arguing with you. Not when I could find other uses for your mouth."

She gasped, pressing herself more firmly against the wall, away from him. Erotic images assaulted her mind's eye. Of herself, kneeling before him. Tasting him, taking him into her mouth. She had never done that before. Not with him, not with anyone.

Strange, now she thought about it. Other people traded that particular sex act so casually, and she had never even shared it with her husband.

It didn't disgust her. To the contrary, it intrigued her. Aroused her. And yet, she was shrinking away from him as though she were afraid. She would not be so easily cowed. Would not allow him to claim total control in this way. She was strong. She had not got to where she was in life by folding in on herself. He might be the king, but she was a queen, for God's sake.

"Could you? That would be a first, then." She lifted her hand, curved it around his neck, losing her fingers through his hair. "Shall I get on my knees and bow down before Your Majesty?"

It was his turn to draw back, dark colors slashing his high, well-defined cheekbones. "I did not mean…"

Of course he didn't. He never meant such salacious things. Ever. He had likely only been thinking of a kiss. He probably hadn't even intended for her to take her dress off.

On the heels of that thought, her hand moved to her shoulder and flicked the strap of her dress down. "Words are powerful," she said, pushing at the other strap so they both hung down. "Once they're spoken you can't erase them. Even if you didn't intend for them to be taken in a certain way. Once you speak them, they belong to whoever hears them." She reached behind her back, grabbing a hold of the zipper tab and drawing it down to the middle of her back. The top of her dress fell, exposing her bare breasts to him.

"Tabitha," he growled, his tone a warning.

"What is it? Is my obedience not to your liking? Is this yet another one of our miscommunications?" She pushed the dress down her hips, taking her panties with it, standing before him, naked, and, somehow, not embarrassed.

"You seemed so confident this was what you wanted only a moment ago."

He said nothing as she lowered herself to the patio in front of him. She was shaking. And she wasn't entirely certain if it was the desire or rage. Or if it was some twisted, unholy offspring of the two, taking her over completely. She wasn't entirely certain it mattered. Just as she was sure inexperience wouldn't matter here either.

She didn't know what sorts of things Kairos had done with women before her. They barely talked about their own sex life, so they'd had no reason at all to discuss experiences either of them had had prior to their marriage. Of course, for her, there hadn't been so much as a kiss. As far as he went? He was a mystery to her.

But one thing she knew for certain, if he was as faithful to her as he claimed to be, no one had done this for him in at least five years. Time healed all wounds, and likely erased memories of oral pleasure. At least, she could hope.

She reached up and grabbed hold of his belt buckle, working the leather through the metal clasp. Her hands were shaking, as much from nerves and determination as from desire. It was impossible for her to tell if this was really her defining move in a power play, or if she was simply acting out of need. Out of lust. She supposed that didn't matter either.

He reached down, grabbing a fistful of her hair, stopping her short. "Tabitha. I would not ask this of you."

She looked up at him, at the desperation in his dark eyes, and something twisted, low and painful inside of her. "Why do you think it's a sacrifice?"

"It offers nothing to you."

"Isn't that what this two weeks is about? My service to you?" She immediately regretted the words the moment they left her mouth. That it was too late to call them back. As she had only just said to him, once words were spoken they could not be erased.

"No," he said, his voice rough, "I do not require you to lower yourself in this way."

Her eyes stung, a deep, painful ache that started behind them and worked its way forward. She said nothing. Instead, she tugged his pants and underwear down slightly, exposing his rampant masculinity to her. She didn't often examine his body. More often than not, they made love in the dark. If she ever saw him naked, it was most likely an accident.

Her breath hissed through her teeth as she ran her palm over his hardened length. He was beautiful. Five years, and she had never had the chance to truly appreciate that. Five years and she had never knelt before him in this way, had never even contemplated doing what she was about to do. She had been so determined to keep control, so absolutely hell-bent on maintaining the facade of the perfect ice queen that she'd even allowed her fantasies to become frozen.

She regretted it now, bitterly. Wasted time freezing in the cold when she could have been warm. Like sleeping out in a snowbank only to discover that the front door had been unlocked the whole time, the lit hearth in a warm bed available to her if she had only tried.

Why had she never tried?

She curled her fingers around him, leaning forward and flicking the tip of her tongue out across his heated flesh. His hips flexed forward, a harsh groan escaping his lips. His fist tightened on her hair, so tight it hurt. Yet, she didn't want him to release her. Didn't want him to pull away.

He didn't. And so she kept on. Exploring the entire length of him slowly, relishing the flavor of him. She raised her eyes and met his as she shifted, taking him completely into her mouth.

"Tabitha," he said, his tone warning even as he tugged her head back sharply.

She resisted him, not allowing his hold to interrupt

her exploration, tears pricking her eyes as he pulled hard on her hair. It occurred to her then how debauched the whole scene must look. How very unlike her and Kairos it was. Her naked, at his feet, with him mostly dressed, standing out there on the terrace of his fine, well-ordered home, the gentle beauty of the ocean acting as a backdrop to their licentious activities.

That thought only aroused her further. She had no confusion about what she felt now. None at all.

She was starving. Starving for a banquet that had been laid out before her for five long years while she wasted away in an abstinent state. And she was going to have her fill.

She rested her hands on his thighs, could feel his muscle shaking beneath her palms. Could feel just how rigorously she tested his control. She was drunk on the power of it, drunk on him. On a desire that she had kept buried so deep, so well hidden, even she might have been convinced that it wasn't there.

But now that she had brought it out, opened the lid, set it free, she was consumed by it.

She didn't know this creature. This creature down on her knees, uncaring that the cement bit into her skin, unconcerned with the fact that she was naked, outside, with the sun shining on her bare skin. She was not, in this moment, the sophisticated woman she had fashioned herself into in order to walk freely in Kairos's world. But she wasn't the girl from the trailer park either. She was something new, something wholly and completely different. And in that was a freedom she had not anticipated.

She had not moved from one cage into another, as she had imagined she might. Rather, she had slipped through the bars completely.

Suddenly, she found herself being hauled to her feet. "Not like this," he said, his tone dark and rough. "I need to have you properly."

She expected him to release his hold on her, to allow her to go back into the house and walk up the stairs, so that they might find a bed or some other civilized surface to complete their exceedingly uncivilized activities.

But as much as she had surprised herself in the past few minutes, Kairos surprised her even further. He turned toward the table, sweeping his hand across the high-gloss surface and sweeping their plates onto the ground, the porcelain shattering, the silver clattering on the hard surface.

Then she found herself being laid down on the pristine white tablecloth, his large body covering hers as he tested her readiness with the blunt head of his erection. He bent his head, kissing her neck, blazing a trail down to her breasts, sucking one nipple deep into his mouth as he sank into her body.

He filled her so completely, so utterly. She shuddered with the pleasure of it. This act had become so painful in the past couple of years. So intimate, the act of two bodies becoming one, and yet a brick wall might as well have existed between them even while they lay as close as two people possibly could.

But that wasn't happening now. Now, she felt him go so deep she was certain he touched her heart. There was no darkness to shield her body from his gaze, none to protect her from the look in his eyes. So she met them, boldly, even though she knew she was taking a chance on finding no connection there. On seeing nothing but emptiness.

They weren't empty. They were full. Full of heat, fire and a ragged emotion she could think of no name for.

It didn't matter, because soon she couldn't think at all. She was carried away on a tide of pleasure, molten waves wrapping themselves around her body until she was certain she would be consumed completely, dragged to the bottom never to resurface.

Just when she thought she would burst, when she was certain she couldn't endure another moment, pleasure exploded deep inside of her, rippling outward. She held on to him tightly, counting on him to anchor her to earth. Then he began to shake, his movements becoming erratic as he gave himself up to his own release.

She turned her head to the side, looking down at the ground, puzzled by the spray of glass she saw. And then it all slowly came back to her, piece by piece. They were on the table. He had broken the plates. The glasses. Had left the food strewn all over the ground for the birds.

He had been…he had been consumed by desire for her.

It was only then she realized that the table surface was uncomfortable. And even with that realization she didn't want to move. Because he was still inside of her, his chest pressed against hers. And she could feel his heart beating. Could feel just how affected he had been by what had passed between them. Could see the evidence all over the ground.

"What happens if we get hungry later?" The question fell from her lips without her permission. But she hadn't eaten very much of her dinner, and it seemed an important thing to know.

"There is plenty in the pantry. There are biscuits."

"American or European?"

"European," he said.

It seemed a little bit absurd to be discussing cookies in such a position.

She was about to say as much when she found herself being swept up into his arms again. She expected to be set on the ground, but he kept her scooped up, held tightly against his chest. "You don't have shoes," he said. She looked down, and saw that he was still wearing his. He stepped confidently over the remains of their plates, shards of glass cracking beneath each of his steps. He brought them both into the house, continuing through the living room and up the stairs. "There will be no question of you sleeping alone."

"We never share a room," she said.

Never. Not from the first moment. The first heart-breaking night of their marriage when he had left her sitting alone, having just lost her virginity with nothing more than a warm bath for comfort.

"We only have two weeks, *agape*," he said, not heeding her request that he refrain from endearments, "and if two weeks is all there is, then I will take every moment."

For the second time in the space of less than twenty-four hours, Kairos watched Tabitha sleep. He found it fascinating. Yet another facet to his wife he hadn't seen over the course of the past few years. Surely she must've dozed off on flights, long car rides. She *must* have.

But he couldn't picture it. The only image he had in his head was that of Tabitha sitting with rigid posture, her hands folded in her lap. Did he truly take so little notice of her? Or was she simply so uncomfortable in his presence that she couldn't do anything but sit as though her life depended on her balancing a book on her head.

She was thoroughly exhausted now. From what had transpired downstairs during dinner.

Erotic images flashed before his mind's eye. Of her kneeling before him. Of him begging her not to.

It was an act he simply wasn't comfortable with. He didn't want someone serving him in that way. Giving him pleasure while he reciprocated nothing. And yet, the moment her tongue had touched him he had been lost. He had not been holding her hair to move her away from him, but rather to anchor himself to the ground.

He was lying next to her now, still naked, but not touching her. She was sleeping on her side, her elbow beneath her cheek, her knees drawn up slightly. She looked young. Vulnerable. Everything she was. Though she wore the facade of a stone wall, he knew she was soft beneath it. He just chose to ignore it when it suited him.

She stirred, rolling onto her back, stretching her arms up over her head, her breasts rising with the motion.

Kairos had never been one to gaze at art. He found it a pointless exercise. The world had enough to offer in terms of beauty without adding needless glitter to it. But she was art, there was no other word for it. She looked as though she was perfectly formed from marble, warm life breathed into her making her human, but still almost impossible in her loveliness. And he was turning into a fool, thinking in poetry, which was something he held in even lower esteem than art.

Her blue eyes opened slowly, confusion drifting through her expression. "Kairos?"

"Yes. Two weeks. The table."

She blinked. "Oh. Yes. That happened."

"Yes."

"I'm hungry," she said, pushing herself into a sitting position, causing her breasts to move in yet more interesting ways.

"I think I can help with that."

CHAPTER NINE

TABITHA WAS BAREFOOT, wearing nothing but Kairos's white dress shirt, the crisp fabric skimming the tops of her thighs. She was certain that her makeup had come off sometime between dinner, being ravished on the table and sleeping for at least three hours afterward.

She didn't make it a habit of being so uncovered in front of him. He never saw her with messy hair, or mascara streaked down her cheeks. And she never saw him as he was now. Shirtless, wearing nothing but a pair of black dress pants. His feet were bare too, and she found something strangely erotic about it.

This was the sort of thing she imagined most couples would take for granted after five years. Rummaging around for food late at night, barely dressed after an evening of sex on the dinner table.

Well, she imagined that sex on the dinner table wasn't all that typical regardless of the type of relationship you had.

The memories made her face heat, made her body feel restless.

She didn't know who she was. Not anymore. The thought should scare her, because she'd left normalcy and control, the things she had prized for so many years, shattered on the floor of the balcony.

But she was going to eat cookies with Kairos, after just getting a taste of the man she'd always suspected lurked somewhere beneath the starched shirts and perfectly straight ties.

It was hard to care about anything else.

"You promised cookies," she said, backing against the kitchen counter, folding her hands in front of her reflexively. It was the position she often assumed around Kairos. It kept her posture straight, kept her from reaching out and touching him, or anything silly like that. It was more of a concern right now than it usually was.

It seemed silly. She should be satisfied, at least marginally. That was hands down the best sex they'd ever had. And what had happened between them a month ago had been pretty amazing. Still, this had nearly obliterated the memory of that.

Forget all the years that had come before it.

"I did," he said, turning toward one of the cabinets and opening it.

She watched much closer than necessary as he reached up to grab a tin that was placed on the top shelf. The muscles in his back bunched and shifted as he moved. She felt a strange, reckless sensation wind its way through her body. Like a shot of adrenaline straight to the system.

"The cookies," he said, turning to face her, the Americanized term sounding strange on his lips. "As promised. Because *I* keep my promises."

"Do you intend to badger me constantly?" she asked, reaching out and taking the tin from his hands. "Make sure I keenly feel the depths of the wound left in you by my betrayal?"

"If badgering is what it takes," he said, "then certainly."

"I promised you two weeks. I don't see the point in you haranguing me constantly." She pried the lid off the tin and reached inside, pulling out a piece of shortbread and lifting it to her lips. She nibbled on it slowly, watching his expression to see if she might find any clues to what he was thinking. As usual, there were none.

"I'm not haranguing you," he said. "I'm simply a man who knows what he wants."

"Yes, you want me to keep on being your wife. For your continued convenience."

"Yes, for my continued convenience. For the welfare of our child as well, if you have forgotten."

Her stomach sank. The truth was, for a moment, she *had* forgotten. It was so easy to forget about the tiny life she carried inside her womb. After all, she had found out less than twenty-four hours ago. And in the time since then she had been extradited to a private island by her estranged husband, made love to enthusiastically on a table and had eaten cookies barefoot in a kitchen. All of it was a bit out of the ordinary.

It was difficult for her brain to decide which particular extraordinary detail to hold on to. She had a feeling it was protecting her from reality a bit, too. Preserving her from the stark truth that she was going to bring a child into a very unsettled situation.

"Of course I haven't forgotten," she said, because the alternative would most certainly break the spell that was momentarily cast over him. He would take a dim view to her forgetting that she was carrying his baby. The baby was the only reason he was attempting reconciliation with her, after all.

"Honesty, Tabitha," he said, his tone chastising, "we have an agreement that we will strive for honesty over this two weeks."

"Sex is easier," she returned, ignoring the heat that assaulted her cheeks. "And more fun."

A strange expression passed over his face. "You have no argument from me on that score."

"Cars," she said, looking at his handsome face, trying to do something to get a handle on the heat that was still thrumming through her veins.

"What about them?" he asked.

"Why do you like them? It's strange. You're a very practical man. Cars don't seem especially practical."

"I don't suppose they are," he said, leaning back against the counter, curling his fingers over the edge and gripping it tight. "But I...I never had hobbies. While my peers were out going to parties and...whatever else they did, I was studying. Not just to get through school, and then university, but studying everything my father did so that I could emulate him. I didn't deviate from his lesson plan for my life. One of the very few normal things I learned was how to drive. It was a practical skill, after all, so he allowed one of his men to teach me. I learned quickly and...for me, that was my only bit of freedom. I would take drives across the country. Alone. Otherwise I was never alone. There was always security detail, or my father or one of his advisors. So that's why I like cars. Freedom and solitude."

She swallowed hard, an unexpected lump of emotion lodging itself in the center of her chest. She hadn't expected anything so complete. So honest. "Your father didn't teach you himself?"

"No," he said. "He was very busy."

She nodded. "Of course."

She hadn't known the king well. By the time they'd married, the old man's health was declining and he hadn't had the energy to take many visitors, much less a commoner daughter-in-law put into place because of his disappointing younger son's scandalous behavior.

"I didn't want him to teach me anyway," he said.

"Why not?" she asked.

"Because I loved it. My father had a way of taking things I loved and turning them into something forbidden. Something I couldn't have." A muscle in his jaw ticked. "I didn't want him to do that with the cars."

"What did he do?"

"He was so very concerned about forming me into the kind of leader Petras needed. A man of principles. A man of control. Levelheaded. When I…when I showed too much enthusiasm, he was eager to snuff it out."

"Why?" she asked, her heart twisting for him.

"Because. He knew that distractions could become weaknesses. Easily."

He pushed away from the counter, closing the space between them, close enough she could feel the heat from his body. Far enough that she couldn't quite touch him. But oh, how she wanted to. How she craved this man.

It wasn't a new hunger, but it was reinvigorated. The tastes of him she'd had made her crave him all the more. Where before, she could control it…now it felt somewhere beyond her.

"Was it there the whole time?" he asked, his voice rough.

Her heart slammed into her chest and she looked down at her hands, frowning deeply when she noticed a large chip in her polish. Strange. She'd just painted them. "Was *what* there?"

"This. This insanity. Was it in you? In me? Was it between us from the very start, needing only a bit of anger to act as an accelerant?"

She lifted her shoulder. "I don't know."

Except she had a feeling she did. It was in her. She knew it. Perhaps it was in both of them. Which made them a deadly combination if ever there was one.

All it took was a little bit of anger. All it took was a little bit of anger to ignite a spark and start a blaze. But whether or not that blaze would be contained to last, or whether he would turn to violence, she didn't know.

She pressed the edge of her thumbnail against the polish on her ring finger and stripped a large flake of coral away.

She blinked, quickly realizing she'd been responsible for the other chip as well. Something she'd always done to her manicures when she was younger. Something she'd trained away.

She was regressing.

"It has never been like this for me. Not with any other woman. I have never..." A crease appeared between his dark brows. "I have never allowed a woman to do for me what you did out on the terrace."

"Oral sex?" she asked, her brows raised. She was a little bit embarrassed by her own frankness, but she hadn't been able to hold it back. Anyway, what was the point of being embarrassed to say something when you had already done it? It didn't make much sense.

"Yes," he said through clenched teeth. "It is not something I ever saw much use in."

"The way I hear tell of it, most men find it extremely useful."

"Have you done that before? For other men?" There was an edge to his voice now. Jealousy. That Kairos could be jealous over who had received her favors made her feel reluctantly satisfied.

She looked up at him, her heart thundering. "If I had?"

"I would call him a lucky bastard. And I would *probably* not put a price on his head."

"That's quite proprietary of you, Kairos," she said. "Very out of character."

"Have I been *in* character for any moment in the past month, Tabitha? Answer me that."

"Not in your character as I know it," she answered carefully.

"Not as I know it either. Staying in control is usually so much easier."

"I test your control?"

"Do you not see?"

"I haven't—" she took another bite of her cookie "—not for five years."

"I suppose I became much more desperate when I thought I might lose you. I could feel this," he said, the admission raw, "this thing between us. I realize now that I could always sense it there."

His words echoed with truth, reflecting everything she knew down deep inside.

"But I never wanted… It is not what I wanted for my marriage," he continued. "My parents were never happy. My father was distant, a man who put his country before all else, because what is a king but a servant to his people? He was not a loving father. He was not warm. He could be very hard. Especially on Andres. But I considered what he gave to me to be guidance. Necessary. He knew that I would someday be as he. A king. But he was not married to you. He was married to a temperamental, flighty woman who let every bump in the road upset her. Who felt things too deeply. I vowed that I would find a woman who was different. You were perfect. Such perfect reserve. And then, the first time I ever touched you, the first time we made love, there was something else there. The very thing I didn't want. That kind of uncontrollable desire that leads to poor decisions made in anger and desperation."

"I didn't want that either," she said, her voice soft.

"I know you didn't want it. Now you resent me for making sure that I did what we both claimed we needed in a marriage? For keeping you at a distance when you asked for that distance?"

"I told you," she said, studying her wrecked manicure, "it doesn't make sense. It's too tangled up in all of my issues to approach sense."

"I suppose it makes as much sense as me being angry at myself. I had you on that desk when you presented me with the divorce papers and most of my anger was directed at me. For having a chance to have you, five long years to make love to you in any way I chose. Squandered. In the interest of control. Control I felt a deep conviction over, but that in the end I despised. You tell me how that makes sense."

"I can't tell you how. Only that it does. Because it mirrors much of what I feel."

"I think that's enough honesty for one evening, don't you?" he asked, his tone growing hard suddenly, his dark eyes shuttered.

"I'm not done with the cookies," she said, taking another one out, this one dipped in chocolate.

"Then, I will wait. Because I find I'm not done with you."

"Oh," she said, putting the cookie back in the tin. Suddenly, she didn't care much about the cookie.

"Come on, *agape*. Let's go to bed."

Kairos had never spent the night with a woman. Not even his own wife. He questioned why he hadn't now. Because it was a thing of brilliant luxury. Luxury and satisfaction he had never known, to wake up with a soft, beautiful woman twined around his body. During their nap the evening before, they had not touched while they'd slept, but sometime during the night she had moved nearer to him, or he nearer to her. Her soft legs were laced through his.

Last night he'd had her more times than he could count. Every time he thought he was satisfied, desire would reach up again and grab him by the throat, compel him to have her. Another side effect of not sleeping with your wife was that intimacy was confined to a single moment. Something planned, something carefully orchestrated. There was always a definite start time. Then an end when he returned to his own bed.

The lines blurred when you didn't leave the room.

He found he quite liked the lines blurred.

He drew the covers back slightly, the pale morning light washing over her curves, revealing bruises on her skin. One on her back, four at her hips. His fingerprints.

He gritted his teeth, regret warring with arousal inside of him. There was something primal and masculine in him that celebrated the fact his mark remained. The fact that he had declared her his with these outward signs.

She no longer wore his wedding ring, but she wore his touch like a brand.

What kind of monster was he?

"Tabitha," he asked, "are you awake?"

"No," she mumbled, rolling over onto her stomach, her blond hair falling over her face like a golden curtain. "If I were awake my eyes would be open."

His chest tightened, his stomach twisting. There was something charming about her like this. Not bound by her typical control, not conscious of the fact that she thought of him as little more than a stranger.

"You answered my question," he said.

"It would be rude not to," she muttered.

"I suppose that's true."

She turned over again, baring her breasts to his gaze, and he felt himself growing hard again.

She must be sore. He needed to practice restraint. He found he did not want to. For the first time in his life he was starting to think restraint was overrated. At least, where sex with one's wife was concerned.

"Why are you looking at me like that?" she asked, opening her eyes to a squint.

"Like what?"

"Like you want to…eat me. Or perhaps ask me deep questions."

"It is a bit early for either, I'm afraid. I require caffeine."

"I don't suppose I'm allowed to have very much caffeine," she said, her tone regretful.

"One cup of coffee will hurt nothing. Let's go downstairs."

"I have to get dressed."

"Why?"

She blinked. "I don't know. Because it seems like the thing to do?"

"Certainly don't dress on my account."

She shot him a deadly glare and got out of bed, crossing the room completely naked and making her way to the wardrobe. There was a white, silk robe in there, and she retrieved it, wrapping it over her curves much to his dismay. "This will do," she said.

"I suppose." He got out of bed, retrieving his pants from the night before and dragging them on, not bothering with underwear or his belt.

He had the strangest urge to pick her up and carry her downstairs, just as he had done when they'd gone upstairs last night. That made no sense. And if Kairos was anything, it was sensible. At least, he had been before the past few weeks. Impending fatherhood and divorce did that to a man, he supposed.

They made their way down the stairs in silence, setting about to prepare cereal and coffee, keeping it simple as both of them preferred to do. He was not accustomed to lingering over large breakfasts. Typically, he was eager to dive into his day. He realized now that he had abandoned the palace with only Andres in his stead, and very little explanation for why.

He dismissed the thought, for the first time in his life dismissing the weight of his responsibility.

That's what a spare was for, after all. To be used in cases of death, dismemberment or divorce. Divorce that needed to be stopped.

It was time Andres took his position a little bit more seriously anyway.

"And what plans have you made for us on this fine day," Tabitha asked, seated across from him at the table inside the dining area. He would have preferred to eat outside, but he had not yet cleaned up the mess of glass and food they had created last night. A drawback to not having staff in residence. The consequences of his actions were very much his own. Fine when he was engaging in normal activities. Less so when he was throwing his wife atop the most convenient surface and consigning anything in his way to the category of collateral damage.

"What makes you think I have some kind of grand plan?"

"Well, I would have thought my captor might be running the show."

"Your captor," he said. "I thought that we had moved beyond that."

"You are still holding me here, are you not?"

"You have agreed."

She sniffed. "Under sufferance."

"Oh, yes, your suffering is great. I believe I made you suffer a minimum of five times last night."

He was gratified to see her cheeks turn a deep shade of rose. A strange sense of satisfaction overtook him. He enjoyed her like this.

He did not think she was goading him because she was angry, not seriously. Rather, he had the feeling that she liked the sparks that crackled between them when they sparred. It was new. Like the unleashed sexual energy between them, this unveiled annoyance was new. Typically, they both buried their barbs much deeper.

"I didn't think a gentleman spoke to a lady in such a way," she said, her tone arch.

"I have found that being a gentleman is boring. Surely you must find being a lady similarly dull."

"In certain environments, yes."

"The bedroom being one of them."

"You may have a point." She lifted her coffee mug to her lips and took a sip. She turned her head, gazing out toward the ocean, the sun bathing her face in a warm glow. The corners of her lips turned up slightly, the breeze rippling through her blond hair.

It was a foreign moment, unlike any he'd had in recent memory. Where they were both relaxed. Companionable, even if only for a few moments.

"Perhaps we should go for a walk?"

"Not while I'm in my robe," she said.

"No. Of course not. But perhaps, you can look and see if my staff were so kind as to provide you with a swimsuit, and we could go down to the ocean."

"We never do things like this."

"I know. But this is the time for us to explore things we've never done. That is the purpose."

"Yes, so you said. I just didn't think it extended to long walks on the beach."

"Why not? Perhaps you will discover we enjoy it. Perhaps it is something we will want to do with our child."

Her smile turned sad. "You do play dirty."

"I will play however I must. If I can make myself seem indispensable to your vision of a happy family, then I'll win. I'm not above using any means necessary."

"I did not take you for being cutthroat, Kairos."

"I hide it well. I rarely need to use it. My title insulates me from much pushback. From much criticism at all. Even if it exists, the teeth aren't sharp enough to do me any harm."

"Will *you* be wearing a swimsuit? I'm wondering if I can look forward to a show."

"I suppose it would be impractical of me to attempt to swim without one."

"Okay, now I'm starting to fear that you've been body snatched. My husband is talking about spending leisure time on the beach. And also, participating in recreational activity."

"No, sadly for you, I remain Kairos. I have not been snatched and replicated by a more biddable man. But if nothing else, I hope this proves to you that even if it is not in my nature to behave a certain way, I can try to change. I can try to accommodate your needs, even if I don't understand them perfectly."

She nodded slowly, and he had a feeling that she found something in his speech unsatisfactory. But then, that was not terribly unusual.

"All right, I'm going to go change. I'll meet you back down here," he said. Because if he joined her in her room, they would never leave.

Not that he minded. But he supposed it ran counter to appealing to her emotions.

"All right. Let's see if either of us can rise to the challenge of being leisurely."

Whoever had done the shopping for Tabitha's wardrobe deserved a raise. That was all Kairos could think as he walked behind her on the beach, taking in the sight of all the bare skin that was on display for his enjoyment. It was a white bikini, one that scarcely contained her perfect figure. The sort of thing she would never have worn on a regular basis.

But this was not a regular basis. This was outside the status quo. And he meant to take advantage of that.

For the moment, that meant admiring Tabitha in her bikini.

"You're staring at me," she said, not looking back at him.

"How do you know?" he asked, feeling a stirring of humor in his chest.

Such a rare feeling. He felt light, happy almost. Yes, things were unsettled between them, but the chemistry they were exploring was off the charts. And right now, he was on a pristine, private beach and she was barely clothed. There was nothing to dislike about the moment.

"I can feel you looking," she said.

"I was not aware you had a sixth sense, *agape*. I learn more secrets about you every moment."

"I don't have all that many."

He caught up to her, keeping pace with her strides. "But you do have some?"

"I told you the biggest one," she said, the humor leaching from her tone as she said those words.

"Are there more? Surely there must be. You are not defined by one traumatic event. Tell me. I want to know more about you."

"I was born in Iowa."

"I don't know anything about Iowa."

She laughed. "No one does. Join the club."

"Did you like it there?"

She laughed. "Do I still live there, Kairos?"

"No. But one cannot be the queen of Iowa. So I suppose in your case, you did not have to *dislike* it to leave."

"The queen of Iowa does have a nice ring to it, though."

"Perhaps not as elegant as the queen of Petras."

"Perhaps not."

He leaned closer to her, taking her hand in his, pausing for a moment when she went stiff beside him. "Tell me more."

"My mother was single until I was eight. Then she married my stepfather. You know how that ended. It was… It was not all bad. She wasn't. He wasn't. He was… the only father figure I ever had. He was kind to me." She closed her eyes. "I remember once he bought me a present for…no reason. My mother never did things like that." Her eyes fluttered open again. "But they were very wrapped up in each other, and I was an only child. Mostly, it was lonely."

"What about friends? Didn't you have friends?"

"Some. People studying advanced subjects in school. Other students who actually enjoyed getting good grades." She paused, a fine line creasing her brow. "Someone came to speak at the school when I was young. A doctor. She had grown up in the area, with no money, nothing. It was a very poor town, and seeing someone come out of it and do what she did was inspiring. She told us that if we worked hard enough we can all achieve it. She talked to us about scholarships. About the kinds of things we could hope to find if we needed to succeed on merit rather than on status or money. I felt like she was speaking to me. I was smart, but we had nothing. My resources were all inside of me. And I was determined to use them. It was all I was given on this earth. I didn't want to waste them."

"From where I'm standing, I would say you didn't." How had he ever seen this woman as soft? She was pure steel. Brave as hell. She was braver than he was, truth be told. All he'd done was fall into line with what was expected of him. She had defied expectation at every turn. Had been brought into this world with no opportunity and from it had fashioned herself into royalty. He imagined there were very few people who could say the same.

"But you don't get into good universities without hard work," she said.

"I would imagine not. I got in with a pedigree."

"People do, but I got in by being exceptional. I had to be. There's so much competition for scholarships. Especially the type I needed. Full rides. Living expenses paid. I needed every bit of help I could scrounge up for myself. My mother went to prison for killing my stepfather during my last year of school. But I just…kept working. I was so close to being eighteen, social services sort of let me be. And I…stayed in the house by myself."

"Tabitha…" His heart ached for her. For this woman who had been so lonely for so long.

"It was all right. I mean, it wasn't in some ways, but in others… I could study in peace. I just kept going to school. And when I got to university, keeping what I had was dependent on maintaining a near-perfect grade point average. I could never afford to have boyfriends. Couldn't waste any time or energy on parties. I had to be single-minded. And I was."

"And a year into school you decided to move to Petras to take a job as my assistant," he said. "Why exactly?"

"As I said, I wasn't after a university experience. I wasn't about making friends. I wanted to secure my future. The internship allowed me to complete my classes, and to gain the kind of work experience that most people would give a body part away to acquire. To work for the royal family? For someone with my background that's more valuable than money. That's a connection. The kind of connection someone like me can't typically hope to ever obtain."

"And then you married me instead."

"You made me an offer I couldn't refuse."

His heart expanded, a sense of fullness pervading his chest. He could hardly breathe. "You're very brave, Tabitha. I never fully appreciated that."

She looked down, tucking a strand of hair behind her ear. "I don't know if I'm especially brave. I was just more afraid of repeating the same life I'd already had as a child than I was of striking out on my own and failing."

"I've heard it said that courage isn't the absence of fear."

"No. Without fear we would not move very fast."

"Is that why you were running from me?"

She frowned, turning away from him and continuing on down the beach. For some reason that action pushed a long-ignored memory to the front of his mind.

"Don't go." He was twelve years old. He might as well be a man. He never cried. And yet, he could feel emotion closing down hard on his throat, strange prickling feeling pushing at the backs of his eyes.

The hall was empty except for him and his mother. He knew that she wasn't simply going out for a walk. She didn't have anything in her hand beyond her purse. But still, he knew. As certain as if she had announced it, he knew that this was the last time he would ever see her.

"Stay here, Kairos," she said, her voice steady. If there was any regret inside of her, she certainly wasn't showing it.

"You can't go," he said, calling on his most commanding tone. Of course, his voice chose that exact moment to crack in two, as it had been doing with increasing fre-

*quency lately. "I am the prince," he continued, drawing
strength from deep within him. "I forbid you."*

*She paused, turning to face him, the expression in her
eyes unfathomably sad. "It will end eventually, whether
I leave now or not. Do you think I have anything your
father wanted? No. But he wanted you. He wanted Andres. In that way, I didn't fail. Remind him of that when
he's raging about this tomorrow."*

*She turned away from him again, continuing down
the long hallway. And he forgot to be brave. Forgot that
he was supposed to be a man.*

*A cry escaped his lips and he ran after her, wrap-
ping his arms around her, pressing his head against her
back and inhaling the familiar scent of her. Honey and
tuberose, mixed with the powder she applied to her face.*

*His cheeks were wet, tears falling easily now. "Don't
go. I won't give you orders again. I'm begging you, please
don't leave. Mom, please."*

*She rested her hands against his forearms, then curled
her fingers around his wrist. She pushed down hard, extricating herself from his hold. "I have to."*

*And then she walked away from him. At the palace
door.*

And he never saw her again.

He was breathing hard, his chest burning, his brain swimming with memories he usually kept locked down deep.

And then he looked at Tabitha.

He was treading on dangerous ground with her. He
wasn't neutral. And this wasn't strictly sexual. It never
had been.

Dammit. He had to get it together. He needed this time
to convince her to stay with him. But he would never,

ever be…that again. Never again would he allow himself to feel so much for someone that the loss of them would break him.

Never again would he be reduced to shameful begging in his own home to keep a woman with him.

He was different now. Harder. He was the man his father had commanded him to be. Not the boy who'd clung to a woman who felt nothing for him and wept as though his heart were breaking.

"I didn't work years to improve my position in life only to settle for an existence that makes me unhappy."

"What does happiness have to do with anything?" Kairos asked. "Happiness is just a socially acceptable word for selfishness. We all talk about how we need to be happy. About how our happiness must come first. In which case, leaving her husband and children isn't abominable. It's brave. Because you were only preserving your own happiness, am I right?"

"That isn't true."

Anger fired through his blood, the memory of his mother walking away still at the forefront of his mind, superimposing itself over this moment. Over this woman. "Of course it is. You can wander off into the far reaches of the world and eat, pray, love to your heart's content regardless of who you leave behind because you're on a journey to your essential truth and damn anyone else's."

"That isn't what I'm doing. We were both drowning in that marriage, don't pretend we weren't."

"I have a feeling we might have drowned either way," he said.

"I'm trying. I said I would try. Must you make this unpleasant?"

He had a feeling that he must. Fighting with her did

something to ease the swollen feeling in his chest. And he found he was much more comfortable with anger than he was with anything tender or painful.

There was nothing wrong with attempting to forge a stronger physical connection between the two of them. But he needed to remember who he was. What his responsibilities were. And what they wanted. He could not afford to be preoccupied with her in any emotional sense.

He had to maintain control while making her lose it.

Had to find a way to convince her to stay with him while maintaining the distance he required.

He had imagined that global distance would be beneficial. That it would prevent his wife from leaving him. He had been wrong. He needed distance. She had to need him.

"My apologies, *agape*," he said. "I'm much more useful when it comes to interacting with heads of state than I am with making pleasant conversation."

"I'm not sure I have very much practice with casual conversation myself."

"That could be a problem. I'm given to understand that children like to make conversation about very small things. Such as insects and the shapes of clouds."

A strange, soft expression passed over her face and had made his heart clench tight. "Well, I have very little to say on the subject of insects. But I do think that cloud looks like a unicorn."

He moved so that he was standing beside her, oriented so that he was facing the same direction she was. "I don't see it."

"What do you see?"

"A war horse. With a lance growing out of his forehead."

"That's a unicorn."

"Clearly, we have different perspectives on things."

Then she smiled, and he thought that he must be doing something right. As long as he continued on, insulating himself against any sort of attachment beyond the practical, he would be able to bind her to him.

He had been blinded by the sex. By the unexpected connection it had provided. But now, in the bright light of day, when she was not on her knees before him, offering up the most tempting image and indulgence he had ever experienced, he had a bit more clarity.

His path was clear. And he would allow nothing to make them deviate from it.

CHAPTER TEN

KAIROS HAD ANOTHER romantic dinner prepared for them out on the terrace. It was dark, the stars in the sky shining brightly as warm air mingled and cooled with mist from the sea, and washed over her skin as she closed her eyes, taking a moment to enjoy the beauty of it. Of what it felt like to be here.

There were only nine days left. Nine days until she had to make a decision about whether or not she was going to leave him. But then, she wasn't entirely sure there was a decision to be made.

Yes, she could have his money if she left after fulfilling the terms of his bargain. But she was starting to think that would be nowhere near enough. Neither would shared custody. Because in that scenario she wouldn't get to be with him. She would never see what kind of father he was to their child. Her child would have a life divided in half. She would never be able to watch the way he interacted with Kairos. Would never be able to fully understand what his life at the palace was like.

Right now, tiny as it was, her baby lived inside of her. She couldn't imagine relinquishing so much time with him once he was born.

She realized that yet again, she was worrying about

the future. Existing in the present, but only by half. She had spent her entire life that way. Living for a moment she wasn't yet in. It struck her, suddenly and sharply.

"I don't know if I've ever really been happy before," she said, looking up from her plate and meeting his gaze.

He looked at her, his expression guarded. He had been a bit more cautious with her since their walk on the beach the other day. Had not been quite so relaxed. Initially, she had attributed it to some kind of leisure fatigue on his part. She had rarely seen Kairos being anything but the stately ruler with posture so stiff he would make a military general envious. Now she wondered. It was something else.

But unless he told her, she wouldn't know. That, right there, was the summation of their entire relationship.

"Another bit of commentary on my skills as a husband?" he asked, his tone dry.

"No. Commentary on myself. I'm always thinking ahead. No matter where I was, it was never enough. It's never been enough. I arrive at a goalpost and I'm immediately looking ahead to the next. I spent all of high school anticipating how I would get into a university. Then I spent all that time calculating my next move. Spent every moment of my internship with you figuring out how I would parlay that into a fabulous gold star on my résumé, what job I would get when it was finished. And then, by the strangest twist of fate I could ever have imagined, I ended up being queen of the nation. I have no goal beyond that, Kairos. You can't go up from there. I was—and am—at the very top. Secure for life, in a position where I can make a difference in the world. And I've still never been happy."

"I was born a prince, I'm not certain I've ever been

particularly happy about it," he said, his tone hard. "But we are in a position to do much good. Isn't that more important than happiness?"

"I suppose. As is security. Or at least, in my experience it's difficult to be happy without security. But… Don't you think it's possible to have happiness as well?"

"I don't give it much thought."

"I think for me I've never allowed myself to rest because of the fear."

He froze then, his dark eyes flat. "Is that so?"

"Yes. I don't…I don't think I've ever honestly feared that I would turn into my mother. You're right, Kairos. I never feared that I would actually pick up a gun and shoot you in a jealous rage. But I… Attachments frighten me. How do you know who you can trust? She was my mother. She raised me from the cradle. I never imagined she would do something like that. I never saw it coming. How do you… I have always struggled to figure out how you trust someone after that. I knew her longer than I had known anyone, and still, she did something so far outside of what I imagined she might be capable of."

"I do understand something of that. It might have escaped your notice but my trust has been betrayed a time or two in my life."

Guilt twisted her stomach, because she knew that she was part of that now. A part of the betrayals that he had experienced.

"I've been thinking a lot about it. A lot about happiness. About trust. I've been waiting to feel a magical sense of both for a very long time. For my position in life to hand me happiness, for time to grant me trust of the situation I'm in. Neither has come. And so, I'm left with only one conclusion."

"That is?"

"I have to choose it. I'm going to have to make a decision to be content. I mean, for the love of God, I'm a queen with a handsome husband, a private island, a palace and a baby on the way. Choosing happiness should not be that difficult. But I think in order to achieve that I'm going to have to choose trust as well. I've been so reluctant to do that. Because the idea of having my trust misused scares me. The idea of trusting *myself* scares me. But…I can't predict the future. Neither can I control you. I can't control any of the circumstances around us, all I can do is make choices for myself. If I want to trust you, then I have to decide to trust you." She looked down, then back up again. "Trust is just like happiness. You can't wait for the evidence. Then it isn't trust. You have to choose it. And be ready to be damned along with that choice if it comes to it. But I trust you."

"So simple, *agape*?"

"Why not? So many things in life are hard. We have no control over them. I know you're well familiar with that too. Who can dictate the things that live inside of us if not us? Why do we look around, trying to claim dominion over things we cannot, while we let the things we could dominate us?"

"I didn't realize I was going to get psychology with my meal."

"I thought it paired nicely with the fish, as we can't have wine."

"And here I thought anthropology went better with fish."

"Not my field of expertise."

"A disappointment," he said. "You always seem expert in everything you try."

"Everything?" she asked, arching a brow.

His gaze turned hot. "Yes," he said, his voice rough now. "Everything."

"Hmm. Well, but then, you haven't got much experience with some of what we've been doing." She had a feeling she was edging into forbidden territory, but she wanted to ask him about this.

"This is true," he said.

"You were not a virgin when we married."

He paused, his fork halfway between the plate and his mouth. "No," he said.

"So it isn't inexperience that caused you to go without a woman…without…what I gave you recently."

"True. Are you really in the mood to examine my past relationships?"

"No," she said. "Not especially. I only want to know why. I mean, you had sex with other women but not… not that. Is it control?"

He set his fork down. "I…I'm not certain how to answer that."

"With the truth. Not your carefully reasoned version, or what you think I might want to hear. Or even what you think makes sense. The real reason. The truth."

He looked as though she'd hit him, and for a second, she felt sorry for him. But not much beyond a second. "I never felt like I deserved such a thing." The words fell from his lips reluctantly, and she could tell that even he was mystified by them.

"Why?" she asked.

"I've never liked the idea of sitting back and taking something like that as my due. You can't… You have to earn things. And serve. You can never just…take."

"I mean, I agree. Reciprocation and being generous is

certainly appreciated, but what does that have to do with letting your partner show you she wants you?"

"I've never felt I could afford such a thing. To give in to such selfish desire," he said, uncomfortable now. Clearly.

"Don't you think now after so many years…don't you think you might deserve something for you, Kairos?"

He curled his hand into a fist and she watched the tendons there shift. Everything about him was so strong. So beautiful. "Are you through eating?" he asked.

"Yes."

"I find that I am ready for bed."

Her heart fluttered, excitement firing through her body. She never tired of this new, more physically attentive Kairos. He didn't bother to hold back the attraction that burned between them. This was sex for the sole purpose of forging a deeper connection between them, finding pleasure with each other, rather than timing their unions around her cycle. It was an entirely different experience, and she loved it.

"Then, I am too," she said, without hesitation.

It occurred to her, as he swept her into his arms and carried her away from the terrace, that he might have been redirecting the conversation. That he was replacing the promise of honest talk with sex.

But she wouldn't allow those thoughts to poison the moment. She had chosen happiness. She had chosen trust. And so, she would cling to those things, as she clung to him.

In his arms, it wasn't difficult to feel perfectly content in the present. To feel secure.

And to trust that everything would work out in the end.

* * *

In spite of her resolution to trust more, she found herself overtaken with a sense of disquiet over the next couple of days. Kairos was definitely distancing himself again. She had lived under the carefully constructed frost blanket he preferred to lay out over everything for too many years not to recognize when he was gearing up to roll it out again. He made love with her every night, yes, but she didn't wake up held securely in his arms as she had done initially here on the island.

Instead, she awoke with a yawning stretch of space between them. He slept on the side of the bed nearest the door, and she couldn't help but think that one morning she would wake up and he would have gone completely. As though he were inching ever closer to the exit with each passing night.

Trust, she reasoned, was not blind stupidity. Trust was going to have to extend to herself as well, not just to him. She had to trust her own instincts where he was concerned. Something had changed, and it wasn't anything good. It was reverting back.

She couldn't help but wonder if he had gotten too close to that fire she talked about earlier, and was running from it now. If all of the intimacy, not just the sex, was getting to him. For the first time, they had really begun to talk. To peel back the layers beneath their clothes and look at who they were, not who they pretended to be.

This thing between them was uncomfortable. That much she knew. It always had been. That was why they had both turned away from it so resolutely.

She was done with that. Sadly for him, she wasn't going to allow him to run.

They had less than a week. Less than a week to fix

this thing between them. She wanted to stay with him. She had made that decision. But she wanted their marriage to be something more. She was not going to determine to remain his wife only to have things revert back to their icy state.

No, she was going to effect change. Permanent change.

Conversation didn't seem to work with him. The only way through to Kairos seemed to be using her body. When he decided to transform her from personal assistant to wife, it had been because of her mind. Because they connected on a logical level.

She was done appealing to logic. She was going to make the appeal with her body. She was going to come at all of this from a different direction. She wondered now if she had tried to seduce him sooner if things would have changed before she walked out.

There was no denying the heat that shimmered between them.

But intimacy had been missing from their sexual encounters in the past. Honesty had been missing.

She intended to reach for both tonight. To strip him bare completely, not just of his clothes, but everything else.

She had dug into the back of that wardrobe, every piece of clothing provided her by a stranger, and found a bright red dress that she would normally never have chosen. She felt as though it was painted over her curves, clinging so tightly to everything, she was certain that each and every flaw her body claimed as its own was on very loud display.

She had never worried terribly much about her figure. Why, when her husband spent so little time looking at it? But now, she intended to use it as a weapon. To be sufficient ammunition to blast that mountain of a man down to his knees.

She took a breath and looked at herself in the mirror. She hardly recognized the woman she saw there. Her blond hair was spilling over her shoulders, unrestrained. She had not styled it within an inch of its life, had not tamed it into submission. Rather, it looked a little bit wild. She was wearing lipstick that matched the dress, also much bolder and brighter than she tended to be.

But a seduction of this importance required bold and bright.

She walked down the sweeping staircase, her fingertips skimming the rail. She had repainted her nails to match the dress and to get rid of the chipped polish she had been wearing for the past few days. She wasn't going to nervously pick at this manicure. In part, because she wasn't going to be nervous.

She gritted her teeth, repeating that mantra over and over again. As though, if she thought it enough times it would make it true.

Then she saw Kairos, standing at the foot of the stairs, wearing a white shirt that was unbuttoned at his throat, revealing a tempting wedge of bronzed skin, just a hint of his dark chest hair. She loved his chest. Could spend hours exploring it with her hands, her lips and her tongue. She found that she had very few inhibitions where he was concerned. That, at least, had made the past week fun.

She smiled as her foot hit the floor and she stood, waiting to see if she could discern his reaction to her appearance.

He was stoic, as ever, his expression schooled into hard granite. But it was that grim set of his mouth, that determination in his eyes that let her know that he was in fact affected. His jaw was so tight, the veins in his neck were standing out, his hands clenched into fists, the enticing muscles of his forearms flexed with the strength that it took for him to restrain himself.

Yes, she was certainly having an effect.

"Are you dressed for dinner?" he asked.

"Actually, I'm dressed for dessert."

Kairos was not entirely certain when he lost control of the situation. Whether it was the moment he caught sight of Tabitha descending the stairs in that dress that clung to her body like a lover, outlining her full breasts, slim waist and perfectly rounded hips. Whether it was when his eyes zeroed in on her lips, painted a bold red, and he immediately imagined her leaving that color all over his skin.

Or whether it was sometime much earlier. Whether it had been slowly sifting through his fingers like sand through an hourglass from the moment they first arrived on this island. He had brought her here to force her to come around to his way of thinking. But standing here, his world seemingly turned on end, he was beginning to wonder who was in charge.

She closed the distance between them, pressing her breasts against his chest, curling her fingers around the back of his neck and drawing his head down for a kiss. It was slow, achingly so. He wanted to wrap her in his embrace, crush her up against him and claim her completely. To show her that she was not the one in control here. But he didn't want this to end. He was so desperate to see what she had planned.

Even while everything in him denied it.

Distancing himself from Tabitha over the past few days had not been a simple task. He had tasted paradise, unrestrained, unmitigated bliss at her hands, and then he had put up a wall. Had drawn a veil between them, blunting their every interaction since. Not allowing himself to get lost in it, not completely, not again. He knew his reasoning was sound, but it was a torture that he had not counted on.

She flicked her tongue out, tracing the edge of his upper lip slowly. Heat fired along his veins, molten fire pooling in his stomach. And he almost lost his control completely in that moment. She pressed her palm against his chest, against where his heart raged, almost out of control, then slid her fingertips down over his stomach, to his belt buckle. She looked up, her eyes meeting his, and his breath caught in his throat.

She meant to do this slow, that he could see clearly. It also might kill him, that he could see clearly too.

She worked his belt through the loop slowly, an echo to that first time she had gone down on him out on the terrace. She finished undoing the clasp on his pants, slipped her hands beneath the fabric and curled her delicate fingers around his aching flesh. His breath hissed through his teeth, his entire body going rigid beneath her touch.

She deepened her kiss as she stroked him, mirroring the rhythm of her hand with her tongue. An involuntary shudder wracked his entire body and she squeezed him tightly as she bit his lower lip.

"Tabitha," he growled. Begging. Cursing. Warning.

"What?" she asked, her tone a model of innocence.

"Do not test me," he said, not even knowing entirely what he meant. Only that he was desperate to push her away, but he wasn't strong enough. Physically, of course he was strong enough. She was a soft, petite woman, and physically he could overpower her if he chose. It was his spirit that wasn't strong enough. He was powerless beneath her touch. And if one of them was going to make the choice to walk away from this moment, it would have to be her. Because he could not. He had tried over the past few days to practice restraint and he was all out of it.

Not just the past few days, the past five years. Five long years of being married to a woman such as her and holding his desire for her in check. He could not. He could not endure the restraint any longer.

"Oh, *agape*, I have come here to test you. And I hope very much you fail," she said, angling her head and kissing his neck, her teeth scraping the sensitive skin there. "I came here to give myself to you. As a gift. One without strings. One you can use as selfishly as you wish. You can enjoy this, enjoy me, to your heart's content."

A feral sound escaped his lips, and he tightened his hold on her, sliding his hands down her thighs and lifting her up, her dress riding up past her hips, her legs wrapped around his waist as he carried her from the base of the stairs into the living area.

He moved over to the couch, lowering himself down onto it, keeping a hold of her hips. He sat, with her straddling his lap, her arms wrapped around his neck, his grip on her tight. She arched against him, pressing the heat of her against his heart and arousal, a short, luxurious sound of pleasure resonating through her as she did.

"I like this view," he said, sliding his hand up her waist and moving it to cup her breast, teasing her nipple with his thumb. "It is a beautiful dress. But I think I would prefer it on the floor."

He reached around, taking hold of the zipper tab and drawing it downward, letting the dress fall around her waist, revealing pale, perfect breasts. He leaned in, lowering his head and drawing one tightened bud into his mouth before circling it slowly with the tip of his tongue. She shivered beneath his touch and a surge of satisfaction claimed him. Stole every thought from his mind. He could think of nothing else but having her, consuming her, giving her mindless pleasure as she had done for him.

He tightened his hold on her, reversing their positions so that she was sitting down on the couch and he was overhead. He lowered himself onto the floor, grabbing hold of her dress and pulling it from her body, finding her completely bare beneath it. He swore, lowering himself further so that he was down on his knees, a supplicant worshipping at the temple of her beauty.

She was so beautiful, so perfectly aroused and uninhibited for him. He was so hard it was a physical pain. He wanted nothing more than to free himself completely from his clothes and bury himself deep inside of her.

But then it would be over. Far too quickly. And she was not half so mindless as he needed her to be.

He realized then that this was the definition of being thoroughly seduced. To the degree that Tabitha was no longer even the aggressor. His body was convinced that this was absolutely his idea and that there was no other course of action. He was not going to fight against it.

He moved his hands slowly along her inner thighs, avoiding the most feminine part of her. Relishing it when she shifted beneath his touch, a needy, disappointed sound escaping from her as he avoided the place he knew she was desperate for him to touch.

"Kairos," she said, her tone holding a hint of steel. A hint of demand.

"Patience, *agape*," he said.

"Why?" she asked, "I've waited five years for you to look at me like this. Why should I wait another moment?"

She was not wrong. He had never done this for her before. Had never tasted her.

He regretted it bitterly.

But he would not allow the regret to linger for much longer. Because he would satisfy that desire soon. Would satiate his appetite for her. But only after he had made her beg for it.

He moved his hand between her thighs, his finger gliding through her slick flesh, over the bundle of nerves there. She arched her back, letting her head fall back, thrusting her breasts forward, her chest rising and falling quickly with her sharp, uncontrolled breaths.

He teased the entrance to her body with his fingertips, spurred on by every restless shift of her hips as she sought out deeper penetration. "You want me," he said, his voice so rocky he barely recognized it. "You really want me."

"Yes," she gasped. "Kairos, stop teasing me."

"So wet for me, my sweet wife. I know you didn't marry me because of any passion between us. But you *do* want me." He didn't know why he felt compelled to hear her say it. To hear her confirm it yet again. Perhaps because she had left him. Perhaps because he knew she had been unhappy for so long. Because he knew he had not satisfied her physical needs as well as he could have.

Because he needed to know, beyond a shadow of a doubt that he was not alone in this deep, howling need that overtook him completely. That made him feel restless and needy. That made him feel as though he would die if he was denied her. Forget oxygen, Tabitha was the most essential element for his survival.

And he needed to know that he wasn't alone.

"I want you," she said.

"More than you have ever wanted another man?"

"I have *never* wanted another man. You're the only one. The only man I've ever kissed. The only one I've ever touched."

On a feral growl, he moved his hands, gripping her hips hard and tugging her toward the edge of the couch as he lowered his head, tasting her deeply, all semblance of restrained seduction gone completely. He was starving for her. And she was the sweetest dessert he had ever conceived of. He had been a fool to have her all these years and never have her in this way. He had been a fool to have her in his life, in his bed, and to hold himself back from her.

He was lost in her, lost in this. Lost in the needy sounds she made, in the sweet, soft surrender of her entire body. She shuddered beneath him as release overtook her. And still, he didn't stop. Didn't stop until she was sobbing, until she was begging, until another climax overtook her and she was trembling.

"I can't," she said, her tone spent.

"You can," he said, not sure where his confidence came from, not certain how he could make such a proclamation about her body. Only that in this moment, he felt as though he owned a part of it. A part of her. "You will." He kissed her inner thigh before rising up and wrapping his arm around her waist, lowering her down onto her back and positioning himself over her. "I need you," he said, kissing her lips deeply as he thrust into her.

She cried out, arching up against him, pressing her breasts against his chest, pushing her hips up against his as he buried himself inside of her. She met his every movement with one of her own, met each kiss, each sound of pleasure.

He tried to go slow, tried to keep things measured, controlled. But he was beyond any of that now. Beyond anything but his intense need for her. Arousal roared through his veins like a beast, overtaking him, consuming him. And he gave up on control. Gave up on slow. On gentle or restrained. He slipped his hands beneath her bottom, drawing her up hard against him as he thrust in deep. As he increased the intensity, as he let the world fade away, he lost himself completely in the tight, wet heat of her body.

Her internal muscles clenched tightly around him, and he felt another orgasm radiating through her. It called irresistibly to the beast inside of him. As though it was just the thing he had been waiting for. It grabbed him by the throat and he could do nothing but submit to it. To the wild, unquenchable pleasure that gripped him tightly and shook him until he was left there, bleeding out on the ground, completely and utterly defeated by the strength of the desire that had claimed him.

When it was over, he realized where he was. Naked, utterly vulnerable, utterly claimed by the woman beneath him.

He had no walls up, no defenses.

And it was unacceptable.

He pushed away from her, forcing his fingers through his hair, resting his elbows on his thighs as he leaned forward, trying to catch his breath.

"Kairos?" Her voice was soft, questioning, and he hated himself for the bastard that he was. Hated that she was now asking for things that he could never give.

And it was his fault. Because he had given in to her.

Because he had sought to bind her to him while know-ing he would never be able to give all of himself. Still, even feeling like the lowest form of life on the planet, he knew he could do nothing else. He knew there was no other course of action to be taken. He needed her. Needed her in his life forever, and at the same time he knew his own weaknesses. Knew that he had to keep his defenses strong.

This could not be endured.

"Thank you for a lovely dessert, Tabitha," he said, ris-ing to his feet. "I find I am in need of a bit of solitude."

He rose to his feet.

"Kairos," she said, her voice shaky. "Stay."

It was all so familiar. So blindingly, painfully famil-iar. In this scenario, she was the boy he'd been, aban-doned, shunned.

And he had become the one leaving.

No. He was doing this for her. To spare her any more pain. To spare himself, the country, from what might hap-pen if he were to ever surrender to his own base needs.

He was not the villain here. Even if she couldn't see it now.

He turned away from her, walking from the room. And no matter how much he burned to take one last look at her, he refused. Denied himself now as he should have done from the first.

He had been weak tonight. He would not be so again.

CHAPTER ELEVEN

"KAIROS?"

The sound of Tabitha's voice pierced Kairos's sleep. He had gone back to his room after their encounter in the living room, and he had stayed there for the rest of the evening. At some point, in spite of his discomfort, he must have fallen asleep.

"What?" he asked, not quite awake enough to sort through whether or not it was strange she was waking him up in the middle of the night.

"Kairos," she said, again. There was something in her voice that jolted him completely into wakefulness. Something tremulous, something terrified.

"What is it?"

"I'm bleeding." The word ended on a sob. "Kairos, I'm bleeding."

He shot out of bed, giving no thought to clothes, giving no thought to anything but figuring out what was happening. "What do you mean you're…?" It hit him then, exactly what it meant. "The baby."

He flipped the light on, and got a look at her face, her eyes large, her skin waxen. He had never seen Tabitha look quite like this. It occurred to him then that *she* might also be in danger. "How much blood?"

"Enough."

"How do you feel?"

"Terrified."

"I meant do you feel like you've lost too much blood?"

Her eyes grew rounder still. "Too much blood for someone who's having a baby."

"I need to call someone," he said. In that moment, his brain was blank, and he had no idea who to call. Why could he think of nothing? He was renowned for being cool under pressure. He was king of an entire nation, after all. But everything he knew, everything he thought, everything he felt was wrapped up in utter terror.

A helicopter. They needed a helicopter.

That jolted him out of his frozen state, and he reached for the phone that was sitting on his nightstand, dialing his right-hand man of the palace with one touch. "The queen is having an emergency," he said, his voice frayed. "We need a helicopter. Now. Medical personnel onboard would be ideal, but if that isn't possible, speed is more important."

"Of course, Your Highness," his man said. "We should be able to send one from the closest island and have you back in Petras in less than an hour. Further instructions will be texted to you, as far as where you should wait to be picked up."

Kairos hung up the phone, looking toward Tabitha. "Help will be here soon," he said.

She only looked at him with very large eyes, and he realized how empty and useless his words were. "Will it be too late?"

Suddenly, all of his power, his title, his status, meant nothing. Everything he had worked his entire life to become was reduced to useless ash. He didn't know the answer to the only question that mattered. He had no control over the outcome of the only thing Tabitha cared about in this moment. He could be a king, or he could be a homeless man, standing on a street corner begging for change. It wouldn't make a difference in this moment. Never before had he been so aware of his own failings. Of his own limitations.

"I don't know," he said, hating himself for not having a better answer.

She closed the distance between them, collapsing against him. He wrapped his arms around her, holding her against him, feeling unworthy that she was seeking comfort in his arms. He had nothing concrete to give her. He was of no use.

The minutes stretched on, a concrete bit of evidence of the relativity of time. It felt like hours since he had made that phone call. He found a pair of pants for himself, but bothered with nothing else. He would need to be decent when the helicopter arrived, but he could not take the time to cover more than society demanded.

Tabitha said nothing. Periodically, she would make a small, distressed sound that would pierce his heart and send a wave of pain through his body. The silence, the endless minutes, gave him plenty of opportunity to reflect on the evening. On his actions.

He had lost his control. He had been rough with her, little more than an animal. And now this. Surely it could not be a coincidence. It was a direct result of him losing himself. Losing sight of what he must be. Of what was important. In pursuit of his own emotions, he had compromised her. Their future. The future of the entire kingdom. Five years, and this was the only time they had ever successfully conceived a child, and now they were losing it.

Because of him.

Because he had become everything he despised.

At that moment his phone vibrated, and he looked down and saw a message giving instructions on where they were to meet the helicopter. "Hold on," he said, scooping Tabitha up into his arms and carrying her down the stairs, outside into the windy night. The approaching helicopter whipped the trees brutally, the sound thundering through his body. "Hold on," he said again, unsure whether she could hear him over the noise.

The giant machine touched down, and Kairos crossed the space, Tabitha held securely in his arms. Too little too late. Everything he was doing now was too little too late.

He got inside the helicopter, never releasing his hold on Tabitha. "Is anyone in here a medical professional?" The pilot and the only other men inside the cockpit shook their heads. "Then just fly as quickly as you can."

Tabitha felt weak, dazed. But then, she imagined an emergency, early-morning helicopter flight and all of the emotional trauma that had gone with it was bound to leave anyone feeling weak and dazed.

She had been in the hospital for a couple of hours now, waiting on results. She'd gotten an ultrasound, but of course the tech hadn't been able to tell her much of anything. She had to wait for the doctor. And they were also waiting for results of her blood work.

She had dozed off and on. Kairos, as far she could tell, had not even sat down since they'd arrived. She wanted to believe it was concern for her, but after the way he had distanced himself from her last night, she had serious doubts about that. A sinking feeling settled over her, dragging her down. As if she had much farther down to go.

Just then, the door to the hospital room opened and the doctor came in.

"Queen Tabitha," she said, her voice soft. "King Kairos. I'm very sorry to see you at such a stressful time."

A distressed sound filled the room, and Tabitha realized it had come from her. Hearing apology on the doctor's lips had sent a sharp, piercing pain through her. If the doctor was sorry, there was no good news for her. No good news for her baby.

"Your Majesty," the doctor said, "don't lose faith. I don't love the results that I have in front of me, but they could be worse. We were not able to see a heartbeat on the sonogram. But you have not miscarried. There is definitely something. It could very well be that it is just too early to see anything yet. Your hCG levels are quite low. I'm hoping that in a week's time we will be able to see the heartbeat, and that these levels will have doubled, which will give us an indication for how viable the pregnancy is."

Tabitha's ears were ringing. The words the doctor had just spoken were rattling around in her head, as she made an attempt to translate them.

"So she hasn't lost the baby," Kairos said, moving to stand nearer to her hospital bed.

"No," the doctor said, "at least, she hasn't miscarried. It's impossible for us to determine whether or not the fetus is viable at this point."

A tear rolled down Tabitha's cheek. She wanted the doctor to be angry, to be upset, and she knew that was counter to anything helpful. Still, she felt as if the world was falling apart. The least everyone around her could do was look as if they could see that. Like they could feel it too. Instead of throwing around all these technical terms with a calm, clinical tone that set her teeth on edge.

"Well, that's good," Kairos said, his tone as modified as the doctor's.

"The bleeding could have easily been the result of a blood vessel rupture, and might not indicate any serious issue at all."

"Until then…" Kairos spoke. "Should she be on bed rest? Should she be doing anything special?"

"If she's going to miscarry, at this stage bed rest won't help. Whatever activity she feels up to should be okay." The doctor finally turned her attention to Tabitha. "Get rest when you feel you need it. Sleep as much as you need to. Just listen to your body."

"I'm sort of angry at my body at the moment," Tabitha said. "It isn't doing what it's supposed to."

"It's hanging on as best it can," the doctor said. "Don't be too hard on it. Or yourself. If you're comfortable with it, I would like to discharge you tonight, so you can spend the week resting at the palace."

"And if she needs anything?"

"I can be there as quickly as possible, or she can be brought here. But I really do think that since we're in for a bit of a wait, it's best if you just go home and make yourself comfortable."

"A week?" Tabitha asked.

"Yes. Unless… If you miscarry between now and then, we will have our answer. But hopefully, things will stay stable. And when you come back we'll have good results."

Tabitha blinked hard, trying to hold back any more tears. "Okay." She took a deep breath. "Okay."

"Do you have any more questions for me?"

"That will be all," Kairos said.

Tabitha didn't have the energy to protest him making proclamations on behalf of the both of them. She closed her eyes, waiting until she heard the doctor's footsteps recede from the room.

"Are you ready?" he asked.

She swallowed hard. "I suppose so."

She stayed silent on the ride home and when he helped her walk into the palace, leading her back to her bedroom. She had not been here in over a month. It felt foreign, strange. She wished very much that she could go back to the island. Go back to earlier yesterday evening. She had felt happy. She had felt as though pieces were finally falling into place. Yes, she knew that she was still going to have to fight to claim him, but she'd been ready to do it. They'd had their fourteen days. And now it was shortened, taken from them. Now they were back here, in the palace, in the middle of reality. Facing an uncertain future. The possibility of a grief that she didn't feel prepared to handle.

It wasn't fair. She had finally gotten up the nerve to leave him, only to fall pregnant with his child. And now, after working so hard to forge a connection with him, to try and repair their marriage, she might be losing the baby.

What was the point of any of it?

She extricated herself from Kairos's firm hold, and crawled onto her soft bed, turning away from him, drawing her knees up to her chest.

"Are you all right?"

"No," she said, surprised at the strength in her response. "No, I'm not all right. This is wrong. All of it is wrong."

"I know."

"Not like I know it," she said, being petulant. Being unfair. Because it was her body that was enduring all of this uncertainty and pain. Because she was the one who cared so much that she had to walk away rather than spend a lifetime in pain, loving a man who didn't love her back.

The realization made her stomach clench tight. She loved him. Of course she did. She was such a fool, she never even let herself think the words for fear of the deeper implications. For fear of how much pain it would cause her in the future. But it didn't make it less true.

She wanted to be sick. Realizing that she loved him now, even as the beautiful future she had begun to imagine for them slipped away. If she lost this baby, what would be left for them? More years of trying? Or would he finally be done with her?

She knew the answer. He would stay with her. He had already made that clear. It was one reason he had pushed Andres to marry Zara, because then they could provide the country with an heir.

Misery stole over her. They were going to be right back where they started. Unless he felt differently now.

"I'm very sorry that you're having to go through this," he said.

"Aren't you going through it too?" Now she was just being spiteful. He'd said that he knew. That he understood. And she had attempted to lay a bigger claim to it than he had. Now he was giving her that claim, and she was angry because he didn't seem as affected as she was.

"Of course I am," he said. "You have no idea how important this child is to me. As the ruler of the country, it has been instilled in me from birth what my responsibilities are in this role. Producing an heir is at the forefront of those responsibilities at this stage of my life."

She sat up, anger overtaking some of the weariness. "Is that the only reason it matters to you?"

"Of course not. How can you even ask me that? I have my doubts of what manner of father I'll be. My own father had an iron fist and he certainly put me on the path to being a good ruler. But in terms of being a father, and not just a drill instructor? I'm not certain he was successful on that score. I want more for our child. I want to be different. And I don't know how to give it. I'm already worried about it. I've already thought about what it would be like to hold this baby. To walk on the beach with him or her, as we did together this week. Do not insult me by asking if the throne is the only reason I care."

"It's all you talk about."

"It's the easiest thing to talk about."

Silence settled between them. She wasn't sure what to say to that. He was right. Talking about the kingdom, the throne, was much easier than discussing feelings. Fears. Much simpler than talking about the feelings that were crowding her chest, making her feel as though she couldn't breathe. Love. Stupid, terrible love that she didn't want to feel.

"This has to work," he said, his tone desperate.

Yes, it did. Because if they didn't have the baby, what did they have? Nothing more than a cold union, and no reason to try and hold it together. She felt as though she was going to have a panic attack. She couldn't breathe.

"Tabitha," he said, his tone suddenly harsh. "Are you okay? You look like you're going to pass out."

"I need to lie down."

"Yes."

She rested her head on her pillow, pulling the covers up to her chin. "Today was terrible."

"Tomorrow will be better," he said, his tone firm and distant.

"Stay with me?" She knew that she shouldn't ask. She knew that it betrayed too much. But she just wasn't in a place to protect her pride at the moment.

There was nothing but silence in place of where his answer should be. She waited. And he said nothing.

"Please," she said.

"I had better not. You need to get some rest. You do not need me taking up any of your mattress. I'll be in my room if you need me. Keep your phone by your bed, call me if necessary."

She gritted her teeth, pain, anger lashing at her. "And will you deign to answer these texts? We both know you ignore me very often."

"I promise I won't," he said, his tone like iron.

She said nothing else to him. Instead, she waited for him to leave. She closed her eyes, turning away from him, listening to his footsteps, to the sound of the door closing. Her head was swirling with too many possibilities. Too many thoughts. It was a good thing the media didn't know about the baby yet. There was no way she could handle any of this publicly, when she had no idea how to deal with it privately.

And why are you thinking about the media at a time like this?

Because that was easier than thinking about her husband.

He was already distancing himself. Truth be told, he had been even before the medical scare.

It was then she realized that for all the talking she had done about her past, he still hadn't done any talking about his own. Yes, on paper, she knew exactly what had happened during Kairos's childhood. She knew his mother had left when he was only twelve. But she didn't know how he felt about it. Didn't know how it had impacted him at the time. Or how it impacted him now. She had told him everything—about the way her stepfather had died. About why she had worked so hard to change her life.

And all the time he had listened, but he had never given her anything in return. He had quieted any thoughts and concerns with kisses, and she had let him.

Suddenly, she sat up, rolling out of bed and walking toward her bedroom door before she could fully process what she was doing. She was tired. She was distraught. She needed to speak to Kairos.

She padded down the hall to his bedroom, which was situated right next to hers. She didn't bother to knock, rather she just opened the door. He was standing by his bed, his back facing her, his bare skin filling her vision. No, she couldn't afford to get distracted by such a thing. Anyway, right now, she was too physically tender to allow sex to cloud what was happening between them.

He turned sharply, his brows locked together. "Are you okay? You don't need to come to get me. I'll come to you. You should be lying down."

"Nothing new happened. But I was thinking. We…we need to talk, Kairos."

"Do we? I think we both need to rest."

"Of course you do. Because you don't want to talk to me. You're more than happy to allow me to talk to you.

In fact, you encourage it. You don't give me anything in return."

"Do I not give you anything? You could have fooled me. I thought I gave you quite a bit on the couch last night."

"Sex is not intimacy," she said, her voice vibrating with emotion. "It certainly can be. It has been for me. But I don't think it is for you. I think you use it to distract me. To distract yourself. I have given you so much of myself this past week. I told you about my past. I told you why I left you. What I wanted. For us, for our future. I feel like you've given me none of that in return."

"What is it you want from me, Tabitha?"

"Honesty. It's time for you to talk to me. I made the choice to trust you, Kairos, and I need you to trust me too. I need to know that we're going to have more than this distance between us."

"I can't promise that."

"Why not? You're going to have to do what I did. You're going to have to make a decision. You should be able to promise too."

"Well, I'm not going to do that. I can't."

"Why not?"

"It is not possible for me. Tabitha, I have to be strong. I have to be the king. I cannot afford to look back and examine my past. And I will not. I cannot afford to be vulnerable. Not to you, not to anything. We will have our child, and everything will make sense. I have to confess to you now that we may never have the marriage that you want. But it is still no less than I ever promised you. I have to serve Petras first. It requires me to maintain a certain amount of distance."

"Kāiros," she said, her throat closing uptight, sorrow filling her chest.

"You will not be unhappy. I think we understand each other better now. I understand you. And this… This is my honesty. It is all I can give. I am sorry if it hurts you. I truly am. But there is nothing to be done."

She nodded, swallowing hard as she turned away from him. She had tried. She had failed. She didn't know if there was anything else she could do.

"Good night," she said, walking out of the room and heading back toward hers. She closed the door firmly behind her, feeling that there was something definitive about it. About this separation. It felt very final.

No matter what, he was never going to drop his guard. He had said it now, admitted to it. He thought everything would be fine because they would have their child, and it would give her purpose. The connection she craved. But if they didn't, then she would be left with nothing. And even if they did, there was not enough between her and Kairos to want to stay in the union. She loved him. She needed him to love her too, and nothing less.

That, she realized, was the happiness she had been searching for.

She had moved through life looking for status, looking for money, for security. But she had forged no connections. Until her marriage to Kairos. And even then, in a palace, with beautiful clothes, she had been unhappy. There was more to life than that. There was love. That was what she truly craved. No money could buy it, no title could bestow it. And she could not force Kairos to feel it for her.

She lay down on the bed, the cool sheets doing little to ease the hot thrum of anxiety rioting through her veins.

She was going to have to make a decision about where to go from here. But not tonight.

Tonight she was just going to sleep. She was going to cling tightly to better thoughts of the future. She wrapped her arms around her midsection and closed her eyes tight. She was going to cling to her baby too. Pray that she made it through the night without more bleeding. Pray that she made it through with this at least.

For the first time it was easy for her to wish that she could just stay in the present. Here in the palace, married to Kairos, such as that marriage was. Pregnant with his baby. With her baby. But no matter how much she knew these things for certain, who knew what would happen tomorrow? Who knew where she would be? She didn't have a clue.

Tears started to fall from her eyes, and she didn't bother to wipe them away. Didn't bother to keep control, or pretend it didn't hurt.

This was all because of love. And even now, she couldn't regret it. She had been afraid of this. Of hurt, of heartbreak. And still, even having the worst fear confirmed, even knowing that opening herself up would only cause her pain, she regretted nothing.

At least this was honest. At least this was real. At least she wasn't hiding.

She would rather be wounded in the light than slowly fade away in the darkness. No matter how much it hurt.

CHAPTER TWELVE

KAIROS FOUND THAT he couldn't sleep. He spent the rest of the early morning hours doing paperwork in his office, then went to the dining room for coffee and breakfast. He was shocked when he saw Tabitha sitting at the table, a mug of tea in front of her, along with a piece of toast. She was dressed impeccably, in her usual style. A pristine black dress, a single strand of pearls, her blond hair pulled back into a bun. The only indication that she had not slept well was the dark circles under her eyes.

"Are you well?" he asked, moving to the head of the table to sit down.

"I'm still pregnant, if that's what you're asking."

"Yes, that is what I was asking." Except it wasn't. He wanted to ask her how she had slept. He wanted to ask if he had wounded her terribly last night. But he could not.

"All right, then, now that that's out of the way. There is something else we need to discuss."

"I would like to have some coffee first."

"And I don't want to wait. In this instance, I feel I should get my way. As I'm the one who is pregnant and in distress."

"I'm in a decent amount of distress, having not had any sleep or caffeine."

She shot him a pointed, deadly glare. "Why didn't you stay with me last night?"

"Because you needed rest."

"And you were going to keep me up all night, telling me ghost stories?"

"No, not ghost stories. But I may not have respected the fact that you needed rest, and not my lecherous advances."

"I have a bit more respect for your control than that, Kairos. I hardly think you're going to accost your recently hospitalized wife."

He gritted his teeth. "You don't know that. Neither do I, frankly. The way that I treated you before the bleeding started was appalling."

"On that score we can agree."

He thought back to how roughly he handled her, how desperate he'd been. He would never forgive himself if anything happened to their baby. Because of him. It would all be because of him.

"I am sorry," he said, his voice rough. "Do forgive me for how rough I was. I lost myself in a way I did not believe possible."

"What are you talking about?"

"I was too rough with you."

"That isn't what I thought you were talking about. I thought you meant after. When you left me. I was upset about that. I needed you to stay. I needed you to hold me. You had… Kairos, you had never done that to me before. It had never been like that. I needed to stay with you, to rest in that experience with you. Otherwise, it's just sex. It isn't intimacy at all."

Relief washed over him, but along with it came anger. Frustration. "I told you, intimacy is not something we can share. Not in the way you want it. You wanted honesty, and I am willing to offer. I'm just sorry it isn't the grand revelation you were hoping for."

"I don't understand why. I still don't understand."

"I cannot make you understand," he said, his temper fraying now. "There is nothing I can say beyond what I have already said."

"Tell me something. Tell me something real about you. Tell me… Tell me what happened when your mother left. Tell me what it is like to have your father raise you."

"I have told you about my father already. He was cold, he was distant. He was trying to make me strong. And I understand why. I cannot resent him for it, even if I cannot claim to have felt happiness in my childhood. It made me the man that I am, the man that I must be."

"Stop it. You're not a robot. You're a human being. Stop pretending that you don't have any feelings. Stop pretending that a childhood being raised by a drill sergeant was fine just because it turned you into what you consider to be an ideal ruler. It's false, Kairos. It all rings so incredibly false. And I can't live a life that way anymore. I simply can't. I spent too many years hiding. Too many years pursuing empty things, looking for happiness that I was never going to find hiding behind a wall. I was so deeply concealed I couldn't even see the sun. Yes, I didn't feel very many bad things, but I didn't feel good things either. Right now? I have never been more terrified than I am right now. I have never prayed so hard for something to work out. I want this baby more than you can imagine. And the very idea of losing it fills me with so much pain… I can barely even think of it at all. But I wouldn't trade it. Not for anything. I wouldn't go back and protect myself by never becoming pregnant.

Because it's touched deeper parts of myself that I never even knew existed. It makes me hope. With a kind of intensity I didn't know I could feel. And it's the same…it's the same with you."

The back of his neck prickled, cold dread living in his chest and radiating outward. "What do you mean?"

"This can't last," she said, her tone filled with sadness, with regret.

"What can't?" he bit out.

"This. Us. I can't go back to the way things were. And if this scare with the baby has taught me anything, it's that what we tried to build on the island still isn't strong enough."

"No. That isn't true," he said, terror clawing at him now.

"It is. Because I can't fight against a brick wall. Not forever. And yes, for a while, I thought maybe it could be different. I thought maybe I could make it work for the sake of the baby. But if that's the only reason we're doing this, then we're not building a strong enough foundation. We only make each other miserable. We'll make our child miserable."

"Or, do you secretly believe you're going to lose it? Are you hoping that you will?"

He regretted his words when he saw her reaction to them. She drew back, as though he had slapped her. "Of course I don't. I want more than anything for our child to be born healthy. But, Kairos, we might lose the baby. And then why are we together? If there isn't an answer to that question, we shouldn't be together no matter what happens."

"You don't think that the heat between us is a reason to stay together?"

"No. Because it isn't enough. Because I can't get so

close to what I want and then have you pull away. It's cruel. I can't exist this way, not anymore."

"Why are you changing things?" he roared, standing up from his seat, rage propelling him forward. "We had a bargain from the beginning. Are you such a liar, such a manipulative bitch?" He hated himself. Hated the words that were coming out of his mouth, but he couldn't stop them. He felt as though the floor was dropping out from beneath him. He had given her everything he was able to give her, and still it wasn't enough. Still she was leaving him. How dare she? He was the king. She was carrying his child. She was his wife.

"Because I changed. I'm sorry. I love you, Kairos. If you can't love me back—I don't mean just *saying* that you love me to make me stay—I mean showing me. I mean giving me parts of yourself. Giving me your soul, not just your body, then I can't stay. Because it hurts too badly."

He felt as though she had reached inside his chest and grabbed hold of his heart, squeezing it tight. She stood up, taking a step away from him, and he felt as if she was going to pull his heart straight from his chest now. That if she took another step away she would take it with her.

Perhaps you should be grateful if she did.

He couldn't breathe.

"Do not leave me," he said.

"What would you give me? And I don't mean clothing, or money, or even pleasure. What will you give me of yourself? Kairos, I've witnessed terrible things. Things that no child should ever have to see. I spent my life hiding because it fractured my view of people. Because for a long time I believed that everyone was hiding something dark and frightening beneath the surface. I had to choose to trust you, and it was the hardest thing I have ever done. So when you tell me that you can't give more to me, I believe you. And I'm not going to sign up for blind faith. For going on for another five years, living in hope that someday you might fall for me. That someday you might break down the wall you've put up around yourself."

"I am a king. I have to put a wall around myself."

"Why?"

He didn't like these questions. Didn't like that her words tested the logic of his argument. "Because I must," he answered. He refused to dig deeper. Refused to uncover that dark well, the lid to the center of his chest, the one that housed the truth of all this. The outcome would be the same, so there was no point. No point at all.

"And I must do this. I have to go, Kairos. I have to."

She turned away from him and he found himself staring down his worst fear. As the woman who rooted him to the earth, who kept his heart beating, began to walk away from him. He had lowered himself completely and begged for his mother to stay, and it had made no difference. And here he was again, facing down his fear. He had to wonder if that moment on the beach wasn't a cautionary tale so much as it was a premonition.

She kept walking away, and he said nothing.

Tell her to stay.

His entire body seized up, his throat closing. And still, he said nothing.

He watched her walk out, her shoulders straight and still. Proud in that way Tabitha always was. And so silent, even when she was hurting. Five years he'd been married to her and most of the time she'd been in pain.

Because of him.

At least this way, she's free of you.

He was free of her too. He should be grateful. He did not need a wife. Everything would be fine with the child, there was no other option. The child would be fine. He would have his heir, and the country would be secured.

That was all that mattered. There was no honor in being a divorced king, but his father had been. This country had been absent a queen for a very long time.

And so it would be again.

He laughed into the empty space, a bitter, hollow sound. He had always aspired to be the king his father was. And now, he had become so.

A king without a queen, who had surrounded his heart in a wall of stone as cold as the castle that he lived in.

Without her, it would be all the colder. But he would welcome it, embrace it. It would make him the leader he had always needed to be. It was a small sacrifice to make for the good of the nation.

A good ruler led with his head and not his heart. A good thing too. Because when Tabitha walked out, she took his heart with her.

And still, he let her leave. In the end, he counted it a blessing.

Finer feelings were for men who had not been born with a kingdom to protect.

He clenched his jaw tightly, and curled his fingers into fists, tightening his hold until his tendons ached. He welcomed the dull pain because it distracted him from the sharp, bitter anguish in his chest. An ache he had a feeling he would have to become accustomed to.

But it was nothing he had not dealt with before. He would make room for this pain next to the one left by his mother. And he would go on as he always had.

There was no other option.

CHAPTER THIRTEEN

FOR THREE NIGHTS, Kairos was plagued with nightmares. Images of a woman walking away from him, of his voice not working, his feet being stuck to the spot. He hated this. This feeling of powerlessness. And in his sleep, it refused to abate. During the day, he did what was required of him. He even issued an official statement regarding the separation of himself and the queen.

Part of him had imagined that if he took official steps to deal with the divorce, it would set things right inside of him. That it would make things feel final. But nothing took away the dreams.

He threw the covers back on his bed and stood, walking out the double doors that led to a balcony that overlooked the mountains and the forest back behind the palace. There was still snow on the ground here in Petras at the higher elevations, and it blanketed everything in glittering frost, making the time spent on the island seem even more surreal. Even more removed from time.

He was continually waiting for a sense of relief to hit. With Tabitha gone, he would not have to contend with the more conflicting elements of their relationship. He would be free to focus again with a kind of single-mindedness he hadn't fully managed since they married.

The icy air bit into his bare skin and he did nothing to shield himself from the cold as he walked farther out onto the balcony, resting his hands on the balustrade and looking out over all of the land that he bore responsibility for. This was his birthright. This was what he would leave to his child, should he ever truly have one.

Usually, he felt some sense of pride looking down at Petras. Tonight, the bare landscape seemed as empty as he was. It did not seem full of promise, at least, not for any future he cared about. He should be angry. Angry that Tabitha had proven to be as false as every other woman in his life.

But he was not. Because for whatever reason, he could not make comparisons between Tabitha and his mother, not now. Yes, that moment had reminded him of the day his mother had walked away, but she was not his mother.

And he'd never truly been afraid of that. He'd told himself he was. That he needed a cold, loveless union to prevent himself from falling prey to a fickle, passionate woman. But that had never been his real fear. *He* was his real fear.

When he had fallen to his knees and wept after his mother had left, when he had refused to leave his room, to get out of bed for days after she had gone, his father had told him that he showed the same signs of weakness that had caused his mother to abandon her duty.

And Kairos had known it to be so. After their mother had left, many people looked at Andres and thought that he was a reflection of the queen. Flighty, free-spirited, and given to reckless, spontaneous action. But Kairos had known the truth.

Andres—while giving the impression of being the feckless spare—did everything with a measure of cold calculation. He did it for the response of the people around him, did it to test their loyalty. And he did it to great effect. But it was Kairos who had that deep well of emotion down in his soul. The one that he could not control. The one that would cause him to act recklessly, to abandon his duty if emotion dictated.

He had wanted to be his father. Desperately. To be the kind of leader that the country needed. But he had known that he wasn't. He was his mother, through and through. Weak, emotional. And so, he had sought to destroy it. To go out of his way to erect barriers between those deadly emotions and his decisions. So he had trapped both himself and Tabitha in a union that could have been, and should have been so much more than he was willing to allow it to be.

Because he was afraid. Afraid of what he might do. Afraid of how weak he might truly be.

You just have to choose. You have to choose to trust.

No. He could not make that choice. Couldn't choose to trust himself or Tabitha.

He gritted his teeth against the anguish that assaulted him. He wanted her. Just thinking about her sent a wave of longing over him. A wave of longing that was destined to go unmet for the rest of his life.

He thought back again to the night his mother had left. To the look in her eyes. Sadness. Fear. She had been afraid. He had never fully realized that before this moment. How could he? When she had left, he had been little more than a boy, concerned entirely with his own emotions and not at all with hers. She was the enemy of that tale, and nothing more. That had been reinforced by his father, and also by his increased understanding of the way she had treated Andres when he was a boy.

But, for some reason, now all he could see was the fear. It twisted the memory, changed it. Made the moment into something different altogether. She wasn't walking away from him. She was running. Running from the palace. From that life. Likely, from the weight of responsibility.

Oh, how he knew that fear. That very same fear. He was running, even now.

He turned away from the balustrade, walking back into the bedroom, and pulled on his pants. Then he took a sharp breath and walked out the door, stalking down the hall, headed for his office. He badly needed a drink. Something, anything to quiet the demons that were rioting through his mind.

He pushed open the door, making his way to the bar at the far end of the room, shutting out all of the memories currently assaulting him of what it had been like to take Tabitha in here. To put her up on that desk and release five years of desperate sexual tension in one heady moment.

He ignored the images that were assuming control of his consciousness and poured a measure of liquor into a glass. Behind him, he heard the door open. He turned, part of him expecting to see Tabitha there for some strange reason.

But no. Tabitha was gone. And it was only Andres.

"What are you doing up?" Kairos asked.

"I got up to ask you that question. It isn't every day I see you wandering around the palace without a shirt. Actually, it isn't any day." Andres walked into the room, over toward the bar. He took the whiskey bottle out of Kairos's hand and set about to pouring himself a generous portion. "Do you want to talk about it?"

"I would rather be publicly flogged, then tarred in honey and rolled over an anthill."

"Excellent. Pretend that I didn't ask, but that I'm commanding we talk about it instead."

"Excuse me, Andres. If you have forgotten you are the spare? I am your king."

Andres waved a hand. "All hail." He took a sip of his drink. "Does this have something to do with your wife?"

He looked down at his glass. "She left."

"Right. This is after your last-ditch reconciliation attempt of the past week and a half or so."

"Yes."

"I hate to be the one to tell you this, Kairos, but that is not how a reconciliation is supposed to work."

"I'm not in an exceptionally good mood, Andres. So unless you want to find yourself in the…stocks or something, you might want to watch the way you speak to me."

"I don't know what century you're living in, but there are no stocks in the town square anymore."

"I might be tempted to build some."

"Tell me what's happening," Andres said, all teasing gone from his tone now. "It can't end like this between the two of you."

"Why not?"

"Because you love her. And I know she sure as hell loves you, though I can't quite figure out why."

Kairos lifted the glass to his lips, trying not to betray just how frightening he found Andres's words. "She said she loved me."

"I see," Andres said. "As one who nearly destroyed his own chance at happiness, take my advice. If a woman like that loves you, then you would be a fool to refuse her." Andres paused for a moment. "Actually, it's very close to advice you gave me. You told me that if Tabitha looked at you the way that Zara looked at me, you would never let her go. But she does, Kairos. She always has. I know you don't find emotion easy. I certainly don't, or haven't, in the past. But that doesn't mean it isn't worth it."

"What did you think of our father, Andres?"

Andres frowned. "I don't know. He didn't have very much time for me. I wasn't of any great value to him."

"And our mother?"

"You know she had no patience for me," Andres said, speaking of how she used to leave him at home during royal events. Afraid that he would cause a scene, that he would somehow find a way to sabotage things.

"Did you ever…? Did you ever wonder why?"

Andres laughed, a short, bitter sound. "Well, as it's the source of all of my emotional issues, I have wondered a time or two."

"They have much to answer for, our parents," Kairos said.

"As do I," Andres said. "Have I ever told you, with all sincerity, how sorry I am about what happened with Francesca? Because I am. Very sorry."

"I know," Kairos said. "And to be honest with you…I was only ever relieved. It was never her for me. Never."

"That doesn't excuse me. Neither does our mother's exit. I know it wasn't only me. But I did blame myself. Now, I understand that there must have been other things happening. I just don't know what."

Kairos nodded slowly. "Yes. I was there. The night that she left. I tried to—I tried to stop her. Looking back, I feel like she seemed afraid."

"It's strange you should say that. What I think of her

now, that's what I think. She didn't seem so much angry at me, as afraid of…something."

"Did you ever want to find her?"

"No one knows what happened to her."

"No," Kairos said, his voice broken. "That isn't true."

"Kairos?"

"I know where she is," Kairos said. "I have known. I went searching for her after our father died. Or rather, I had someone do a bit of searching. I haven't made contact. But I do know that she's living in Greece, using a different name."

"I don't think I want to speak to her," Andres said.

"And I don't blame you. Not with the way she treated you. But I…I might need to."

"You do what you have to. But I may not be able to support you with this."

"Tabitha's pregnant," he said. He had been determined not to tell his brother, particularly as everything was in a precarious position at the moment, but he found he couldn't hold back any longer. He needed Andres to understand why he was going to pursue contact with their mother. Especially after all she had put his brother through. "It isn't going well. The doctor's concerned that she will miscarry. But she is pregnant, for now."

Andres cursed. "I…I'm not entirely certain what to say to that. Whether or not to congratulate you."

"It's difficult. That's why…that's why I tried to save our marriage."

"Is that the only reason?"

"No. Of course not."

"Did you tell her that?"

"I don't know what to tell her. I don't…I don't know how to do this. I spent too many years training myself not to feel things. I don't recognize any of it now. I don't know how to move forward now."

Andres nodded slowly. "I think you're lying to yourself. I think you know full well how to proceed. I think you know full well how you feel. I just think that you also happen to be terrified."

Kairos couldn't argue with that. "That's why I need to talk to our mother. I have to find something out."

"And you don't think you'll give the poor woman a stroke? Calling her after twenty years of no contact?"

"Well, I think she nearly gave me one when she left me crying on the palace floor as a twelve-year-old boy. We can consider ourselves even."

"I thought I was a little bit more well-adjusted since my marriage, but all of this emotion still makes me slightly uncomfortable."

"Extremely."

"Do whatever you have to do, Kairos, but do not let Tabitha get away." Andres turned and walked out of the office, leaving Kairos alone.

Now, all he had to do was wait until it was late enough for him to call a woman he hadn't seen in more than two decades.

He was afraid. He didn't know if he could trust her, or himself.

But if he had learned one thing from Tabitha it was that you had to make choices. And he was making them now.

"Hello. Is this Maria?" Kairos could scarcely breathe around the lump in his throat as he waited for the response to come down the telephone line.

"Yes," the response came, questioning, uncertain.

"Then I am hoping I've reached the right person. It

is entirely possible I have not. But I am King Kairos of Petras. And if that means anything to you, then you are the person I'm looking for."

There was nothing in response to that but silence, and for a moment, Kairos was certain she had hung up the phone.

"Hello?" he asked.

"I'm here," she said. "I'm here."

"You are my mother."

"Yes," she said, her voice a whisper.

"I am very sorry to call you suddenly like this. Especially because I do not have time to make light conversation. There are some things I need to know. And it may be difficult."

"You don't have to apologize to me. I'm the one who should be apologizing."

"Perhaps," he said, ignoring the knot that tightened in his chest. "But there will be plenty of time for that. Later."

"I hope so. What is it you need to know, Kairos?" she asked, her voice wrapping itself around his name like an embrace.

"I need to understand why you left. And I need to know why... I need to know why you treated Andres as you did. He will not ask."

"He grew up to be quite a lot of trouble, didn't he?" The question wasn't full of judgment, but rather a soft, sad sort of affection.

"You have read the tabloids, I take it?"

"Some. I could never resist the chance to look upon you again. Even if only for a moment."

"He has settled. He has a wife. He is a good husband to her. Where I fear...I am not so accomplished as a spouse." He took a deep breath. "This is why I need to know. I need to know why you left."

"It took me a very long time to answer that question for myself," she said, her voice sounding thin. "A lot of therapy. A lot of regrets. Please, know that I regretted it. Even as I was leaving. But there was no going back."

"My father's doing?"

"Yes. He could not… He said he could not forgive me. And that the damage was already done. It wasn't only that he refused to take me back…he refused to let me see you."

It didn't surprise him to hear that about his father. And perhaps, because it was so unsurprising, he couldn't find it in him to be angry. He only felt a strange sense of relief over the fact that she had thought of them again. She had wanted to come back. Selfish, perhaps. But he found comfort in it.

"I knew it would come to that point with him," she continued, her voice sad. "I always had. My family raised me to be the queen. To marry the king. I was trained. But I always feared that I would not be equal to the task. Your father would get so angry when Andres would act up. That's why I stopped having him come to events. I was afraid he would start taking it out on him. As it was, he simply took it out on me."

"He didn't hurt you?"

"Not physically. But…it was very trying. I was afraid of where it might lead eventually. I was just so afraid of doing something wrong. And you boys were a reflection on me. In your father's eyes, if you did something wrong, it was directly related to a weakness of mine. And I…I wasn't strong enough to fight against that. I was so low. And I just left you with him. That was the hardest thing later. Once I was gone. Realizing that I had abandoned you to stay with that cold man who… But I didn't feel I was helping you. Not by being there. I certainly wasn't helping Andres. I couldn't be the mother that he needed. I did more harm to him than I ever did good. Once I realized that…I just…I didn't feel I did a good enough job as queen. And I didn't feel I did a good enough job as a mother. At that point, I had convinced myself that you were better off without me. I was just so afraid that if I didn't leave, he would make me go. And for some reason, that seemed worse. And if I waited for that…well, I might have done more damage to you both by then and I was so afraid of that."

Kairos nodded, before realizing that she couldn't see him. "Yes," he said, his voice rough, "I can understand that."

"You can?" she asked, her voice so filled with hope it broke his heart.

"Yes. I have been afraid too. But someone very wise once told me that sometimes we just have to make a choice. A choice to trust. The choice to let go."

He realized, right then, that he had a choice to make. To release his hold on the past, to refuse to allow any more power over the present. Tabitha was right. You couldn't wait for these things to go away. Couldn't wait until a magical moment of certainty, couldn't wait for a guarantee. It didn't exist.

There was no magic. Sometimes, you had to get up and move the mountains all on your own.

"That is very wise. But I'm not certain I deserve for anyone to choose to let my sins go."

"I'm not certain that matters either," he said. There were so many years between this moment, and that moment in the hall in the palace when his mother had left. So much bitterness. So much pain. Part of him railed against the idea of releasing it, because shortly, it couldn't be so simple.

In truth, he knew it wouldn't be simple. But it was the only way forward.

"Come and visit us," he said. "When you can. The palace will facilitate your travels."

"Oh," she said. "Are you… You're certain you want to see me?"

"You left because of fear. I pushed my wife away because I was afraid. There is nothing more to fear now. Anger, hurt, it doesn't have to stand in the way. At least, not if we make the choice to put it away."

"You would do that for me?"

"For me. For me, first. Don't get the idea that I turned into anything too selfless. I realized that I had to speak to you, to put all of this to rest first before I could move on with my life. I want very much for us to get on with life. All of us."

"I would very much like that too, though I don't deserve it."

"Heaven forbid we only got what we deserved. If that were the case, then there would be no point in me going and trying to fix things with Tabitha," he said.

"Go. You should always go. I didn't. And I will never stop regretting it."

"No more regrets. For any of us."

CHAPTER FOURTEEN

Tabitha felt wrung out. She hadn't had the energy to try and secure herself a place other than Kairos's penthouse, and to his credit, he hadn't come after her. Also, to his discredit, he hadn't come after her. She didn't know what she wanted. She didn't know what she had expected. Something. To hear from him.

You expected him to stop you.

Yes, two days ago when she had walked out of the palace, she had expected him to prevent her from leaving. But he hadn't. He had simply let her go. Damned contrary man.

The bright spot was that she had no more bleeding. She was feeling well, and not terribly drained. At least, not physically. Emotionally, she felt exhausted. She was sad. As though there was a weight in each of her limbs, pulling her down, trying to bury her beneath the earth. She was beginning to think it might succeed. That the weight would win. That the overwhelming heaviness would become too great a burden, that she would simply lay her head down and not get up and spend the rest of her days in bed, watching life go by.

Why did she have to love him so much? It was more convenient when she believed herself simply unhappy because of distance. Not unhappy because she was the victim of unrequited love.

She walked out of the bedroom, into the kitchen, feeling extremely contrary, because she wanted to lie down desperately, but she also needed to get something to eat. She stopped as soon as she walked into the main part of the room. She pressed her hand to her chest, as if it would keep her heart from beating right out of it.

"Kairos," she said, stopping cold when she saw her husband standing there.

He looked as if he hadn't slept in the past two days. His black hair was disheveled and there were dark circles under his eyes. His white dress shirt was undone at the collar, the sleeves pushed up to his elbows. He looked devilish and devastating. Like every good dream she could hope to have for the rest of her life. So close, so real, but untouchable.

"Are you all right?"

"Is that going to be the first question you ask me every time we see each other from now on?" And she realized just then that they would see each other again. At least, if all went right with the pregnancy, which she desperately wanted.

They would be forced to see each other at sonograms. At the hospital when she went into labor. Every time they passed their child back and forth. She would have to watch him walk away, taking a piece of her heart with him. Not just because he was holding their child, but because he was leaving too.

There would be no clean break, no getting over it. And if he remarried... If he had more children with another woman... She would be forced to see that too. And photographs of it in the papers, and clips of it on TV. A woman standing in her position.

She pressed her hand to her stomach, and doubled over, a harsh cry escaping her lips.

"Tabitha!" Suddenly, his strong arms were around her, holding her close. "Tabitha, what is it?"

"I can't do this," she said, her voice nearly a sob. "How can I see you and not have you? How can I watch you with another woman? How can I watch her take my place, and hold my child and bear more of yours? Kairos, this can't be endured. I can't."

"You're the one who left," he said.

"Yes, I left. Because I can't live with you when you don't love me either. Why do you have to make everything impossible?" She straightened, and he took a step back, but she followed the motion, pressing herself against his chest, hitting him with her closed fist, even while she rested her head there, listening to the sound of his beating heart. "Why do I still love you?"

"I never quite understood why you loved me in the first place," he said, his deep voice making his chest vibrate against her cheek.

"I don't either. I was very careful. I was supposed to marry a man so cold he could never melt the walls I built up. You didn't hide it well enough."

"What?"

"How wonderful you are. Even when I couldn't see it, I could feel that it was there. And I just wanted…I want everything you hide from me."

"I want to stop hiding," he said, his voice rough.

She lifted her head, looked into his dark eyes. "You what?"

"I called my mother. And I…I have to tell you something. I never wanted to tell you about the night my mother left. It was a defining moment for me. A mark of my great failure, a warning against what I might become. My greatest weakness."

"You aren't weak. If there's one thing I know about you, Kairos, it's that."

"But I have been. Just not…in the way that I recognized weakness. I have been afraid. Like you, I've been afraid of being hurt again. Afraid of undoing everything I have learned. And that if it happens, I will no longer be able to do what I need to do as king of this country. It isn't that I feel nothing, Tabitha. I feel things, so deeply, and I spent a great many years trying to train that away."

"What happened when your mother left?"

"I saw her. I saw her walking out and I knew. I knew because I always felt I was more like her than I was like my father. She felt things so deeply. At first, it was one of the very beautiful things about her. But I… Talking to her, I understand. My father took that softness and twisted it. He made her feel like there was something wrong with her. Like her feelings were going to bring down the kingdom. I understand, because he did the same with me. He saw me crying after she left. I started the moment I fell to my knees and begged her to stay, and she walked out anyway. And I didn't stop. He saw me, twelve years old and weeping like a baby for my mama, and he told me that I could not afford such emotion. Such weakness. But you see, it is this false strength that has become my greatest enemy. It has kept me safe from heartbreak, but it has destroyed any chance I might have had at a normal life. At love. And when you told me you loved me…I didn't know how to respond. Or, rather, I didn't know how to be brave enough to respond."

"Kairos, of course you're brave. You're the strongest man I've ever known."

"Who was reduced to trembling by your declaration."

"Love is terrifying. It's certainly the most terrifying thing I've ever confronted."

"But everything of value comes at a price, does it not? Otherwise it would have no value. And so, I think the price for love is that you must lay down your fear. Your anger. Your resentment. Because you cannot carry them and carry love along with them. But no one can put them down for you. And very often, time is not enough to reduce the burden. So you must set them down. As you said, for you, trust had to be a choice. You chose to trust me, and I used it badly. For that, I am sorry."

"I was going to say that's okay. But it really isn't. You hurt me. So badly."

"I know." He reached up, cupping her cheek. "I know. Tabitha, my arms are empty now. I set everything down. Everything that will get in the way of you. Of the love that I want to give you." He wrapped his arms around her, pulling her into his embrace. "I put it all away so that I could carry my love for you. It's all I want. It's all I need."

Her heart was thundering hard, her throat tight, aching. She could hardly believe the words she was hearing. She was afraid for a moment that she might be dreaming. "You love me?"

"I have. From the beginning. But there was too much in the way. Too many things I didn't need. All I need, all I have ever needed, is you. You make me a stronger man. My love for you is what makes me think that I should be."

"We don't even know... Kairos, if I lose this baby, I don't know if there will ever be another one." She swallowed hard. "Five years, it took five years for us to conceive this one and now..."

"It doesn't matter. It...it matters, because of course I want to have children with you. But as far as whether or not I stay with you, there is no condition placed upon your ability to bear children. The country will do just fine with Andres's children if need be. Or with the children of the distant cousin if we must. The country will survive, that much I know. But I will not survive without you."

She tilted her head up, pressed a kiss to his lips. "I love you," she said, her heart so full it could burst.

"I love you too. Whatever lies ahead, we will face it together." He took hold of her hand, curled his fingers around it and pulled it against his chest, placing it right over his beating heart. "I am stronger because of you," he repeated. "Never forget that. You're the one who showed me that we always have a choice. That you can choose to let go of the painful things in the past, so that you can have a future."

"I'm so busy being happy, I realized that for myself," she said. "Because I'm so glad that now, no matter what our pasts, we're going to have a future together."

"Yes, my love, we will."

"I'm so glad, *agape*," she said, smiling up at him.

"I imagine I'm allowed to call you that again."

"Yes, because now I know you mean it."

"Do you see it?"

"What?" Tabitha asked, holding on to Kairos's hand so tightly it hurt.

"That little flicker there." Kairos pointed that out on the sonogram monitor, and they both looked at the doctor.

"You have a heartbeat," she said, smiling at Tabitha. She

moved the wanderer over Tabitha's stomach, and a slight frown creased her brow. "Actually, I see another one."

All of the breath left Tabitha's lungs in a gust. "Two?"

"Yes." The doctor paused, highlighting two different places on the screen. "There," she said, pointing, "and there."

"What does that mean?" Tabitha asked, knowing that she was feeling sick. But for the past week she had been certain they would find a living baby inside of her. She could hardly process what they were seeing now.

"Twins," the doctor said.

Tabitha looked up at Kairos, who was looking a bit pale and shell-shocked. "It looks like you'll be getting your heir and spare all in one shot," Tabitha said.

"Neither of them will be a spare," Kairos said, his tone fierce.

"Of course not. But that is what they call it. And it's what you call your brother."

"I'm going to outlaw the term," he said, his eyes glued to the screen. "Twins. You're absolutely certain?"

"Completely," the doctor said. "It's very likely the bleeding was nothing, and she was simply too early in her pregnancy last week to see a heartbeat."

"Well," Kairos said, bending down and kissing her cheek. "You are certainly full of surprises, my queen."

"Quite literally, at the moment."

Kairos laughed. "Yes. Very much."

Tabitha sighed happily, her eyes on the screen, on the evidence of life in front of her. "I'm glad you put all your burdens down, Kairos."

"Is that so?"

"Yes. Because for the next eighteen years we're definitely going to have our hands full."

EPILOGUE

NEW YEAR'S EVE was officially Kairos's favorite holiday. It had been for the past five years. Ever since that New Year's Eve when his wife had been waiting in his office at midnight, ready to demand a divorce.

Because since then, everything had changed. Most importantly, he had changed.

He looked around the large family area in the palace. Everything was still decorated for Christmas, the massive tree in the corner glittering. This was the last night they would have it. The last night before all of the holiday magic was removed and everything returned back to normal.

The children were already protesting. The twins, along with Zara and Andres's brood—which was in Kairos's estimation a bit much at three, with one on the way—were not ready for the holidays to be over.

"I don't want to go to bed," Christiana said, pouting in that way of hers that was both aggravating and irresistibly charming. At four, she had discovered that she could use her cuteness against her parents to great effect.

"I don't either," said Cyrena, turning an identical pout his direction.

"It is nearly midnight," he said.

"It is not," Christiana said.

"Well," Tabitha responded, "it is somewhere in the world."

Andres laughed. "That isn't good enough," he said, "not for my niece. She's far too clever for that."

"Worry about your own children, Andres," Kairos said.

"Mine do not know their numbers yet. I live in fear of that day."

"And when they learn to spell," Zara said, placing her hand over her rounded stomach.

"The horror," Kairos said. "Okay, girls. It is truly bedtime. But I am certain if you ask her very nicely, Grandma Maria would love to come and read to you."

His mother smiled at all of them from her position on the couch. Reconciliation was never easy. It had been particularly difficult for Andres. And as far as Kairos went, it came and went like the tide for the first year or so, as he dealt with anger, sadness at all the missed years and then determination not to miss any more because of mistakes that were long past the point of correcting.

All they could do was move forward now. And now, when he saw his mother with his children, with Andres and Zara's children, he knew that none of them regretted their decision to release their hold on the past.

"Of course I will," she said. "I never tire of reading to them."

She ushered the children out of the room, and then Andres looked at Zara. "Are you exhausted yet, princess?"

"Very," she said, "and my feet hurt."

"Well, we can go back up to my bedroom, and I will rub your feet. And possibly some other things."

Zara smacked him on the shoulder, then followed

him out of the room anyway, leaving Kairos and Tabitha alone.

It was then that Tabitha turned to him, smiling at him, unreserved, unrestrained. Perfection. "Do you think we'll make it until midnight tonight?"

"I do always try to stay awake until midnight on New Year's Eve. Just in case you decide to ask for a divorce. I would hate to sleep through it."

She laughed. "Not a chance." She looked around the room. "Can you imagine if we had given up then? Can you imagine what we would have missed?"

"I don't like to. I'm so grateful that you gave me a second chance."

"So am I." She leaned against him, wrapping her arm around his waist. "Do you remember when I told you how hard it was for me to be happy in the present? How difficult it is for me to simply be in the moment?"

"Yes," he said.

"It isn't now. I have lived in a million perfect moments since you said you loved me. And this is one of them."

Kairos looked around at the Christmas decorations, the evergreen twisted around the pillars, the large tree and the clear lights that glittered in the midst of the dark branches. And he had to agree. The perfect moment, the perfect woman.

The perfect life.

* * * * *

AWAKENED
BY HER
DESERT CAPTOR

ABBY GREEN

This is for Iona, Heidi, Fiona and Susan...
my support network. Love you ladies

PROLOGUE

THE PRIEST'S EYES widened as he took in the spectacle approaching down the aisle, but to give him his due he didn't falter in his words, which came as automatically to him as breathing.

It was a slim figure, dressed from head to toe in black leather, the face obscured by a motorcycle helmet's visor. The person stopped a few feet behind the couple standing before the priest, and his eyes widened even further as a young woman emerged from under the motorcycle helmet as she took it off and placed it under one arm.

Long red hair cascaded dramatically over her shoulders just as he heard himself say the words, '…or for ever hold your peace…' a little more faintly than usual.

The woman's face was pale, but determined. And also very, very beautiful. Even a priest could appreciate that.

Silence descended, and then her voice rang out loud and clear in the huge church. 'I object to this wedding. Because last night this man shared my bed.'

CHAPTER ONE

Six months previously...

SYLVIE DEVEREUX STEELED herself for what was undoubtedly to be another bruising encounter with her father and stepmother. She reminded herself as she walked up the stately drive that she was only making an appearance for her half-sister's sake. The one person in the world she would do anything for.

Lights spilled from the enormous Richmond house, and soft classic jazz came from the live band in the back garden, where a marquee was just visible. Grant Lewis's midsummer party was an annual fixture on the London social scene, presided over each year by his smiling piranha of a wife, Catherine Lewis—Sylvie's stepmother and mother to her younger half-sister, Sophie.

A shape appeared at the front door and an excited squeal presaged a blur of blonde as Sophie Lewis launched herself at her older sister. Sylvie dropped her bag and clung on, struggling to remain upright, huffing a chuckle into her sister's soft, silky hair.

'I guess that means you're pleased to see me, Soph?'

Sophie, younger by six years, pulled back with a grimace on her pretty face. 'You have *no* idea. Mother is even worse than usual—literally throwing me into the arms of every eligible man—and Father is holed up in his study with some sheikh dude who is probably the grimmest guy I've ever seen, but also the most gorgeous—pity it's wasted on—'

'*There* you are, Sophie—'

The voice broke off as Sylvie's stepmother realised who

her sister's companion was. They were almost at the front door now, and the lights backlit Catherine Lewis's slender Chanel-clad figure and blonde hair, coiffed to within an inch of its life.

Her mouth tightened with distaste. 'Oh, it's you. We didn't think you'd make it.'

You mean you'd hoped I wouldn't make it, Sylvie desisted from saying. She forced a bright smile and pushed down the hurt that had no place here any more. She should be over this by now, at the grand age of twenty-eight. 'Delighted as ever to see you, Catherine.'

Her sister squeezed her arm in silent support. Catherine stepped back minutely, clearly reluctant to admit Sylvie into her own family home. 'Your father is having a meeting with a guest. He should be free shortly.'

Then her stepmother frowned under the bright lights, taking in what Sylvie was wearing. Sylvie felt a fleeting sense of satisfaction at the expected wave of disapproval. But then she also felt incredibly weary...tired of this constant battle she fought.

'You're welcome to change in Sophie's room if you wish. Clearly you've come straight from one of your... er...shows in Paris.'

She had actually. A matinée show. But she'd left work dressed in jeans and a perfectly respectable T-shirt. She'd changed on the train on the way. And suddenly her weariness fled.

She stuck a hand on her hip and cocked it out. 'It was a gift from a fan,' she purred. 'I know how much you like your guests to dress up.'

The dress really belonged to her flatmate, the far more glamorous Giselle, who was a couple of bra sizes smaller than her. Sylvie had borrowed it, knowing full well the effect it would have. She knew it was childish to feel this urge to shock constantly, but right now it was worth it.

Just then there was movement nearby, and Sylvie followed her stepmother's look to see her father standing outside his office, which was just off the main entrance hall. She barely registered him, though. He was with a man—a tall, very broad, very dark man. The most arresting-looking man she'd ever seen. His face was all sculpted lean lines, not a hint of softness anywhere. Dark slashing brows. Grim indeed, if this was who Sophie had been talking about.

Power and charisma was a tangible force around him. And a very sexual magnetism. He was dressed in a light grey three-piece suit. Dark tie. Pristine. The white of his shirt made the darkness of his skin stand out even more. His hair was inky black, and short. His eyes were equally dark, and totally unreadable. She shivered slightly.

The two men were looking at her, and Sylvie didn't even have to see her father's face to know what his expression would be: a mix of old grief, disappointment and wariness.

'Ah, Sylvie, glad you could make it.'

She finally managed to drag her mesmerised gaze from the stranger to look at her father. She forced a bright smile and moved forward. 'Father—good to see you.'

His welcome was only slightly warmer than her stepmother's. A dry kiss on her cheek, avoiding her eyes. Old wounds smarted again, but Sylvie pushed them all down to erect the *don't care* façade she'd honed over years.

She looked up at the man and fluttered her eyelashes, flirting shamelessly. 'And who do we have *here*?'

With evident reluctance, Grant Lewis said, 'I'd like you to meet Arkim Al-Sahid. We're discussing a mutual business venture.'

The name rang a dim bell, but Sylvie couldn't focus on how she knew it. She put out her hand. 'Pleasure, I'm sure. But don't you find discussing business at a party so *dull*?'

She could almost feel the snap of her stepmother's censure from behind her, and heard something that sounded like a strangled snort from her sister. The man's expression had a faint sneer of disapproval now, and suddenly something deep inside Sylvie erupted to life.

It goaded her into moving even closer to the man, when every instinct urged her to turn and run fast. Her hand was still held out and his nostrils flared as he finally deigned to acknowledge her. His much bigger hand swallowed hers, and she was surprised to feel that his skin was slightly calloused as long fingers wrapped around hers.

Everything suddenly became muffled. As if a membrane had been dropped around the two of them. A pulse throbbed violently between her legs and a series of out-of-control reactions gripped her so fast she couldn't make sense of them. Heat, and a weakness in her lower belly and limbs. A melting sensation. An urge to move even closer and wind her arms around his neck, press herself against him, along with that urge to run, which was even stronger now.

Then he broke the connection with an abrupt move, extricating his hand from hers. Sylvie almost stumbled backwards, confused by what had happened. Not liking it at all.

'Pleasure, indeed.'

The man's voice was deep, with a slight American accent, and his tone said that it was anything but a pleasure. The sensual lines of his mouth were flat. That dark gaze glanced over her, dismissing her.

Immediately Sylvie felt cheaper than she'd ever felt in her life. She was very aware of how short her gold dress was—skimming the tops of her thighs. Her light jacket didn't provide much coverage. She was too voluptuous for the dress, and she felt every exposed inch of it now. She was also aware of the fall of her unruly hair, its natural red hue effortlessly loud and attention-seeking.

She made a living from wearing not much at all. And

she'd grown a thick skin to hide her innate shyness. Yet right now this man's dismissal had blasted away that carefully built-up wall. Within mere seconds of meeting him—a total stranger.

Aghast to note that she was feeling a sense of rejection, when she'd developed an inbuilt defence mechanism against ever experiencing it again, Sylvie backed away.

Relief surged through her when her sister appeared, slid an arm through their father's and said with forced brightness, 'Come on, Daddy, your guests will be wondering where you are.'

She watched as her father, stepmother and sister walked off—along with the disturbing stranger who sent her barely a glance of acknowledgement.

On legs that felt absurdly shaky Sylvie finally followed the group outside and determined to stay out of that man's dangerous orbit, sticking close to Sophie and her group of friends.

A few hours later, though, she found herself craving a moment's peace—away from people getting progressively drunker, and away from the censorious gaze of her stepmother and the tension emanating from her father.

She found a quiet spot near the gazebo, where a river ran at the end of the garden. After sitting down on the grass and taking off her shoes she put her feet in the cool rushing water and breathed out a sigh.

It was only after she'd tipped her head back and had been contemplating the full moon, low in the sky, for a few seconds that she felt a nerve-tingling awareness that she wasn't alone.

She looked around just as a tall, dark shape moved in the shadows of a nearby tree. Stifling a scream, Sylvie sat up straight, heart pounding, and asked, 'Who's there?'

The shadow detached itself, revealing the other reason for her need to escape: so she could find an opportunity to dwell on why she'd had such a confusing and forcible reaction to the enigmatic stranger.

'You know exactly who's here,' came the arrogant response.

Sylvie could make out the glitter of those dark eyes. Feeling seriously at a disadvantage, sitting down, she stood again and shoved her feet back into her shoes, her heels sinking into the soft earth, making her wobble.

'How much have you had to drink?' He sounded disgusted.

Anger at the unjust question had Sylvie putting her hands on her hips. 'A magnum of champagne—is that what you expect to hear?'

She'd actually had nothing to drink, because she was still on antibiotics to clear up a nagging out-of-season chest infection. Not that she was about to furnish *him* with that little domestic detail.

'For your information,' she said, 'I came here because I believed I'd be alone. So I'll leave you to your arrogant assumptions and get out of your way.'

Sylvie started to stalk off, only noticing then how close they were—close enough for Arkim Al-Sahid to reach out and touch her. Which was exactly what he did when her heel got caught in the soft earth again and she pitched forward into thin air with a cry of surprise.

He caught her arm in such a firm grip that she went totally off balance and was swung around directly into his chest, landing against him with a soft *oof.* Her first impression was of how hard he was—like a concrete block.

And how tall.

Sylvie forgot why she'd been leaving. 'Tell me,' she asked, more breathily than she would have liked, 'do you hate everyone on sight, or is it just me?'

She could make out the sensual line of his mouth, twisting in the moonlight.

'I know you. I've seen you… Plastered all over Paris on those posters. For months.'

Sylvie frowned. 'That was a year ago—when the new show opened.' *And that wasn't really me.* She'd been chosen for the photo shoot as she was more voluptuous than the other girls…but in truth she was the one who bared the least of all of them.

She knew she should pull back from this man, but she seemed to be unable to drum up the necessary motor skills to do so—and why wasn't he pushing her away? He was obviously one of those puritans who disapproved of women taking their clothes off in the name of entertainment.

His silent condemnation angered her even more.

She arched a brow. 'So that's it? Seeing me in the flesh has only confirmed your worst suspicions?'

She saw how his gaze dropped down between them, to where she could feel her breasts pressed against him. Her skin grew hot all over.

His voice sounded husky. 'Admittedly, there is a lot of flesh to see.' His gaze rose again and bored into hers. 'But then I guess not half as much as is usually on show.'

That ripped away the illusion of any cocoon. Sylvie tugged herself free of his grip and pushed against him to get away. She was too angry, though, not to give him a piece of her mind before she left.

'People like you make me sick. You judge and condemn and you've no idea what you're talking about.'

She took a step back towards him and stuck a finger in his chest, hating how aware she was of his innate masculinity.

'I'll have you know that the L'Amour revue is one of the most upmarket cabaret acts in the world. We are world-class trained dancers. It's not some seedy strip joint.'

His tone was dry. 'Yet you *do* take off your clothes?'

'Well…' The truth was that Sylvie's act didn't actually require her to strip completely. Her breasts were slightly too large, and Pierre preferred the flatter-chested girls to do the full nudity. It provided a better aesthetic, as far as he was concerned.

Arkim Al-Sahid emitted a sound of disgust. Sylvie wasn't sure if it was directed at her or himself.

And then he said, 'I couldn't care less if you stripped naked and hung upside down on a trapeze in your show. This conversation is over.'

Sylvie refrained from pointing out that that was actually Giselle's act, assuming he wouldn't appreciate it.

He'd turned and was stalking away before she could say anything more anyway, and Sylvie bubbled with futile indignation and hurt pride. And something else—something deeper. A need to not have him judge her so out of hand when his opinion shouldn't matter.

She blurted out the words before she could stop herself—an irritating side effect of her red hair: her temper. She hated being a cliché, but sometimes she couldn't help it.

He halted in his tracks, his broad frame silhouetted by the lights of the party and the house in the distance.

Slowly he turned around, incredulity visible on his face.

For a moment Sylvie had to choke back a semi-hysterical giggle, but then he said in an arctic tone, '*What* did you say?' and any urge to giggle died.

She refused to let herself be intimidated and drew back her shoulders. 'I believe I said that you are an arrogant, uptight prat.'

Arkim Al-Sahid prowled back towards her. Deep in the garden as they were, he was like a jungle cat, in spite of his still pristine three-piece suit. All predatory and menacing. There was a thrill in her blood that was extremely inappropriate as she found herself backing away… Until her back slammed into something solid. The gazebo.

He loomed over her now…larger than life. Larger than anyone she'd ever known. He caged her in with his hands either side of her head. Suddenly her heart was racing, her skin prickling with anticipation. His scent was exotic and musky. Full of dark promise and danger and wickedness.

'Are you going to apologise?'

Sylvie shook her head. 'No.'

For a long second he said nothing, and then, almost contemplatively, 'You're right, you know…'

Her breath stopped… Was he *apologising*? 'I am?'

He nodded slowly, and as he did so he lifted a hand and trailed one finger down over Sylvie's cheek and jaw to where the bare skin of her shoulder met her dress.

She was breathing so hard now she felt as if she might hyperventilate. Her skin was on fire where he touched her. *She* was on fire. No man had ever had this effect on her. It was overwhelming, and she was helpless to rationalise it.

'Yes,' he said in a low voice. 'I'm very *uptight*. All over. Maybe you could help me with that?'

Before she could react his arm had snaked around her waist, pulling her into him, and his other hand was deep in her hair, anchoring her head so that he could plunge his mouth down onto hers, stealing what little breath she had left along with her sanity.

It was like going from zero to one hundred in a nanosecond. This was no gentle, exploratory kiss. It was explicit and devastating. Sylvie's tongue was entwined with Arkim Al-Sahid's before the impulse to let him in had even registered. And there wasn't one part of her that rejected him—which was so out of character for her that she couldn't appreciate the significance right now.

Her hands were on his chest, fingers curling into his waistcoat. Then they were climbing higher to curl around his neck, making her reach up on tiptoe to get closer.

Adrenalin and a kind of pleasure she'd never experienced before coursed through her blood. It radiated out from the core of her body and to every extremity, making her tingle and tighten with need.

His hand was on her dress now, at her shoulder, fingers tucking under the fabric, pulling it down.

There was something wild and earthy beating inside her as his mouth left hers and trailed down over her jaw, down to where her shoulder was now bare.

Sylvie's head tipped back, her eyes closed. Her entire world was reduced to this frantic, urgent beat that she had no will to deny as she felt her dress being pulled down, and cool night air drifting over hot skin.

Her head came up. She felt dizzy, drugged. 'Arkim…' She was dimly aware that she didn't even know this man. Yet here she was, entreating him to…to stop? Go on?

When he looked at her, though, those black eyes—like hard diamonds—robbed her of any ability to decide.

'Shh…let me touch you, Sylvie.'

His mouth wrapped around her name…it made her melt even more. His other hand was on her thigh, between them, inching up under her dress, pushing it up. This was more intimate than she'd ever been with any man, because she didn't let many get close, but it felt utterly right. Necessary. As if she'd been missing something her whole life and a key had just been slotted into place, unlocking some part of her.

Tacitly, her legs widened. She saw a glimmer of a smile on Arkim's face and it wasn't cruel, or judgemental. It was *sexy*.

He lowered his head to her now bared breast and closed his mouth over the pouting flesh, sucking her nipple deep and then rolling and flicking it with his tongue. Sylvie nearly shot into orbit. Electric shocks pulsed through her and tugged between her legs, where she was wet and aching…

And where Arkim's fingers were now exploring... Pushing aside her panties and sliding underneath, searching between slick folds and finding where her body gave him access, then thrusting a finger deep inside.

Sylvie's hands tightened, and it was only then that she realised she had them clasped on Arkim's head as his mouth suckled her and his finger moved in and out of her body, making a strange and new tension coil unbearably tight within her. Was this what he'd meant about being uptight? Because she felt it too. Deep in her core. Tightening so much it was almost unbearable.

Overcome with emotion at all the sensations rushing through her, she lifted Arkim's head from her breast, looking into those dark, fathomless eyes. 'I can't... What are you...?'

She couldn't speak. Could only feel. One minute she'd thought he was the devil incarnate, and now...now he was taking her to heaven. She was confused. His whole body was flush against hers, his leg pushing hers apart, his fingers exploring her so intimately...

Frustrated by her lack of ability to say anything, she leant forward and pressed her mouth to his again. But he went still. And then suddenly he was pulling away so fast Sylvie had to stop herself from falling forward. He stood back and looked at her as if she'd grown two heads, his horrified expression clear in the moonlight. His tie was askew and his waistcoat was undone. His hair mussed up. Cheeks flushed.

'What the hell...?'

Sylvie wanted to say, *My thoughts exactly*, but she was still struck mute.

Arkim backed away and said harshly, 'Don't *ever* come near me again.' And then he stalked off, back up the garden and into the light.

Three months ago...

Sylvie couldn't believe she was back at the house in Richmond again so soon. She usually managed to avoid it, because Sophie lived in central London in the family's *pied-à-terre*.

But the *pied-à-terre* wasn't suitable for this occasion: a party to celebrate the announcement of her little sister's engagement...to Arkim Al-Sahid.

Sylvie could still hear the shock in her sister's voice when she'd phoned her a few days ago: *'It's all happened so fast...'*

Nothing would have induced Sylvie to come into the bosom of her family again except for this. No way was she going to let her little sister be a pawn in her stepmother's machinations. Or *that* man's.

The man she'd been avoiding thinking about ever since that night. The man who had at first dismissed her and then... She shivered even now, her skin prickling with awareness at the thought of meeting him again.

The memory of what had happened was as sharp and humiliating as if it had happened yesterday. His voice. The disgust. *'Don't* ever *come near me again.'*

The shrill tones of Sylvie's stepmother hectoring some poor employee nearby stopped her thoughts from devolving rapidly into a kaleidoscope of unwelcome images.

Her hands closed over the rim of the sink in the bathroom as she took in her reflection.

Despite her best efforts she could still remember the excoriating wave of humiliation and exposure when she'd watched Arkim Al-Sahid walk away and realised that her breast was bared and her legs still splayed in wanton abandonment. Panties pulled aside. One shoe on, one off. And she'd been complicit—every step of the way. She couldn't even say he'd used force.

He'd crooked his finger and she'd all but come running. Panting. Practically begging.

The true magnitude of how easily she'd let him—more or less a complete stranger—reduce her to a quivering wreck was utterly galling.

Sylvie cursed herself. She was here for Sophie—not to take a trip down memory lane. She stood up straight and checked her appearance. A far cry from the gold dress she'd worn that night. Now she was positively respectable, in a knee-length black sleeveless shift and matching high heels, her hair pulled back into a low bun. Discreet make-up.

She didn't like to think of the reaction in her body when her sister had informed her of the upcoming nuptials. It had been a mix of shock, incomprehension, anger—and something far more disturbing and dark.

Sylvie made her way into the huge dining room, which had been set up for a buffet-style dinner party. She was acutely aware of Arkim Al-Sahid, looking as grimly gorgeous as ever, and made sure to stay far away from him. It meant, though, that she couldn't get Sophie to herself. And she needed to talk to her.

The evening was interminable. Several times, as Sylvie made mind-numbingly boring small talk, she felt the back of her neck prickle—as if someone was staring at her... or more likely *glaring* at her. But each time she looked around she couldn't see him.

Not seeing her sister anywhere now, Sylvie determined to find her and went looking. The first place she thought to look was in her father's study/library, and she opened the door carefully, seeing nothing inside the oak-panelled room filled with heaving shelves of books but the fire, which was dying down low.

The warmth and peace called to her for a minute, and she slipped in and closed the door behind her.

Then she saw a movement coming from one of the high-backed chairs near the fire. 'Soph? Is that you?' The room had always been her little sister's favourite hiding place when she was younger, and Sylvie felt a lurch near her heart to think of her sister retreating here.

But it wasn't Sophie—which became apparent all too quickly when a tall, dark shape uncoiled from the chair to stand up.

Arkim Al-Sahid.

Instinctively Sylvie backed away, and said frigidly, 'At the risk of being accused of following you I can assure you I wasn't.' She turned to go, then stopped and turned back. 'Actually, I have something to say to you.'

He folded his arms. 'Do you, now?'

He was as implacable as a stone pillar. It infuriated Sylvie that he could so effortlessly arouse seething emotions within her. She stalked over to the chairs and gripped the back of the one he'd been sitting in. She hated it that he looked even more enigmatic and handsome. As if the intervening months had added more hard muscle to his form. Made his features even more saturnine.

He was dressed in similar pristine fashion to last time—in a three-piece suit. He sent a dismissive look up and down her body, and then said with a faint sneer, 'Who are you trying to fool? Or are we all going to be treated to an exclusive performance, in which you reveal the truth of what lies beneath your pseudo-respectable façade?'

Sylvie's anger spiked in a hot rush. 'At first I couldn't understand why you hated me on sight, but now I know. Your father is one of America's biggest porn barons, and you've made no secret of the fact that you disowned him *and* his legacy to forge your own. You don't even share his name any more.'

Arkim Al-Sahid's body vibrated with tension, his dark eyes narrowing on her dangerously. 'As you said, it's no secret.'

'No...' Sylvie conceded, slightly thrown off balance by his response.

'And your point?'

She swallowed. Lord, but he was intimidating. Not a hint of humanity anywhere in his whipcord form or on that beautiful face.

'You're marrying my sister purely to gain social acceptance, and she deserves more than that. She deserves love.'

Arkim emitted a short, curt laugh. It was so shocking to see his face transformed by a smile—albeit a mocking one—that she almost lost her train of thought.

'You're for real? Since when does anyone marry for *love*? Your sister has a lot to gain from this union—not least a lifetime of security and status. At no point has she indicated that she's not happy for this engagement to proceed. Your father is keen to secure her future—which is no surprise, considering how his eldest daughter turned out.'

Sylvie kept her expression rigid. Amazing how this man's opinion sneaked under her guard with such devastating effect and struck far too close to the heart of her— which was the last place he should be impacting.

He continued. 'I'm not stupid, Miss Devereux. This is as much a business transaction for him as it is a chance to secure his daughter's future. It's not a secret that his empire took a big hit during the downturn and that he's doing all he can to bolster his coffers again.'

Business transaction. She felt nauseous. Sylvie knew vaguely that her father's fortune had taken a dip...but she also knew perfectly well that her stepmother was the real architect behind this plan. She was a firm believer that a woman's place was by her rich husband's side, and no doubt had convinced Grant Lewis that this was their ticket to security for the future.

She ungritted her teeth and desisted from belabouring the point of whether or not love existed. Clearly in his world it didn't.

'Sophie's not right for you—and you are certainly not right for *her*.'

An assessing look came over that starkly handsome face. 'She's perfect for me. Young, beautiful, intelligent. Accomplished.' He looked her up and down. 'And above all she's refined.'

Sylvie held up a hand, hating it that that stung. 'Please—save your insults. I'm perfectly aware where I come on your scale of condemnation. Clearly you have issues with certain industries, and you've deemed me worth judging on the basis of what I do.'

'What you *are*,' he said harshly.

Her hands clenched into fists. 'You didn't seem to have much of an issue with what I *am* the last time we met.'

His face flushed dark red and Sylvie felt the bite of his self-condemnation as sharply as if he'd just slapped her.

'That was a mistake—not to be repeated.'

Something about that lash of recrimination made her want to curl up and protect herself. The look on his face was pure…disgust. And it would have been worse if it was solely for her. But she could tell it wasn't. It was for himself.

Hurt lodged deep in her belly like a dark, malevolent thing, tugging on other hurts, reopening old wounds. Reminding her of the disgust on her father's face when he'd looked at her after her mother had died…

She desperately wanted to lash back and see this man's icy condemnatory control snap. Acting on blind instinct, and on that hurt, she stepped out from behind the chair and right up to Arkim Al-Sahid. She pressed her body to his, lifting her arms to wind them around his neck.

His nostrils flared and those black eyes flashed. His hands were on her arms, his grip tight. 'What the hell do you think you're doing?'

But he didn't pull her arms down. Sylvie's entire body was quivering with adrenalin at her bravado.

'I'm proving that you're a hypocrite, Mr Al-Sahid.'

And then, in the boldest move she'd ever made in her life, she reached up and pressed her mouth to his. She moved her lips over his and through the frantic thumping of her heart she could feel excitement flooding her at the sheer proximity of their bodies. Brain cells were scrambled in a rush of heat.

She could feel the tension holding his body rigid… But what he couldn't disguise was the explicit thrust of his arousal against her belly. That evidence was enough to send a thrill of exultation through Sylvie and help her block out the memory of how he'd pushed her away the last time.

Except then she started to forget why she'd even started this. Her body moved against him, closer. Arms locked tighter. And after a heart-stopping infinitesimal moment his hands loosened from her arms and slid down the length of her torso to her hips, gripping her there as his mouth started to move on hers—slowly at first and then, like a storm gathering strength, with an almost rough intensity.

For a long moment everything faded into the distance as the kiss became hotter and more intense. Arkim Al-Sahid's hands pulled Sylvie even closer—so close that she could feel his heart beating. And then something shifted. He went very still, before abruptly breaking the kiss.

Sylvie was left grasping air when he thrust her away from him. She stumbled backwards and found herself landing heavily in the chair behind her, her breathing laboured, her heart out of control. Dizzy.

Arkim's mouth twisted and his voice was rough. '*No.* I will not do this. You *dare* to try and seduce me on the evening of the announcement of my engagement to your sister? Is there no depth to which you won't descend?'

Sylvie was going cold all over. The lust which had risen up like wildfire dissipated under his murderous gaze. Her brain felt woolly…it was hard to think. Why had it been so important to kiss him like that? What had she been trying to prove? How did this man have the ability to make her act so out of character?

She looked up at him. 'It wasn't like that. I'd never do anything to hurt Sophie.'

Arkim made a rude sound just as a knock sounded at the door and it was opened.

Sylvie heard a voice say, 'Sorry to disturb you, Mr Al-Sahid, but they're ready to make the announcement.'

Sylvie realised that whoever was at the door wouldn't be able to see her in the chair just as Arkim Al-Sahid answered with a curt, 'I'll be right there.' The door closed again and he looked down at her, black eyes glittering with disgust and condemnation. 'I think it would be best for all of us if you left now, don't you?'

CHAPTER TWO

Present day—a week after the ruined wedding...

ARKIM AL-SAHID LOOKED out over the view from his palatial office and apartment complex, high in the London skyline. And even though the past week had brought to life a lot of his worst nightmares all he could think about right at that moment was of how he'd only met Sylvie Devereux twice in the past six months—three times if you counted her memorable appearance in the church—and yet each time he'd let his legendary control slip.

And now he was paying for it. More than he'd ever thought possible.

Anger was a constant unquenchable fire within him. He was paying for the fact that she was a privileged spoilt brat, who didn't take rejection well. Who had acted out of her poisonous jealousy of her younger sister to ruin their wedding.

Yet his conscience pricked him. It had been *him* who had fallen for her all too obvious charms. He'd had to fight it from the moment he'd laid eyes on her, when she'd stood in the reception hall of her father's house with her hand on her hip, her beautiful body flaunted to every best advantage.

He could still see her eyes landing on him, widening, the familiar glitter of feminine awareness, the scenting of his power. Sensing a conquest. And then she'd sashayed over as if she owned the world. As if she could own him with a mere flutter of her eyelids. And, dammit, he had almost fallen right then—as soon he'd seen those amazing eyes up close.

One blue and the other green and blue.

An intriguing genetic anomaly in a perfect face—high cheekbones, patrician nose and a mouth so lush it could incite a man to sin.

His body had come to hot, pulsing life under that knowing feline gaze, showing him that any illusion that he mastered his own impulses was just that: a flimsy illusion.

His mouth compressed now as he stared unseeingly out of the window, as if he could try to compress the memories.

The full repercussions of his weakness sat like lead in his belly. The marriage to Sophie Lewis was off. And Arkim's very substantial investment in Grant Lewis's extensive industrial portfolio was teetering on the brink of collapse. Losing the deal wouldn't put much of a dent into Arkim's finances, but the subsequent loss of professional standing *would*.

He was back to square one. Having to prove himself all over again. His team had been fielding calls from clients all week, expressing doubts and fears that Arkim's solid business reputation was as shaky as his personal life. Stocks and shares were in freefall.

The tabloids had salivated over the story, featuring a caricaturised cast of characters: the stoical and long-suffering father; the scandalous daughter bent on revenge borne out of jealousy; the sweet innocent bride—the victim—and the ruthless social-climbing mother.

And Arkim—son of one of the world's richest men, who was also one of its most infamous, dominating the world's porn industry.

Saul Marks lived a life of excess in Los Angeles, and Arkim hadn't seen him since he was seventeen. He'd made a vow a long time ago to crawl out from under his father's shameful reputation, even going so far as to change his name legally as soon as he'd been able to—choosing a name that had belonged to a distant ancestor of his mother's as he hadn't thought her present-day immediate family would appreciate their bastard relative making a claim on their name.

Arkim's mother had come from a wealthy and high-born family in the Arabian country of Al-Omar. She'd been studying in the States at university when she'd met and been seduced by Saul Marks. Naive and innocent, she'd been bowled over by the handsome charismatic American.

When she'd become pregnant, however, Marks had already moved on to his next girlfriend. He'd supported Arkim's mother, but wanted nothing to do with her or the baby...until she'd died in childbirth and he'd been forced to take his baby son into his care after Zara's family in Al-Omar had expressed no interest in their deceased daughter's son.

Arkim's early life had been a constant round of English boarding schools and impersonal nannies, interspersed with time spent with a reluctant father and his dizzying conveyer belt of lovers, who invariably came from the porn industry. One of whom had taken an unhealthy interest in Arkim and given him an important life lesson in how vital it was to master self-control.

But a week ago, when the society wedding of the decade had imploded in scandalous fashion, all those ambitions and his efforts to distance himself from shame and scandal had turned to dust.

And all because of a red-haired witch.

A witch who had somehow managed to sneak under his impenetrable guard. It was galling to recall how hard it had been to let her go that night in the study. How hard *he'd* been. From the moment he'd first seen her appear. Looking like a schoolteacher. With her hair pulled back, her face pale. Covered up.

He'd only come to his senses because there had been

something in the way she'd kissed him—something he hadn't believed… Something innocent. Gauche. But it was a lie—as if she'd been trying to figure out what he liked. Acting sweet and innocent after she'd just been completely brazen. Attempting to seduce him away from her sister.

The only thing that had got Arkim through the past week of ignominy and public embarrassment had been the prospect of making Sylvie Devereux pay. And the kind of payment he had in mind would finally exorcise her from his head, and his body, once and for all.

For months she'd inhabited the dark, secret corners of his mind and his imagination. She'd been the cause of sleepless nights and lurid dreams. Even during his engagement to her far sweeter and infinitely more innocent sister.

Apart from the injury Sylvie had caused to Arkim with her selfish behaviour, she'd also recklessly played with her sister's life. The young woman had been inconsolable, absolutely adamant that she wouldn't give Arkim another chance. And could he blame her? Who would believe the son of a man who lived his life as if it was a bacchanal?

The words Sylvie Devereux had said in the church still rang in his head: *'This man shared my bed.'* And yet even now his body reacted to those words with a surge of frustration. Because she most certainly had *not* shared his bed. It had been a bare-faced lie. Conjured up to create maximum damage.

Sylvie Devereux wanted him so badly? Well, then, she'd have him—until he was sated and he could throw her back in the trash, where she belonged.

But it would be on *his* terms, and far out of the reach of the ravenous public's gaze. The damage to his reputation stopped right here.

Sylvie looked out of the small private plane's window to see a vast sea of sand below her, and in the distance, shimmering in a heat haze, a steel city that might have come directly from a futuristic movie.

The desert sands of Al-Omar and its capital city, B'harani.

Some called it the jewel of the Middle East. It was one of its most progressive countries, presided over by a very dynamic and modern royal couple. Sylvie had just been reading an article about them in the in-flight magazine: Sultan Sadiq and his wife Queen Samia, and their two small cherubic children.

Queen Samia was younger than Sylvie, and she'd felt a little jaded, looking at the beaming smile on the woman's face. She was pretty, more than beautiful, and yet her husband looked at her as if he'd never seen a woman before.

She'd seen her father look at her mother like that.

Sylvie ruthlessly crushed the small secret part of her that clenched with an ominous yearning. The cynicism she'd honed over years came to the fore. Sultan Sadiq might well be reformed now, but she could remember when he'd been a regular visitor to the infamous L'Amour revue and had cut a swathe through some of its top-billed stars.

Not Sylvie, though. Once she was offstage and dressed down, with her hair tied back, she slipped unnoticed past all her far more glamorous peers. She courted endless teasing from the other girls—and from the guys, who were mostly gay—having earned the moniker of 'Sister Sylvie', because of the way she would prefer to go home and curl up with a book or cook a meal rather than head out to party with their inevitably rich and gorgeous clientele. A clientele that appreciated the very discreet ethos of the revue *and* any liaisons that ensued out of hours.

But even they—her friends, who were more like her family now—didn't know the full extent of her duality… how far from her stage persona she really was.

'Miss Devereux? We'll be landing shortly.'

Sylvie looked up at the beautiful olive-skinned steward-ess, with her dark brown eyes and glossy black hair. She forced a smile, suddenly reminded of someone with simi-lar colouring. Someone infinitely more masculine, though, and more dangerous than this courteous flight attendant.

That fateful day almost two weeks ago rushed back with a garish vividness that took her breath away. Remind-ing her painfully of the searing public scrutiny, judgement and humiliation. And *his* face. So dark and unforgiving. Those black eyes scorching the skin from her body.

He'd moved towards her, his anger palpable. But her stepmother had reached her first, slapping Sylvie so hard that her teeth had rattled in her head and the corner of her lip had split. It was still tender when she touched her tongue to it now.

And then she saw in her mind's eye her sister's face. Pale and tear-streaked. Eyes huge. Shocked. *Relieved.* That relief had made it all worthwhile. Sylvie didn't re-gret what she'd done for a second. Sophie hadn't been right for Arkim Al-Sahid.

Her feeling of vindication had been fleeting, though. The truth was, when she'd stood behind them in that church her motivation for stopping the wedding had felt far more complex than it should have.

Arkim was the only man who'd managed to breach the defences Sylvie hadn't even been aware she'd erected so high. She'd bared herself to him in a way she'd never done with anyone else—which was ironic, considering her profession—only to be cruelly pushed aside...as if she was a piece of dirt on his shoe. Not worthy to look him in the eye.

But her sister *was* worthy. Her beautiful blonde, sweet sister. Just as Sophie was worthy of their father's affec-tions. Because *she* didn't remind him of his beloved dead first wife.

Maybe it was this stark landscape that was making her think about all of that—and *him*. Forcing him up into her consciousness. She buckled her seat belt, diverting her mind away from painful memories and towards what lay ahead. The problem was that she wasn't even entirely sure what lay ahead.

She and some of the other girls from the revue had been invited over to put on a private show for an important sheikh's birthday celebrations. Sylvie wasn't flying with the others because they'd travelled before her. She'd only been asked to join them afterwards—hence her solo trip on the private jet.

It wasn't unusual for this kind of thing to happen. Their revue had performed privately for A-list stars around the world, much as a pop star might be asked to perform, and they'd done a residency one summer in Las Vegas. But this... Something about this made Sylvie's skin prickle uncomfortably.

She tried to reassure herself that she was being silly. The other girls would be waiting for her, they'd rehearse and perform, and then they'd be home before they knew it.

They were landing now, and she noticed that they were quite far outside the city limits, with nothing but desert as far as the eye could see. The airport didn't look like a busy capital city's airport. Just a few small buildings and a runway carved into the arid landscape. She pushed the nervous flutters down.

Once the small jet had taxied to a gentle stop Sylvie was escorted to the door of the plane—and the heat of the desert hit her so squarely that she had to suck in a breath of hot, dry air. Sweat instantly dampened the skin all over her body. But along with the trepidation she felt at what lay ahead was a quickening of something like exhilaration as she took in the clear blue vastness of the sky and the rolling dunes in the distance.

She was so far away from everything that was familiar in this completely alien landscape, but it soothed her a little after the last tumultuous couple of weeks. It was as if nothing here could hurt her.

'Miss, your car is waiting.'

Sylvie looked down to see a sleek black car. She put on her sunglasses and went down the steps and across the scorching runway to where a driver was holding the back door open. He was dressed in a long cream tunic, with close-fitting trousers underneath and a turban on his head. He looked smart and cool, and she felt ridiculously underdressed in her jeans, ballet flats and loose T-shirt. Like a gauche westerner.

Someone was putting her cases into the boot, and Sylvie smiled as the driver bowed deferentially, indicating for her to get in.

She did so—with relief. Already craving the cool balm of air-conditioning. Already wanting to twist her long, heavy hair up and off her neck.

The door was closed quickly behind her and then a lot of things seemed to happen simultaneously: she heard the snick of the door locking, the driver slid into the front seat and the privacy partition slid up, and Sylvie realised that she wasn't alone in the back of the car.

'I trust you had a pleasant flight?'

The voice was deep, cool—and instantly, painfully, recognisable. Sylvie turned her head and everything seemed to go into slow motion.

Arkim Al-Sahid was sitting at the far side of the luxurious car, which was now moving. A fact she was only vaguely aware of. She went hot and cold all at once. Her belly dropped near her feet. Her breath was caught in her chest. Shock was seizing at her ability to respond.

He was dressed in his signature three-piece suit. As if they were in Paris or London. En route to some civilised place. Not here, in the middle of a harsh sun-beaten land. Here in the middle of nowhere. Here where she'd just thought nothing could touch her.

Arkim Al-Sahid looked so dark, and his face was etched in lines of cruelty.

A small voice jeered at Sylvie, *Did you really think he would do nothing?* And underneath the shock was the pounding of her heart that told her that perhaps, in some very deep and hidden secret space, she *hadn't* thought he would do nothing. But she'd never expected this...

He reached forward and her sunglasses were plucked off her face and tucked away into his pocket before she could react. She blinked, and he came into sharp, clear focus. Dark hair brushed back from a high forehead. Deep-set eyes over sharp cheekbones. His patrician nose giving him a slightly hawk-like aspect.

And that mouth... That cruel and taunting mouth. The mouth that even now she could recall being on hers. Hard and demanding, sending her senses into overdrive. It was curved up into the semblance of a smile, but it was a smile unlike anything Sylvie had ever seen. It was a smile that promised retribution.

When she remained mute with shock, one dark brow arched up lazily. 'Well, Sylvie? I'll be exceedingly disappointed over the next two weeks if you've lost the ability to do anything with your tongue.'

Arkim tried to ignore the frantic rate of his pulse, which had burst to life as soon as he'd seen her distinctive shape appear in the doorway of the plane. Slim, yet womanly. Even in casual clothes.

Her glorious red hair glowed like the setting sun over the Arabian sea. Her face was as pale as alabaster, her skin perfect and flawless. Her eyes were huge and almond-shaped, giving her that feline quality, her left eye with that distinctive discolouration. It did nothing to diminish her appeal—it only enhanced it.

Irritation rose at her effortless ability to control his libido.

Arkim was about to say something else when she got out a little threadily, 'Where are the other girls?'

He felt a twinge of guilt, but pushed it down deep. He glanced briefly at his watch. 'They're most likely performing, as arranged, for the birthday celebrations of one of the Sultan's chief advisors—Sheikh Abdel Al-Hani. They'll be on a plane first thing tomorrow morning.'

If possible, Sylvie paled even more. It sent a jolt of something horribly like concern through him, reminding him of when her stepmother had slapped her in the church and how his first instinctive reaction had been to put himself between them. *Not* something he relished remembering now.

But now the shocked glaze was leaving her face, colour was surging back into her cheeks and her eyes were sparking. 'So why am I not there too? What the hell *is* this, Arkim?'

Nurturing the sense of satisfaction at having Sylvie where he wanted her, rather than his other more tangled emotions, Arkim settled back into his seat. 'Believe it or not, people here call me Sheikh too—a title conferred upon me by the Sultan himself…an old schoolfriend. But I digress. This is about payback. It's about the fact that your jealous little tantrum had far-reaching consequences and you aren't going to get away with it.'

Sylvie put out a hand and Arkim noticed it was trembling slightly. He ruthlessly pushed down his concern. Again. This woman didn't deserve anything but his scorn.

'So…what? You're kidnapping me?'

Arkim picked a piece of lint off his jacket and then looked at her. 'I'd call it a…a *holiday*. You came here of

your own free will and you're free to go at any time...
It's just not going to be that easy for you to leave when
there's no public transport and no mobile phone coverage,
so I'm afraid you'll have to wait until I'm leaving too. In
two weeks.'

Sylvie clenched her hands into fists on her lap, her jaw
tight. 'I'll damn well walk across the desert if I have to.'

Arkim was calm. 'Try it and you'll be lucky to last
twenty-four hours. It's certain death for anyone who
doesn't know the lie of this land—not to mention the fact
that someone as fair as you would fry to a crisp.'

Sylvie was reeling, and trying hard not to show it. She
felt as if she'd fallen through a wormhole and everything
was upside down and inside out. Panic tightened her gut.

'What about my job? I'm expected back—it was only
supposed to be a one-night event.'

Arkim's face was scarily expressionless. It made her
want to reach across and slap him, to see some kind of
reaction.

'Your job is unaffected. Your boss has been recom-
pensed very generously for the use of your time. So much
so, in fact, that I believe he can finally start the renovations he's been wanting to do for years. As a result of my
generous donation the revue is actually closing for a month
from next week, while they do the work.'

She had to choke back a lurch of even greater panic;
it was common knowledge how much Pierre wanted to
renovate—he'd been begging for loans from banks for
months. And this would be perfect timing...before the
high tourist season.

She spluttered. 'Pierre would never let one of his girls
go off on an assignment alone. He'll raise hell when I don't
return, no matter how much you've offered him!'

Arkim smiled, and it was cold. 'Pierre is like anyone
else in this world—mesmerised when large sums of money

are mentioned. He's been assured that your services are required as dance teacher to one of the Sheikh's daughters and her friends, who want to learn the western way of dancing. The fact that you're here with me instead is something he doesn't need to be aware of.'

Sylvie folded her arms, trying to not let on how scared she was. She injected mockery into her voice. 'I'm surprised. I would have thought your morals wouldn't allow you to come within ten feet of me—much less arrange a private performance.'

Arkim was no longer smiling. 'I'm prepared to risk a little moral corruption for what I want—and I want you.'

She sucked in a breath at hearing him declare it so baldly. 'I should have known you'd have no scruples. So you've effectively *bought* me? Like some kind of call girl?'

Arkim's mouth curled up into that cruel smile again. 'Come now…we both know that that's not so far from the truth of what you are.'

This time Sylvie couldn't hold back. She was across the seat and launching herself at Arkim, hand outstretched, ready to strike, when he caught her wrists in his hands. They were like steel manacles, and she fell heavily against his body.

Instantly awareness sparked to life, infusing her veins with heat and electricity. Even now, when she was in the grip of panic and anger.

'Let me *go*.'

Arkim's jaw was like granite, and this close she could see the depths of anger banked deep in his eyes. He was livid. She felt a quiver of real fear—even though, perversely, she knew he wouldn't hurt her physically.

'No way. We have unfinished business and we're not leaving this place until it's done.'

Sylvie was excruciatingly aware of her body, pressed to Arkim's much harder and more powerful one. Of the way her breasts were crushed against him, as they'd been crushed against him once before…when he'd thrust her back from him and looked at her as if she'd given him a contagious disease.

'What are you talking about?' she asked, hating the tremor in her voice.

The expression in his eyes changed for the first time, flashing with a heat that Sylvie felt deep in her belly.

'What I'm talking about is the fact that I'm going to have you—over and over again—for however long it takes until I can think straight again.' A note of unmistakable bitterness entered his voice. 'You've done it, Sylvie— you've got me.'

She finally broke free from Arkim's grip and sat back, as far away as she could. 'I don't want you.' *Liar*, whispered an inner voice. She ignored it. She hated Arkim Al-Sahid. 'As soon as this car stops I'm out of here, and you can't stop me.'

Arkim merely looked amused. 'Each time we've met you've demonstrated how much you want me, so protesting otherwise won't work now. Where we're going has no public transport, and it would take you about a week to walk to B'harani—days in any other direction before you hit civilisation.'

Sylvie crossed her arms over her chest, a feeling of claustrophobia threatening to strangle her. 'This is ridiculous.' The thought of being alone with this man in some remote desert for the next two weeks was overwhelming. 'You can't force me to do anything I don't want to do, you know.'

He looked at her, and there was something so explicit in his gaze that she felt herself blushing.

'I won't need to use force, Sylvie.'

And just like that the humiliation she'd felt that night in the study of her father's house came back and rolled over her like a wave.

She fought it. 'This just proves how little you really felt for my sister. Hurting me will only hurt *her.*'

The expression on Arkim's face became incredulous at the mention of Sophie 'You *dare* speak to me of hurting your sister? When *you* were the one who callously humiliated her in public?'

Words of defence trembled on Sylvie's tongue, but she bit them back. She would never betray her sister's confidence. Sophie had just been a pawn to him. It never would have worked. She had to remember that. She'd done the right thing.

But then she saw something in the distance and became distracted.

Arkim followed her gaze and said, 'Ah, we're here.'

Here was another, even smaller airfield, with a sleek black helicopter standing ready.

Slightly hysterically Sylvie remembered something she'd learnt when she'd taken self-defence classes after a—luckily—minor mugging in Paris. The tutor had told the class the importance of not letting an attacker take you to another location at all costs. Because if he did get you to another place, then your chances of survival were dramatically cut down.

It would appear to be common sense, but the tutor had told them numerous stories of people who had been so frightened they'd just let themselves be taken to another place, when they should always have tried to get away during the initial attack.

And okay, so technically Arkim wasn't attacking Sylvie, but she knew that if she got into that helicopter her chances of emerging from this encounter unscathed were nil.

The car came to a stop and he looked at her. 'Time to go.'

Sylvie shook her head. 'I'm not getting out. I'm staying in this car and it's going to take me back to wherever we landed. Or to B'harani. I hear it's a nice city—I'd like to visit.'

She hoped the desperation she was feeling wasn't evident.

He turned to face her more fully. 'This car is driven by a man who speaks only one language, and it's not yours. He answers to me—no one else.'

The sheer hardness of Arkim's expression told her she was on a hiding to nothing. A sense of futility washed over her. She wouldn't win this round.

'Where is it that you're proposing to take me?'

'It's a house I own on the Arabian coast. North of B'harani and one hundred miles from the border of Burquat. Merkazad is in a westerly direction, about six hundred miles.'

The geographical details somehow made Sylvie feel calmer, even though she still had no real clue where they were. She'd heard of these places, but never been.

Something occurred to her. 'This…' her mouth twisted '…this fee you've paid Pierre. I assume it's conditional on my agreeing to this farcical non-existent dance tuition?'

Arkim nodded. 'That's good business sense, I think you'll agree.'

Sylvie wanted to tell him where he could stick his business sense, but she refrained. She didn't doubt that there really was no option but to go with Arkim. For now.

'Once we're at this…this place, you won't force me to do anything I don't want to?'

Arkim shook his head, eyes gleaming with a disturbing light. 'No, Sylvie. There will be no force involved. I'm not into sadism.'

His smug arrogance made her want to try and slap him again. Instead, she sent him a wide, sunny, smile. 'You know, work has been so crazy busy lately I'm actually looking forward to an all-expenses-paid break. The fact that I have to share space with *you* is unfortunate, but I'm sure we can stay out of each other's way.'

Arkim just smiled slowly, and with an air of sensual menace, as if he knew just how flimsy her bravado was.

'We'll see.'

Sylvie had never been in a helicopter before, and she'd been more mesmerised than she cared to admit by the way the desert dunes had unfolded beneath them, undulating into the distance like the sinuous curves of a body. It all seemed utterly foreign and yet captivating to her.

Her stomach was only just beginning to climb back down from her throat when she heard a deep voice in her ear through the headphones.

'That's my house, Al-Hibiz, directly down and to your left.'

Sylvie looked down and her breath was taken away. *House?* This was no house. It looked like a small but formidable castle, complete with ramparts and flat roofs. It was distinctly Arabic in style, with ochre-coloured walls. Within those walls she could see lush gardens, and in the distance the Arabian sea sparkled. What looked like an oasis lay far off in the distance, a spot of deep green. It was like something out of a fairytale.

It distracted her from the shock she still felt after realising that Arkim was co-piloting the helicopter, and the way his hands had lingered as he'd strapped her in, those fingers resting far too close to her breasts under her thin T-shirt.

He should have looked ridiculous, getting into the cockpit still dressed in his suit, against the backdrop of the stark desert, but he hadn't. He'd looked completely at home, powerful and utterly in control.

And now the helicopter was descending onto a flat area

just outside the walls of the castle, which looked much bigger from this vantage point.

Sylvie could see robed men waiting, holding on to their long garments and the turbans on their heads as the helicopter kicked up sand and wind. When the craft bounced gently onto the earth she breathed out a deep sigh of relief, unaware of how tense she'd been.

The helicopter blades stopped turning and a delicious silence settled over them for a moment, before Arkim got out and the men approached. She watched as he greeted the men heartily in a guttural language that still managed to sound melodic, a wide smile on his face.

It took her breath away. It was the first genuine smile she'd ever seen on his face. Admittedly their previous encounters hadn't exactly been conducive to such a reaction. Not unless she counted that sexy smile when his hand had explored between her legs—

'Time to get out, Sylvie. I'm afraid the chopper has to go back and you're not going to be in it.'

She scowled, hating to be caught out in such a memory. She fumbled with the seat belt and swatted his hand away when he would have helped. Eventually it came undone and she extricated her arms, unaware of how the movement pulled her T-shirt taut over her breasts, or of how Arkim's dark gaze settled there for a moment with a flash of hunger. If she'd seen that she might well have barricaded herself into the helicopter, come hell or high water.

But then she was out, and swaying a little unsteadily on the firm sun-baked ground.

Staff dressed in white rushed to and fro, loading luggage into the back of a small people carrier, and then Arkim was leading Sylvie over to what looked like a luxurious golf buggy. He indicated for her to get in, and after a moment's futile rebellion she did so.

She really was stuck here now—with him.

He got in beside her and drove the small open-sided vehicle to the entrance of the castle, where huge wooden doors were standing open. They entered a beautiful airy courtyard, with a fountain in the centre. A deliciously cool gentle mist of moisture settled on her skin from the spray.

But the vehicle had stopped now, and Arkim was at her side, holding out a hand. Sylvie ignored it and stepped out, not wanting to see what would undoubtedly be a mocking look on his face.

When he didn't move, though, she had to look at him. He gestured with a hand and—damn him—a mocking smile.

'Welcome to my home, Sylvie. I expect our time here to be...cathartic.'

CHAPTER THREE

SYLVIE PACED BACK and forth in the rooms she'd been shown to by Arkim. *Cathartic! The arrogant, patronising son-of-a—*

A knock sounded on the door and she halted, her breathing erratic. Her hands balled into fists at her sides—she wasn't ready to see Arkim again.

Cautiously she approached the ornately decorated door and opened it, ready to do battle, only to find two pretty, smiling women on the other side. They had her two wheelie suitcases. One filled with now redundant dance costumes, the other with her own clothes.

She forced a smile and stood back. They entered meekly and she observed their pristine white dresses. Like long tunics. They wore white head coverings too, but not veils obscuring their faces. They looked cool and fresh, and Sylvie felt sticky and gritty after the tumultuous day.

As they were leaving again one of the girls stopped and said shyly, 'I'm Halima. If you need anything just pick up the phone and I will come to you.'

She ducked her head and then was gone, leaving Sylvie feeling a little slack-jawed. She had her own *maid*?

Arkim had left her here with a curt instruction to rest and said that he'd let her know when dinner would be ready. Sylvie could see the sky outside turning blood-red from the setting sun, and for the first time took in the sheer opulence of the rooms.

She was in a reception area that would have housed her small Parisian apartment three times over. It was a huge octagonal space, with a small pond in the centre with a tiled bottom and sides, where exotic fish swam lazily.

There were eight rooms off this main area. Two guest bedrooms, a dining room, and a living room complete with state-of-the-art sound system and media centre which had had all channels available when Sylvie had flicked it on.

The decor throughout was subtle and understated. The stone walls of the castle had been left exposed. and modern artwork and an eclectic mix of antiques enhanced the rather austere ancient building. Huge oriental rugs adorned the floors, softening any sharp edges further. The windows were all open to the elements, and even though it was sweltering outside, the castle had been designed so that balmy breezes wafted through the open rooms.

There was also a gym, and an accompanying thermal suite with hot-tub and sauna/steam room. And then there was the main bedroom suite, dressed in tones of dark red and cream. A fan circled overhead, distributing the air to keep it cool.

She'd never considered herself much of a sensualist, beyond tapping into her inner performer for her work, but right now her senses were heightened by everything she'd seen since she'd arrived in this country.

The bed was situated in the middle of the room, and strewn with opulent coverings and pillows. It had four posters and luxurious drapes, which were held back in place by delicately engraved gold curtain ties. The bed looked big enough to hold a football team with room to spare, let alone one person... *Or two*, inserted a snide voice, which Sylvie ignored.

One thing she was sure of: Arkim Al-Sahid would *not* be sharing her bed. Yet something quivered to life deep inside her and she couldn't seem to take her eyes off it... an image filled her brain of naked pale limbs entwined with much darker ones.

For years Sylvie had seen her peers indulge in casual sexual relationships and on some level had envied them that ease and freedom. She'd gone on dates…but the men involved had all expected her to be something she wasn't. And when they'd pushed for intimacy she'd found herself shutting down. The prospect that they'd somehow 'see' the real her and reject her was a fear she couldn't shake.

It was galling that she seemed to be hardwired to want more than casual sex—based on a fragile memory of the happiness and joy that had existed between her parents before her mother had so tragically died. She'd somehow clung to it her whole life, letting it sink deep into her unconscious.

It was even more galling, though, that Arkim Al-Sahid could look at her with explicit intent and have the opposite effect from making her shut down. When he looked at her she felt as if something was flowering to life deep inside her.

Irritated with the direction of her thoughts, and telling herself she was being ridiculous, Sylvie walked over to the French doors of the main bedroom and stepped outside. Heat washed over her like a dry caress, sinking into her bones and melting some of the tension away in spite of her wish to stay rigid at all costs.

She had her own private terrace, complete with a sparkling lap pool, its turquoise tiles illuminating the water. Low seats were scattered in twos and threes around low tables, with soft raw silk cushions. Lanterns hung from the walls, but weren't lit. Sylvie could imagine how seductive it might be at night, with only the flickering lights and the vast expanse of a star-filled night sky surrounding her.

And then she berated herself for getting sucked into a daydream so easily. Pushing the images out of her head, she walked over to the boundary wall, with its distinctive Arabic carvings. Outside she could see nothing but desert and dunes. A bird of prey circled lazily against the intense blue of the sky.

It compounded her sense of isolation and entrapment, and yet…much to her chagrin…Sylvie couldn't seem to drum up any sense of urgency. She realised that she was exhausted from the shock and adrenalin of the day.

A sound made her whirl around from the wall, her heart leaping into her throat. But it was only Halima again, with her shy smile.

'Sheikh Al-Sahid has sent me to tell you that he would be happy for you to join him in an hour for dinner. He said that should give you time to freshen up.'

Sylvie felt grim. 'Did he, now?' She thought of something and said, 'Wait here a moment—I'd like you to give him something, please.'

When she came back she felt unaccountably lighter. She handed the girl a folded-up note and said sweetly, 'Please give this to Sheikh Al-Sahid for me.'

The girl scurried off and Sylvie closed the door. A wave of weariness came over her, dousing any small sense of rebellious triumph. She set about unpacking only the most necessary items from her case, having no intention of staying here beyond a night. Whatever she had to do to persuade Arkim to let her go, she'd do it.

She was disappointed but unsurprised to see that her mobile phone didn't work. Exactly as he'd told her. She put it down and sighed, then took off her clothes, finding a robe. When she got to the door leading into the bathroom she had to suck in a breath. The sinks and the bath seemed to be carved out of the stone itself, with gold fittings that managed to complement the stark design without being tacky.

The bath was more like a small pool. When she'd filled it up, and added some oils she'd found in a cleverly hidden cabinet, exotically fragrant steam wrapped around her in a caress.

She drew off the robe and took the few steps down into

the bath, trying not to feel too overwhelmed by the sheer luxury. The water closed over her body and as she tipped her head back she closed her eyes and pushed all thoughts of Arkim Al-Sahid out of her mind, trying to pretend she was on a luxury mini-break and not in the middle of an unforgiving desert, cut off from civilisation with someone who hated her guts.

Arkim stood looking out over the view, at the fading twilight casting the dunes into mysterious shadows. He had claimed this part of his maternal ancestral home for himself. His mother's family had no interest in him, and he'd told himself a long time ago that he didn't care. They'd rejected her and he wanted nothing to do with them—even if they came begging.

He'd come here initially as an exercise in removing himself from his father's sphere. He'd never expected this land to touch him as deeply as it had done on first sight. Almost with a physical pull. His mind automatically felt freer, less constrained, when he was here. He felt connected with something primal and visceral.

When he'd made his first million this property had been his first purchase, and he'd followed it up with properties in Paris, London and New York. He'd surpassed his goals one by one. All of them. Only to fall at the last hurdle: gaining the stamp of social approval and respect that would show everyone that he was *not* his father's son. That he was vastly different.

He thought of Sophie Lewis now and his conscience twinged. He hadn't thought of her very often. In truth, he'd had his doubts—their relationship had been very... platonic. But Arkim had convinced himself that it suited him like that. Her father had been the one to suggest the match, and the more Arkim had thought about it the more the idea had grown on him.

In contrast to her flame-haired provocative sister, Sophie had been like a gentle balm. Shy and innocent. Arousing no hormone-fuelled lapses of character. He'd courted her. Taken her for dinner. To the theatre. Each outing had soothed another piece of his wounded soul, making him believe that marriage to her would indeed offer him everything he'd ever wanted—which was the antithesis of life with his father.

He would be one of those parents who was respectable—respected—who came to school to pick up his son with his beautiful wife by his side. A united front. There would be no scandals. No children born out of wedlock. No mistresses. No sordid rumours and sniggering behind his back. No child of *his* would have to deal with bullying and fist fights when another kid taunted him about the whores his father took to his bed.

But the gods had laughed in his face at his ambitions and shown him that he was a fool to believe he could ever remove the stain of his father's legacy from his life.

He looked at the crumpled piece of paper in his hand and opened it out again to read.

Thank you for the kind 'invitation' to dinner, but I must decline. I've already made plans for this evening.
Sincerely, Sylvie Devereux.

Arkim had to battle both irritation and the lust that had held his body in an uncomfortable grip since he'd seen Sylvie earlier that day. He fought the urge to go straight to her room to confront her. No doubt that was exactly what she wanted.

He'd annoyed her by bringing her here and she was toying with him to get her own back. His mouth tipped up in a hard smile. No matter. He didn't mind being toyed

with as long as she ended up where he wanted her—
underneath him, naked and pliant and begging for mercy.
Begging forgiveness.

When Sylvie woke it was dawn outside. She felt as if she'd
slept for a week, not just the ten or so hours she *had* slept.
Strangely, there was no disorientation—she knew exactly
where she was.

She was still in the robe and she sat up, looking around
warily, as if she might find Arkim lurking in a corner, glaring at her. She wondered how he'd reacted when she hadn't
shown for dinner. She wasn't sure she wanted to know…

She got up and opened the French doors, the early
morning's cool breeze a balm compared to the stifling
heat which would no doubt come once the sun was up.
She walked to the boundary wall again and sucked in a
deep breath. The intense silence wrapped around her. She
couldn't remember the last time she'd experienced this level
of stillness—if ever. It seemed to quiet something inside
her…some sense of restlessness. It was disconcerting—as
if she was betraying herself by finding an affinity with any
part of this situation.

She went back inside and dressed in jeans and a clean
T-shirt, loath to make any kind of effort with clothes or to
leave her rooms in case it showed acquiescence to Arkim.
But she was also feeling somewhat trapped, and she didn't
like it.

In the end Halima appeared, fresh-faced and smiling,
with a tray of breakfast, bringing it into the dining room.

Sylvie's stomach rumbled loudly and she realised that
because she'd turned down dinner the previous evening
she'd not eaten since she'd been on the plane the day before. She was starving, and when Halima pulled back a
cloth napkin to reveal a plate of fragrant flat breads Sylvie had to bite back of a groan of appreciation. It was a

mezze-style feast, with little bowls of olives and different cheeses, hard and soft. And a choice of fragrant coffee or sweet tea.

Before she left, Halima said, 'Sheikh Al-Sahid sends his apologies. He's been detained by a business call otherwise he would have joined you. He said he will meet you for lunch.'

Sylvie forced a smile. She couldn't shoot the messenger. 'Thank you.'

After Halima left and Sylvie had eaten her fill, she wandered around her rooms for a bit, feeling increasingly claustrophobic. She knew she should really do some exercises to keep herself flexible, especially after travelling, but she was feeling too antsy to focus. She left her rooms and walked down long stone corridors that gave glimpses into intriguing courtyards and other open spaces.

Through one open courtyard she saw a terrace with tall ornate stone columns and a vast pool that stretched around the side of the castle. It was breathtaking. Idyllic.

Sylvie backed away from the seductive scene and explored further. Some doors were closed, and she refrained from opening them in case she stumbled into Arkim.

Eventually she found herself at the main door, which led out to the central courtyard. Adrenalin flooded her system when she saw the golf buggy that Arkim had used to bring them into the castle the previous day. The key was in the ignition. And from here she could see that the main doors to the castle complex were open.

She had a sudden vision of Arkim wearing down her defences, slowly but surely. If he kissed her again she was very much afraid that she'd melt—just as she had before, when she'd lost all control of her rational functions.

The truth was that she didn't have an arsenal of experience to fend off someone like Arkim, and the thought of him ever discovering how flimsy her façade was made her go cold with terror.

She didn't think. She reacted. She got into the golf buggy and turned the key, setting it in motion. Her heart was clamouring as she sped out of the castle complex.

Less than an hour later Sylvie's feet sank into the sand. She was on top of a dune, with the now dead golf buggy in front of her. Futile anger made her kick ineffectually at the inanimate object. It had started sputtering and slowing down about ten minutes before, eventually conking out.

The sun beat down mercilessly and there was nothing as far as the eye could see except sand, sand and more sand. Heat waves shimmered in the distance.

Of course it was only now that Sylvie realised just how stupid she'd been to react to her own imagination like that and set off in a panic. She had no water. No food. No idea where she was. Even if she'd had the means she wasn't sure which way she'd come!

Her T-shirt was stuck to her skin and her jeans felt red-hot and too tight. Right now she would have given any-thing for a cool white tunic and a head-covering. She could feel her skin prickling uncomfortably under the sun, and the roof of the buggy offered scant protection.

She gulped and, absurdly, tears pricked her eyes. Arkim Al-Sahid had driven her to this desperate measure. She wished she'd never laid eyes on the man. She wished he'd never kissed—

Something caught at her peripheral vision and she looked. For a second she wondered if she was seeing things, and then as the image became more distinct her eyes widened.

It was a man on top of a horse... Except this looked like no ordinary horse. It was a huge black stallion. And the man...

Sylvie felt as if she might have slipped back a few centuries. At first she thought it must be one of Arkim's staff, because he was dressed in white robes, with a *keffiyeh* around his head. His face was obscured by the material, leaving only his eyes and dark skin visible. And was that a jewelled dagger stuck into the roped belt around his waist?

He drew up alongside her, the horse rearing up, making Sylvie back away skittishly. Even now—even though her accelerated pulse told her otherwise—she was hoping she was mistaken.

But the man who jumped off the horse had such grace and innate athleticism that her mouth dried.

He tied the horse to the buggy and then stalked towards her, growing bigger and taller as he did so. Right up until the moment that he ripped aside the material covering his mouth and face Sylvie was still hoping it was anyone but…*him*. Of course he'd found her. This man seemed to have a heat-seeking radar, able to pin her to the spot no matter where she was.

'You damned little fool. What the *hell* did you hope to achieve by this stunt?'

She tried to ignore how Arkim's almost savage appearance made her feel as if she was losing it completely. He looked even more ridiculously handsome against this unforgiving backdrop.

She shouted back. 'I was trying to get away from *you*, in case it wasn't completely obvious.'

Arkim's eyes glittered like obsidian. 'In a golf buggy? With none of your things?' He was scathing. 'Did you really think you could just bounce merrily across hundreds of miles of desert and roll into the nearest petrol station to refuel?'

Humiliated beyond measure, Sylvie launched herself at Arkim, hands balled into fists and beating against his chest.

He caught her arms easily and held her immobile. Tension crackled between them, and for a heart-stopping moment Sylvie thought he was going to kiss her—but then a piercing sound shattered the air and they both looked up to see two Jeeps coming towards them over the top of the dune, horns blasting.

Sylvie felt so jittery all she wanted was to escape back to the castle as quickly as possible and lock herself in her rooms. She was caught between a rock and a hard place. Literally. The thought didn't amuse her.

The Jeeps pulled up and concerned-looking staff spilled out. Sylvie immediately felt guilty for having precipitated this search.

Arkim wordlessly led her over to the nearest vehicle and said a few words to the driver. Then he opened up the back door for her. When she would have expected to get in, he handed her a bottle of water. She looked at him and he was grim.

'Drink, you'll be dehydrated.'

Sylvie couldn't argue with that, and she was thirsty, so she took several large gulps. Then Arkim reached into the back of the Jeep again and pulled out a long white robe. He thrust it at her.

'I'm supposed to put this on?' Sylvie said waspishly.

Arkim's expression darkened. 'Yes. You're already burning.'

Her skin *was* still prickling, but Sylvie was afraid that it was more to do with his effect on her than the sun—even though when she looked her arms were ominously pink.

Mutinously she pulled on the long-sleeved robe, and was surprised at how much cooler she felt instantly—which was crazy when she was pulling on *more* clothes.

Then he was unwinding his *keffiyeh* from his head, and before she could stop him he'd placed it over her hair, like a shawl. He started to wind it around her head, tucking it in, until there was only one long piece left that he drew across her mouth and tucked in at the back.

She was effectively swaddled. And it was only then that she realised that the Jeeps were driving off into the distance, towing the buggy behind them. Arkim's scent was disturbing, and all around her. The thought that this fabric had been across his mouth was almost too intimate to take in.

He held his horse by the reins and was leading it over. Sylvie pulled down the material covering her mouth. 'What are you doing? Where are the Jeeps going?'

He stopped in front of her, the huge horse prancing behind him. 'We are going for a little trip.'

Before she could ask more, Arkim had his hands around her waist and was lifting her effortlessly onto the horse. His sheer strength took her breath away and she clung to the saddle, her brain reeling at being so high up. She hadn't been on a horse since she was a teenager...

Arkim put his foot in the stirrup and vaulted on behind her, his agility awesome. And suddenly he was all around her. Strong muscled thighs gripping hers, his torso against her back, his arms coming around her to take the reins.

'Cover your mouth.'

Sylvie was too stunned to move. 'Wh—where are we going?'

Arkim angled himself so he could see her and made a rude sound. 'Don't you *ever* do anything you're told?' The material was firmly pulled back over her mouth and he said, 'It'll stop sand getting in.'

Sylvie couldn't say anything else, because Arkim was turning the horse around and they were galloping in the opposite direction from where the Jeeps had gone. For a semi-hysterical moment Sylvie thought that perhaps she'd pushed Arkim so far he was just going to dump her in the desert and leave her to die a slow, painful death.

Gradually, though, as they galloped into the seeming nothingness of the sandy landscape, almost against her will she felt herself relaxing into Arkim's body, letting him take her weight. One of his arms was around her torso, holding her to him, and she felt the intimate space between her legs soften and moisten.

She was fast losing all sense of reality. The real world and civilisation felt very far away.

After about twenty minutes Arkim drew the stallion to a stop, its muscles quivering under Sylvie's legs. He got off the horse and Sylvie looked down to see his arms outstretched towards her. His mouth was stern.

'Bring your leg over the horse, Sylvie.'

She wanted to disobey, but she knew Arkim would pull her off the horse anyway. Better to do it with a modicum of decorum and not let him see how intimidated she was. And she was scared… Even though she knew—in some way she didn't like to investigate—that he wouldn't harm her.

Her hands landed on Arkim's wide shoulders and his hands clamped around her waist as he lifted her down as effortlessly as before. She saw the reins on the ground and said nervously, 'Won't the horse just go?'

'Aziz won't move unless I say so. And we won't be long.' Arkim's tone brooked no disobedience—from her or the horse.

Sylvie broke away from Arkim's hands. The *keffiyah* was still around her mouth and she pulled it down as she looked around at a sea of nothing but blue sky and dunes.

'Why are we here?'

Arkim planted himself in front of her, hands on hips. 'Because this is where you would have ended up if the buggy hadn't run out of fuel. This is where we might have found you in two days, if we were lucky enough, dehydrated and burnt to a crisp.'

Sylvie looked at him and shivered. 'You're exaggerating.'

Arkim looked livid. He grabbed her arms with his hands. 'No, I'm not. Men who know this area, who have lived here for years, can still get caught out by the desert. Right now it looks calm, wouldn't you agree?'

Sylvie nodded hesitantly.

Arkim's mouth thinned. 'It's anything but. There's a sandstorm due to hit any day now. Have you ever been in a sandstorm?'

She shook her head.

'Imagine a tidal wave coming towards you—except in this case it's made of sand and debris, not water. You'd be obliterated in seconds. Suffocated.'

Genuine horror and fear finally made her realise just how reckless she'd been. She seized on the surge of anger. He made her feel as if she was a tiny ship bobbing about in a huge raging sea.

'Okay, fine—I get it. What I did was foolish and reckless and silly. I didn't know. I didn't mean to put everyone to so much trouble...' A very unwelcome sense of vulnerability made her lash out. 'But, in case you don't remember, it's *your* fault I'm even here!'

Arkim looked down at that beautiful but defiant face and felt such a mix of things that he was dizzy. He shook his head, but nothing rational would come to the surface. All he could see was *her*.

He gave in to the urgent dictates of his blood and lowered his mouth to the lush contours of hers—and drowned.

His tongue swept into her mouth in a marauding move and he quickly became oblivious to everything except the rough stroke of his tongue against Sylvie's, demanding a response.

She resisted him for long seconds, but he felt her

gradually relax, as if losing a battle with herself. Once again there was an almost unbelievable hesitance—as if she didn't know what to do. The thought that she could do this—get under his skin so easily, make him doubt himself—made Arkim's blood boil.

He held the back of her covered head and put his hand to where her neck met her shoulder in an unashamedly possessive move, his thumb reaching for and finding that hectic pulse-beat, which was telling him that no matter how ingrained it was in her to act, she couldn't control *everything*.

And finally he felt her arms relax and start to climb around his neck, bringing her body into more intimate contact with his. Her mouth softened and she...acquiesced. The triumph was heady. Her tongue stroked his sweetly, sucking him deep—as deep as he imagined the exquisite clasp of her body would be around his in a more intimate caress.

He wanted to throw her down on the ground right here and pull up that robe, yank down her jeans, until he could find his release. The desire was so strong he shook in a bid to rein it in. And that brought him back from the brink of losing it completely.

Reality slammed into him. He was in the middle of the desert, under the merciless sun, about to ravage this woman. Make her his...brand her like some kind of animal.

He wanted to push her away from him and yet never let her go.

He hated her. He wanted her.

He pulled back from the kiss even though everything in his body and his blood protested at the move. He felt the unrelenting beat of the sun on his head. Her eyes opened after a moment, wide and blue...and that intriguing blue-green. Her cheeks were flushed. Lips swollen.

And then suddenly she tensed and scrambled free of

his arms. Arkim might almost have laughed—even now she was intent on playing this game of push and pull. Acting her little heart out.

'Have you forgotten that you're a civilised man?'

Even her voice sounded suitably shaky. But Arkim barely cast her a glance as he reached for the horse's reins. 'I don't have to be civilised here.'

That was why he'd brought her here in the first place— because he didn't trust himself around her in more civilised surroundings. It was as if he'd known the desert was the only place big enough to contain what he felt for her.

He picked up the reins, ignoring the dull throb of unsatisfied desire in his system…the way his arousal pressed against his trousers under his robe.

'You really can't turn it off, can you?'

Sylvie scowled at him. She should have looked ridiculous. The *keffiyah* was askew on her head, and slivers of bright red curling tendrils of hair peeped out from under its folds. She crossed her arms. 'Turn what off?'

'Your constant need to act out some role—pretend you don't want this.'

'I'm *not* acting. And I *don't* want this! I don't know what happened there…a moment of sunstroke…but it won't be happening again.'

Arkim almost felt pity for her. He reached out and rubbed a thumb back and forth over her plump lower lip. 'Oh, don't worry—it'll be happening again, and you'll be fully participant in it when it does.'

Sylvie slapped his hand away. She might have screamed at his arrogance, but he was lifting her up onto the horse again before she could take another breath. And, in any case, what could she say after she'd just melted all over him?

It was pathetic. *She* was pathetic. She turned to mush

when he came near her. So she'd just have to keep him at a distance.

But then he got up on the horse behind her again, and predictably Sylvie's body went into a paroxysm of anticipation as one arm snaked around her torso, holding her to him, and his other hand expertly gathered the reins to urge the horse on. Of course he would *have* to be an expert horseman too. Was there anything this man *couldn't* do? Apart from act in a civil manner to her?

His lower body was pressed against her backside now, and she could feel the thrust of something unmistakably hard. Her face flamed, and it had nothing to do with the sun. She yanked the material of the *keffiyah* back over her mouth. He wouldn't have to ask her to cover up. She'd never uncover herself again in this man's presence.

CHAPTER FOUR

SYLVIE SAT CURLED up on one of the vast couches in the living area of her suite. When she'd returned to her rooms a couple of hours ago she'd found Halima waiting for her, with ointment for her sun-tender skin and some lunch snacks—and plenty of water. Arkim's efficiency at work. Afterwards she'd changed into loose pants and layered on a couple of her sleeveless workout tops to keep her arms bare.

On their return Arkim had taken her into an expansive stables area at the back of the castle, and when he'd helped Sylvie off the horse she'd felt wobbly-legged and suitably chastened after being shown the very real dangers of the desert.

Arkim hadn't accompanied her back to the castle; he'd sent for one of his staff to do it. Sylvie had recognised him as one of the drivers of the Jeeps and had apologised to him for having dragged them out to look for her. She wasn't even sure if he'd understood her, but he'd shaken his head and looked embarrassed, as if it was nothing.

The night was falling outside now: the sky was a stunning deep violet colour and stars were appearing. Questions abounded in her head. Questions about Arkim. Seeing him against this backdrop was more intriguing than she liked to admit. And she hated to acknowledge it but she was also fascinated by the barely repressed emotions below the surface of his urbanity. He was different here. More raw. It should be intimidating. But it excited her.

What was his connection to this place? And if he had a connection here, how could he—a man who had this desert in his blood, so timeless and somehow base—agree to marry purely for business and strategic reasons?

A noise made her tense and she looked round to see the object of her thoughts in the doorway to her living room. Dressed in a robe again, with his head bare, he looked… powerful. Mysterious.

Sylvie's belly tightened. 'Come to check your prisoner is still here?'

Arkim's mouth lifted slightly at one corner, as if he were wryly amused, and Sylvie felt it like a punch to the gut.

'Somehow I don't think even *you* would be so foolish as to try and escape again.'

Sylvie scowled. 'Next time I'll prepare better.'

His smile faded. 'There won't be a next time—believe me. You won't be leaving until I do.'

She stood up, frustration running through her blood. 'Look, this is crazy. I need to get back to Paris. I have to—'

Arkim interrupted her. 'You have to eat.'

She could see staff now, coming up behind him, carrying things.

He stood aside and said, 'I've arranged for dinner to come to you this evening. We'll have it on the terrace.'

She felt completely impotent. What could she do? Storm off to another part of the castle in protest?

She preceded Arkim out to where the staff were setting up on the terrace, and when she saw lanterns being lit, sending out soft golden light, her heart flipped. She'd imagined this seductive scenario…

Plates of fragrant steaming food were being placed on a low table and the scents teased Sylvie's nostrils. She was an unashamed foodie, and the prospect of an exotic feast was too much temptation to resist.

Halima arrived then, with a bottle of champagne which she put in an ice bucket by the table. Sylvie scowled at it, just as Arkim came into her line of vision and held out a hand.

'Please, take a seat.'

Sylvie sat down cross-legged on a low chair, and watched as Arkim lowered himself athletically into a similar pose on the other side of the delicately carved table. It should have made him look less manly, but of course it didn't.

'How are your arms?'

She glanced down, noting with relief that the vivid pink had faded and they weren't so hot. In this day and age of knowledge of sun damage she'd been very stupid.

She said, 'Much better. Halima's ointment was very effective.'

She looked at Arkim and words of apology for running off earlier trembled on her tongue. But he wasn't looking at her—he was piling a plate high with different foods before handing it to her. Like a coward, she swallowed the words back and took the plate, telling herself that he would only spurn an apology.

There was a faint popping sound as he expertly opened the champagne and poured her a glass of the sparkling wine. She accepted it after a moment's hesitation.

Arkim arched a brow. 'You don't like champagne?'

'I don't drink much of any alcohol, I never really acquired the taste.'

Arkim made a noise and she looked at him, seeing him fill his own glass as he said, 'You forget that I've seen you inebriated.'

Sylvie frowned, and then that night in the garden flooded back. Hotly she defended herself. 'My shoe got stuck in the ground. I was still on antibiotics from a chest infection that night—the last thing I'd have done was drink alcohol.'

He just looked at her, eyes narrowed, and she glared at

him. After a long moment he shrugged and said, 'It hardly matters now, in any case.'

Sylvie was disconcerted by how much it *did* matter to her. She looked away from him and put down her glass without taking a sip, choosing to focus on the food instead and trying to block him out. *Ha!* As if *that* was possible.

Arkim could see how tense Sylvie's body was as she resolutely avoided his eye and picked at the food. Her jaw was so tight he thought she might break it if she had to chew. Her vibrant hair was piled high in a haphazard bun, tendrils trailing down to frame her face. His fingers itched to undo the knot and let her hair fall around her shoulders and down her back.

He diverted his attention from the urge he felt to undo that knot and watched with growing incredulity, and something much earthier, as Sylvie seemed to be absorbed by the food—spearing large morsels and evidently taking extreme pleasure out of the discovery of the various tastes. It was incredibly sensual to watch.

She seemed to be completely oblivious to Arkim and he sat back slightly, the better to observe her. He knew she *wasn't* oblivious to him, though—it was there in the tension of her body, and in the pulse beating under the delicate pale skin of her throat.

He'd noticed for the first time this evening that his impression of her being tall actually wasn't correct. He might have registered it before if she hadn't distracted him so easily, but she'd always seemed a lot taller. Maybe it was because she consistently stood up to him in a way no one else did.

That revelation wasn't welcome. It made him think of the fact that he'd overheard her trying to apologise to a member of his staff earlier. He'd have assumed it was for show, but she had been almost out of his earshot, so patently not doing it for his benefit.

Sylvie was actually only just above average height, and her whole frame was on the petite side. He didn't like the way this fact made his conscience smart a little. It made him see a vulnerability he'd blocked out before, and reminded him of the way her stepmother had slapped her in the church...

She leaned forward at that moment, to get some bread, and her full breasts swayed with the movement. Arkim's whole body seemed to sizzle, and he was reminded of exactly who he was dealing with here—a mistress of selfishness and manipulation.

'You like the food?' he asked now, in some kind of effort to wrench his mind off Sylvie's physical temptations, angry with himself.

She glanced at him—a flash of blue and green. She nodded and swallowed what she was eating. Her voice was low, husky, when she said, 'It's delicious. I've never tasted flavours like this before.'

'The lamb is particularly good.'

He speared a morsel of succulent meat with his fork and held it across the table. When she reached for it with her hand he pulled it back and looked at her. She scowled.

'Coward,' Arkim said softly.

Something in him exulted when he saw the fire flash in her eyes as she took the bait and leant across the table to take the piece of meat off his fork and into her mouth.

Her loose tops swayed, giving Arkim an unrestricted view of her lace-clad breasts. Full and perfectly shaped. She moved back before he could make a complete fool of himself by grabbing her and hauling her across the table.

Her cheeks were flaming. And he didn't think it was from the spices in the lamb. Their mutual chemistry was obvious. So why would she fight it like this?

He leant back on one arm again. She took a sip of champagne and he watched the long, graceful column of her throat work, jealous of even that small movement. She might have passed for eighteen, with her face free of make-up.

Something niggled at him—where was the *femme fatale*? So far he had to admit that the Sylvie he had here was nothing like the woman who had provoked him beyond measure each time he'd seen her before. Not least when she'd appeared in the church, dressed from head to toe in motorcycle gear. The soft black leather jacket and trousers had moulded to her body in a way that had been indecent—and even more so in a church.

He'd expected her to be a lot more sophisticated, knowing... Giving in to her situation and manipulating him as much as she could. That was how the women he knew operated—ultimately they would follow the path of least resistance and take as much as they could.

That was what had attracted him to Sophie Lewis and made him believe he could marry her—her complete lack of guile or artifice. A rare thing in this world.

And that was as far as the attraction had gone.

Arkim ignored the voice. But he had to acknowledge uncomfortably that if the wedding had gone ahead and he'd married Sophie Lewis he wouldn't be here now with her sister. And for a sobering and very unpalatable moment Arkim couldn't regret that fact.

A deeper, darker truth nudged at his consciousness— the very real doubts he'd had himself about the wedding as it had come closer and closer. But he wasn't a man who spent fruitless time wondering about what might have been. And he didn't entertain doubts. He made decisions and he dealt in reality, and this was now his reality.

Sylvie was avoiding looking at him and he hated that.

He said, 'Your eyes... I've never seen that before.'

* * *

Sylvie was straining with every muscle she had not to let Arkim see how much he was getting to her, lounging on the other side of the table as he was, like some kind of robed demigod. When she'd leant across the table—provoked into taking that food off his fork—and she'd seen him looking down her top, she'd almost combusted.

Distracted, and very irritated, she said, 'They're just eyes, Arkim. Everyone has them. Even you.'

She risked a look and saw that half-smile again. *Lord*.

'Yes, but none as unusual as you. Blue and blue-green.'

Sylvie hated the frisson she felt to think of him studying her eyes. 'My mother had it too. It's a condition called heterochromia iridum. There's really nothing that mysterious about it.'

Arkim frowned now. 'Your mother was French, wasn't she?'

Sylvie nodded, getting tenser now, thinking of Arkim's judgmental gaze turning on her deceased mother. Sophie must have mentioned it to him.

'Yes, from just outside Paris.'

'And how did your parents meet?'

Sylvie glared at him. 'You're telling me you don't know?'

He shrugged lightly and asked, 'Should I?'

For a moment she processed that nugget. Maybe he genuinely didn't.

From what she'd learnt of this man, he would not hesitate to take advantage of another excuse to bash her—so, anticipating his scathing reaction, she lifted her chin and said, 'She was a dancer—for a revue in Paris that was in the same building where I now dance. It had a different name when she was there and the show was…of its time.'

'What does that mean?' he drawled derisively. 'Not so much skin?'

Sylvie cursed herself for being honest. Why couldn't she just have said her mother had been a nurse, or a secretary? Because, her conscience answered her, her mother would never have hidden her true self. And neither would Sylvie.

'Something like that. It was more in the line of vintage burlesque.'

'And how did your father meet her? He doesn't strike me as the kind of man who frequents such establishments.'

Sylvie pushed down the hurt as she recalled sparkling memories full of joy—her father laughing and swinging her mother around in their back garden. She smiled sweetly and said, 'Just goes to show that you can't always judge a book by its cover.'

Arkim had the grace to tilt his glass towards her slightly and say, 'Touché.'

She played with her champagne glass, which was still half full. She grudgingly explained, 'He was in Paris on a business trip and went with some of his clients to the show. He saw my mother…asked her out afterwards… that was it.'

Sylvie would never reveal the true romance of her parents' love story to this cynical man, but the fact was that her father had fallen for Cécile Devereux at first sight—a *coup de foudre*—and had wooed her for over a month before her mother had finally deigned to go out with him— an English businessman a million miles removed from the glamorous Cécile Devereux's life. Yet she'd fallen in love with him too. And they'd been happy. Ecstatically.

Familiar emotion and vulnerability rose up inside Sylvie now and she knew she didn't want Arkim to probe any further into her precious memories.

She took a sip of champagne and looked at him. 'What about *your* parents?'

Arkim's expression immediately darkened. It was visible even in the flickering light of the dozens of candles and lanterns.

'As you've pointed out—you know very well who my father is.'

Sylvie flushed when she recalled throwing that in Arkim's face in her father's study. She refused to cower, though. This man had judged her from the moment he'd laid eyes on her.

She thought of how he was doing everything he could to distance himself from his parent and she was doing everything to follow in her mother's footsteps. The opposite sides of one coin.

'I don't know about your mother—were they married?'

His look could have sliced through steel. Clearly this wasn't a subject he relished, and it buoyed her up to see him lose that icy control he seemed to wield so effortlessly. It reminded her of how she'd wanted to shatter it when she'd first met him. Well, it had shattered all right—taking her with it.

Arkim's tone was harsh. 'She died in childbirth, and, no, they weren't married. My father doesn't *do* marriage. He's too eager to hang on to his fortune and keep his bedroom door revolving.'

Sylvie didn't like the little dart of sympathy she felt to hear that his mother had died before he'd even known her. She moved away from that kernel of information. 'So, you grew up in America?'

His mouth tightened. 'Yes. And in England, in a series of boarding schools. During holidays in LA I was a captive audience for my father's debauched lifestyle.'

Sylvie winced inwardly. There was another link in the chain to understanding this man's prejudices.

Hesitantly she said, 'You've never been close, then?'

Arkim's voice could have chilled ice. 'I haven't seen him since I was a teenager.'

Sylvie sucked in a breath.

Before she could think how to respond, Arkim inserted mockingly, 'Living with him taught me a valuable lesson from an early age: that life isn't some fairytale.'

The extent of his cynicism mocked Sylvie's tender memories of her own parents. 'Most people don't experience what you did.'

His eyes glittered like black jewels. He looked completely relaxed, but she could sense the tension in his form.

The question was burning her up inside. 'Is that one of the reasons why you agreed to marry Sophie? Because you don't believe real marriages can exist?'

'Do you?' he parried.

Sylvie cursed her big mouth and glanced away. She longed to match his cynicism with her own, but the truth was that even after witnessing how grief had torn her father apart she *had* seen real love for a while.

She looked back. 'I think sometimes, yes, they can. But even a happy marriage can be broken apart very easily.' *By devastating illness and death.*

He looked at her consideringly for a long moment and she steeled herself. But then he asked, 'What was your mother like?'

Sylvie's insides clenched harder. She looked at her glass.

'She was amazing. Beautiful, sweet…kind.' When Arkim didn't respond with some cutting comment, she went on, 'I always remember her perfume…it was so distinctive. My father used to buy it in the same shop for her whenever he was in Paris. It was opposite the Ritz hotel, run by a beautiful Indian woman. He took me with him once. I remember she had a small daughter…' Her mouth quirked as she got lost in the memory. 'I used to sit at my mother's feet and watch her get ready to go out with my father. She used to hum all the time. French songs. And she would dance with me…'

'Sounds just like one of those fairytales—too good to be true.'

Arkim's voice broke through the memories like a rude klaxon. Sylvie's head jerked up. She'd forgotten where she was for a moment, and with whom.

'It *was* true. And good.'

She hated it that her voice trembled slightly. She wouldn't be able to bear it now if Arkim was to delve further and ask about her mother's death. That excruciating last year, when cancer had turned her mother into a shadow of her former self, would haunt Sylvie for the rest of her life. She'd lost both her parents from that moment.

She felt prickly enough to attack. 'Why did you agree to marry my sister? Really?'

Arkim was expressionless. 'For all the reasons I have already explained to you.'

Beyond irritated, and frustrated at the way he made her feel, Sylvie put down her napkin and stood up, walking over to the wall. She heard him move and turned around to face him, feeling jittery.

He stood a few feet away. Too close for comfort. Before she could say anything, Arkim folded his arms and said, 'I won't deny I had my doubts...'

Sylvie went still.

'That night in the study, when you found me... I wasn't altogether certain that I was going to go through with it. But then you appeared...' Something like anger flashed in his eyes. 'Let's just say that you helped me make up my mind.'

Sylvie reeled. He might have called it off? And then his words registered. Anger flared. 'So it was *my* fault?'

He ignored that. 'Why did you break up the wedding? Was it purely for spite?'

The realisation that Arkim might have called the whole thing off was mixing with her anger, diluting it. Making her heart beat faster. Words trembled on her lips. Words that would exonerate her. But she couldn't do it; she'd promised her sister.

She lifted her chin. 'All you need to know is that if I had to do it over again I wouldn't hesitate.'

Arkim's face hardened even more. He didn't like that. But his drawling voice belied his expression. 'The motorbike was a cute touch. Did you learn how to ride one especially for dramatic effect?'

Sylvie flushed. 'I used to have one in Paris—to get around. Until it got stolen. I hired one that day…more for expediency than anything else.'

He sneered now. 'You mean a quick, cowardly getaway so you didn't have to deal with the fallout…?'

Before Sylvie could formulate a response, Halima and some other discreet staff appeared at that moment, defusing the tension a little, and removed the remains of their dinner from the table.

When they were gone Sylvie was still facing Arkim, like an adversary in a boxing ring. The revelation that she'd inadvertently influenced his decision to marry Sophie was crowding everything else out of her head. Presumably it had been because she'd reminded him of exactly the kind of woman he *didn't* want. And that stung.

She pushed down her roiling emotions and tried to appeal to his civilised side. 'Arkim…you've made your point. You need to let me go now.'

His expression remained as hard as granite. Unforgiving. Sylvie shivered. This man wasn't civilised here.

And then he said, 'I've paid a substantial sum of money for your presence and I believe that I'd like to see you dance for me.' The shape of his mouth turned bitter. 'After all, thousands have seen you dance, so why shouldn't I?'

The thought of performing in front of this man made

Sylvie go cold, and then hot. 'Now?' Her voice squeaked slightly.

A ghost of a smile touched his lips. 'No, tomorrow evening. You'll perform a very *private* dance. Just for me.'

She straightened her spine. 'If you're expecting a lap dance, I hate to disappoint you but I really don't do that kind of thing.'

He moved close enough to reach out and trail a finger down over her cheek and jaw, and said softly, 'I'm looking forward to seeing what you *do* do.'

She slapped his hand down, terrified of the way his touch made her melt so easily. Terrified he'd kiss her again. 'And why on earth should I do anything you ask me to?'

Arkim's jaw clenched, and then he said baldly, 'Because you owe me, and I'm collecting.'

The following evening Halima held up one of Sylvie's rhinestone-encrusted outfits and stroked it reverently. 'This is so beautiful.'

The thought of the robed young woman wearing it, baring her skin so comprehensively, made Sylvie feel a little uncomfortable, and she gently took the garment out of Halima's hands to hang it up, along with the other costumes the girl had insisted on taking out of her suitcase.

She hadn't been able to eat since breakfast that morning, and her belly had been doing somersaults all day at the thought of dancing for Arkim. She'd realised that of course he'd be expecting her to rebel, refuse. And then maybe he'd initiate another cosy dinner and tell her more things about himself that would put her on uneven ground where her feelings towards him were concerned.

As she'd lain in bed last night and gone over everything he'd told her she had found her antipathy hard to cling on to. So she'd decided to keep him at arm's length and do the opposite of what he was expecting and dance for him.

She realised with some level of dark irony that if he was reverse psychoanalysing her, then it was working.

And if Sylvie was being completely honest with herself, a part of her still wanted to provoke Arkim—make him admit that he was just like everyone else.

It was that damned icy façade of his that had sneaked under her skin and made her want to break it apart as soon as he'd looked at her for the first time with such disdain. And where had breaking that control apart got her? To one of the hottest places on earth. About to strip herself bare in front of a man who wanted her, yet despised her.

Words trembled on Sylvie's tongue. Words to instruct Halima to go and tell the Sheikh that she wasn't available this evening after all. But she couldn't back down now.

She surveyed herself in the mirror as Halima clipped a veil behind her head, obscuring her mouth, so only her heavily kohled eyes were visible. Her hair was tucked and hidden under another veil.

Sylvie wondered if Arkim would appreciate the fact that the act she'd decided to do was based on the story of *Scheherazade*. Somehow, she didn't think he'd be amused.

She took a deep breath and turned to Halima. 'Now all I need is a sword...do you think you can find one here?'

The young girl thought for a moment, then brightened. 'Yes!'

Anticipation lay heavy and thick in Arkim's bloodstream as he waited for Sylvie to appear. He'd given instructions for her to be brought to one of the ceremonial rooms, where traditionally the Sheikh would greet and entertain his important guests. The room was open to the elements behind Arkim. Lanterns lit the space with golden flickering shadows.

Just then he noticed that a strong gust of wind whipping through the open space had almost put out one of the candles. The storm. It was coming. It made Arkim feel reckless. Wild. He'd gone out on Aziz earlier that day, tracking it, seeing the wind pick up. The stallion had moved skittishly, wanting to get back to cover.

There was a raised marble dais in the centre of the room, where the Sheikh would usually sit to greet his guests, and it was also sometimes used for ceremonial performances and dances. Arkim didn't doubt that he was about to bring this space into serious disrepute by having Sylvie dance here, but he couldn't seem to care too much.

He took a sip of his wine. *Where was she?* He tensed at the thought that she was defying him again.

Just as he was about to put down his glass and stand up and go to her, his blood fizzing, she appeared. She was slight and lissom...in bare feet. Arkim blinked as blood roared up into his head and south to another part of his anatomy.

She didn't look in his direction or acknowledge him as she stepped up onto the dais. He wasn't sure what he'd been expecting, but it wasn't this. She was wearing gold figure-hugging trousers that were flared at the ends and partially slit up the sides, embellished with jewels and lace. They sat low on her hips, along with a belt from which tassels dropped and moved and swayed with her body.

Her middle was toned and bare, and encircled with a delicate gold chain that sat just above the curve of her hips. A cropped black top with long trailing sleeves was tied in the front, between her breasts, worn over a gold-coloured and very ornate-looking bra.

Her breasts were...perfection. Full and luscious, beautifully shaped. Her provocative cleavage was framed by the top.

She still hadn't even so much as flicked a glance in his direction, and he noticed properly for the first time that the lower half of her face was obscured by a black veil, and that a black covering also hid her hair. Arkim wanted to rip it off and see those red tresses tumbling around her shoulders.

All that was visible of her face were her heavily kohled eyes. She was bending down now, doing something with speakers, and then a slow, sultry and distinctly Arabic beat filled the space.

Arkim's eyes widened when he saw her pick up a large curved sabre—he'd been too distracted to notice it before. He frowned. It looked disturbingly like the one that hung in the exhibition room that housed all his precious antiques and old weapons.

Sylvie faced away from him now, and all he could see was the tempting curve of her buttocks, the tantalising line of her waist and hips, and that gold chain glinting in the flickering glow of the lamps. And then she lifted the sword high in her hands over her head and slowly turned to face him. Those distinctive eyes met his, and she started to move sinuously to the beat of the music.

And Arkim's brain stuttered to a halt.

He was aware of pale skin, dips and hollows, a toned belly. She played with the huge sword as if it was a baton—twirling it in one hand and then in the other. She was on her knees now, one leg raised at a right angle, and arching her body backwards like a bow, with the sword resting on its tip behind her and her free arm stretched out in front of her. The line of her throat was long and graceful, and curiously vulnerable.

The music seemed to be pounding in time with Arkim's blood. And then it changed and became a little faster, with a different beat.

Sylvie straightened up and bent forward with impressive flexibility, bringing the sword back in front of her to place it on the ground and push it away. And then, still bending forward, she lifted the veil and head covering

off her head. She undid the tie on her black top and removed that too.

Now her hair tumbled down, free and wild, and the
ornately decorated gold bra was revealed. He could see
the faint sheen of perspiration on her pale skin and his insides tightened with pure, unadulterated lust. Would her
skin be sheened like that when he joined their bodies for
the first time?

She came onto her knees, facing Arkim again, and
started undulating her body in a series of movements—
hips, arms, chest—disconnected but connected. He'd seen
belly dancers before, but never like this. Bright red hair
trailed over her shoulders and down to her breasts. He
wanted to reach out and curl a tendril around his hand,
pull her towards him.

She was looking at him now, but blankly. A sizzle of
irritation ran through his blood. When women looked at
him, they *looked*.

She moved lithely to her feet and brought her whole
body into the dance. This should be boring him to tears.
But it wasn't. He hated to realise that he was most likely in
the kind of thrall that had mesmerised men for hundreds
of years when a woman danced like this for him.

And then he realised it was *her*. There was something profoundly captivating about Sylvie and the way
she moved. It was knowing, and yet there was something
Arkim couldn't put his finger on…something slightly *off*.
As if a piece of the jigsaw was missing.

She'd stopped dancing now, her chest moving rapidly
with her breath, her hair tangled in waves and falling down
her back as she stood with one hand on her hip and the
other stretched out towards him, as if she were offering
him something.

She hadn't even stripped. But arousal sat heavy in Arkim's body and bloodstream. He felt like a fool. Sylvie

had told him that she didn't do lap dances, but somehow that was exactly what he had expected. Something tawdry and fitting for the picture he'd built up of her in his head.

But this whole performance had been sweetly titillating— like a throwback to a more innocent time. A time that Arkim had never had the pleasure of knowing. He'd never really experienced innocence. His own had been corrupted when he had been so young.

Anger rushed through him and he stood up. He did a slow hand-clap and then said, as equably as he could, 'Who exactly are you trying to fool with a routine suited to the top of a table in a restaurant?'

Sylvie's arm dropped and she looked at him, cheeks flushed. Arkim's body throbbed all over. But he held on to what tiny bit of control he had—rigidly.

Her gaze narrowed on him. 'I take it that you didn't care for it, then? Too bad you can't get your money back.'

Her voice was breathy, and there was something defiant in those flashing blue-green eyes. It sent his churning cauldron of emotions into overdrive. She was taunting him. He thought of all the people she'd bared herself to, and yet she wouldn't for him. The thought that she might have an inkling of just how badly he wanted her scored him deep inside.

He didn't want to go near Sylvie for fear of what might happen if he did. As if some beast inside him might be unleashed and she'd see just how close to the edge of his control he was. He felt feral. As if he needed desperately to prove to himself that she was who he believed she was.

'You'll dance again, Sylvie. And this time you'll perform exactly as you do for the thousands of people who have seen *all* of you. I won't accept anything less. Be back here in half an hour.'

CHAPTER FIVE

SYLVIE WATCHED ARKIM stalk out of the huge space, adrenalin still fizzing in her blood. Vulnerability and frustration vied with her anger at his high-handedness. And a need to wipe the disdainful look off his face.

More anger coursed through her when she thought of what Arkim had been expecting and what he clearly still expected: *You'll perform exactly as you do for the thousands of people who have seen* all *of you.*

She was surprised he hadn't had a pole installed so she could shimmy up and down it. Clearly she'd done such a good job of doing absolutely *nothing* to amend Arkim's bad opinion of her, she'd merely raised his expectations.

It had taken more nerve than she'd thought she possessed to come in here and dance for him. It had taken all her strength to look at him and through him—even though he'd sat there like some kind of lord and master, surveying her as if she was some morsel for his delectation.

But she'd still been acutely aware of that powerful body, its inherent strength barely leashed. He'd dressed in western style, in dark trousers and an open-necked shirt. And somehow, after seeing him in nothing but pristine three-piece suits and then the traditional Arabic tunic, it was a little shocking—as if he was unravelling, somehow.

Suddenly there was a flurry of movement as staff entered the cavernous space and rushed to close the huge open doors.

Sylvie had been so caught up in her own thoughts that she hadn't noticed how the sky had darkened outside—dramatically. There was so much electricity in the air she could swear it was sparking along her skin.

And then Halima appeared, a look of excitement on her pretty face. 'The Sheikh has told me to help you. We must close all your doors and windows—the storm is coming.'

As Halima ushered her out of the room, eager to do her Sheikh's bidding, Sylvie's rage spiked—as if in tandem with the escalating weather outside. If Arkim wanted a damn lap dance so badly, then maybe she should give him exactly what he wanted.

They got back to Sylvie's rooms, and Halima was about to close the French doors but turned around, eyes wide. 'You can see the sandstorm coming!'

'Really?' Curiosity distracted Sylvie momentarily and she went to the doors to look outside. She sucked in a breath when a powerful gust of wind made the curtains flap. She hadn't noticed how strong the winds had become.

'Look—see there? In the distance?'

Sylvie followed Halima's finger and saw what looked like a vast cloud against the darkening sky. It took her eyes several seconds to adjust to the fact that it was a bank of sand, racing across the desert towards them. It was like a special effect in a movie.

'My God...' she breathed, more in awe than in fear at the sight. 'Will we be okay?'

Halima shut the doors firmly and nodded. 'Of course. This castle has withstood much worse. We will be quite safe inside, and by morning it will be gone. You'll see.'

Sylvie shivered at the thought of all that energy racing across the desert—the fury she'd seen in the cloud-like shape. Not unlike the fury she'd seen in Arkim's eyes...

Halima left Sylvie to get ready, telling her she must make sure all the other doors and windows were closed.

Sylvie was grateful for that when she surveyed her outfit in the mirror a short time later. She might have winced if she hadn't still been so angry.

She'd customised one of her short skirts and now it barely grazed the tops of her thighs. The rest of her legs were covered in over-the-knee black socks. She wore a simple white shirt, knotted just under her bust, leaving her midriff bare. Underneath the skirt she wore a pair of black dance shorts, embellished with costume gems sewn into the edges, and under the shirt she wore a glittering black bra top.

She tied her hair back now, in a high ponytail. Her eyes were still heavily kohled, lashes long and dark. Lips bright red.

She felt like a total fraud, just aping what she'd seen in a million images and movies as to what constituted a lap dance outfit. It was ridiculously similar to something a famous pop-star had worn in one of her videos.

The fact was that the L'Amour revue prided itself on doing avant-garde strip routines, burlesque in nature. They didn't do anything as hokey as this. Sylvie's mouth firmed—Arkim clearly wasn't appreciative of the more subtle side of her profession.

Just then there was a knock at the door and Sylvie grabbed for her robe, slipping it on over her clothes. She didn't want Halima to see her like this. She felt tawdry.

The girl appeared. 'The Sheikh is ready for you, Miss Devereux.'

Sylvie tightened the belt of her robe and took a deep breath. 'Thank you.'

But as she walked to the ceremonial room again, behind the young girl, she felt the anger start to drain away. Doubts crept in. She was *not* what Arkim thought she was, and yet here she was—letting him goad her into pretending to be something she wasn't.

Because he'd never believe you, inserted a small voice.

She was at the door now, and her circling thoughts faded as Halima gently nudged her over the threshold.

The door closed behind her. The interior was darker than it had been, with the encroaching storm turning the world black outside. Too late to back out now. Girding her loins, Sylvie straightened her shoulders and walked in.

Arkim was sitting in his chair again, with a table beside him holding more wine and food. The anger surged back. He was so arrogant. Demanding. Judgemental. Cold.

She did her best to avoid his eyes, but she was burningly aware of him. He looked dark and unreadable when she sneaked a glance at his face. He seemed so in control. As if nothing would ruffle his cool.

Sylvie *badly* wanted to ruffle his cool.

She put on her music again, aware of the tension spiking in the room when the slow, sultry, sexy beat filled the space. She saw the chair that she'd asked Halima to provide in the centre of the dais, and she slowly unbelted her robe and then slid it off, throwing it to one side.

Did she hear an intake of breath coming from his direction?

She ignored it and walked up to the chair, turning to face Arkim with her hands on the back of it. And now she looked him straight in the eye. Unashamed. Exuding confidence even if she was quivering on the inside.

She started to move, using a mixture of what she'd seen some of the other girls do for their routines and her own modern dance moves. And a hefty dose of inspiration from one of her favourite movies of all time: *Cabaret*.

She kept eye contact with Arkim, even though her confidence threatened to dissolve when his gaze moved down, over her body, over her splayed legs as she sat in the chair. She dipped her head down between her legs before coming back up, deliberately making sure her cleavage would be visible, and running her hands up her bare thighs.

His gaze was so black it seemed to suck all the light out of the room—or was that the storm? Sylvie didn't know. She only knew that as his eyes tracked her movements she became more and more emboldened. She felt as if she was becoming one with the music. The throbbing bass beat was deep in her blood…telling her where to move next. Telling her to stand up, to put her hands on the seat of the chair and bend over, while sending a sideways look to Arkim. Telling her to straighten and then arch her back as she pulled her hair tie off so her hair tumbled down around her shoulders.

And telling her to open the buttons on her shirt, down to where it was tied under her breasts, so that they would be revealed.

Something dangerous was pounding through her blood—the same something that had coursed through it that night in the garden, when Arkim had pressed against her, letting her feel how aroused he was by her…even though he disapproved of her.

Sylvie felt powerful—because she could sense his control cracking. Arkim's cheeks were flushed, eyes glittering darkly. Jaw clenched. This was what she wanted…to make him admit he was a hypocrite.

Without really thinking about what she was doing, Sylvie stepped down from the dais and walked over to Arkim. His chin tipped up and their gazes clashed—just as the music faded away and stopped, bursting the bubble of illusion around them.

She knew instantly that she'd made a tactical error. Desperate to try and regain her sense of power, she started to walk away from his chair—but a big hand shot out and gripped her wrist, stopping her in her tracks.

She looked down at him, heart bumping violently. That obsidian gaze glittered up at her, and she saw the fire in their depths. The knowledge that she'd managed to ruffle him wasn't as satisfying as she'd expected when she was this close to him.

He stood up and they were almost touching. The air sizzled.

'What the *hell*,' he said in a low voice, 'do you think you're doing?'

The disgust Sylvie read in his eyes made her pull her wrist free of his grip with a jerk. She was aware that the huge sand cloud was approaching closer and closer through the massive windows behind Arkim, about to envelop them totally, blotting everything out. It made her feel reckless—as if everything was about to be altered for ever.

'Isn't this what you expected of me?' she asked tauntingly. 'I'm giving you exactly what you want.'

'*Exactly* what I want?' he asked.

And before she could say anything, just before the sandstorm inexorably claimed the castle in its path, Arkim speared both hands into her hair, angling her face up to his.

'I'll show you exactly what I want,' he said gutturally.

Arkim crushed Sylvie's mouth under his, his need too great to be gentle or finessed. He wanted to devour her.

Her lips were soft, but she kept her mouth closed and there was tension in her body. Damn her. She would *not* deny him. Not after that cheap little show. Yet even in spite of the tackiness he'd still been turned on. *Again.* And she was right—he'd asked for this.

That knowledge wasn't welcome.

Neither was her resistance.

Arkim was aware of the changing quality of sound around them. How everything was muffled. The sandstorm must have enveloped them by now. But all of that was secondary to the woman in his arms. The woman who would pay for turning his life upside down.

He took his mouth off hers and looked down to see those extraordinary eyes glaring at him. If he wasn't acutely aware of how her body quivered against his he would have let her go, been done with her. A reluctant lover was not something he was interested in—not that he had much experience of that.

But Sylvie wanted him. It had sparked between them from the moment their eyes had met—from the moment he'd rejected her outright. And in spite of that rejection they were here now, as if this course had always been inevitable.

There was no turning back until this was done and she'd paid. And he was sated.

He relaxed his hands in her hair, started to subtly massage her skull. It felt fragile under his hands.

'What are you doing?' she said huskily.

Her hands were against his chest, but she wasn't pushing him away. His arousal was so hard he ached with the need to sheathe himself inside her body, feel her contract around him. But her innate fragility did something to him…it tempered his anger, turned it into a need to seduce. To make her acquiescent.

'I'm making love to you.'

Her hands pushed against his chest now. 'Well, I don't want to be made love to.'

Arkim shook his head, his fingers all the while massaging her skull in slow, methodical movements. 'You've admitted you want me. And I think you *do* want to be made love to—very much. After all, you're a highly sexed woman…aren't you, Sylvie?'

Sylvie looked up into his eyes. Even in heels she felt tiny next to him. Puny. Weak. His fingers were in her hair, massaging her… She felt like purring. Not like pushing him away. But she had to. *Highly sexed?* If he found out what she really was—

She went cold at the thought and pushed him again, but his chest was like a steel wall. Immovable. At the same time she was aware that she wasn't scared; the fight to get away from him was as much a fight with herself as it was with him. More so. And he knew it—the bastard.

His hands were moving now...down to her jaw, cradling her face. Something dangerous lurched inside Sylvie—some emotion that had no place there. It seemed to be the hardest thing in the world to free herself completely and move away.

Arkim's scent was heady, masculine. It enticed her on a very basic female level. He didn't even say anything this time. He just bent his head and kissed her again, those sensual lips moving over hers with masterful precision and an expertise she couldn't resist even though she tried.

She tried to keep her mouth closed, like before. But Arkim was biting gently on her lower lip, making it tingle, making her want more... She felt some of her resistance give way, treacherously, and he took advantage like the expert he was—slipping his tongue between her lips, finding hers and setting her world on fire.

His hands moved over her shoulders, down her back, urging her into him, against the hard contours of his body. Her scanty costume offered little protection. She was helplessly responding to his kiss, to the tantalising slide of his tongue against hers, urging her to mimic him, initiate her own contact.

Sylvie couldn't think. Everything was blurry, fuzzy. Except for this decadent pleasure, seeping into her veins and making her feel languorous. Treacherously, she didn't want this moment to stop. *Ever.*

Her hands were moving, lifting of their own volition, sliding around Arkim's neck so that she could press closer. She was aware of her breasts, crushed to his chest, tightening into hard points. One of his hands was on her lower back and it dipped down further, cupping one buttock, squeezing gently. Between her legs she felt hot, moist...

But as Arkim's hand slipped even lower, precariously close to where Sylvie suddenly wanted to feel him explore her, she had a startling moment of clarity—this man hated her. He believed that she was little more than a common tart, debauched and irredeemable, and she was about to let him be more intimate with her than anyone else had ever been.

Disgusted with her lack of control, Sylvie took Arkim by surprise and pushed herself free of his embrace. For a second when he opened his eyes they looked glazed, unfocused, and then they cleared and narrowed on her. She felt hot and dishevelled. And exposed.

She put her arms around herself. 'I told you. I don't want this.'

Colour slashed Arkim's cheekbones. He was grim. 'You want this, all right—you're just determined to send me crazy for wanting it too.'

Something enigmatic lit his eyes, and for a split-second Sylvie had the uncanny impression that it was vulnerability.

That impression was well and truly quashed when he said coldly, 'I don't play games. Go to bed, Sylvie.'

He turned on his heel, and he was walking away when something rogue goaded her to call after him, 'You don't know a thing about me. You think you do, but you don't.'

Arkim stopped and turned around, his face etched in stern lines. It made Sylvie want to run her fingers over them, see them soften. She cursed herself.

'What don't I know?' he asked, with a faint sneer in his tone.

'Things like the fact that I'd never sleep with someone who hates me as much as you do.'

He walked back towards her slowly and Sylvie regretted saying anything. He stopped a few feet away.

'I thought I hated you…especially after what you did

to ruin the wedding…but actually I don't feel anything for you except physical desire.'

Sylvie was surprised how strong the dart of hurt was, but she covered it by saying flippantly, 'Oh, wow—thanks for the clarification. That makes it all *so* much better.'

To her surprise, Arkim just looked at her for a long moment, and then he reached for the robe that lay on the ground near their feet and handed it to her, saying curtly, 'Put it on.'

Now he wanted her to cover up… Why didn't that make her feel vindicated in some way?

She slipped her arms into the sleeves and belted the thick material tightly around her waist. Arkim was still looking at her intently, but it had a different quality to any expression she'd seen before. She felt exposed, and a little disorientated. For a moment when he'd handed her the robe she could have sworn he'd seemed almost…apologetic.

As much as she didn't want to hear his scathing response again, she was tired of playing a role that wasn't really her. 'There's something else you don't know.'

Arkim arched a brow.

She took a deep breath. 'I've never actually…stripped. The main act I do in the show is the one with the sword. I do other routines too, but I've never taken all my clothes off. What I did just now… I made it up… I was just proving a point.'

He frowned, shook his head as if trying to clear it. 'Why don't I believe that?'

Sylvie lifted her chin. 'Because you judged me before you even met me, and you have some seriously flawed ideas about what the revue actually is. Why would I lie? It's not as if I have anything to lose where you're concerned.'

She saw a familiar flash of fire come into Arkim's eyes and went on hurriedly.

'The man who runs the revue—Pierre—he knew my

mother. They were contemporaries. When I arrived in Paris I was seventeen years old. He took me under his wing. For the first two years I was only allowed to train with the other dancers. I wasn't allowed to perform. I cleaned and helped keep the books to pay my way.' Sylvie shrugged and looked away, embarrassed that she was telling Arkim so much. 'He's protective of me—like a father figure. I think that's why he doesn't allow me to do the more risqué acts.'

When she glanced back at Arkim his face was inscrutable. Sylvie realised then that he probably resented her telling him anything of the reality of her life.

When he spoke his voice was cool, with no hint of whether or not he believed her. 'Go to bed Sylvie, we're done here.'

She felt his dismissal like a slap in the face and realised with a sense of hollowness that perhaps she should have been honest from the beginning. Then they could have avoided all of this. Because clearly Arkim had no time for a woman who didn't match up to his worst opinions.

He turned to walk away again and she blurted out before she could stop herself, 'What do you mean, "we're done"?'

Arkim stopped and looked at her. He seemed to be weighing something up in his mind and then he said, 'We'll be leaving as soon as the storm has passed.'

Then he just turned and walked out, leaving Sylvie gaping. *'We'll be leaving...'* She'd done it. She'd provoked him into letting her go. She'd finally made him listen to her—made him listen as she tried to explain who she really was. And now he didn't want to know. Yet instead of relief or triumph all Sylvie felt was...deflated.

'I don't feel anything for you except physical desire.' Arkim's own words mocked him. He couldn't get the flash

of hurt he'd seen in Sylvie's eyes out of his head. And he tried. He couldn't deny that it made him feel…guilty. Constricted.

He'd lied. What he felt for her was much more complicated than mere physical desire. It was a tangled mess of emotions, underscored by the most urgent lust he'd ever felt.

He didn't ever say things to hurt women—he stayed well away from any such possibility by making sure that his liaisons were not remotely emotional. Yet he seemed to have no problem lashing out and tearing strips off Sylvie Devereux at every opportunity.

It should be bringing him some sense of pleasure, or satisfaction. But it wasn't. Because he had the skin-prickling feeling that there was something he was missing. Something in Sylvie's responses. He would have expected her to be more petulant. Whiny. More obviously spoilt.

She'd shown defiance, yes, and even though her dash into the desert had been foolhardy she'd shown resilience.

Arkim sat in his book-lined study with its dark, sophisticated furniture and classic original art. He'd always liked this room because it was so far removed from what he remembered of his childhood in LA: his father's vast modern glass mansion in the hills of Hollywood. Everything there was gaudy and ostentatious, the infinity swimming pool full of naked bodies and people high on drugs.

And now he felt like a total hypocrite. Because when Sylvie had stood in front of him in some parody of what strippers wore—because *he'd* all but goaded her into it— he'd been as hard and aching as he could ever remember being. The insidious truth that he really was not so far removed from his father whispered over his skin and made him down a gulp of whisky in a bid to burn it away.

He'd brought her here and asked for it—and she'd called his bluff spectacularly. She was turning him upside down and inside out with her bright blue and green gaze that seemed to sear right through him and tear him apart deep inside. Showing up everything he sought to hide.

The fact that she'd seemed intuitively to sense the maelstrom she inspired within him had galvanised him into kissing her into submission. And yet she'd been the one who had stood there proudly and told him she wouldn't sleep with someone who hated her.

He'd walked away from her just now because she'd shamed him. The irony mocked him.

Arkim couldn't deny it any more: Sylvie made no excuses for what she did and she had more self-worth than most of the people he encountered, who would look down their noses at her. As he had.

When she'd mentioned going to Paris at seventeen he'd felt a tug of empathy and curiosity that no other woman had ever evoked within him. He'd been seventeen when he'd last seen his father. When he'd told him he wasn't coming back to LA and when he'd decided that he would do whatever it took to make it on his own.

Arkim stood up and paced his study. It felt claustrophobic, with the shutters closed against the storm which raged outside—not unlike the turmoil he felt within.

The truth was that he wanted to know more about Sylvie—more about why she did what she did. About her in general. And he'd never felt that same compulsion to know about her sister.

He'd told Sylvie that they'd be leaving as soon as the storm was over—a reflexive reaction to the fact that she affected him in a way he hadn't anticipated. He'd thought it would be easy, that she'd be easy. The truth was that the storm might pass outside, but it would rage inside him until he quenched it.

If he left this place without having her she would haunt him for the rest of his life.

* * *

When Sylvie woke the next morning everything was dark and quiet. She got up and padded to the shutters over her windows, not sure what to expect. Maybe the castle would be completely buried in sand? But when she opened them she squinted as beautiful bright blue skies were revealed. What looked like just a thin layer of sand lay over the terrace—the only clue to the formidable weather of the previous evening.

Her mind skittered away from thinking of what else had happened. She wanted to cringe every time she thought of how she must have made such a complete fool of herself—prancing around in those stupid clothes. Even more cringeworthy was recalling how for a few moments she'd got really into it, and had seriously thought she might be turning Arkim on.

But he'd been disgusted. Yet not disgusted enough not to kiss her. And she'd responded—which said dire things about her own sense of self-worth.

Thank God she'd managed to pull back. To show some small measure of dignity. If she hadn't, she could well imagine that Arkim might have laid her down on that stone floor and had her there and then—and discovered for himself just how innocent she was. Sylvie balked at that prospect.

The sunlight streaming into the room reminded her of the fact that Arkim had said they'd be leaving. She sank back on the bed. She'd done it. She'd managed to resist him and disgust him so completely that he was prepared to take her home. In spite of the mutual physical lust that sparked between them like crackling fire whenever they got close.

She hated to admit it, but that sense of deflation hadn't lifted. Had she enjoyed sparring with Arkim so much? Had she wanted him to take her in spite of what he thought of her? In spite of her brave words last night?

Yes, said a small voice, deep inside. *Because he's connected with you on a level that no other man ever has.*

Sylvie felt disgusted with herself. Was she so wounded inside after her father's rejection of her that this was the only way she could feel desire? For a man who rejected her on every level but the physical?

Someone knocked on the door and she reached for her robe, pulling it on. Halima appeared, smiling, with breakfast on a tray. She set it up on a table near the French doors and opened them wide.

'The storm has passed! It will be good weather for your trip with the Sheikh.'

'My trip…?' Sylvie said quietly, assuming Halima meant her trip home.

The other girl chattered on. 'Yes, the oasis is so beautiful this time of year…and the way it emerges from the desert—it's like a lush paradise.'

Sylvie frowned, confused. 'Wait—the oasis? Arkim—I mean, the Sheikh isn't leaving to go home today?'

Now Halima looked confused. 'No, he is preparing for his trip and you are going with him. I am to pack enough things for a few days.'

Sylvie's heart-rate picked up pace, along with her pulse. What was Arkim up to now?

She rushed through her breakfast and got washed, and when she re-emerged into the suite Halima was waiting with her bag packed.

Sylvie had dressed in simple cargo pants and a T-shirt. Halima took one look and tutted, saying something about more suitable clothing. Sylvie followed the girl into the dressing room, which Sylvie hadn't explored fully yet, having been intent on using her own clothes. But now Halima was opening the wardrobe doors, and Sylvie gasped when she saw what looked like acres of beautiful fabric: dresses, trousers… All with designer labels.

'Whose are these?' she breathed, letting the silk of one particularly beautiful crimson dress move through her fingers. The thought of them belonging to another woman—or women—was stinging Sylvie in a place that was not welcome.

'They're yours, of course. The Sheikh had them delivered especially for you before your arrival.'

Shock made Sylvie speechless for a moment, and then she said carefully, 'Are you sure they aren't left over from the last woman he had here?'

Halima turned and looked at her, incomprehension clear on her pretty face. 'Another woman? But he's never brought anyone else here.'

Sylvie knew she wasn't lying—she was too sweet... innocent. Her heart started beating even harder. She'd assumed this exotic remote bolthole was one of Arkim's preferred places to decamp with a mistress. She would never have guessed she was the first woman he'd brought here.

'Here—you should change into this.'

Sylvie blinked and saw Halima holding out a long cream tunic with beautiful gold embroidery. Like a more elaborate version of the tunic Arkim had put on her when he'd found her in the desert. *'You're burning.'* His reprimand came back.

'Is this a cultural thing?' Sylvie asked Halima as she slipped out of her trousers.

'Well, yes. Where you're going *is* more rural, and conservative. But it's also practical. It protects you from the heat and sun.'

'Where you're going.' Sylvie was very aware that she had given no indication to the girl that she was *not* going on this trip. Was she going to just...*go*? Acquiesce? Her pulse tripped again at the thought, and a wave of heat seemed to infuse her skin from toe to head.

The tunic was matched with close-fitting trousers in a

beautiful soft cotton material. They too were embroidered with gold. And then Halima was placing a gossamer-light matching shawl around her shoulders. Soft flat shoes completed the outfit.

Sylvie caught sight of herself in a mirror and sucked in a breath. Her hair stood out vibrantly against the light colours of the clothes. She looked…not like herself—but perversely *more* like herself in a way she'd never seen before.

Halima tweaked Sylvie's shawl over her head, and then they were walking down the corridor. She felt a little like a bride being walked to face her fate.

Sylvie chastised herself for being so compliant. Of course she wanted to leave. Of course she had no intention of going off to this admittedly, intriguing-sounding oasis with a man who felt nothing for her and yet made her body come alive in a way that made her want to descend with him into a pit of fire.

She was going to tell Arkim she had no intention of—

All her thoughts faded to nothing when they rounded the corner into the main hall and Sylvie saw Arkim waiting for her.

CHAPTER SIX

HE SIMPLY TOOK her breath away. It was as if she'd never seen him before. He was so tall and exotic, in a long dark blue tunic. Still stern...

It made her yearn for things: to see him smile, unbend. To know more about him. Dangerous things.

The staff left their bags between two Jeeps and melted away into the shadows. Sylvie was aware that this was the moment when she should make it absolutely clear that she had no intention of going with Arkim to this oasis. But she was rooted to the spot—caught and mesmerised by those obsidian eyes.

There was an intense silent conversation happening between them. He was issuing a direct challenge with that fathomless gaze. A challenge that she felt in every pulsing, throbbing beat of her blood. A challenge of the most sensual kind. A challenge to step up and own her femininity in a way she'd never done before. A challenge to go with him.

She felt giddy...breathless. The palms of her hands were damp with perspiration that had nothing to do with the heat.

It came down to this: did she want this man enough to throw her self-respect to the winds and risk the bitter sting of self-recrimination for ever? Did she want to give him the satisfaction of knowing that he was right? That ultimately she couldn't resist him? And did she want to risk the worst kind of rejection?

He moved, and her breath hitched at the sheer grace and beauty of his masculinity. He stopped in front of her. She could see the tension in his form and on his face. It made something inside her soften, uncoil. Closer, like this, he was infinitely more seductive, less formidable. And infinitely harder to resist.

'There are two Jeeps behind me.'

Sylvie had seen them. She nodded.

'The one on the left will take you back to the airfield where we landed the other day—if you want it to. The one on the right is the one I'm taking to the oasis. I told you last night that we'd both be leaving, but I've decided to stay. I want you to stay with me, Sylvie. I think there are things about you that I don't know…that I want to know. And I want *you*. This isn't about the past or the wedding any more. I've made my point. This is about…*us*. And it's been about us since the moment we met.'

His mouth twisted.

'Perhaps our failing all along has been that we didn't pursue this attraction at the time. If we had we wouldn't be standing here now.'

Sylvie's chest contracted with a mixture of volatile emotions. 'Because you'd be married to my sister? That's heinous—'

His finger against her lips stopped her words. He looked disgusted. He took his finger away, but not before Sylvie had the strongest urge to take it into her mouth.

'No. I *never* would have pursued your sister with marriage in mind if we had had an affair.'

Affair. The word hit her hard. Arkim didn't need to clarify the fact that Sylvie would never in a million years be a contender for marriage or a relationship.

Right now she felt very certain that she would be getting into the Jeep on the left. But then his mouth softened into those dangerously sensual lines and he slid a hand around her neck, under her hair. Suddenly she couldn't think straight.

'If we don't do this…explore our mutual desire…it'll

eat us up inside like acid. If you're strong enough to walk away, to deny this, then go ahead. I won't come after you, Sylvie. You'll never see me again.'

She wanted to pour scorn on Arkim's words. The sheer *arrogance*! As if she *wanted* to see him again! She should be pulling away from him and saying *good riddance*. But there was a quality to his voice… Something almost… rough. Pleading. And the thought of never seeing him again made her want to reach out and grip the material of his tunic in her fist. Not walk away.

God. What did that mean? What did that make *her*?

Arkim took his hand away and stepped back. Sylvie almost reached out for him. She teetered on the cliff-edge of a very scary and precipitous drop into the unknown. His words seduced her: *There are things about you that I don't know…that I want to know.*

A fluttering started low in her belly. Nerves, excitement. The thought of going with him…getting to know him more…letting him be intimate with her…was terrifying. But the thought of leaving…going back to her life and not knowing him…was more terrifying.

Sylvie's gut had been guiding her for a long time now—taking her out of the toxic orbit of her stepmother and her father's black grief at the age of seventeen—and it was guiding her towards the Jeep on the right-hand side before she could stop herself.

Arkim displayed no discernible triumph or sanctimony. He just held the passenger door open for her to get in, closed it, and got in at the other side. Sylvie was aware of the staff re-materialising, to put their bags in the back of the Jeep, and once that was done Arkim was pulling away and out of the castle.

She tried to drum up a sense of shame for her easy capitulation but it eluded her. All she felt was a fizzing sense of illicit anticipation.

Endless rolling desert and blue skies surrounded them. It should have been a boring landscape but it wasn't. And the silence that enveloped them was surprisingly easy as Arkim navigated over a road that was little more than a dirt track.

Eventually, though, Sylvie had to say the words beating a tattoo in her brain. She looked at him, taking in his aristocratic profile. 'Halima told me you've never brought anyone else to the castle.'

His hands tightened on the steering wheel momentarily and his jaw twitched. 'No, I haven't taken anyone else there.'

She hated it that she cared, because it meant nothing, and the feeling of exposure after having mentioned it made her say frigidly, 'I should have guessed that you'd prefer to keep this...*situation* well out of the prying gaze of the media. The last thing you want is to be publicly associated with someone like *me*.'

Arkim glanced at Sylvie, and she was surprised to see his mouth tip up ever so slightly at one side. 'I think our association became pretty public when you broke apart the wedding and claimed that I'd spent the night in your bed.'

She flushed. She'd conveniently forgotten that. She never had been a good liar. Afraid he'd ask her again about her motive for doing such a thing, she said hurriedly, 'This oasis—it's yours?'

Arkim finally looked away again to the road—but not before Sylvie's skin had prickled hotly under his assessing gaze. 'Yes, it's part of the land I own. However, nomads and travellers use it, and I would never disallow them access as some others do. It's really their land.'

There was unmistakable pride in Arkim's tone, and it made Sylvie realise that, whatever their tangled relationship was, this man was not without integrity.

Genuinely curious, she asked, 'What's your connection to Al-Omar?'

Arkim's jaw tightened. 'This is where my mother is from—hence my name. The land belonged to a distant ancestor. She grew up in B'harani; her father was an advisor to the old Sultan, before Sadiq took over.'

'And do you see any of your family here?'

Before he'd even answered Sylvie might have guessed the truth from the way his face became stern again.

'They disowned my mother when she brought shame on the family name—in their eyes. They've never expressed any interest in meeting me.'

Sylvie felt a surge of emotion and said quietly, 'I'm sorry that she had to go through that. She must have felt lonely.'

How bigoted and cruel of them, to just leave her. But she didn't think Arkim would appreciate any further discussion on the subject, or hearing her saying she felt sorry for him.

She looked out of the window and took the opportunity to move things on to a less contentious footing. 'It is beautiful here…so different to anything I've ever seen before.'

There was a mocking tone to his voice. 'You don't miss the shops? Clubs? Busy city life?'

She immediately felt defensive. 'I love living in Paris, yes. But I actually hate shopping. And I work late almost every night, so on the nights I *do* have off the last thing I want to do is go out to a club.'

Arkim seemed to consider this for a moment. Then he settled back into his seat and angled his body towards her, one hand relaxed on the wheel and the other on his thigh.

'So tell me something else about yourself, then… How did you end up in Paris at seventeen?'

Sylvie cursed herself. She'd asked for it, hadn't she? By changing the subject. She looked at him and there was something different about him—something almost conciliatory. As if he was making an effort.

Because he wants you in his bed.

She ignored the mocking voice. 'I left home at seventeen because I was never the most academic student and I wanted to dance.'

She deliberately avoided going into any more detail.

'So why not dance in the UK? Why did you have to go to Paris? Surely your aspirations were a little higher?'

Arkim sounded genuinely mystified instead of condemning, and Sylvie felt a rush of emotion when she remembered those tumultuous days. Her hands clenched into fists in her lap without her realising what they were doing.

Suddenly one of his hands covered hers. He was frowning at her. 'What is it?'

Shocked at the gesture, she looked at him. The warmth of his hand made her speak without really thinking. 'I was just remembering… It was not…an easy time.'

Arkim took his hand away to put it on the wheel again, in order to navigate an uneven part of the road. When they were through it, he said, 'Go on.'

Sylvie faced forward, hands clasped tightly in her lap. She'd never spoken of this with anyone—not really. And to find that she was about to speak of it now, to this man, was a little mind-boggling.

Yet even *his* judgement could never amount to the self-recrimination she felt for behaving so reactively. Even though she couldn't really regret it. She'd learnt so much about herself in the process.

'As is pretty obvious, my stepmother and I don't get on. We never have since she married my father. And my father… Our relationship is strained. I rebelled quite a bit—against both of them. And Catherine, my stepmother, was making life…difficult for me.'

'How?' Arkim's voice was sharp.

'She wanted me to be sent to a finishing school in Switzerland—a way to get rid of me. So I left. I went to Paris to find some old contacts of my mother's. I'd always wanted to dance, and I'd taken lessons as a child… But after my mother died my father lost interest. And when Catherine came along she insisted that dance classes weren't appropriate. She had issues with keeping my mother's memory alive.'

That was putting it mildly. Her father had had issues too, and his had had more far-reaching consequences for Sylvie. Her stepmother was just a jealous, insecure woman. She'd never known Sylvie well enough for her rejection to really hurt. But her father *had* known her.

'So you took off to Paris on your own and started working at the revue?'

Sylvie nodded and settled back into her seat, the luxurious confines of the vehicle making it seductively easy to relax a little more. 'I had about one hundred pounds in my pocket when I met up with Pierre and found a home at the revue. I had to pay my way, of course. He let me take dance classes, but only if I cleaned in my spare time.'

'You took no money from your father?'

Sylvie glanced at Arkim's frown and slightly incredulous expression and wondered why she was surprised at his assumption that she would have. 'No, I haven't taken a penny from my father since I left home. I'm very proud of the money I make—it's not much, but it's mine and it's hard-earned.'

He schooled his expression. This information put everything he knew about Sylvie on its head and pricked his conscience. It was so completely opposite to everything he'd always assumed about her: that she was a trust fund kid, petulant and bored, seeking to disgrace her family just because she could. It sounded as if she'd sought refuge in Paris out of rebellion, yes, but also because she'd more or less been pushed away.

Very aware of that direct gaze on him, he said a little gruffly, 'You should rest for a bit—it'll take another hour or so to get there.'

Sylvie's eyes flashed at his clear dismissal of the subject, but gradually the tense lines of her body relaxed and she curled her legs up on the seat. Her head drifted to one side, long red hair trailing down over her shoulder.

Her lashes were long and dark against her cheeks. She wore no make-up, and Arkim noticed a smattering of small, almost undetectable freckles across the bridge of her nose. Had that been the sun? Because he didn't remember seeing them before. They gave her an air of innocence that compounded the naivety he'd seen in her dancing.

His chest felt tight. He looked back to the desert road, feeling slightly panicked. He shouldn't have indulged his base desire like this. He'd already behaved completely out of character by bringing her to Al-Omar in the first place—like some medieval overlord. He should have called the helicopter and got them both back to civilisation. He'd made his point—he'd demonstrated his anger.

But his hands gripped the steering wheel tight and he kept on driving. Because he wasn't ready to call it quits, to let her go. And she'd made a very clear choice to stay, and the triumph he'd felt in that moment still beat in his blood. Why would he turn back now, when they could exorcise this lust between them and get on with their lives?

'We're here.'

Sylvie opened her eyes and looked out of her window, straightening up in her seat as wonder and awe filled her. Maybe she was still dreaming? Because this was paradise. They were surrounded by lush greenery—greener than anything she'd ever seen before.

Arkim had got out of the Jeep and was opening her door. She got out on wobbly legs, eyes on stalks.

Two big tents were set up nearby—dark and lavishly decorated, with their tops coming to a point in the centre. Smaller tents sat off at a distance, separated from the others by trees. Sand dunes rose up around the camp, almost encircling it on one side, and on the other side was a rocky wall. When Sylvie shaded her eyes to look, she saw the most exquisite natural pool.

She walked over, stunned. The water was so clear she could see right down to the rocks at the bottom. The air was warm and soft—a million miles from the harsh heat she'd experienced since she'd arrived.

She felt Arkim's presence beside her but was afraid to look at him because her emotions were all over the place—especially so soon after waking up. It was as if she was missing a layer of skin.

'This is obviously a very special place,' she finally managed to get out, without sounding too husky.

'Yes, it is. I think it's the most peaceful spot on this earth.'

Sylvie looked at him at last and saw that he was staring down into the water. When he lifted his head and looked at her his gaze was so direct that it took her breath away. It was the most unguarded she'd ever seen him, and she could see so many things in his eyes. But the one that hit her right in the belly was desire.

She had a feeling that whatever lay tangled between them—all the animosity, misjudgement and distrust—it was slipping away and becoming irrelevant. What was relevant was here and now. Just the two of them—a man and a woman.

It was so primal that Sylvie was almost taking a step towards Arkim before she realised that someone was interrupting them, telling him something.

Arkim's gaze slipped from Sylvie's and she held herself rigid, aghast that she'd come so close to revealing herself like that. Was she really so ready to jump into his arms? Even though she'd already tacitly capitulated by coming here?

Sylvie composed herself as Arkim talked to the man, and then he was turning towards her. 'Lunch has been prepared for us.'

She welcomed the break in the heightened tension and followed him as he led her to an open area outside the tents, where a table had been set up under a fabric covering held up by four posts. It was rustic, but charming.

The table was low, covered in a deep red silk tablecloth, and there was no cutlery. Arkim indicated a big cushion on one side of the table for Sylvie and she sat down, mesmerised by the mouth-watering array of foods laid out on platters. The smell alone was enough to get her stomach growling.

Arkim settled himself opposite her and handed her a plate with an assortment of food which she surmised she was meant to eat with her hands. Silver finger bowls were set by their plates.

Sylvie experimented with something that looked like a rice ball, closing her eyes in appreciation as warm cheese melted into her mouth. When she opened them again she saw Arkim taking a sip of golden liquid and watching her. There was something very sensual about eating with her hands. And then she looked at Arkim's strong hands and imagined them tracing her body… Heat suffused her face.

'Try your drink—it's a special brew of the region. Not exactly wine, but a relation.'

Sylvie hurriedly took a sip, hoping it might cool her down. It was like nectar—sweet but with a tart finish. 'It's delicious.'

Arkim's mouth tipped up. 'It's also lethal, so just a few sips is enough.'

She frowned. 'I thought people didn't really drink in this part of the world?'

'They don't… But there are nomads from this region who have made a name for themselves with this brew. It's a secret recipe, handed down over hundreds of years and made from rare desert berries.'

Sylvie took another sip and relished the smooth glide of the cold liquid down her throat. She realised that she'd always known what sensuality was in an abstract and intellectual way, and that she could exude it when she wanted to, but she'd never really embodied it herself. She felt as if she embodied it now, though, when this man looked at her. Or touched her.

She put the glass down quickly, shocked at how easily this place was entrancing her. And at how easily Arkim was intriguing her by making her believe that things had somehow shifted. They had…but in essence nothing much had changed. She was who she was, and *he* was who he was.

When this man set his mind to seduction it was nigh impossible to resist him, and Sylvie had a sense that she was far more vulnerable to him than she even realised herself. She knew it was irrational, because she'd already agreed to come here, but she felt she had to push him back.

She heard herself saying, 'Why go to the trouble of bringing me here when we both know this isn't about romance? You say you don't hate me, but what you do feel for me isn't far off that.'

Arkim looked at Sylvie from where he lounged across the table. Her hair glowed so bright it almost hurt to look at. Her skin was like alabaster—like a pearl against the backdrop of this ochre-hued place.

He replied with an honesty he hadn't intended. 'You've

turned my life upside down. You irritate me and frustrate me…and I want you more than I've ever wanted another woman. What I feel for you is…ambiguous.'

Sylvie looked at him, and this time there was no mistaking the hurt flashing in her eyes. Before Arkim could react she stood up and paced away for a moment, and then she swung round, hair slipping over one shoulder, tunic billowing around her feet.

She crossed her arms. 'This was a mistake. I should never have come here with you.'

Arkim cursed his mouth and surged to his feet. Yet again Sylvie was exposing all his most base qualities. He couldn't believe how uncouth he was around this woman. He moved towards her and she took a step back. He controlled his impulse to grab her.

'You're here because you want to be, Sylvie—plain and simple. This isn't about what's happened. This is about us—here and now. Nothing else. I won't dress it up in fancy language. There is a physical honesty between us which I believe has more integrity than any fluctuating and fickle emotions.'

He saw how she paled, but how her pulse stayed hectic. Arkim felt as if he held the most delicate of brightly coloured humming-birds in his palm and it was about to fly away, never to be seen again.

He wanted her full acquiescence—for her to admit she wanted him. It unnerved him how much he wanted that when he hadn't given much consideration to her feelings before now.

Another truth forced its way out. 'You were right last night. I don't know you, but I want to. Sit down…finish eating. Please.'

Arkim was tense, waiting. But eventually Sylvie moved jerkily and sat down again. None of her usual grace was evident. She avoided his eyes as he took his seat again and they ate some more, awareness and tension crackling between them like a live wire.

After a minute she wiped her mouth with a napkin and took another sip of her drink. Then she looked at Arkim, her blue-green gaze disturbingly intense.

'So…what was it like growing up in LA?'

Relief that she was engaging stripped away Arkim's guardedness. His inner reaction to her question was a list of words. *Brash. Artificial. Excessive.* But he said, 'I hated it. So much so that I've never been back.'

Sylvie assimilated that, and then said, 'I've been to Las Vegas and I hated it there. It's so fake—like a film set.'

A spurt of kinship surprised Arkim. 'LA is massive—sprawling. Lots of different areas separated by miles of freeway…no real connection. Everyone is looking for a place in the spotlight—striving to be skinnier, more tanned, more perfect than the next person. There's no soul.'

'They say no one walks in LA.'

Arkim smiled and it felt odd—because he wasn't used to smiling so spontaneously in the presence of anyone, much less a woman.

'That's true. Unless you go somewhere like Santa Monica, and then it's like a catwalk.'

'You really haven't seen your father since you left?'

He shook his head. 'Not since I was seventeen.' Then he grimaced. 'That's not entirely accurate. I would have left voluntarily, but I was still too young. He threw me out.'

'Why?'

Arkim steeled himself. 'Because he caught me having sex with his mistress—a famous porn actress.'

He saw myriad expressions cross Sylvie's face: shock, hurt, and then anger.

She put her napkin down, eyes flaming, jaw tight. 'You absolute hypocrite! You have the gall to subject me to your judge and jury act and all the time—'

'Wait.' Arkim's voice rang out harshly.

He hadn't even been aware of the impulse to lean across the table and capture Sylvie's wrist in his hand before he realised that was what he was doing. Panic made his gut clench. For the first time in his life he found that his words were tripping out before he could stop them—along with an urge to make her understand.

Because if Sylvie damned him then there truly was no hope for his redemption at all...

'I didn't seduce her. She seduced me.'

Sylvie looked at Arkim, her wrist still caught in his firm grip. There was something almost desperate in his eyes. Her anger, which had flared so quickly, started to fizzle out. 'What do you mean?'

He let her wrist go and stood up, moving away from the table to pace, running a hand through his hair. Sylvie had never seen him like this. On the edge of his control.

He turned to face her, his face etched in stark lines. 'I was back from England for the summer holidays. My father had refused to let me stay in Europe for the summer, even though I'd offered to pay my own way by working. I'd done my A levels. I was just biding my time until I had to go to college. My father knew I hated LA, so he taunted me with it.'

His mouth twisted. 'Cindy was everywhere I was. Especially when my father wasn't around. And invariably she was half-naked.'

Self-disgust was evident in his voice.

'I thought I could resist her... I tried for the whole summer. I was only a few days from returning to the UK and she found me by the pool. I was too weak. The worst thing was that she stayed in control the whole time while I lost it. My father found us in the pool house.'

He didn't have to elaborate on what had happened next

for Sylvie to join the dots. She shouldn't be feeling anything other than what he'd dished out to her—judgement and condemnation... But she couldn't help it. Sympathy surged in her breast. She could well imagine that whatever judgement she might hurl at Arkim, he'd already judged himself a thousand times over—and far more harshly than anyone else could have.

'You were seventeen, Arkim. There's probably not a straight teenage hormonal boy on the planet who could have resisted the seduction of an older and more experienced woman—much less a porn star whose job is controlling sex.'

Arkim's harsh lines didn't relax. 'She only did it because she wanted to make my father jealous...to push him into some kind of commitment. She gambled the wrong way, though. He threw her out too.'

He turned away from her then, to look out at the view. His back was broad, formidable. As if he didn't want her to look at him.

'Do you know I saw my first orgy when I was eight?'

Sylvie put a hand to her mouth, glad he wasn't looking at her reaction. She took her hand down after a moment. 'Arkim...that's—'

He turned around again. He was harsh. 'That was my life. Someone saw me watching, and of course I couldn't really understand what was happening. It was after that that my father sent me to school in England. He got off on the idea of sending me to school with English royalty. But it saved me, I think. I only had to survive the holidays, and I learned to avert my eyes from the debauched parties he liked to throw.'

The thought of such a small child witnessing such things and then being sent away... Sylvie stood up. 'That was abuse, Arkim. And what that woman did to you— seducing you like that—it was a form of abuse too.'

Arkim smiled, but it was infinitely cynical and Sylvie suddenly loathed it.

'*Was* it abuse? When it was the most exciting moment of my life at that point? She showed me how much pleasure a man can feel. I submitted to her. Even though I hated myself for it.'

For a second Sylvie felt a blinding flash of jealousy so acute she nearly gasped. The thought of this man being helpless, submitting to a woman who had given him pleasure... and who was not *her*...was painful.

Thankfully he didn't seem to notice her seismic reaction and he said, 'Do you know what it's like to grow up under the influence of someone with no moral compass?'

Sylvie shook her head, clawing back control.

He was grim. 'It's like you're tainted by his deeds—no matter what you do to try and distance yourself. It's a tattoo on your skin—for ever. And I failed the test. I proved I was no better than my father—a man who debased a sweet, innocent woman from a foreign country and all but dumped her by the road when she needed him most.'

His words sank heavily into the silence, and just like that Sylvie saw Arkim's intense personal struggle. Saw why he'd always reacted so strongly to her. She understood now how very attractive a respectable marriage would be—it would offer him everything he'd never had. It all made sense. And her heart ached.

The approach of another staff member broke the bubble surrounding them. The man said something to Arkim that Sylvie couldn't understand. She was reeling with all this new information, feeling such a mix of things that she hardly knew how to assimilate it all.

The man left and Arkim turned to her, his face expressionless again, as if he *hadn't* just punched a hole in her chest with his revelations.

'There are some nomads who want to meet with me. You should rest for a while—it's the hottest part of the day.'

Sylvie felt his dismissal like a glancing blow, but before she could say a word Arkim was striding away. A middle-aged woman dressed all in black appeared by her side. She had a smiling face and kind eyes. She said something Sylvie couldn't understand and gestured for Sylvie to follow her. With no other choice, she did, and was led to the smaller of the two big tents.

The woman slipped off her shoes before she went in so Sylvie copied her, not wanting to cause any offence.

It took her eyes a moment to adjust to the darker interior, and when they had her jaw dropped. It was refreshingly cooler inside, and the entire floor area was covered in oriental rugs, each in a more lavish design than the last. Her toes curled at the sensation of the expensive material under her feet...it was like silk.

The tent was simply the most decadent thing Sylvie had ever seen. Dark and full of lustrous materials. Huge soft cushions around a low coffee table; a dressing screen with intricate Chinese drawings. Beautiful lamps threw out soft lights...drawing the eye to the most focal point of the tent: the bed.

It was on a raised platform in the centre of the room. It was a four-poster, with heavy drapes pulled back at each corner. More cushions in lush jewel colours were strewn artfully across the pillows, and the sheets—Sylvie reached out to touch them—they were made of satin and silk. The bed was a byword in shameless opulence.

Sylvie caught the older woman's eye. She was looking at her with a very knowing glint. There was obviously only one reason for Sylvie to be here with the Sheikh.

She blushed furiously, squirming on the spot, and suffered through being shown the bathroom—another eye-poppingly sensual space, complete with a huge copper claw-footed bath—and tried not to die of embarrassment.

When the woman had left, Sylvie paced back and forth, expecting to see Arkim darken the tent's doorway at any moment. She felt panic at the thought of seeing him again. When he didn't appear she sank down into a chair near the bottom of the bed and glared balefully at the entrance of the tent for a few minutes. She realised that Arkim had really meant her to have a nap. He wasn't coming.

A sense of disappointment cut through all the other emotions, mocking her. The last thing she felt like doing was napping—she was so keyed up, her mind racing. But when she got up and sat down on the edge of the sumptuous bed it seemed to draw her into the centre, cushioning her like a cloud.

The last thing she remembered before sleep claimed her was vowing to herself that she would absolutely *not* think again about what he'd just told her—because that way lay all sorts of danger, and feelings that made her far too susceptible to the man.

CHAPTER SEVEN

SYLVIE WOKE SOME time later with a jolt. She'd been having a horrible dream about hundreds of naked faceless people with bare limbs entwined—so much so that she couldn't tell where one person ended and another began. She was tiny in the dream, and trying to find a way out, but gradually getting more and more suffocated…

She scowled and stretched out her stiff limbs. So much for not thinking about what Arkim had told her. She shook off the disturbing tendrils of the dream and looked around, taking in the fact that someone must have come into the tent and lit some more lights. *Arkim?* The thought made her heart beat faster.

She went into the bathing area and, feeling sticky, took off her clothes and dropped them to the floor. She stepped under the shower, which was in a large private cubicle near the bath and open to the elements. Twilight was just starting to turn the sky dusky, and Sylvie couldn't help but be affected by the magic of the place as the deliciously warm water sluiced down over her head and body.

Eventually she switched off the shower, dragged a towel around herself and twisted up her damp hair. She found a robe hanging on the back of the dressing screen. It was a beautiful emerald-green colour, silk—light as a feather. Slipping it on, she relished its coolness against her skin.

And then she went to the door of the tent and looked out. Twilight was descending around the camp in earnest now, bathing it in a gorgeous lilac light. She didn't see anyone moving, but could hear low voices in the distance and smell something cooking. No sign of Arkim. She didn't like the hollow feeling that brought with it. Only a couple of hours ago she'd been ready to leave, and then he'd told her...so much.

She thought of the pool she'd seen when they'd arrived and slipped her shoes on to explore. The air was sultry and warm, even though the intensity of the day had diminished. When she came close to the beautifully peaceful pool she pushed aside foliage and then she stopped dead in her tracks, her heart in her mouth, because it was occupied.

By a butt-naked Arkim.

He stood in the shallows, and all she could see were the firm globes of a very muscular bottom as he bent and threw water over his head. Water ran in rivulets down his back. And then he stood straight and tensed. He'd sensed her. Sylvie stopped breathing. She knew she should turn and run. Do something. But she couldn't move.

And then he turned around.

His hair was slicked back, and he was...*magnificent*. Sylvie had seen plenty of naked male bodies—working at the revue and helping people change between numbers meant personal modesty quickly became a thing of the past. But she'd never seen a man like this. He looked as if he'd been carved out of rock. His chest was broad and leanly muscled. His chest hair was dark and dusted over his pectorals before dissecting his chest and abs to lead down to slim hips and...

Sylvie's heart was beating so fast she wasn't sure how she was still standing. Arkim's penis twitched under her gaze, the shaft getting harder as she watched, rising from the thicket of dark hair between his powerfully muscled thighs.

Somehow she dragged her gaze up and his dark eyes were on her, molten... The very air seemed to contract around them.

When she'd first seen him he'd been dressed in that

three-piece suit, all buttoned up. Here, now, he was stripped bare. Without the armour that told the world he was different, respectable. To Sylvie there was something very poignant about finding Arkim like this, naked.

He stepped out of the pool and gracefully bent down to pick up a piece of material and wrap it around his waist. Sylvie was barely aware. Her entire body and mind was focused solely on this man, on this moment. It throbbed with potential.

She realised with a stunning flash of clarity that she wanted to give herself to him—this man who had never had a moment of purity in his life. Who'd seen things at a young age that had darkened his view of the world for ever.

It was the one thing she had—her innocence. And with every fibre of her being she wanted to gift it to *him*. As if she could assuage the raw edges she'd seen earlier.

Arkim walked up to her and Sylvie's eyes stayed on his, unblinking. She was drawing confidence from his obvious arousal and his intentness on her.

He looked almost ferocious, every line of his body and face unyielding. 'What do you want, Sylvie?'

It wasn't just a question. It was almost a demand.

Sylvie spoke what was in her heart and soul. And in her body. 'I want *you*, Arkim.'

He came closer and lifted a hand, undoing the pin holding up her damp hair, letting it fall loose around her shoulders. He put his hands on her arms and pulled her closer. Closer to that bare wet chest. Until they were touching. Until the points of her breasts hurt with the need to press against him more fully. His erection pushed against her lower belly and excitement flooded her, making her ready.

'Arkim…' she said, not even sure what she was asking for. Why wasn't he taking her right now? Making the most of his conquering?

'You're sure you want this?'

Sylvie hadn't been expecting this consideration. Another dangerously tender emotion ran through her. She didn't hesitate. She moved closer, feeling the delicious press of her breasts against him.

'Yes.'

Just one word. Simple, but devastating.

In a rush of emotion she said, 'I want to give you—' But she stopped, not sure how to articulate exactly what she *did* want to give him. So she just said a little lamely, 'I want to give you myself.'

Arkim's hands were so tight on her arms it almost hurt, but then they relaxed marginally and he bent down for a moment. She felt herself being lifted into his arms, against his chest, and he walked back the way she'd come.

One of her arms was tight around his neck and she ducked her head into his chest, eyes shut tight. Her other hand was on her robe, holding it together. She didn't want to catch the knowing eyes of that woman, or anyone else. She felt too raw and needy.

And also dangerously cossetted, held in his arms like this.

She pushed down all the tangled emotional implications of how she was feeling and focused on the urgent hunger racing through her blood.

When everything felt cooler and darker Sylvie knew that they'd entered an interior space and opened her eyes again. It had to be Arkim's tent—similar to hers, but bigger, more masculine, with bolder colours. And the bed in the centre of the tent was...huge.

Arkim carried her over and put her down on her feet by the side of it. She avoided looking at it by looking at him.

He cupped her face with his hand. 'I've wanted you from the moment I saw you. I saw it as a weakness, as something to be denied...but not any more.'

Sylvie felt vulnerable. She believed him, and his words had all sorts of implications she couldn't think about right now.

Acting on impulse, she raised herself on tiptoe and put her arms around his neck. 'Stop talking…you're ruining the moment.'

Arkim smiled, and it was devilish. It made something soar inside her.

He tugged the belt on Sylvie's robe and it fell open. She unwrapped her arms from his neck and stood before him, heart palpitating wildly as Arkim pushed the robe apart, revealing her naked body to his dark gaze.

He looked at her for a long moment, until Sylvie could start to feel herself trembling lightly. She was someone who knew her own body intimately, as any dancer would, but right now it felt foreign, and she was insecure.

'You're shaking.'

She looked at him and tried a smile. 'You're quite intimidating.'

Arkim's answer to that was to take off the material around his waist before he pushed her robe off her shoulders so that it fell down her arms and to the floor.

'Now we're equal.'

Those words impacted deep inside her. All along she'd fought a battle with this man not to let him make her feel inferior, less than him. The moment was heady.

Arkim turned then, taking her with him as he moved closer to the bed. Sylvie was unbalanced and fell against him, but he caught her easily and drew her down with him, so they landed on the soft surface in a sprawl of limbs.

She was lying on top of his hard body, every inch of her flesh coming into contact with his. She felt dizzy. And then Arkim's hands were smoothing down her bare back and cupping her buttocks, pulling her thighs apart so that they lay either side of his hips.

His mouth reached up to hers and Sylvie felt her hair fall over her shoulders, screening them as she fell into the kiss...wet and rough and intoxicating.

After more long, languorous kisses Arkim moved, so that Sylvie was now the one on her back, and he loomed over her, huge and awe-inspiring in the gloom of the tent. One of his thighs was between her legs and he moved it against her, making her body twitch and ache. The friction caused a delicious tension to coil inside her and she bit her lip.

Arkim's gaze roved over her body hungrily. 'You are more beautiful than I could ever have imagined.'

Sylvie shook her head, feeling breathless because of what was happening between her legs. 'No...*you're* beautiful.'

But he didn't seem to be listening. He was transfixed by her breasts, cupping one now, so that the hard point pouted upwards wantonly. He lowered his head and blew gently on it, making her tingle and ache for more, and then his mouth was on her, and that wicked tongue, flicking and sucking on the turgid flesh.

Her hands were in his hair, fingers funnelling deep, holding him to her. Her back was arched and she was fast losing any sense of reason. Or maybe she'd lost it when she'd laid eyes on this man for the first time. Anyway, it was gone.

He lavished attention on both breasts until they ached and felt swollen, and then his mouth was moving down... over her belly and lower. Sylvie only realised her hands were still on his head when he reached up to take them away. Taking both her hands in one of his, he held them captive over her belly.

Now she really was at his mercy. He moved lower, the bulk of his body forcing her legs apart.

Sylvie lifted her head and looked down. 'Arkim...' Her voice sounded rough, broken. Taut with need.

He looked up at her and said, 'Shh...'

Sylvie's head was too heavy. She let it fall back just as he released her hands, and then both of his hands were on her buttocks, lifting her to his mouth, where his tongue explored the damp folds of her sex, laying her so open she couldn't bear it.

She had to bite down on a fist when she felt his tongue surge deep inside her, and then his teeth were nipping... The tension was coiling so tightly now she thought she might have to scream to release the pressure, and he was relentless.

Sylvie was vaguely aware of bucking towards him mindlessly—and then he reached up and squeezed her breast, and she exploded into a million tiny pieces of pleasure so intense that she couldn't breathe or see.

She'd orgasmed before—you couldn't work in her industry and remain completely unaware of taking pleasure—but it had always been by her own hand, and never this...*mind-blowing*. She'd actually thought it was overrated. Evidently she'd been doing it all wrong, she thought dreamily as her body floated back to earth slowly, lusciously.

She was aware of him moving aside momentarily, with an intense focus in his movements, and then he was back, coming over her and leaning on both arms, the muscles bunched and taut.

Sylvie felt him lodge himself between her legs, and then the potent thrust of his erection against the sensitised folds of her sex. For a moment she thought it might be too soon, that she couldn't possibly— But then he hitched himself against her, the head of his erection sliding tantalisingly between those folds, and her whole body quivered with anticipation.

Instinctively she put her hands on Arkim's arms, as if to hold on for the ride, and her legs opened wider in tacit acceptance.

Sylvie's eyes were huge, staring up at him as if he knew all the secrets of the universe. Arkim didn't know how he hadn't already spilled onto the sheets, like the virginal teenager he'd been all those years ago, when he'd felt her body convulse in spasms of pleasure. But somehow he hadn't...and now he was on the very edge of his control as he felt her body accept his.

He started to sink into her tight, silken hot sheath.

Her *very* hot and *very* tight sheath.

In fact as Arkim's body sought to go deeper he realised that Sylvie's body was tight against him in a way he'd never encountered before...

His brain was overheating, his body screaming for a release of the tension, and those huge limpid eyes were still staring up at him. The hard tips of her breasts scraping against his chest.

Arkim was about to lose it...the heady scent of musk and sex urged him on. He gritted his jaw and thrust hard—and went nowhere.

He heard Sylvie's swift, sharp intake of breath and looked down. His brain was feeling too hot, too fuzzy to try and figure out what was wrong. But something *was* wrong. Very wrong.

Moments ago Sylvie had been flushed with pleasure. Now she looked pale and clammy. Shocked. She was biting her lip and her eyes shone with...*tears*?

Arkim's insides seemed to drop from a height. But even as suspicion crept in he fought the knowledge... She was just small—that was it. A lot smaller than he'd realised she was.

He clenched his buttocks, trying to forge a passage, and

Sylvie's hands gripped his like steel clamps, her nails digging into his muscles.

'Stop—please! It *hurts*.'

And the truth resounded in Arkim's head like a klaxon going off. *Virgin. Innocent.*

It was too much to take in. But he had to. *She was a virgin.*

Arkim pulled back from Sylvie's resisting body, her wince of obvious pain making him feel as if someone had just punched him in the gut. Somehow he got off the bed, stood up... His legs were shaky. He stared at Sylvie but didn't really see her, and then he acted on autopilot, going to the bathing area to take care of the protection.

He caught the expression on his face in the mirror and stopped. He looked dark, feral. He looked...*like his father.* With that insatiable glint in his eye. Narcissistic and intent only on his own self-satisfaction. Uncaring if someone might be innocent, pure. Like his mother. *Like Sylvie.*

He was no better than his father. This proved it more than any teenage humiliation with a porn actress. Something cold settled down over Arkim's heart. Something hard and familiar.

He went back out to the main area of the tent and saw Sylvie sitting on the side of the bed, the sheet wrapped around her body. She looked at him over her shoulder and the dark hardness inside Arkim nearly split apart because she looked so forlorn.

He reached for his trousers and pulled them on, irrational anger growing deep down inside him and crawling upwards to catch him in its hot grip.

'Why didn't you tell me?' He walked around to stand in front of her.

She looked shell-shocked. Arkim drove the emotion down.

'Why?' It burst out of him like the firing of a rifle.

Sylvie flinched, her hands clutching the sheet to her chest. 'I wasn't sure you'd notice. I almost told you...but I didn't know how.'

Arkim felt as if all of his ugliness was exposed. He sneered. 'How about, *Hey, Arkim, I'm a virgin, by the way... be gentle with me.*'

Sylvie stood up then, and Arkim could see how she trembled. The exposed skin of her shoulder and upper chest was very white. Delicate. Fragile. And he'd been like a rutting bull in a china shop.

He wanted to smash something.

'I didn't think you'd notice and I didn't think it was important.'

'Well, I *did* notice and it *is* important.' Arkim stalked away and then back, folding his arms across his chest. 'You're twenty-eight and you work in a strip club—how the hell are you still a virgin?'

Sylvie hitched her chin. 'It's *not* a strip club. And I just...was never interested before now.'

She started to look around for her things and Arkim caught her by the arm. The anger inside him was a turbulent mass. Everything in him wanted to lash out, to blame someone—blame *her*. If she'd told him...

What? asked a snide voice. *Would you have let her go?* Never.

'Why, Sylvie? And it's not just because you weren't interested. You're a sexual being—it oozes from you. I had no idea. If I had—'

She wrenched her arm free, fire flashing in her eyes now, any hint of vulnerability gone. 'You'd have what? Declined the offer?'

She spied her robe on the ground and grabbed it, letting the sheet fall as she tugged it on—but not before Arkim saw that luscious body and his own reacted forcibly.

Then she stopped and glared at him. 'You want to know

the psychological motivation behind my still being a virgin? Really?'

Suddenly he didn't. But she went on.

'My father rejected me as a child. My mother had died—his beloved wife—and I resembled her so much that he couldn't bear to look at me. So he sent me away. He's never been able to look at me since then without pain or grief. The truth is he would have switched me for her any day of the week.'

Arkim's chest ached. 'How can you know that?'

'Because I overheard him talking to someone. I heard him say how he couldn't bear the sight of me—that I was a constant reminder that she was gone and that if he could he'd have her back instead of me.'

Arkim reached out, but she slapped his hand away.

'And as for why I decided to let you be my first lover…? Well, maybe I felt bizarrely secure in the fact that you'd already rejected me on pretty much every level that counts. When you've protected yourself against rejection your whole life, it's almost a relief not to have to fear it any more.'

She stepped back, the robe pulled so tightly around her that every curve was lovingly delineated, and then she left.

Sylvie was so angry and humiliated she could have cried. But her anger kept the tears at bay. What on earth had possessed her to spill her soul to Arkim like that? As if he cared about the sob story of her relationship with her father. Or about her deepest inner fears of being rejected. She'd never even spoken to Sophie of any of this, not wanting to burden her sister with a negative view of their father.

Sylvie paced back and forth, her emotions vying between humiliation and anger, very aware of the dull throb and stinging between her legs. She stopped in her tracks when she thought of the excruciating pain of Arkim trying to penetrate her—his shock when he'd realised why he couldn't.

She sat down gingerly on the side of her own bed. She'd never expected it to be that bad. Up till that moment it had been the most incandescently pleasurable experience of her life. And she'd truly thought that he wouldn't know—that it would always be her own secret.

The tender feelings that had led Sylvie to want to soothe him in some way mocked her now. All the while she'd been thinking she was giving Arkim the supreme gift of her innocence he'd been ready to reject it outright. Evidently her lack of experience was a huge turn-off.

What she'd told Arkim wasn't entirely true—his outright rejection of her hadn't really prepared her for this. Or for how much it would hurt. Far more than the physical pain.

She reminded herself that she'd knowingly risked this when she'd chosen to come here. She had no one to blame but herself. It wasn't a comfort.

Arkim was undoubtedly done with her and his little plan of retribution. He would let her go and she would never see him again.

Feeling raw and weary, Sylvie stood and picked up her bag, started to fill it with the clothes that must have been unpacked when she'd been sleeping. She couldn't see Arkim doing such a menial task, so it hadn't been him in her tent.

Now she felt doubly foolish.

Packing her things with more force than necessary, Sylvie didn't hear anything until a deep and infinitely familiar voice spoke from behind her.

'What are you doing?'

Sylvie's entire body hummed in response. She cursed her reaction and didn't turn around. 'I'm leaving—what does it look like?'

'Why?'

There was some note in Arkim's voice that made her insides flutter dangerously but she ignored it. She steeled herself and dropped the clothes from her hands and turned around. In the dim flickering lights of the tent Arkim looked huge. He'd put a tunic on over his trousers.

'Your reaction just now was hardly indicative of wanting us to spend more time together.'

She thought Arkim winced, but couldn't be sure it wasn't a trick of the light and her imagination.

Then he said, 'I could have handled that better. Did I hurt you?' His voice had turned gruff.

The fluttering in her belly intensified, but Sylvie pushed it down ruthlessly. 'I'm okay.'

And she was. As soon as he'd pulled out the pain had faded and all that was left was some tenderness.

Then she said tartly, 'You obviously weren't prepared for me to be a virgin because all along you've assumed I'm some kind of a sl—'

'Do *not* even say that word.' Arkim stepped forward, the lines in his face harsh.

The hurt was back and more painful. Why was he doing this? Bothering? Sylvie crossed her arms, wishing she'd had the foresight to change out of the robe, which felt very flimsy now.

'Look, you don't have to do this…apologise, or whatever it is you're doing. I get it. Me being a virgin was not a welcome surprise, and I understand that you have no desire to be the one to initiate me.'

Arkim came closer and shook his head, a look of incredulity coming over his face. It was only now that she noticed the growth of stubble on his jaw, remembered how it had felt against her softer skin…*between her thighs*.

'That's not it at all. I didn't handle my reaction well

and I'm sorry for that. I had no right to take out my anger on you. It was just a shock when I expected—' Arkim stopped and ran a hand through his hair and stepped back. He cursed and walked to the door of the tent.

For a heart-stopping second Sylvie thought he was leaving, and her brave façade was just about to crumble when he stopped and put his hand up over the top of the doorway.

He spoke into the inky darkness outside. 'My mother was a virgin. My father seduced her and took her virginity from her. She didn't even enjoy the experience. He was rough...'

Arkim turned around and Sylvie felt her heart beating too fast. She sank down onto the bed. 'How can you know this?'

He was grim. 'She kept a diary. It was in a box of her personal items that my father somehow miraculously kept. I read it when I was a teenager.' His voice was rough. 'When it became obvious you were...innocent I realised that I was doing to another woman exactly what he'd done to her.'

Sylvie shook her head and stood up again, compelled to go over to Arkim with a fierceness she'd never felt before. 'You didn't know... I could have explained, but I didn't.' She bit her lip. 'This is going to sound really stupid, but when you told me about what had happened to you... I wanted you to be the one...'

Arkim reared back slightly. 'You wanted to sleep with me because you felt sorry for me?'

'No.' She stopped, and then admitted sheepishly, 'Maybe, in a way...'

Arkim looked ready to bolt, but Sylvie put a hand on his arm. He stopped, his face etched with injured pride.

'Not like that.' Her mouth twitched slightly. 'Believe

me, you don't inspire *pity* in people, Arkim—anything
but. I wanted to sleep with you because you truly are the
first person who has connected with me on that level…
From the moment I saw you, I wanted you. Even when
you looked at me with disdain it made me want to make
you notice me.'

'I noticed you…' His tone was wry.

Sylvie's cheeks grew hot as she remembered that first
time they'd met. The erroneous impression she'd made.

She let his arm go and shrugged lightly, avoided his
eye. 'I thought that I could somehow gift you something…
pure. The purest thing I have to give. To show you that
not everything is tainted.' She looked at him again. 'You
are nothing like your father. And I am nothing like your
mother. This is *not* the same. You are considerate…you
stopped when you knew I was in pain. It sounds like your
father wasn't even aware of that.'

Something in the air between them changed…sizzled.
The tension shifted to one full of awareness. Wanting.

Arkim lifted a hand and cupped Sylvie's jaw. 'What do
you say we start again?'

Her breath hitched. Start again…? As in from the beginning or just from tonight? But she was too afraid to ask
it out loud, to break this fragile spell. She'd bared herself
completely to him and he was still here. Still wanted her.

'Yes…' she breathed.

Arkim moved closer and Sylvie's skin tingled all over.
Her breasts, still sensitive, peaked to hard points.

'And, for the record, I don't reject you… I absolutely
accept you.' His voice became fervent. 'You are *mine*, Sylvie. No one else's on this earth.' Something dark crossed
his face. 'If I was a better man I'd let you go, but I'm too
selfish to let anyone else have you.'

And then he kissed her, before she could say a word,
and there was nowhere left to run or hide.

The fire swept up around them faster than before, and then he was carrying Sylvie over to the bed, putting her down and sweeping her clothes and bag away with one hand.

He took off his clothes and her hungry gaze roved over him, as if it was her first time seeing him. His erection strained from his body, thick and long. She felt a glimmer of fear, remembering the pain.

But as if reading her mind Arkim came down over her and said, 'I'll make it good…don't worry. It won't hurt again.'

She looked at him and felt her heart turn over. The thought of this man not taking the opportunity to hurt her…she'd never expected it. She couldn't speak. So she just nodded.

He carefully opened her robe and peeled it off her, laying her bare. And then he came alongside her on the bed and proceeded to do everything he'd done before, and more, until Sylvie was writhing, begging… Her sex was hot and damp, aching to feel him again, pain be damned.

'Touch me first,' he said hoarsely, poised above her, his powerful body between her legs.

Sylvie was nearly incoherent, her vision blurry. She looked down to see Arkim's sheathed erection and put a hand down to encircle him. She lamented the protection— she wanted to feel him skin to skin—but even like this… it was awe-inspiring. *He* was awe-inspiring.

She squeezed him gently, moved her hand up and down experimentally, and then she looked at him and saw the huge strain on his face. He was holding back, going slowly for her. Letting her get used to him.

Tenderness welled inside her. She took her hand from him and then placed both her hands on his hips, drawing her legs up in an instinctive feminine move as old as time.

'Now, Arkim—I need you now.'

She saw him struggle, and then give in. His body fused with hers and inch by inch he slowly sank into her. To the point of resistance.

'Sweetheart, relax...let me in.'

The endearment made something melt inside Sylvie and she could feel all the muscles that were clamping so hard against him relax.

Arkim slid a little deeper. She felt so full...almost uncomfortable. But also...*amazing*. Arkim kept going until Sylvie could barely breathe and his hips touched hers. She felt impaled...but *whole*. It was such a new and alien sensation. And then he started to pull out, beginning a dance of movement between their bodies that Sylvie had never known existed. Just when she thought he was withdrawing from her completely he'd thrust back in, and each time it felt a little more imperative that he did so.

Her legs were wrapped around his waist and her hands were on his buttocks now, silently commanding his movements to be stronger, more forceful.

Arkim huffed out laboured-sounding words. 'Should have known you'd be a fast learner...'

Sylvie smiled up at him—but then her smile got stuck as Arkim touched something deep inside her that sent shockwaves and thrills through her. His movements became faster, wilder, as if he couldn't control them any more, and the delicious tension Sylvie had felt before coiled tight within her again, and tighter. Until she begged for release.

Arkim put a hand between them and pressed his thumb against her, and Sylvie couldn't hold back her cry as she broke into shards of light and sensation. Her whole body convulsed with pleasure around Arkim's, her skin damp and slick.

Powerful shudders shook Arkim's body as he finally

took his own release, and through the cataclysm Sylvie
could feel the contractions of her body around his. In that
moment she'd never felt so complete.

CHAPTER EIGHT

SYLVIE FLOATED ON her back, naked in the warm water, and looked up into an endless violet-hued sky. Early evening was practically the only time Arkim would let her out, for fear of the sun damaging her skin, even though she faithfully slathered on factor fifty.

The silky water lapped between her legs. Soothing the tenderness. She couldn't keep back a small smile… The last week had been the most illuminating, mind-blowing week of her life. It had been an intense tutorial in the sensual arts, with a master teacher.

She'd never known… She'd heard people talk about it, but had never really understood just what they'd been going on about. And that deep-rooted fear of rejection had made her shy away from any intimacy.

Not here, though. Every night and most of the day Arkim laid Sylvie bare, over and over again, until she was reduced to a mass of sensation and lusting and craving—no longer a human being. He'd turned her into some kind of animal.

That thought made something tighten inside her and Sylvie flipped over, lazily swimming to the far end of the pool. She wasn't worried about being seen—the staff knew not to come to the pool at this time, and used it only during the day.

She sat on a natural stone ledge in the water, the tops of her breasts exposed, and blushed when she imagined Arkim taking her here—pressing between her legs, urging her to wrap them around his waist as he thrust so deep inside her she'd have to bite down on his skin to contain her cries of ecstasy.

She wasn't entirely sure someone hadn't slipped a drug into her drink or food, and that this wasn't all some kind of crazy hallucination. But the air was warm on her wet skin, and the water was real enough. As was the smell of cooking. And the sounds of people in the distance, laughing and talking softly.

Sylvie hadn't seen much of the nomads—they kept themselves to themselves. And anyway…how could she notice anyone else when Arkim filled her vision larger than a twenty-foot statue?

Physically Sylvie had never been more replete or happy. Emotionally, however… Her insides tightened again.

Since she and Arkim had started sleeping together there had been no more intensely personal confessionals. She had no idea what he thought of her now, beyond the very physical evidence that he wanted her. And she wanted him. *Oh, God.* She wanted him more and more each day. As if the more she had of him the tighter would be the bonds holding them together.

For her.

Sylvie knew one thing: even though he'd said he accepted her, this was a moment out of time for Arkim. He didn't have to say it. Whatever he'd once thought of her— and whatever he thought of her now—was irrelevant. This was just a slaking of lust for him. And when they left here he would turn his back and walk away. Because a man like Arkim Al-Sahid, with all his dark secrets and troubled past, would never choose a woman like Sylvie.

Even if she *had* been a virgin, and that had changed his perception of her, she was still unpalatable in his real world. Sylvie had to remember that, and not get caught up in this interim magic and madness.

In spite of everything that had brought them here he'd given her an incredible gift. The gift of her own sensuality and sexuality. Which was ironic, considering she'd been successfully projecting it for years. He'd taken the broken pieces inside her and forged a new wholeness. And that was what she would take with her when this was over...

She heard a movement and looked up to see Arkim standing at the edge of the pool, with only a towel around his waist. Hair slicked back. He'd obviously just showered. Instantly Sylvie could feel the effect of his presence on her body—blood flowing to erogenous zones, flesh swelling, tingling, becoming engorged.

With his hands on his hips and a scowl on his face he looked truly intimidating. He was looking for her, and Sylvie's breath quickened as his gaze came closer and closer... *Zing!* Eye contact. Heat. Pulsing awareness.

The scowl faded and was replaced by a look of carnal intent. With one hand Arkim undid the towel and twitched it to the ground. He stepped into the pool—gloriously, unashamedly naked.

Like a little wanton, Sylvie had her legs open and ready for him when he came close enough to touch her. He registered her acquiescence with a feral smile that curled her insides.

The head of his erection notched against her sex, slipping between slick folds. His hands cupped and moulded her breasts, teasing the hard points, before he lowered his head so that he could tease first one, then the other, with his hot mouth and tongue and teeth.

Then his mouth was on hers, swallowing her cry as he seated himself with one smooth thrust, deep inside her. Everything quickened. She was so primed she couldn't hold back a series of shattering orgasms, and she felt Arkim's struggle as he fought to hang on... But it was too much. He pulled free of her clasping body at the last moment and the hot spurt of his seed landed on her belly and breasts. His face was drawn back into a silent scream of ecstasy.

The lash of his essence on her skin felt like a brand,

and intensely erotic. But as suddenly as she felt that, Sylvie felt cold, in spite of the heat and languor in her bones. Because she ached with wanting to feel his seed lodged deep inside her, where it might create life, connecting her to this man for ever.

'Are you planning on dropping off the radar for good?'

Arkim scowled into the satellite phone and answered his executive assistant. 'Of course not.'

'Good, because the deal with Lewis is still on—just about. But you need to be here to deal with it.'

After a few more minutes of discussion Arkim ended the call. He was on a horse, on a sand dune, looking down over the oasis.

He could see Sylvie's bright red hair as she played with a group of the nomad children, chasing them. He could hear their squeals of delight from here. Her skin had taken on a golden glow and more delicate freckles, in spite of the high-factor sun cream he insisted she wear every day.

He felt himself smiling, and a sense of deep contentment was flowing over him and through him. Along with that piquant edge of desire never far from the surface whether Sylvie was in sight or not.

His smile faded when he thought of that first night again. He'd been convinced he'd have to take them both back to civilisation after she'd walked out on him— justifiably—with all the hauteur of a queen. What she'd told him about the legacy of her father had eaten away at his guts like acid: *'When you've protected yourself against rejection your whole life it's almost a relief not to have to fear it any more.'* But ultimately he hadn't been strong enough to walk away. Or to send her away. So he'd been selfish. And taken her for himself.

And even though she'd told him so fiercely, *'You're not your father...'* he was afraid that he was. That he still had some deep flaw inside him. Yet somehow, right now, looking down at that bright head, the assertion didn't sting as much as it usually did.

He'd always ensured his lovers never strayed beyond the firm boundaries he laid down. He always went to their places, or met them in hotels. He never brought them to his personal space. Never encouraged them to talk of personal matters.

And he never spirited them away to a desert oasis to lose himself in their bodies before he went crazy...

'Are you planning on dropping off the radar for good?'

It suddenly struck him: *what the hell was he doing?* His smile faded completely and he went cold inside. His reputation still hung in the balance, and it was thanks to that woman's actions. He'd meted out his vengeance. He'd had her under him, begging for release. *But not for forgiveness*. At what point had Arkim forgotten that?

Around the first time Sylvie opened her legs to you...

It started hitting him like a series of blows about the head and face. Just how much he'd let her in. Just how much he'd told her. And all because since the moment she'd arrived she'd been nothing like he'd expected. The biggest revelation of all having been her innocence. Her physical innocence.

He had to force himself to acknowledge now that that was as far as her innocence went. She still hadn't told him her reasons for disrupting the wedding that day.

Something trickled down his neck and spine. A sense of having been monumentally naive. Moments ago— before Arkim had had that phone conversation—he'd been contemplating what might happen after Al-Omar. He'd contemplated keeping Sylvie on as his lover. Because he didn't see an end in sight to this ravenous desire. The more he had of her, the more he wanted.

From his vantage point now he could see the children scattering as someone called them, the cry lifted on the wind.

Sylvie stood and looked up to where he was, shaded her eyes. Arkim felt her pull even from here as the breeze moulded the long tunic she wore to her body, showing off the curves of her high, full breasts.

He imagined a scenario of returning to civilisation and allowing Sylvie to slip under his skin even more indelibly. She was the last woman he needed in his life right now—right when everything hung in the balance *because of her*.

With a sharp kick of his heel on his horse's flank he made his way back to the oasis. He knew what he had to do.

'Look! It's a puppy with eyes like mine!'

Sylvie was sitting cross-legged outside Arkim's tent, more happy than she cared to admit to see him returning from his satellite phone call, even if he did look very grim. She held up a squirming bundle of white fur with a tail, yapping intermittently.

Arkim crouched down and Sylvie held it so he could see the puppy's brown and blue eyes. There was something about Arkim's grimness that made her say nervously, 'Sadim, one of the younger boys, showed him to me. They were excited because of the similarity…the eye discolouration.'

He straightened up again. 'You shouldn't be handling it—dogs around here are feral.'

Sylvie's sense of something being wrong increased. Arkim's tone was harsh in a way she hadn't heard in days.

She stood up too, cradling the dog against her chest, feeling at a disadvantage. 'He's not feral…he's gorgeous.'

The small boy Sylvie had spoken of hovered nearby. With a brusque movement Arkim gestured him over. He took the puppy out of Sylvie's arms, his hands brushing against her breasts perfunctorily, and handed it back to the boy, saying something that made the boy look at him as if he'd just kicked the puppy before he ran off.

Sylvie stared at him. 'What did you do that for?'

Arkim was definitely harsh now. 'Because we don't have time for this. It's time to leave... I have to return to London.'

'Oh, is everything okay?' Sylvie struggled to assimilate Arkim's change in mood and this news.

'I've arranged for the helicopter to come for you in a couple of hours. Halima will ensure your bags from the castle are on board.'

'For me?' Sylvie repeated faintly, aware that Arkim hadn't really answered her question.

His face was expressionless, and it made Sylvie think of the passionate intensity he'd shown in bed only a few hours before. It suddenly felt like a long time ago. Not hours.

'Yes, for you,' Arkim reiterated. 'The helicopter will take you to the international airport in B'harani, where one of my staff will meet you and see you on to a plane back to France. I'm taking the Jeep back to the castle as I've some business to attend to there before I return to Europe.'

When she said nothing, feeling cold inside, and as if she'd been hit with a bat, Arkim asked almost accusingly, 'Did you think we could stay here for ever?'

Yes, came a rogue voice. And Sylvie felt like such a fool. She'd been weaving daydreams and fantasies out of something that didn't exist. This oasis and what had happened here was as much of a mirage as the kind a dying man in the desert might see through the heat waves in the distance. For ever unreachable.

She forced herself to look Arkim in the eye. 'No, of course not.'

His voice was stark, stripped of anything remotely soft.

'This can't ever be anything more than what's happened here. You *do* know that, don't you?'

Sylvie felt her old cynical walls—badly battered and crumbled—start to resurrect themselves. What Arkim really meant was, *You didn't really think I'd ever want to be associated with you outside of this remote outpost, did you?*

She couldn't believe she'd let herself fall so hard and so fast for someone who would only ever hold her in mediocre esteem. Who had only seduced her as a form of retribution. And she'd been fully complicit.

'Of course I know that, Arkim.' She tried to inject as much nonchalance into her voice as possible.

She felt brittle. If someone so much as brushed past her now she might shatter. She stepped back—out of the pull Arkim exerted on her with such effortless ease.

'I should pack my things. I don't want there to be any delay when the helicopter gets here.'

'Mariah will bring you some lunch.'

Sylvie forced a smile. 'That's considerate—thank you.'

She turned and walked away before he could see the rise of tumultuous emotions within her. Anger and hurt and self-recrimination. She should have left when she had the chance. She should have protected herself better. She should have known that he would just drop her from a height when he was done with her... She just hadn't expected it to be so soon, so cold, and so brutal.

A month later, London...

Arkim stood at his office window, gazing out on a scene of unremitting grey skies and rain. An English summer in all its glory.

He realised, somewhat moodily, that he seemed to be spending an inordinate amount of time looking out of his window across the iconic cityscape, with an inability to focus.

Since he'd come back to London he'd been braced for the fallout from his very public humiliation. But, to his shock and surprise, when he'd requested a debriefing from his PR team he'd been informed that there *was* no discernible fallout. Yes, he'd lost some business initially, and the tabloid reports in the immediate aftermath had been bruising. Stocks had fallen sharply, but it had been very temporary. And ultimately not damaging.

Arkim was not a little stunned to realise that in the wake of his ruined wedding, the world hadn't stopped turning. The reputation he'd spent so long building up hadn't crumbled to pieces, as he'd feared. Many more scandals had come and gone. He was already old news. People couldn't care less if he'd really slept with Sylvie Devereux.

The deal with Grant Lewis had been signed off on, and the old man appeared to feel no rancour towards Arkim, despite what had happened. Lewis had been in straits far more dire than he'd led anyone to believe, and his eagerness to keep the deal on the table only reminded Arkim of how eroded his well-worn cynicism had become. Lust for power and wealth trumped even scandal.

A hum of ever-present frustration pulsed in his blood. Despite his best efforts to resist the urge, he'd had his team checking the papers and media daily for any news of Sylvie, but to all intents and purposes she'd vanished back into her life.

An image of her face, wide open and smiling, her skin lightly golden from the sun and dusted with freckles, came back to him so vividly that he sucked in a breath.

An ache had settled deep into his being from the moment he'd watched her helicopter take off from the oasis that day and it hadn't subsided. The truth could no longer be ignored or denied. *He still wanted her.*

In the last month he'd been to functions with the most beautiful women in the world, and they'd left him cold. Dead inside. But all he had to do was conjure up a memory of Sylvie—*that day in the pool*—and he was rewarded with a surge of arousal. About which he could do nothing unless he wanted to regress to being the age of fourteen in a shower stall.

The intercom sounded from his desk and Arkim welcomed the distraction, turning around. 'Yes, Liz?'

'There's a young lady downstairs to see you...'

Even before Arkim could ask her name, blood was rushing to his head and heat to his groin.

'Who did you say?' He had to ask, after his assistant had said the name. Surely he'd misheard—?

'Sophie Lewis...your...er...ex-fiancée.'

Disappointment was acute. So acute that Arkim knew he had a problem. And what on earth could Sophie Lewis possibly want with the man who had—allegedly—been unfaithful to her with her own sister?

'Send her up,' he said grimly.

Sylvie had finished rehearsals with Pierre and the rest of the revue for the day and had stayed behind at the dance studios to practise on her own for her modern dance class.

She focused on the music and the athletic movements of her body, clad in dance leggings and a cropped tank top. Her hair was up in a high ponytail and her skin was sheened with perspiration from the exertion. But the burn of her muscles and the intense focus was good. Anything to block *him* and the fact that she would never see him again out of her mind. Block out the fact that he wanted nothing to do with her. That what had happened meant nothing to him...

Sylvie made an awkward move and landed heavily on her foot. Damn. *Damn him for invading her thoughts.*

She bent down over her foot, but thankfully she hadn't strained it. They were close to the opening night for the relaunch of the club—Pierre would never forgive her if she injured herself now…especially when she wasn't even practising the revue's routines.

She stood up straight in front of the long mirror that spanned one whole wall and stretched her neck. She was about to start at the beginning again when she saw something move, and she looked towards where the door was reflected in the mirror to see a big dark shape.

Arkim.

This was really getting to be too much. Now she was seeing things. She blinked. But he didn't go away.

The door was pushed open and he walked in. Dressed in dark trousers and a light shirt, sleeves rolled up, top button open. As if he'd just strolled in from a nearby office.

Slowly, eyes widening, Sylvie turned around, half expecting him not to be there when she faced him. But he was. He was real.

To her utter horror she felt a welling of emotion: a mixture of anger, relief and the sheer need to run to him and wrap herself so tightly around him he wouldn't be able to breathe.

She took a deep, steadying breath, and curled her hands into fists. Had she already forgotten the brutality with which he'd let her go that day at the oasis? Coldly. Summarily.

Praying her voice wouldn't betray her, and lamenting her less than pristine physical state, she said coolly, 'Hello, Arkim.'

'Hello, Sylvie.'

That voice. *His* voice. It reached inside her and squeezed tight. She remembered him saying *Sylvie* with a guttural groan as his climax had made his whole body go taut over hers.

'I can't imagine that you were just passing.'

Arkim put his hands in his pockets and walked into the room, his every step gracefully athletic. Masculine. He was clean-shaven. And he'd had a haircut.

He was still quite simply the most astoundingly handsome man she'd ever seen.

He stopped a couple of feet away. Close enough for his scent to tickle her nostrils and for her body to go into meltdown at his proximity. Her heart seemed to have been in shock, because it started again at about triple its normal rate.

'No, I wasn't just passing. I came especially. To see you.'

She dampened down the surge of excitement. Her hurt at the way he'd sent her off was still acute. She lifted her chin. 'Why? Did I leave something behind?'

Arkim's face was impassive, but she saw a muscle work in his jaw. His throat moved. Sylvie could have spent hours just studying every minute part of his olive-skinned anatomy. *She had.*

'You could say that. *Me.*'

Her eyes clashed with the darkest brown. Incredulity made her mouth gape before she found the wherewithal to say, 'I left *you* behind?'

'Yes…' he breathed, and moved even closer.

His eyes were roving hungrily over her now, making a hot flush spread out all over Sylvie's body from between her legs. This man had changed her utterly, in so many ways. So much so that the minute Pierre had seen her again the older patriarchal man had looked her up and down and said accusingly, 'Something's different…what's happened to you?'

Sylvie had been mortified beyond belief to think that someone might be able to *see* what had happened to her. But she could feel it even when she danced. A new awareness of her body…her sexuality.

She crossed her arms over her chest and glared at
Arkim, the architect of all of this. His eyes met hers again
and she saw the fire in them. But before she could say
anything—not even sure what she *wanted* to say—he
asked, 'What was that dancing you were just doing? It
was different to the way you danced for me.'

Taken aback, Sylvie said, 'It's something I'm working
on for my contemporary dance class.'

'I liked it…it was beautiful.'

And just like that Sylvie's jagged emotions stopped
pricking her. 'You did?'

Arkim reached out and touched a loose tendril of hair.
He nodded. 'You looked as if you were lost in another
world.'

She was finding it hard to breathe. 'I choreographed
the dance.'

It was only when she said it that she felt totally exposed.
A lot of that dance had been born out of the pain she'd felt
for the past month.

She stepped back and his hand fell away. His eyes
flashed. Still the same arrogant Arkim. And what had he
meant when he'd said she'd left him behind?

'What do you want, Arkim? I haven't finished practising, and I only have this space for another twenty minutes.'

'I want to talk to you. And I have something for you
at my apartment.'

'Your apartment?'

'I have an apartment here in Paris. I'm working here
for the next few weeks—in my Paris office.'

Of *course* he had an office and an apartment here. He
would.

But still, she resisted. 'Why, Arkim? Why do we have
to talk? I think we said everything, don't you? Or you certainly did, anyway.'

He looked for a moment, as if he didn't want to say

anything, but then he did. 'Your sister came to see me...
I *know*, Sylvie.'

Sylvie could feel her blood draining south so quickly
that she swayed. Immediately Arkim's hand was on her
arm. To her awful shame, her first thought was not of Sophie but of the fact that Arkim hadn't come because he
wanted her back at all...

'Sophie...came to see you?' Sylvie was vaguely aware
that her phone had been off all day during rehearsals, so
she'd been uncontactable.

He nodded. Grim. 'Look, finish your practice. I'll wait,
and then you'll come with me...yes?'

There was no way Sylvie could focus now. She'd break
her ankle. And that was just at the thought of Arkim waiting for her. She shook her head. 'No, I'll change now and
come with you.'

She had no choice. She had to know what Sophie's visit
to him meant. And that was *all* Arkim wanted to talk to
her about. As long as she remembered that she'd be okay.

He let her go. 'I'll wait for you downstairs. My car is
at the door.'

As Arkim waited in the back of his chauffeur-driven car he
couldn't dampen down the swell of triumph...or the swell
of his erection. His whole body had gone on fire as soon
as he'd seen Sylvie through the door...her lithe dancer's
body moving with such grace and power...in a way he'd
never seen before. Beautiful, elegant...passionate. He'd
been mesmerised. In awe. In lust.

She'd looked wary at seeing him again, even though
he'd felt the resurgence of the powerful sexual connection
between them. Yet could he blame her for being wary?
He'd behaved like an idiot that last day at the oasis... He'd
been acting on a knee-jerk reflex to get rid of Sylvie be-

fore she slid herself even more indelibly under his skin...
but it had been too late.

He had to concede that even if Sophie hadn't come—

His thoughts stopped working as Sylvie walked out
through the door, her vibrant hair tied back in a knot—
damp from a shower? She wore faded skinny jeans that
showed her long legs off to perfection, ballet flats and a
loose off-the-shoulder T-shirt, with the straps of a vest
visible underneath. Her skin was pale again...like a pearl.

Arkim let his driver get out to open the door for her.
He literally couldn't move for fear of making a complete
idiot of himself.

When she slid into the back seat on the other side she
didn't look at him, putting her slouchy bag firmly on her
lap as she strapped her seat belt on. Arkim wanted to
reach across and force her to meet his eyes, force her to
know how much he wanted her before he crushed that soft
mouth under his and found some sense of peace for the
first time in a month.

A flutter of panic at the strength of how much he
wanted her made his gut tighten. How relieved he'd been
as soon as he'd laid eyes on her...

Sylvie Devereux was still completely wrong for him on
so many levels. This was lust. Pure and simple. Unprecedented, but not without its sell-by date.

Then she looked at him with those wide eyes, blue and
blue-green, and Arkim's thoughts scattered to pieces.

'Why did Sophie come to see you?'

Arkim dragged his brain back into some kind of functioning order. 'She told me everything.'

CHAPTER NINE

THE CAR WAS moving at a snail's pace in the early-evening Paris traffic as Arkim's words sank in. And even though Sylvie was preoccupied by what he was saying, and what it meant, she was acutely aware of that big, powerful body so close to hers. Legs spread, chest broad.

She had to get it together. *Sophie.* Hesitantly she asked, 'When you say "everything", do you mean—?'

'I mean,' Arkim said, cutting her off, 'I know that she's gay, Sylvie. She told me everything. About how she was afraid to come out. About how she was railroaded into marriage by her parents because they thought it would sweeten the deal for me. I'd made no attempt to hide the fact that I wanted to settle in England, and I wasn't averse to settling down with a suitable wife.'

The kind of wife who would remove Arkim permanently from his sordid past... Sylvie thought to herself, with a lurch of pain near her heart.

He continued, 'She told me about her girlfriend in college, and how she was too terrified to stand up to her mother...that she's always had trouble standing up to her.' Arkim's mouth twisted. 'I can understand why.'

Sylvie reeled. 'My God...she really *did* tell you everything.'

Arkim nodded. 'She also told me that she'd refused to let you do anything at first, because she didn't want you to damage your already contentious relationship with your father and stepmother, and they'd inevitably blame you even though it had nothing to do with you... But the week of the wedding she was panicking so much that she accepted your offer to step in at the last minute if she needed it. Which is what you did…in your own inimitable way.'

Sylvie blushed, thinking of that daring moment again. Arkim looked equable enough right now, but she knew how deep his emotions went, and how he simmered.

Trepidation gripped her. 'Were you angry with her?'

For a second he just looked at her, and then he said with faint incredulity, 'Even now your first concern is whether or not I got angry with her?'

Sylvie squirmed. 'Well, I know how intimidating you can be.'

Arkim's mouth thinned. 'At first I was angry, yes.' He reacted to the look that crossed Sylvie's face. 'I had a right to be. Both of you made me a laughing stock. If Sophie had just come to me and explained I would have understood. I'm not such an ogre. *Hell*.'

He turned away in disgust, to look out of the window. Sylvie felt immediately chastened. She knew that he wouldn't have taken it out on Sophie…all of Arkim's anger was only ever for *her*.

She pushed down the sense of futility. 'You're right,' she said in a quiet voice. 'I should have come to you myself and said something… If we'd been able to stop the wedding a week before it would have avoided the messy scandal it became. But I knew how unlikely it was that you'd believe anything I said…'

Some of the tension seemed to leave his shoulders. He turned back, those black eyes like pools of obsidian. To Sylvie's surprise, his mouth quirked ever so slightly on one side.

'I guess I have to give you that… I would have seen it as just another jealous attempt to make me notice you.' His expression became shuttered. 'I believed you were *jealous*…you let me believe that, like a fool.'

She knew she owed him total honesty now—especially

after Sophie's bravery—albeit belated. She forced herself to look at him. 'The truth is…as much as I was doing it for Sophie I *was* jealous. I wanted you…for myself.'

She hadn't even properly admitted that to herself until this moment. Her head felt light.

Arkim's eyes gleamed. He breathed out. 'I *knew* it…'

For a second she thought he was about to reach for her, and her whole body tingled, but then a discreet tap came from nearby. It took a minute for her to figure out that the driver was knocking on the partition, alerting them to the fact that they'd pulled up outside a building on a quiet street.

Sylvie felt a little dizzy. She looked out of the window and didn't immediately recognise much, except for the fact that they were in a very expensive part of Paris. Her voice was husky. 'Where are we?'

'My apartment building on the Île Saint-Louis.'

She looked back to Arkim. She felt confused, she wasn't sure where they stood any more.

He said, 'I have something for you upstairs.'

She joked weakly, 'That's not a very original chat-up line.'

He was serious. 'It's not a chat-up line. I really *do* have something for you.'

'Oh.' She instantly felt silly. The driver—as if knowing just the perfect moment to capitalise on her doubts—appeared at her door and opened it. By the time she was standing, clutching her bag, Arkim was waiting for her, darkly handsome and very vital-looking against the grey stone of the old building.

How was it that he could look so devastating, no matter what milieu he was in? she grumbled to herself as she let him lead her into the building. She felt very dishevelled when she saw the marble floor and discreetly exquisite furnishings. And the uniformed concierge who treated Arkim like royalty.

There was a lift attendant, and Sylvie almost felt like giggling. It was so far removed from the constantly out of use elevator in her rickety building in Montmartre.

The lift came to a smooth stop and Arkim led her into a luxuriously carpeted hall, with one door at the end. He opened it and she walked in cautiously, her eyes widening as she took in the parquet floors and quietly sumptuous decor.

The reception rooms were spacious, with floor-to-ceiling French doors looking out over Paris and the Seine. The furniture was antique, but not fussy. Comfortable, inviting.

Drawn by something she'd spotted, she walked over to the opposite side of the room and stood before a black and white photo.

'It's Al-Hibiz.'

Arkim's voice was close enough to set Sylvie's nerve endings alight. 'Yes,' she said, remembering her first view of the majestic castle. A terrible sense of longing for that wide open landscape washed over her. *The oasis.*

This was torture, being so close to Arkim again and yet not really knowing what he wanted from her. She whirled around and he was a lot closer than she'd expected, within touching distance.

'Arkim?' Her voice croaked humiliatingly.

He was staring at her mouth. 'Yes…'

So she looked at his…at the strong sensual lines. And his jaw, so resolute. From the moment she'd first seen him she'd had that instinct to smooth the stark lines of his face.

She didn't know who moved first, but it was as if attracting ions finally overcame the tension between them, and then she was in his arms, her whole body straining against his, her arms tight around his neck. Their mouths were fused, tongues tangled in a desperate hungry kiss, the breath being sucked out of each other's bodies to mix and mingle and go on fire. Arkim's hands shaped and cupped Sylvie's buttocks, lifting her up, encouraging her legs to wrap around him.

She wasn't even aware that Arkim had collapsed onto a couch behind them until she pulled back from the kiss to gasp in air and realised that her thighs were wedged open, tight against his, and she could feel the potent thrust of his arousal against where she ached.

She felt shaky. The fire had blasted up around them so quickly. 'Arkim...what are we—?'

He put a finger to her lips. He looked fierce. 'Don't say anything—please. I need this. I need *you*. Now.'

There was something raw in his tone...something that resonated deep inside her. Who was she kidding? She needed this too. Desperately.

She levered herself against him, pushing back. Infused with a sense of confidence borne out of what this man had given her at that oasis, Sylvie stood up and slowly and methodically took off her clothes until she was naked.

He looked...stunned. Hypnotised. In shock. In awe.

Sylvie came back and straddled him again, every inch of her skin sensitised just from his look. His hands came to her waist and she felt a slight tremor in them. She reached down between them and undid his trousers, pulled him free, smoothing her hand up and down the silken length of his erection, her whole body flushing red with lust.

The fact that she was naked and he was still almost fully dressed was erotic in the extreme. But when Arkim's mouth latched on to her nipple, Sylvie's fleeting sense of being in control quickly evaporated, and he skilfully showed her who was the real master here. She was rubbing against him, thick and hard between her legs, feeling her juices anointing his shaft.

Arkim groaned and dropped his head against her and said, 'I need to be inside you...*now.*'

Sylvie raised herself up in wordless acquiescence while Arkim extricated protection from his pocket, smoothing the thin latex sheath onto his penis.

His hands were back on her waist—tight, urgent. He positioned her so that her slick body rested just over his tip and with exquisite care, as if savouring the moment, he brought Sylvie down onto his erection. She inhaled as he filled her, almost to the point of pain but still on the side of pleasure. When he was as deep as he could go he held her there for a moment, before it got too much and he had to move again...

There was nothing but the sound of their laboured breathing in the quiet apartment as the frenzy overtook them. Her knees were pressed to his thighs, her hands gripping his shoulders. Her whole body tightened and quickened as Arkim thrust hard and deep up into her, hips welded to hers. He was so deep...deeper than ever before. She could feel her heart beating out of time. And when the explosion hit there was nowhere to hide.

Sylvie's head was thrown back, her eyes shut, every muscle and sinew taut, as waves and waves of release flowed through her body, wrenching her soul apart. And Arkim was with her every step of the way, his own body as taut as a whip under hers.

It was so excruciatingly exquisite that it almost felt like a punishment. As if Arkim was doing this on purpose, just to torture her. It was shattering.

And when the waves subsided Sylvie subsided too, unable to keep herself upright, collapsing against Arkim's chest, her head buried in his neck.

She felt like a car crash victim. As if some kind of explosion had really just happened, knocking her out of orbit. The fact that his heart was thundering under hers was no consolation. Her skin was hot, sticky, but she was too wiped out to care.

She whispered into his damp neck, 'What are we doing?'

She felt Arkim's chest swell underneath hers, making her sensitive breasts ache. His voice rumbled around her.

'We're doing that again…as soon as I can move…'

Much later, when it was dark outside, Sylvie woke alone in a massive bed. She was disorientated for a moment, and then the pleasurable aches and tingles in her body and the tenderness between her legs helped her to remember the last few cataclysmic hours.

Arkim had been true to his word. As soon as he'd been able to move he'd carried Sylvie into the bedroom, stripped, and proceeded to make love to her all over again. Then they'd taken a shower…and barely made it back to the bed before making love again.

Sylvie groaned and rolled over, mashing her face into a soft pillow. What was she *doing*?

She flipped back again and looked up at the exquisitely corniced ceiling, her mind racing with the implications of what it all meant. Arkim knew now. He knew everything. Everything she hadn't been able to tell him out of loyalty to her sister.

Feeling curious, and wondering where he was, Sylvie sat up, wincing as tender muscles protested. She saw a robe at the end of the bed and reached for it, sitting up to pull it on. It dwarfed her slim frame but she belted it tightly around her, blushing when she thought of her clothes, which must still be strewn in that elegant reception room.

She padded barefoot out of the bedroom and back towards the main part of the apartment. As she was passing a door that was slightly ajar she noticed a dim golden light and heard a suspicious-sounding *yap*.

She pushed open the door to find a study, three walls

lined with bookshelves and books. A huge desk was in front of the window, its surface covered with a computer, laptop and papers... But her eyes nearly popped out of her head when she saw Arkim sitting on the ground, his back against the only bare wall in the room, wearing only a pair of sweats and cradling a familiar-looking puppy in his arms.

They both looked up at the same time, and it would have been comical if Sylvie hadn't been so shocked. The little dog shot out of Arkim's arms and raced over to Sylvie, yapping excitedly, its stubby little tail waggling furiously. She crouched down and was almost bowled over by his enthusiasm, his tongue licking wherever he could reach.

When she was over her shock she looked at Arkim, who was still sitting there, looking for all the world as if nothing untoward was going on. 'What on earth...? How did you get him here?'

And why? Sylvie wanted to ask, but was afraid.

Arkim shrugged one shoulder negligently. 'I brought him back to the castle with me that day...and then I just ended up bringing him to Europe.'

Sylvie's breath felt choppy all of a sudden, and her heart was thumping hard. In a flight of fancy in her head she was imagining all sorts of reasons that were all very, *very* dangerous.

She buried her nose in his fur. When she looked up again she said, 'He's all cleaned up...what is he?'

Arkim's mouth quirked. 'A Highland Westie mixed with something indeterminate.'

'Have you got a name for him yet?'

He shook his head. 'I couldn't think of one. But I want to give him to you...so you choose a name.'

Sylvie's mouth fell open and the dog squirmed to be free, so she let him out of her arms to go sniffing at something exciting nearby. 'But…but I can't take him. My apartment is tiny, and Giselle is allergic to animal hair.'

Arkim frowned. 'Giselle?'

Sylvie waved a hand. 'My flatmate. Arkim…why are you doing this?'

He rose lithely from his seat on the floor, his chest dark under its smattering of hair in the golden light. He came over to her and held out a hand. Sylvie took it and he pulled her up. He led her over to a seat and sat down, pulling her into his lap. He smoothed her trailing hair over one shoulder.

She felt extremely unsure of her footing, and vulnerable. 'Arkim—'

'That day…' he interjected.

She nodded.

'I regretted sending you away like that.'

Sylvie's heart palpitations were back. 'You did?'

He nodded, his black eyes on hers, not letting her look away. 'I was a coward. You were getting too close… I asked you if you'd thought we were going to stay there for ever, but the truth is I think that's exactly what *I* wanted. Never to leave. And it just hit me: I had a life to get back to and I'd almost forgotten it existed. That *I* existed outside of that place. I honestly haven't been able to stop thinking about you. We're not done, Sylvie… I need more time with you.'

'What exactly are you saying, Arkim?' Sylvie didn't like the unpalatable questions being thrown up by his choice of words. *'I need more time with you…'* It sounded finite. Definitely finite.

'I want you to move in with me. Stay with me for as long as…'

'For as long as what?' she asked sharply, tensing all over. Because she very badly wanted him to say, *For as long as you want. For ever.*

'For as long as this lasts…this crazy, insatiable desire.'
Finite. Definitely finite.

She pulled away from Arkim and stood up before he could see how raw she felt. The puppy sniffed around her feet and she picked him up and held him against her, almost like a shield. How could Arkim manipulate her like this? Give her a reminder of the exquisite pleasure he could wring from her body…tell her he regretted the way he'd behaved…the puppy…and now this. When her defences were down.

Because this is the man who all but kidnapped you and held you in his castle at his pleasure when he wanted revenge.

She pushed aside the memories crowding her head. She needed to lay it out baldly for herself. 'So you're asking me to become your mistress? Is that it? And the dog is meant to sweeten the deal?' She made a sound of disgust and turned round to face the window. How could she have been so stupid…so—?

She was whirled around again to face Arkim, looming tall and intimidating.

'No…it's not like that. I mean…yes, I want you to stay— but as my lover…not as a mistress.' He sounded almost bitter. 'Believe me, I know by now that you would never languish idly at someone's beck and call. And the dog… I hadn't even consciously realised I wanted him for you, but I got your address from Sophie and I brought him with me. I don't take mistresses,' he said. 'I thought you'd know me well enough by now to know that I don't indulge women like that. I don't do frills or niceties.'

No. He didn't. He could tear a woman's heart and soul to shreds just by being him. Raw. Male. Uncompromising. Tortured, but with a deep core of emotion that made her heart break.

'You were right, you know,' he said heavily.

Sylvie finally found her voice. 'About what?'

Arkim grimaced. 'About my motivations for agreeing to marry Sophie. She represented something to me—something I'd always craved. A respectable family unit.'

And that just confirmed for Sylvie what she'd already guessed. Some day Arkim would find a woman worthy of being his perfectly respectable wife, and then he *would* do frills and niceties. She didn't doubt it.

The hatred she felt for that future woman shocked her. But it also made her see her own weakness. She wanted more too. She wanted to take every atom of what Arkim was offering and gorge herself before he cast her aside again. Or—if she had the strength—gorge herself so that she could walk away before he could do it for her.

She lifted her chin. 'If I stay with you and we…we do this, I won't give up my job.'

Arkim was very still. 'I wouldn't expect you to.'

Sylvie felt a spurt of relief mixed with pain. As long as she stayed in her 'job of ill repute' she'd remember who she was—and so would he. There would be no dangerous illusions or dreams, no fantasies that things could be different. Because they never could be. She was *not* the woman who would share Arkim's life and mother his children. And she needed to remember that.

She forced a lightness to her voice that she wasn't feeling and said, 'Well, then, if this dog is really mine I'd better think of a name.'

'That's a *good* boy, Omar…'

Arkim stood at the door and watched Sylvie hand the puppy a treat from her pocket as she lavished him with praise, rubbing him behind his floppy ears. As far as he could tell the dog wasn't doing anything that vaguely resembled obeying commands, but Sylvie was too besotted to care.

He recalled the spontaneous urge he'd felt to take the dog with him when he'd been leaving the oasis, obeying some irrational impulse because it had been the last thing Sylvie had touched. And then he'd spent a month tripping over the damn thing in London, talking to it as if it could understand him.

An alien lightness vied with a familiar surge of arousal just to see her sitting on the floor, her hair in a plait down her back. She was obviously just back from work, still dressed in leggings and a loose top. Arkim was used to women in couture creations and the latest ready-to-wear casuals. Yet Sylvie would blow them all out of the water with her inherent grace and elegance, dressed just like this.

She insisted on taking the Métro every day, refusing his offer of a driver and car. And he hadn't even realised that his kitchen functioned until he'd come in one evening and found Sylvie taking a Boeuf Bourguignon out of the oven. Far from making him break out in a cold sweat at the domesticity, he'd found it surprisingly appealing. He'd never known what it was to come home to a cooked meal, and he'd found himself laughing out loud at Sylvie's wry tales of learning to cook when she'd first arrived in Paris.

When she'd told him that she regularly baked for the members of the revue, he'd found his conscience smarting at the thought of how badly he'd misjudged her from that first moment he'd laid eyes on her. Because at first glance she'd epitomised everything he'd grown up to despise in a lewd, over-sexualised world.

In fact she was anything but. He'd been wrong about her. *So* wrong.

It had been two weeks now since she'd moved in…and just like before, the more Arkim had of her, the more he wanted her. It made him nervous. This…this lust he felt was too urgent. Desperate, even. He couldn't let her go. *Yet.*

She looked up then and saw him standing there. Her

eyes widened, brightened, and she smiled. But then the smile slipped slightly and a guarded look came over her beautiful face. It made Arkim want to haul her up and demand that she... *What?* asked a small voice. *Stop shutting you out?*

Ever since that night when she'd agreed to stay Sylvie had locked a piece of herself away from him. She was careful around him—there was some spark he'd come to expect in her missing.

Except for when they made love... Then she could hold nothing back, in spite of herself.

But when they were finished she would curl up on her side, away from him. And Arkim would lie there and clench his hands into fists to stop himself from reaching for her—because he didn't do that, did he? That would send the wrong message...that this was something more than a transitory slaking of mutual lust.

Except it wasn't being slaked. It was being stoked.

'A function?' Sylvie felt a flicker of trepidation. So far she and Arkim had spent their time confined to his stunning apartment. They met here after work and indulged in satisfying their mutual lust until they couldn't move. Then they got up, went to work and repeated the process.

Every morning Sylvie woke up praying that this would be the morning when he didn't affect her so much...to no avail. And when they'd had dinner the other night... dinner she'd made...it had felt far too easy...seductive. She couldn't do that again.

Arkim was leaning against the doorframe, looking edible in a dark three-piece suit, his jaw stubbled after the day.

'It's a charity benefit thing...to raise money for cancer awareness. I thought you'd have an interest.'

Sylvie was shocked that Arkim obviously remembered her telling him that her mother had died of cancer.

'Well, of course I do… But… I mean, I didn't think you'd want to be seen with me. In public.'

Some fleeting expression passed over his face and then he came over and pulled her up from the floor, his hands resting under her arms. 'The reason we haven't gone out together is because the minute I see you I need you. And I need you now.'

Everything in Sylvie exulted. She felt exactly the same. The insatiable desire to cleave herself to this man.

She was barely aware of Omar—she'd named him after Al-Omar—pawing her calf, looking for attention.

'What about the function?' The thought of going out in public with Arkim was alternately terrifying and exciting.

'We're still going… But first…a shower?'

Sylvie hid her reaction to the fact that he was prepared to be seen in public with her and said, mock seriously, 'I think your dedication to water conservation is to be commended.'

Arkim snorted and tugged her to the bedroom, shutting the door firmly on Omar, who skidded to a stop outside the closed door and proceeded to whine pitifully and unnoticed for the next half an hour.

'Are you sure I look okay?'

Arkim was the epitome of civilised style in a black tuxedo. Sylvie hated feeling so insecure, but the full magnitude of what this public outing meant was sinking in—and not in a good way. She was nervous of people recognising him, recognising *her*, and the inevitable scrutiny.

He reached for her hand, lacing his fingers through hers. 'You look amazing. Just think of this as one of your father's events…you looked pretty confident to me in that milieu.'

She fought back a blush to think of how forward she'd been and plucked at the silky emerald-green material of her dress. The dress was gorgeous—a slinky column of pure silk—it covered her from throat to wrist to ankle but, perversely, it felt more revealing than anything she'd ever worn before, skimming close to her curves and cut on the bias.

It had been waiting for her in a silver embossed box when she'd emerged from her shower with Arkim, barely able to walk after his *very* careful ministrations. Every feminist principle in her had risen up to refuse it…but she'd taken one look and fallen in love. It reminded her poignantly of a dress her mother had owned—which Catherine had inevitably thrown out—and so, like a traitor, she'd accepted it.

She'd styled her hair into movie star waves and hoped that it wasn't too much. She knew how snobbish these events were, and if anyone recognised her… She gulped.

'Relax… I know how you feel—believe me.'

Sylvie was jolted out of her introspection and she looked at the wry expression on Arkim's face. Of course he knew. He was the son of one of the most infamous men in the world. When she thought of how proud he was… Her heart felt ominously achy at the thought of people looking at him and judging him.

As he did you, she reminded herself. And even though she could understand his motives now the hurt still lingered.

The car was drawing to a smooth stop outside one of Paris's most iconic and glamorous hotels. Arkim got out, and Sylvie drew in a deep breath as he opened the door and held out a hand for her. They joined a very glitzy throng of beautiful people entering the foyer with lots of expensive perfume and air-kissing. Arkim held Sylvie's hand, and she found she was clinging to him.

She reminded herself that she needed to be vigilant around him. She didn't want to lose herself again so easily. So she forced herself to relax and took her hand out of his, ignoring his look as she squared her shoulders and entered the massive ballroom where the function was being held.

His hand stayed on the small of her back, though, as waiters offered them drinks and they navigated their way around the room, constantly stopping when Arkim was recognised by various people.

Sylvie found, much to her relief, that she was usually given a quick once-over and then summarily dismissed. She didn't mind. She preferred that to scrutiny or recognition any day of the week.

When they were momentarily alone again Sylvie asked curiously, 'When do they announce dinner?' She was beginning to feel hunger pangs after their earlier activity.

Arkim grimaced slightly and gestured with his head to where a waiter was passing, with some teeny-tiny hors d'oeuvres that looked more like art installations than food. 'That's dinner, I'm afraid, I think most people here haven't eaten in about ten years.'

Sylvie grinned at his humour—and then her stomach growled in earnest and she blushed, ducking her head with embarrassment.

Arkim slid an arm around her waist and pulled her into his tall, hard body, creating a wave of heat that slowly engulfed her. When she looked at him again he said, 'Isn't there some leftover Boeuf Bourguignon at home?'

His use of the word *home* caused butterflies. She fought to stay cool. 'I believe there is...'

Arkim's gaze moved down to her mouth and now *he* looked hungry. 'Then let's get out of here. I've had enough.'

The thought of leaving now, getting out of the evening intact, without any awkward public meetings, was very appealing. Apart from what the explicit hunger in his eyes promised... Well, she *had* made a promise to herself to gorge, hadn't she?

Sylvie looked up at him and felt as if she was drowning. As if she was fighting a losing battle. 'Okay, then— let's go.'

They were walking out through the vast marbled lobby—hand in hand because Arkim refused to let her tug free—and Sylvie was floating on a cloud of dangerous contentment at the thought of being alone with him again, when a group of men stopped in front of them. Arkim stopped, making her jerk to a halt beside him.

She looked up, expecting it to be someone he knew. But the men were looking at *her*. At her body. At her breasts. Before Sylvie had even assessed the situation properly, icy-cold humiliation was crawling up her spine.

'Well, well, well...it's your favourite L'Amour revue artist, James.'

CHAPTER TEN

SYLVIE RECOGNISED THEM—sickeningly. They were regulars at the show—English ex-pats, working in Paris—and one of them had had a brief fling with Giselle, her flatmate. She remembered the guy blearily hopping around their tiny apartment the morning after, looking for his clothes.

Arkim snarled from beside her, 'She doesn't know who you are—now, get out of our way.'

Now all the men's attention was on Arkim. Sylvie wanted to curl up and die. He looked livid. A muscle throbbed in his jaw.

'And who are *you*, mate? Are you paying her well for the night? Cos if you've lost interest we'd be more than happy to stump up some cash for a good time.'

One of the others interjected then. 'She doesn't put out, remember?'

Sylvie felt as if she was in some kind of nightmare. She tried to speak. 'I'm sorry… I really don't think we've met…' But her voice came out all thready and weak, and now the tallest of the men—still a good few inches shorter than Arkim—was standing toe to toe with him.

'Think you're some hotshot, eh? Well, it happens that I recognise you too—*you're* the guy that got stood up at the altar.'

'Oh, God!' Sylvie hadn't even realised she'd spoken out loud. She felt nauseous.

Arkim let her hand go and pushed her away from him, saying in a voice edged with steel, 'Get into the car and wait for me—*now.*'

Sylvie started to back away, horror filling her at the murderous look on Arkim's face, but as she turned around one of the men who so far hadn't said anything blocked her.

'And where do you think *you're* going?'

Sylvie clenched her jaw. 'Get out of my way.'

He came closer and she could smell the reek of alcohol on his breath. 'Now, now…that's not nice, is it? I've *seen* you, you know…'

He stroked a finger up her arm and Sylvie fought not to flinch in disgust.

'You're my favourite of them all…but I'd like to see a lot more of you…'

Sylvie had just positioned her knee for maximum damage, in case he touched her again, and heard an almighty *crack* behind her. She whirled round to see Arkim staggering back, holding a hand up to his eye.

She flew to his side just as the hotel security officers rushed forward. Arkim, still holding a hand to his face, spoke to someone who looked like a manager. The eight or so English guys were rounded up within seconds, and it was only then that Sylvie realised just how drunk they all were, as they were led away with belligerent faces.

Her hand was in Arkim's again, and he was taking her out to the car so fast she had to trot to keep up, holding her dress up. Her stomach was churning painfully, and she breathed out as the car pulled away from the front of the hotel.

She looked at Arkim and winced when she saw his eye, shut tight. She knelt on the seat beside him, swatting aside his hand when he tried to stop her. 'What happened? How did you get hit?'

He looked at her with his one good eye. 'I recognised one of the men.'

Sylvie felt shaky. She reached for a bottle of water and unscrewed it, lifting some of the material at the bottom of her dress and wetting it to dab at his eye ineffectually.

'And?' she prompted, feeling sick all over again.

'He said something about you that I know isn't true.'

Her insides cramped.

'I told him that if he didn't take it back I'd spread the word about his out-of-control recreational drug use. So he hit me.'

Sylvie sat back on her heels, anguished. 'I'm so sorry, Arkim.'

His one good eye glared at her. 'What are you apologising for? *They* were at fault.'

'Yes, but if they hadn't recognised me...'

Arkim didn't say anything, and his silence spoke volumes.

With relief Sylvie saw that they were drawing close to the apartment. The traffic at this time of evening was light, and Arkim didn't live far away. The car pulled to a stop and Arkim got out, his movements jerky. Sylvie didn't wait. She clambered out, still holding her dress up in one hand. The feeling of contentment she'd had earlier had been well and truly shattered by a rude awakening.

In the apartment she could hear Arkim moving restlessly around the drawing room, the clatter of the drinks tray. He was angry. She wrapped some ice in a towel and brought it in, saying as authoritatively as she could, 'Sit down—let me look at you.'

He scowled at her. His jacket was off, his bow tie undone. His eye was closed and swelling. He looked thoroughly disreputable, and it only added to his appeal.

He sat down, legs spread, stretching an arm across the back of the couch. Approaching him, Sylvie felt as if she was approaching a bad-tempered lion. But she did it, and then observed, 'Your eye isn't bleeding—that's good.'

'You're a nurse now?'

Sylvie pushed down a flare of irritation at Arkim's

snappy mood. 'No, but I do tend to be the one people come to with minor injuries at work.'

Arkim made a *harumph* sound. Of *course* everyone went to her for treatment at work. He could just imagine her: compassionate, kind, soothing. Yet another unwelcome reminder of how badly he'd misjudged her all along.

He knew he was being a boor, but his gut was still too churned up after the confrontation for him to be sanguine. Sylvie pressed the ice near his eye, and he was aware of her wincing when he sucked in a pained breath.

The words that man had said came back to him: *'She tastes as sweet as she looks, doesn't she?'*

Arkim had had to call on a level of control he'd never used before. And what scared him even now was the instant volcanic jealousy that had swamped him. The tiniest implication that the man had been intimate with Sylvie had been enough to send him into orbit.

He still felt edgy, volatile. Sylvie was kneeling on the couch beside him, the silk of her dress straining across her breasts, outlining their luscious shape. Adrenalin still lingered in Arkim's blood. He needed to channel it…dilute it somehow. Sylvie shifted and her body swayed closer. His arousal spiked, mixing with the adrenalin, making him crave an antidote to this churning in his gut.

He put down his glass of alcohol and reached out and put his hands around Sylvie's waist. She took the ice away and looked at him. Her hair was tumbling over her shoulders, a glossy wave of bright red. She looked concerned. Eyes huge with worry. Remorse.

'Arkim—'

He took the ice pack out of her hands and threw it aside, then pulled her into him, his intent unmistakable.

Sylvie protested, even though he could feel her breath coming faster, moving her chest against his. 'You're hurt. We can't—'

He put a finger on her mouth, then cupped the back of her head. In spite of his need to devour, consume, he found that something happened as he touched her mouth with his. The tension in his body was fading away…and he was touching her as reverently as if she was made of china.

She braced herself with her hands on his chest. Desire rose up, fast and urgent, replacing the need to be reverent, and Arkim fumbled clumsily with his clothes and body, sheathing himself with protection. Sylvie rose above him, pulling her dress up, eyes glazed with lust, cheeks flushed.

Arkim tore Sylvie's delicate lace panties off and drew the head of his erection up and down her slick folds, tantalising her, torturing himself, until she was slick and hot. Too impatient to wait, she rose up and took him in her hand, then slowly slid down, taking all of him inside her body. It was so exquisite Arkim had to grit his jaw tightly.

They moved with a kind of slow but languorous intent…rocking, sliding…and when the need became too great Arkim held Sylvie's hips in place and lost himself inside her, burying his head in her breast, feeling her hands on his head, as his soul flew apart and finally he found the oblivion he was looking for.

A couple of hours later Sylvie was lying on her side, naked, her hands under her face, watching Arkim's chest rise and fall. He'd taken her to bed and made love to her again, and the after-shocks of pleasure still pulsed through her body at intermittent intervals. The intensity of the way he'd taken her on the couch still took her breath away. It was as if he'd been consumed with a kind of fury.

His face was in profile to her, showing the proud line of his nose. From here she couldn't see his injured eye. Sylvie couldn't help but feel that in spite of the passion with which Arkim had taken her just now something had altered since that confrontation at the hotel.

A cold weight settled in her belly as an ugly reminder reared its head. She'd been meaning to discuss something with Arkim for the past couple of days and had been avoiding it like a coward. Because she was afraid that it would prove to be some kind of a test. A test of where she really fitted into his life.

As his chest rose and fell evenly she envied him his peace, when *her* body and brain felt as if they were tying themselves into a million knots. Knowing she wouldn't rest, Sylvie slipped out of bed and got dressed, going into the living room.

She sat cross-legged on the couch and Omar jumped up into her lap. As she petted him absently and looked into the muted darkness she knew that she had no choice but to talk to Arkim. And after what had happened this evening she knew that he would have no hesitation in letting her go. For good, this time.

Dawn was breaking outside when Arkim woke. His head was throbbing and he wondered why—until he lifted a hand and winced when it came into contact with his black eye.

Sylvie. Anger jerked him fully awake in an instant. The memory of those men...eating her up with their eyes. And one of them had touched her. He'd seen it. His hands curled into fists just from thinking about it, remembering, his blood pressure increasing.

No woman had ever roused Arkim to the point of wanting to do violence on her behalf. But he'd been ready to take on all those men. His anger had been volcanic. It was something he hadn't felt in a long time...since the day that woman had controlled him for her own amusement and his father had thrown him out like unwanted baggage.

Sylvie. Arkim looked around. He was alone in the room...no sounds were coming from the bathroom. He wanted her even now, even after making love to her like some kind of feral youth on the couch earlier. Damn her. Would he *ever* not want her?

Not wanting to investigate the way his gut clenched at that prospect, Arkim got out of bed and pulled on a pair of sweats, feeling as if he'd done about ten rounds in a boxing ring. He frowned as he padded through the apartment, hearing nothing but silence. Not even Omar.

He checked all the rooms and came to the living room last—and finally he saw her. She was standing with her back to the door, looking out of the window. He noticed that she was dressed in jeans and a shirt. There was something tense about the lines of her body that made him stay where he was.

'You're dressed.'

The lines of Sylvie's body got tenser. She turned around slowly. Her hair was pulled into a low bun at the back of her head. She confounded him—she could go from looking like the sexiest movie star goddess to something like this, much more simple and plain, and yet his body reacted the same way every time.

He leaned against the door and crossed his arms, grateful for the fact that his sweats were loose. His susceptibility to this woman was something that still made him feel uncomfortable. Exposed.

Sylvie's arms were crossed too. 'There was something I wanted to tell you earlier, but I never got a chance.'

Feeling a flutter of panic, and not liking it, Arkim said, 'Is it so important it can't wait till later?' He stood up straight and held out a hand. 'Come back to bed…it's too early for talk.'

Sylvie smiled, but it was touched with something Arkim hadn't seen in some time. Cynicism.

'No, it can't wait…'

Arkim went over to the drinks cabinet and helped himself to a shot of brandy. He saluted Sylvie. 'Medicinal purposes.'

She paled at that, and Arkim paused with the glass half-way to his mouth. 'What is it?'

She looked at him, that blue-green gaze unnervingly direct. 'Pierre has offered me a bigger role in the show.'

The tight ball in Arkim's gut seemed to ease. *That was it?* 'That sounds good.' So why did she look so serious?

'It is good... But if I accept it I'll have to take off my clothes for the first time...like the other girls. Pierre has never pressured me about this before... I told you, he's been like a father to me. But he says now that if I want to stay I have to start delivering a fuller performance.'

For a second Arkim just heard a roaring in his ears. Images rushed through his head: Sylvie's pale breasts bared for thousands of people to see... Her perfect body... No wonder her boss wanted to exploit her.

And those men last night...they would look at her—every night if they wished. And taunt Arkim with the knowledge that they'd seen as much of his lover as he had.

He realised his hand had tightened so much around the glass that he risked breaking it. He forced himself to relax, to focus.

Sylvie continued. 'The truth is that I don't know if I should do it or not. I've been thinking...about doing something else.'

Relief vied with something much darker inside Arkim. Sylvie was looking at him far too carefully. As if his response mattered. As if she wanted him to tell her what to do.

The sheer volatility of his emotions was like acid in his stomach, inhibiting his response. If he told Sylvie he cared what she did she would have control over him...she would know his vulnerability. It would make a statement about what was happening here, would demonstrate a possessiveness of her that had already earned him a black eye. In public. In front of his peers.

He went cold—because he hadn't even contemplated that side of it yet.

He'd just weathered one public scandal...was he now in danger of being dragged into another one?

It was too much. Too reminiscent of that day when he'd lost his innocence and his self-respect. When he'd been found, literally, with his pants down and that woman's mouth around his— He blanked the poisonous memory. He wasn't going back there for anyone.

Carefully, he took a sip of his drink. He didn't even feel the burn. His voice when he spoke was cool. Calm. Belying the tumult underneath. 'I don't really know what you want me to say. It's your life, Sylvie. You should do whatever you think is best for you.'

She looked at him for a long moment, but it was a kind of dead-eyed stare. She was so pale that Arkim almost made a move towards her, but then she seemed to break out of her trance-like state and uncrossed her arms, her gaze narrowed.

'Yes, it *is* my life, and I *do* know what's best for me. Which is why I'm going to leave now.'

Arkim frowned. 'Leave...?'

Sylvie glanced down to where Omar was sitting at her feet, looking up at her adoringly, his tongue hanging out. But she didn't bend down to pick him up. Arkim saw her hands form fists, as if to stop herself.

She looked back at him, her jaw tight. 'Yes, leave. The new show opens in a week and there's a huge PR campaign starting tomorrow. In light of what happened last night I think it's best if we call it quits now.' Her chin lifted. 'I would prefer not to be responsible for any further public incidents, and when the new show takes off... Well, it's only more likely to happen.'

Something hard and dark and cold settled into Arkim's belly. 'So you're going to do it, then? Take Pierre up on his offer?'

Her face was like a pale smooth mask. She shrugged lightly. 'It's all I've ever known. They're my family... I'd be a fool not to want to progress in one of the most famous shows in the world.'

'By taking off your clothes?' Arkim almost spat the words.

Sylvie's gaze sparked. 'What's it to you? I have to worry about my career, Arkim. If I don't take this opportunity now there's a million girls coming up behind me who'll do the job.'

Arkim had to grit his jaw. He wanted to say, *What about the way you were dancing that day when I found you again?*

She had been so passionate and beautiful. But that wasn't really her, was it? If she was prepared to do this? Take the last step over the line...? Something within Arkim snapped and the words spilled out before he could stop them. 'What if I asked you to stay?'

A flare of colour came into Sylvie's cheeks. 'How long for? Another week? A month? Two months? We both know what this is...impermanent. Unless...'

Unless it's more.

The implication of her unfinished sentence made Arkim say harshly, 'Unless it's nothing.'

'It's nothing, then,' said Sylvie faintly.

She walked over and picked up her bag and a jacket, shrugging into it in jerky movements. She was avoiding Arkim's eye as she walked to the other side of the room, where he saw that a larger bag was waiting. So she'd packed already. Because she'd known how he would react? The knowledge sent a sharp pain through his chest.

She turned around to face him, looking very petite and

young. Delicate. He thought of her just a couple of hours ago, astride him, rocking her body against his. She'd been like a fearsome warrior, claiming her pleasure with a ferocity matched only by Arkim's desire to give it to her.

The image was so vivid that it took him a second to realise she'd gone.

No.

He put down the glass, uncaring that it fell to the floor, spilling dark golden liquid. When he got to the hall, he saw her holding Omar close, burying her face in his body before putting him down carefully. Something was constricting Arkim, like a band around his chest.

She didn't face him. She put her hand on the knob of the door and said tautly, 'I can't take him with me—it's not practical... But you will take care of him, won't you?'

Arkim was cold. All over. He hated his father. He'd never known his mother. He'd never known love. What he felt for Sylvie was just too...*overwhelming.*

'Of course.'

He wasn't even aware that he'd spoken. Cold was good. This was what he wanted. He didn't want volatility. Messy passion. *Emotions.*

'Thank you. Goodbye, Arkim.' She opened the door, and just before she stepped through she said huskily, 'Take care of yourself.'

After she'd gone Arkim was dimly aware of something warm on his toes, and he looked down stupidly to see Omar, tail wagging, making a small pitiful sound. He bent down and scooped him up against his chest, then went into the living room and sat on the couch, where the puppy settled trustingly into his lap.

He could smell Sylvie's delicate scent on the air. And something else. *Sex.* He realised that this was where he'd had her...only hours before. Every time he'd lost himself inside her it had felt as if another part of his soul was being altered.

He clenched his jaw so hard it hurt. Pain was good. The pain reminded him that he craved order and respectability above all. He didn't *need* his soul to be altered.

Sylvie Devereux had been a brief and torrid interlude in his life and now he was moving on. For good.

CHAPTER ELEVEN

A week later—L'Amour revue, final dress rehearsal...

'*SYLVIE!* HURRY UP! You're next.'

Sylvie took a deep breath, grabbed her prop sword, and made her way to the spotlit stage. The mood was controlled chaos. The new show was opening in a few hours and they still had lots to prepare. She was in a more elaborate version of the belly dance outfit that she'd worn for Arkim in Al-Hibiz, and the reminder was jarring.

When she got on stage the music started almost at once, so she had to jump straight into the routine. She wasn't overly worried about how precise her movements were because this rehearsal was really for the technical team, to make sure that all the timings for cues and lights and so on were lined up properly.

She had taken off her veil and head-covering and pushed her sword away, ready to move into the second part of the dance, when a loud *'Stop!'* sounded in the dark theatre.

Sylvie's heart stuttered, but she told herself she was imagining that she knew the voice. She was on her feet now and she kept going. It was probably just one of the stage hands.

Suddenly the music stopped.

She whirled around to hear some kind of a scuffle going on in the darkness backstage, and then a man walked out onto the stage from behind the curtains. Even though he was in the shadow of the lights she knew it was Arkim, taller and broader than everyone else.

He was holding something that looked like a vital piece

of audio equipment. Sure enough, he was quickly followed by an irate sound engineer, spluttering and gesticulating furiously, grabbing back his piece of equipment and disappearing again.

Sylvie wasn't sure she wasn't dreaming. 'Arkim...?'

He stepped forward into the spotlight. He wasn't a mirage. And then she became aware of the fact that they had an audience of crew and other dancers.

'What the hell are you doing? We're in the middle of rehearsals—you can't be here,' she hissed at him. But her mind leapt to the million and one possibilities of why he might be there anyway.

She noticed that the swelling on his eye had gone down, to be replaced by a dark bruise. He looked as if he'd just come from a brawl in an alley.

Her fault.

And, adding to her sense of everything being unreal, he was wearing faded worn denims and a close-fitting T-shirt, more casual than she'd ever seen him. It was almost as shocking as the time when she'd seen him naked in the pool at the oasis. His hair was messy and his overall demeanour was edgy and dangerous. He looked a million miles removed from the man she'd first seen in her father's house in his three-piece suit, so controlled. So disdainful.

'Arkim—'

But he cut her off, saying baldly, 'I don't want you to strip. I don't want anyone else to see you.'

Shock reverberated through her. And something scarily like euphoria. But just as quickly she feared that she was reading this all wrong.

She put her hands on her hips, anger flaring. 'It's okay for *you* to see me, but you're so controlling and possessive that you can't bear the thought that your *ex*-property might become a little more public?'

He stepped closer, the inevitable electricity sparking

between them. 'No,' he growled. 'I don't want anyone to see you because you're *mine*.'

Sylvie glared up at him. 'Do I need to remind you that you've let me go—*twice*?' The knowledge of her own weakness around him and the realisation that he'd never choose her to be a permanent part of his life made her say frigidly, 'What is it, Arkim? You're so concerned with your precious reputation that you're afraid my debauched lifestyle will come back to haunt you?'

A muscle in his jaw pulsed. 'No, dammit. I don't want anyone else to see what's *mine*.'

Emotion made Sylvie's chest ache. This man had started out rejecting her before he'd even known her, and even after getting to know her—intimately—he'd still ultimately rejected her. He was just here beating his chest because he couldn't bear the thought of sharing her.

'But I'm not *yours*. You let me go.'

They were so close now they were almost touching. Sylvie was unaware of anything but the man in front of her and those deep, dark eyes. Eyes that could look so cold and dead, but which she knew could turn her heart upside down and inside out.

'I don't want you to go. I want you to stay.'

Hating the little tremor of emotion that made her heart jump with irrational hope, Sylvie threw out a hand. 'We've *had* this conversation. For how long? Another two weeks? A month? And then you'll move on with your perfect respectable life and you'll meet some perfect respectable woman and you'll marry her—like you wanted to marry Sophie because she was so perfect for you.'

'*You* are perfect for me.'

Sylvie's mouth was still open. She shut it abruptly, aghast at everything that had tumbled out. And had he just said…?

'What did you say?'

'I said that you are perfect for me. I don't want anyone else.'

His words impacted like a sledgehammer, knocking her to pieces. And even though she'd registered them she shook her head, took a step back. It wasn't hard to envisage being rejected again, when Arkim woke up one morning and realised she wasn't perfect for him, wasn't really suitable for the life he wanted, and this time his rejection would be comprehensive and fatal. She wouldn't recover. And the worst of it was she *knew* why it was so important to him...she wanted him to be happy.

'This is just lust talking,' she said.

Before Sylvie could react Arkim had closed the distance between them and cupped her face in his hands. He blotted out the world when he lowered his mouth to hers. Sylvie might have expected devastation, bruising passion...but his kiss was like a kind of benediction. A kiss that was gentle and restrained, but with the unmistakable promise of *more*.

And, damn him, she couldn't help but respond. A sob of reaction was working its way up her throat, making her grab his T-shirt in order to stay standing. She just wasn't able to defend herself. The last week had been torture.

Eventually Arkim pulled back, his eyes glittering down into hers. Sylvie felt exposed...vulnerable.

'I know what I want and I want you.'

I want. Not *I love.* And Sylvie needed love. After feeling so bruised all her life from her father's rejection, she couldn't go through that with someone else. Better to be the rejecter. Arkim didn't want her. Not really. No matter what he said or how he kissed her.

She pulled free. 'It wasn't enough of a wake-up call that you got punched in the face? Are you so blinded that you've forgotten what I do? What I am? Wherever we go there's always going to be a risk that someone will recognise me...' She crossed her fingers behind her back at the white lie she was about to tell. 'And especially when I become famous for taking my clothes off completely. I won't be one of the less risqué acts any more, Arkim. Everyone will know what I look like naked.'

Sylvie could see him pale slightly under the olive tones of his skin. His face was starker, leaner than she'd ever seen it. As if he'd lost weight in the space of a week.

'If that's what you really want to do I won't pretend that I'll like it, but I'll support you.'

Sylvie reeled. Her jaw dropped. Eventually she got out, 'You're saying you'd *accept* me, no matter what?' She couldn't believe it for a second. Because if she did... Her heart contracted painfully.

She shook her head. 'This is not you talking... This is lust...desire. And once it's gone, Arkim—' Her voice broke traitorously. 'I won't let you send me away again when you realise that I'm not perfect after all...because I'm a constant reminder of some weakness you feel, of your life with your father.'

She'd moved to turn away, her vision blurring, when Arkim's hand shot out and caught her shoulder. She saw Pierre standing and watching, his gnarled old face incredulous. They had an avid audience. Everyone had gathered to watch the show.

Sylvie let Arkim turn her back towards him, saying in a choked voice, 'Arkim, you have to—'

'Stop talking, Sylvie.'

Her mouth closed. He had to know they were being observed. Why wasn't he leaving? Why wasn't he preserving what was left intact of his reputation?

Maybe because he means what he says? said a small seductive voice.

But before she could do or say anything more Arkim was reaching for the bottom of his T-shirt, pulling it up over his head and off, revealing his very taut and perfect musculature.

There was a collective intake of appreciative breath and a low whistle, which sounded as if it was quickly stifled by an elbow in the ribs.

Sylvie barely noticed, she was so shocked. 'What are you *doing*?'

His hands were on his jeans now. He looked grim. 'I'm trying to prove to you that I'll do whatever it takes to make you trust in me.'

He was starting to undo his top button, and Sylvie realised that he fully intended to strip completely. She put out a shaking hand. 'Stop.' And then she shook her head. 'Why...?'

Arkim dropped his hands, and now he looked bleak. 'Because I need to show you that I'm willing to bare myself totally for you. And that if you wanted me to stand in front of Notre Dame and do it, I would. I need you to know that I won't ever judge you again. I'm proud of you, and of everything you've achieved with such innate dignity and pride. You shame me. Everything I've been aiming for my whole life is empty. Meaningless. Without you.'

Sylvie was struck dumb.

He seared her alive with the intensity in his dark gaze. 'Don't you get it yet? I love you... But it took me a really long time to understand it because I've never loved anyone, so I didn't know what it felt like...and I'm sorry.'

To her absolute shock Arkim proceeded to get down on one knee in front of her. He took something out of his pocket. A small velvet box. He opened it up and took something out, held it up between his fingers. She could see that his hand was trembling.

He took her hand in his and said, 'Sylvie Devereux, I know I've given you every reason in the world to hate me...but will you please consent to be my wife? Because

I love you, and without you I'm just an arrogant, uptight prat.' He squeezed her hand. 'Whatever it is you want to do in this life I will support you, and I will take a thousand blows for you if that's what comes my way. Because you're mine to protect and cherish and love, and I pledge to do this for as long as I have breath in my body.'

Sylvie felt dizzy, anchored to the earth only by Arkim's hand wrapped around hers. She wasn't even looking at the ring, glinting with a green flash of colour in her peripheral vision. She wanted to believe…*so* badly. And then she realised that she was just as guilty as he of wanting to protect herself. She had to trust or she'd never move on from her old hurts.

She spoke with a rush. 'I'm not really taking Pierre's offer… I just said that to try and make you see how inappropriate I was for you. I'm only performing tonight as a favour, because we're stuck for an act. My modern dance teacher is putting together a company, here in Paris, and he wants me to be a part of it—as one of their lead dancers. I won't be taking my clothes off, but I still won't be perfect.'

He smiled a crooked smile. 'You *are* perfect. If you want to ride naked on a horse through the streets of Paris then I'll take off all my clothes too and join you.'

Another voluble sigh came from someone nearby. Sylvie ignored it.

Arkim's hand gripped hers. 'I just want you to be happy…'

And finally it sank in, and spread through her whole body like a warm glow, lighting up the dark corners that had been filled with pain and uncertainty for a long time.

Sylvie realised that Arkim was looking a little strained… He was still waiting for her answer. Unsure.

'Yes,' she said softly, her heart swelling. 'Yes, I'll marry you.' She got down on her knees and faced him, touching his face, tracing his mouth. She looked at him and said shakily, 'I love you so much… I think I've loved you for ever. And I knew it the moment I saw you, even though I couldn't understand how…'

For a second Arkim looked stunned, as if he truly hadn't known what she would say. Then she felt him push the ring on her finger, and glanced down to see a huge emerald flanked by smaller blue sapphires and diamonds. Like her eyes.

She reached for him just as he reached for her, their mouths fusing, bodies pressed close enough to hurt.

And then a very loud and obvious cough from nearby made Sylvie jerk in Arkim's arms. The theatre and their surroundings filtered back into her consciousness as if she were coming out of a particularly delicious dream.

She looked around to see a sea of faces and a lot of suspiciously shiny eyes. Pierre, however, looked familiarly stern. But she could see the glint of affection in his expression.

He eyeballed Arkim. 'If you've quite finished with my dancer, Mr Al-Sahid, I have a theatre to run and a show to put on in less than an hour…'

Arkim had a tight grip on Sylvie's hips and he was still unashamedly half naked. Something Sylvie was becoming more and more burningly aware of. The ring he'd put on her finger felt heavy and solid. A happy weight.

Arkim, totally unfazed by Pierre, looked at Sylvie. 'There's nothing I want more than to take you home right now…but do you want to do the show?'

The Arkim she'd first met might have carried her out of here over his shoulder. Or paid Pierre to release her.

Sylvie looked between the men and then back to Arkim. Her voice was husky when she said, 'Yes, I'd like to do it. It's to be my last performance, and it's thanks to Pierre I got a place with the modern dance company.' Sylvie grinned. 'He only offered me the bigger role because he knew I'd say no and that it was the push I needed to move on…'

Arkim looked at the older man, his eyes suspiciously bright. He stood up and, bringing Sylvie with him, reached out to shake the man's hand. 'Thank you for taking care of her—and for seeing her potential.'

Now Pierre looked suspiciously emotional. Sylvie fought back her own tears and pulled away from Arkim. She had to finish getting ready. He let her go with a look that told her he'd be in the front row, waiting for her. For ever.

Just before Sylvie went out of earshot, though, she thought she heard Pierre say hopefully, 'Mr Al-Sahid, are you *sure* you don't have any dance experience…?'

EPILOGUE

THE PRIEST'S EYES widened as he took in the spectacle approaching down the aisle. There was the slim figure of the bride, dressed from head to toe in white satin and lace, her face obscured by a gauzy veil. Her arm was tucked into the arm of the young woman who was giving her away. She was blonde and very pretty, dressed in dusky pink, and—the priest frowned—very familiar. Because, he realised, he'd watched *her* come down the aisle dressed as a bride only a few short months before. To stand with the same groom.

The groom now turned to look and the priest could sense his nervous tension. He hadn't been half as jumpy the last time.

The woman in pink handed the bride over to the groom with a smile and a look that said, *Take care of her or I'll kill you.* But the priest could tell that the groom needed no such warning. He looked as if he'd kill anyone who dared to come between him and this woman, who was now stepping up to the altar, her hand firmly in his.

But then, before the priest could open his mouth to start the proceedings, the groom lifted the veil from his bride's radiant face and pushed it over her head, before pulling her close to lower his head and press a kiss to her mouth.

Eventually, after realising that this was the same woman who had so sensationally interrupted the last wedding, the priest coughed loudly. They separated, the bride's face flushed, her eyes shining.

The priest was feeling rather hot under the collar by now himself, and said testily, 'If you're quite ready, shall we proceed?'

They both looked at him and the groom smiled.
'We're ready.'

And thankfully, when the moment came for anyone to
object, there was nothing but happy silence…

* * * * *

TWINS HEIRS
TO HIS THRONE

OLIVIA GATES

Prologue

"Only family is allowed to visit Mr. Voronov, Ms. Stavros."

"At least…"

The nurse cut Kassandra's protest off, stonewalling her again. "Only family is allowed to learn information about his condition."

"But…"

Refusing to give concessions they both knew she wasn't allowed to grant, the nurse rushed away, dismissing her like everyone else had. For the past damned week. Since his accident.

The dread and desperation she'd been struggling to keep at bay rose until she felt her blood charring.

Leonid. Lying somewhere in this hospital, injured, out of reach, with her deprived of even knowing his condition. She wasn't family. She was nothing to him,

not to the rest of the world. Nobody knew of their year-
long affair.

With no one left to approach for information or reassurance, she staggered to the hectic waiting area of the
highest-ranking New York City university hospital. The
moment she slumped down on the first vacant seat, the
tears she'd been forbidding herself to shed since she'd
heard of his accident spilled right out of her soul.

Nothing could happen to him. Her vital, powerful
Leonid. She couldn't live without him, could barely remember her life before she'd first laid eyes on him three
years ago.

That night, she'd been the star model and one of the
top designers in a charity fashion show. As she'd walked
out onto the catwalk, her gaze, which normally never
focused on anyone in the audience, had been dragged
toward a point at the end of the massive space. Then another unprecedented thing had happened. She'd almost
stumbled, had stopped for endless, breathless moments,
staring at him across the distance, overwhelmed by his
sheer gorgeousness and presence.

Though tycoon gods populated her Greek-American
family, and she moved in the circles of the megarich and
powerful, Leonid was in a league of one. Not only was
he a billionaire with a sports-brand empire, but a decathlon world champion...and royalty to boot. He was
a prince of Zorya, a kingdom once part of the former
Soviet Union, and annexed to Belarus since its disin-
tegration. Though the kingdom hadn't existed in over
ninety years, he was still considered royalty in Asia and
Europe—and sports and financial royalty in the rest of
the world.

Not that any of these attributes had contributed to

his being the only man to ever get her hot and flustered with a mere look. He'd continued to scorch her with such looks for two endless years as they'd moved in the same circles. But nothing had come of it. He'd never come closer than the minimum it had taken him to keep her inflamed and in suspense, until she'd believed that the lust she'd felt blasting from him had been wishful thinking on her part.

Then had come the wedding of one of her best friends, Caliope Sarantos, to Maksim Volkov in Russia. Leonid had been one of the groom's guests. After every man but him had asked her to dance, frustrated out of her mind, she'd escaped outside to get some air. She'd found none when he'd followed her, at last, and taken away her breath completely.

She'd since relived those heart-pounding moments endless times, as he'd closed in on her, informing her that she could no longer run from him. Closing her eyes now, she could again feel his arms around her and his lips over hers as he'd dragged her into that kiss that had made her realize why she hadn't ever let another near. Because she'd been waiting for him her whole life.

But before he'd taken her on what had turned out to be a magical roller-coaster ride, he'd made his intentions clear: nothing but passion and pleasure would be on offer. And Kassandra had been perfectly okay with that. At thirty, she'd never wanted to marry, and she'd long given up on meeting a man she could want, let alone that completely. Finding Leonid had added a totally unexpected and glorious dimension to her life. Having him free from expectations had been a sure path to ecstasy and a surefire guard against disappointment.

Being with him had exhilarated and satisfied her

in ways she hadn't known existed. They'd meshed in every way, met when their hectic schedules allowed, away from the world's eyes, always starving for one another. Keeping their relationship secret from everyone, above all her conservative Greek family who'd long disapproved of her unconventional lifestyle, had made everything even more incendiary.

Then Leonid's training for his upcoming championship had intensified, and between that and running his business empire, she'd seen less and less of him. Media scrutiny had made it impossible to even visit him while he'd trained.

That was when she'd realized she was no longer content with their status quo. But before she'd had time to ponder how to demand a change in the terms of their relationship, he'd had his accident.

From the media reports that had hailed him as a hero, she'd learned that a trailer had flown over the center divider of the I-95 heading into NYC, and into the incoming traffic. Before it had managed to pulverize a car carrying a father and his daughter, Leonid had smashed into their car's side, ramming them out of the path of destruction. But the trailer had slammed into his car full force, catapulting his vehicle into a tumbling crash.

She'd almost fainted with horror at the sight of the crumpled wreck his car had become. It was a miracle he had come out alive.

Desperate to be by his side the moment she'd heard the news, the nightmare had only escalated when she hadn't been able to determine where he'd been taken. Now that she'd finally found him, she'd again been denied any information. She was being treated like the stranger everyone thought she was. He was her lover.

And the father of the baby she'd just yesterday found out she was carrying.

Suddenly, her heart boomed. Was that…?

Yes, yes it was. Ryan McFadden. Her old college friend who'd gone on to become a doctor. She'd seen him a couple of years ago, but he'd been working at another hospital at the time. Finding him here was a lifeline.

Before Ryan could express surprise at seeing her, she flung herself at him, begged him to let her see Leonid, or at least to let her know how he was.

Clearly used to dealing with frantic people, Ryan covered the hands clawing his arm. "I know that apart from his time in surgery, he's been conscious since they brought him in."

He was? And he hadn't called her?

But what if… "C-can he talk?"

"Oh, yes. None of his injuries involved vital organs, thankfully."

And he hadn't left instructions to let her in, or to even let her know how he was?

At her deepening dismay, Ryan rushed on. "He was transferred to an exclusive wing with only his medical team allowed in, to guard against media infringement. But I'll gain access to him. If he grants you permission to visit him…"

"He will." She hugged him fervently. "Thank you."

Giving her a bolstering grin, Ryan strode away.

After what felt like forever, he returned, giving her two thumbs up. She found herself flying to him, so he could take her to Leonid.

At the wing's door, Ryan stopped her. "Listen, Kass, I know it's hard for you to do in your current condition, but keep it light and short, for his sake."

Nodding, she wiped away the tears that had gathered in her eyes again. "How…how bad are his injuries?"

"I don't know details, but when he was brought in I heard he'd suffered compound fractures to both his legs."

Her heart imploded all over again. His legs.

To anyone else, it would mean months of limited mobility. To Leonid, it meant his plans for a new world record were over, who knew for how long. Maybe he'd never heal enough to compete on that elite level again. When that was a major part of his being…

Stop it. She couldn't consider worst-case scenarios. Ryan was right. She had to suppress her own anxiety. Leonid needed her support for the first time ever, and she was damned if she would fail him. Putting on a brave face, she opened the door.

He was the first thing she saw as she stepped into the exquisite suite. Only the bed with monitors surrounding it at its far end betrayed its presence in a medical facility.

Leonid, her beloved lion. He lay sprawled on his back, his perfect body swathed in a hospital gown, already diminished, both legs in full casts, arms limp at his sides, eyes closed. His almost shoulder-length hair lay tousled around a face that was unscathed, but his skin was drained of its normal vital bronze color.

Her heart lurched violently, as if to fling her across the room to him, catapulting her feet forward.

As she eagerly bent to kiss his clamped lips, he opened his eyes. Instead of the most vivid blue, they were almost black. And they slammed into her with the force of a shove. But it was what filled them that had her jackknifing up. Her nerves jangled; her balance wavered. She couldn't be reading the aversion in his expression correctly.

But what gripped his face didn't look like pain, or the effect of a drug. There was no distress or fogginess in his eyes, just clarity and…emptiness.

Telling herself it was an expected by-product of everything he'd gone through, she reached for his hand, suppressed a shudder at how cold it was. "Leonid, darling…"

He tugged his hand away, harder than necessary, from her trembling hold. "I'm fine."

Reminding herself that what she felt didn't matter, that only he did, she forced a smile. "You do look…"

His glacial look stopped her flimsy lie in its tracks. "I know how I look. But I *am* fine, considering." A beat. "I hear you kicked up quite a commotion trying to get to me."

He knew? And he hadn't told them to let her in earlier?

His expression became even more inanimate as he looked away. "I kept hoping you'd give up and just leave."

Her throat squeezed, making it nearly impossible to breathe. "I—I realize how you must feel. But there will be other championships…"

He cut her off again. "I'm sick of people placating me."

Telling herself he needed her nearness even if his current mood made him pretend he didn't, she sat down and caressed his corded forearm, trying to infuse him with her strength and let their connection bolster him. "I'm not 'people,' Leonid. I'm your woman, your lover, and you're my…"

His gaze swung to hers, this time filled with frost. "You're free to consider yourself whatever you want, but I'm certainly not your anything."

The lump in her throat grew spikes. But still convinced it was his ordeal talking, she tried again. "Leonid, darling…"

He shook off her hand, his face twisting in a snarl. "Don't you dare 'darling' me. I made my terms clear from the start. The only reason I was with you was because I thought you agreed to them."

Shocked out of her wits at his viciousness, she again told herself she must have gravely underestimated the effects of his injuries and near-death experience, that it was better to withdraw now, before he got even more worked up.

She stood up carefully so she wouldn't sway. "I only wanted to know you're okay… I shouldn't have disturbed you…"

"No, you shouldn't have. But now I'm glad you did."

"Y-you are?"

"That's the one good thing that's come out of this mess. It's giving me the chance to do what I've been trying to do."

Her heart decelerated, as if afraid to beat and let his meaning sink in. "What have you been trying to do?"

"I've been trying to end this."

Her heart stopped. "This? You mean…us?"

His stone-cold gaze slammed into her, compromising what was left of her balance. "There was never an 'us.' I thought we had an arrangement for sexual recreation, to unwind from the stresses of the pursuits that matter in our lives. But you were only pretending to abide by my terms, until I was softened enough, or maybe weakened enough, as you must believe I am now, to change the terms to what you wanted all along, weren't you? You're just another status-hunting, biological-clock-ticking woman after all, aren't you?"

Unable to breathe, she flinched away. "Please…stop…"

He pushed a button that brought him to a seated position, as if to pursue her to drive his point through her heart. "I'm not stopping until this is over, once and for all. I grabbed the opportunity of training to break it off with you naturally, but you only escalated your pursuit. And now that you think me a sitting duck, you're here to pin me down? To smother me with solicitude at my lowest ebb? You think you'll make me so grateful I'll end up offering you a commitment?"

She shook her head, shook all over, the tears she'd suppressed burning from her depths again. "You know it was never like that. Please, just calm down…"

"So now you want to make it look as if I'm raving and ranting? But you're right. I'm not calm. I'm fed up. What else can I do so you'll understand I can't bear your suffocating sweetness anymore?"

Shock seeping deeper into her marrow, she staggered back to escape his mutilating barrage. "Please… enough… I'll leave…"

"And you won't return. Ever."

His icy savagery shredded her insides. It was as if the man she loved had never existed. As if the accident had only revealed the real him, someone who relished employing cruelty to get rid of what he considered a nuisance.

She'd swayed halfway to the door before she stopped.

She couldn't bear telling him. It would only validate his accusations. But he had to know.

Teetering around, she met the baleful bleakness of his stare, and forced the admission out. "I—I'm pregnant."

Something spiked in his gaze before his thick lashes lowered, and he seemed to be contemplating something horrific.

At length, demeanor emptied of all expression, he raised his gaze to her. "Are you considering keeping it?"

Her world tilted. The Leonid she'd known would have never asked this. The real Leonid did because it was clear he'd rather she didn't.

Trying to postpone falling apart until she walked out, she choked, "I only told you because I thought you had a right to know. I guess you would have rather not known."

"Answer me."

The remaining notches of her control slipped. "Why are you asking?" she cried. "You made it clear you care nothing about what I do or about me at all."

He held her gaze, the nothingness in his eyes engulfing her.

Then he just said, "I don't."

One

Two years later...

"After his disappearance from public view over two years ago, Prince Leonid Voronov is back in the spotlight. The former decathlon world champion dropped off the radar after suffering injuries in a car crash that took him off the competitive circuits. Now the billionaire founder and CEO of Sud, named after the Slavic god of destiny and glory, one of the largest multinational corporations of sports apparel, equipment, accessories and services, could be poised to become much more. As one of three contenders for the resurrected throne of Zorya, a nation now in the final stages of seceding from Belarus, he could soon become king. With our field reporter on the scene as the former sports royalty and possible future king exited his New York headquarters..."

Kassandra fumbled for the remote, pushing every button before she managed to turn off the TV just as Leonid appeared on the screen.

But it was too late. She'd seen him. For the first time since she'd walked out of his hospital room twenty-six months ago. That had been the last time the world had seen him, too. He'd dropped off the radar completely ever since.

But he was back. Reentering the world yesterday like a meteor, making everyone gape in wonder as he hurtled out of nothingness, burning brighter than ever.

Everywhere she'd turned in the past twenty-four hours there'd been news of him. She'd avoided getting swept up in the tide of the world's curiosity about his reappearance, at least outwardly. Until now.

Now her retinas burned with the image of him striding out of his imposing Fifth Avenue headquarters. In spite of herself, she'd strained to see how much of the Leonid she'd known had survived his abrupt retirement from his life's passion.

The man she'd known had been crackling with vitality, a smile of whimsy and assurance always hovering on his lips and sparkling in the depths of his eyes. He'd perpetually looked aware of everything and everyone surrounding him, always connected and tapping in to the fabric of energy that made the world. She'd always felt as if he was always ready to break out in a run and overtake everyone as easily as he breathed. Which he'd literally done for eight years straight.

The man who'd filled the screen had appeared to be totally detached, as if he no longer was part of the world anymore. Or as if it was beneath his notice.

And there'd been another change. The stalking swagger was gone. In its place was a deliberate, almost menacing prowl. Whether this and the other changes she'd observed were sequels of the physical or psychological impact of his accident, one thing was clear, even in those fleeting moments.

This wasn't the man she'd known.

Or rather, the man she'd thought she'd known.

She'd long faced the fact that she'd known nothing of him. Not before she'd been with him, or while they'd been together, or after he'd shoved her away and vanished.

For most of that time, Kassandra had withdrawn from the world, too. After the shock of his rejection, she'd drowned in despondence as its implications and those of her pregnancy had sunk in. She'd been pathetic enough to be literally sick with worry about him, to pine for him until she'd wasted away. Until she'd almost miscarried.

That scare had finally jolted her to the one reality she'd been certain of. That she'd wanted that baby with everything in her and would never risk losing it. That day at the doctor's, she'd found out she wasn't carrying one baby, but two.

After the scare and the discovery, she'd forced everything into perspective, then had even progressed to consider what had happened a blessing. Before Leonid, she'd never thought she'd get married. She'd never considered marriage an option between them, not even when she'd wanted to demand a change in their arrangement. But she'd always wanted to be a mother. Especially after her best friends, Selene, Caliope and Naomi, had had their children. She'd known she wanted what they had, that she'd be good at it, that it would complete her life.

As he'd said, one good thing had come out of that

mess. She would be a mother without the complication of having a man around.

Not that it had been smooth sailing. Being pregnant and alone after the unbearable emotional injury of his rejection had been the hardest thing she'd ever gone through. Her family hadn't made it any easier. Their first reactions had ranged from mortification to outrage. Her mother had lamented that she'd deprived her of the traditional Greek wedding she'd planned for her from childhood, while her father had swung between wrathfully demanding the name of the bastard who'd impregnated and abandoned her to forbidding her to have a baby out of wedlock. Her siblings and other relatives had had a combination of both reactions to varying degrees, even those who'd tried to be progressive and supportive.

The only ones who'd been fully behind her from day one had been her trio of close friends. Not only had they always been there for her and vice versa, no questions asked, they'd once been in her situation. Even if *their* stories had progressed toward ecstatic endings.

But when her family realized the price for any negative stance would be never seeing her again, they'd relented. Their disappointment and misgivings had gradually melted, especially her parents', giving way to full involvement in her pregnancy and the preparation for her delivery. After the twins had arrived, they'd become everyone's favorites and considered to be the best thing that had ever happened to Kassandra. Everything had worked out for the best.

She'd reclaimed herself and her stability, had become even more successful career-wise, but most important she'd become a mother to two perfect daughters. Eva and Zoya. She'd given them both names meaning life, as they'd given *her* new life.

Then Zorya had suddenly filled the news with a declaration of its intention to reinstate the monarchy. With every rapid development, foreboding had filled her. Even when she'd had no reason to think it would make Leonid resurface.

It seemed her instincts had been correct, for here he was, back on the scene with a vengeance. In one day, he'd taken the world by storm, a mystic figure rising from the ashes of oblivion like a phoenix.

Leonid's disappearance had been the one thing left unresolved inside her. Everything she'd ever felt for or because of him had long dissipated. But wondering where he'd gone and what he'd been up to had lingered. Now explanations would be unearthed and any remaining mystique surrounding him would be gone, so she could once again resume her comforting routines, untouched by his disruption.

Leonid was a page that hadn't only been turned, but burned.

"Mama."

The tension clamping her every muscle suddenly drained at the chirping call of her eldest-by-minutes daughter, Eva. The girls had started calling her Mama two months ago. She hadn't thought it would be that big of a deal. But every time they said it, which was often now that they knew it activated her like nothing else, another surge of sheer love and indulgence flooded her. Her lips spread with delight as she strode through her spacious, cheerfully decorated Bel Air house to their room.

It had been like this for months. Eva and Zoya always woke up an hour after she put them to bed. It was

as if they loathed wasting precious playtime sleeping, or
thought they shouldn't leave her alone. But since she'd
gone back to work after their first birthday almost six
months ago, and they spent mornings with Kyria Despina, her late uncle's wife and now her nanny, she welcomed the extra time with them.

As she approached the nursery, she could hear the
girls' efforts to climb out of their cribs through the ajar
door. They were able to do it after a few trials now, but
would soon be experts at it. She debated whether to go
in or to let them complete their task and toddle their way
to her in their playroom, as she'd been doing lately. It
was why she'd been leaving the door ajar. She had child-
proofed every inch of her home six thousand ways from
Sunday after all.

Moments passed and neither toddler showed up at
the end of the corridor. Heart booming with the always-
hovering anxiety she'd learned was a permanent side effect of motherhood, she streaked inside and found both
girls standing in their crib, literally asleep on their feet.

The tenacious tots were obeying their regular programming even though their strenuously fun weekend
at Disneyland had left them wiped out.

Scooping them up, she held one in each arm in the
way she'd perfected, cooing to them, letting them know
as they nestled into her and made those sweet sleep
sounds that she'd come, as she always would, that they
hadn't missed that extra time with her they'd wanted.

Once she laid them down again, each turned to her
favorite position and resumed a deep, contented sleep.

Sighing at that tremor of acute love and gratitude
coursing through her, she walked out, closing the door

completely now that she knew they were down for the night.

The moment she exited the room, the doorbell rang.

Frowning, she remembered that the girls' play pals, Judy and Mikey, had again left behind some toys she'd found only after a thorough tidying up. It had become a ritual for Sara, their mother and her neighbor, to come by and collect her children's articles after she'd put them to bed. They usually ended up having a cup of tea to unwind together after their hectic days.

Rushing to the door, she opened it with a ready smile. "We should establish rules about allowing only in-house toys…"

Air clogged her lungs. All her nerves fired, short-circuiting her every muscle, especially her heart.

Leonid.

Right there. On her doorstep.

She'd visualized this encounter countless times in waking trances and suffocating dreams. The perverse yearning had risen time and again for him to show up, look down at her from his prodigious height with eyes full of all he'd deprived her of, and tell her everything that had happened since his accident had been a terrible dream. She'd hoped for it until hope had turned to ashes.

And now…out of the blue, he was here…

Oh, God! He is really here.

Almost unrecognizable. Yet distressingly the same.

Observations accumulated in the white noise that filled her mind, burying her. The most obvious change was his hair. The silk that had been long enough to wind around her hands in the throes of passion was now severely cropped. It still suited him. It actually suited him better, accentuating the dominance of his bone structure.

The other major difference was his body. It hadn't been a distortion of the video or his size relative to others. He *was* bigger. Broader. More heavily muscled. The leanness of the runner had been replaced by the bulk of a supreme fitness athlete.

His every feature and nuance, familiar yet radically different, felt like a knife to the heart.

But on the whole, he looked as if everything human about him had melted away, revealing a creature of polished steel beneath. Even the way he held himself seemed…inhuman. As if he was now a being of pure intellect and purpose, like a cyborg, an animate form of artificial intelligence.

An hour could have passed as she gaped up at him and he stared blankly down at her. He'd always had that power. Time had always distorted when she'd entered his orbit.

"Invite me in, Kassandra."

His bottomless voice yanked her out of the stupor she'd stumbled in.

"I will do no such thing."

"Your porch isn't the place for what I've come to say."

Her mouth dropped open at his audacity. That he could just appear on her doorstep after what he'd done to her, and without even an attempt at apology or even civility, not only demand but expect to be invited in.

"There's no place where you can say anything to me. We have absolutely nothing to say to each other."

"After the past two years, we have plenty."

"The past two years are exactly why there's nothing to be said. Even if there was, I'm not interested in hearing it."

His eyes gave her a clinical sweep, as if assessing her

response for veracity and judging it to be false. It made her loathe her weakness for him all over again.

"I don't know what you were thinking coming here like this, what you expected, but if…"

"If you're still angry, we can discuss that, too."

If? *If?*

"Are you sure you broke only your legs in that accident? Sounds as if you'd pulverized way more. Like the components that made you human."

"I do realize showing up here must have surprised you…"

"Try *appalled* and *outraged*."

He shifted, like the automaton she'd just accused him of becoming, as if moving into a different gear to counter her response. "That's why I showed up. I gathered if I called ahead, you would have been just as resistant to granting me an audience. So I decided to eliminate unnecessary steps."

"And this single step turned out to be as pointless. I'm not granting you an audience since we have zero things to discuss, so you might as well save us both the aggravation and go disappear again. Preferably forever this time."

"If you're concerned I might be here to exhume the past, rest assured I have no wish to resurrect anything between us. I'm not here for you at all. I'm here for my daughters."

Every word sank into her mind like a depth mine. Then the last ones exploded.

I'm here for my daughters.

My daughters.

The rage that detonated inside her, that he would dare say this, or even think it, almost rocked her on her feet.

Biting a tongue that had gone numb with fury, she gritted out, "Leave. Right this second."

Unperturbed, he gave a nonchalant shrug of his daunting shoulder. "I will leave after I've said what I came to say and when we've come to a preliminary understanding. Whether you approve or not, I am the father of your twin daughters, and I am here to—"

Red smeared her vision. "You won't be here much longer or I'm calling the police."

His searing blue gaze remained still, his pupils unmoving, indicating he had no emotional response to her threat and agitation. "I would advise against this. It would disrupt your neighborhood and bring you unneeded speculation and embarrassment. Not to mention you'd have to lie to the police to make them take action against me…"

"I won't be lying when I say you're here uninvited, harassing me and making fraudulent claims to *my* daughters."

"They're my daughters, too."

"Not according to the law, they're not. Nor to them or to the whole world. Any passing stranger they've ever briefly met is more to them than you are."

His formidable head inclined in agreement. "I know that being their biological father on its own means nothing. That's why I'm here, and I'm not going anywhere until I say my piece or until you indicate your willingness to negotiate further."

"What the hell do you mean, negotiate?"

"Over the twins, of course."

She gaped, unable to voice any of the million violent protests ricocheting in her skull and boiling her blood.

"Before you blast me off the face of the earth, I remind you that as their biological father, I do have a right to—"

"You have absolutely no right to Eva and Zoya. None. You relinquished any right to even think of them as yours way before they were born. You made it clear you didn't even want them to be born. You may have forgotten this, but I remember all too well."

"I freely admit I behaved extremely…inappropriately when you came to me after my accident. You can understand I was at my worst at the time."

"And you remained there for over two years?"

"I'm the first to admit it took me longer than acceptable to deal with everything."

Rage deepening at his dismissal of his abandonment of her, she seethed, "I care nothing about why you did what you did, and I'll be damned if I let you pretend it was forgivable and invade my life again. You're sure as hell never coming near my daughters."

"I'm not here seeking forgiveness. I don't waste my time, and I certainly won't waste yours pursuing the unattainable. But I'm here to acknowledge my responsibilities. Whatever I've done, I'm myself again."

"If you think *that* makes it any better, let me disabuse you of that notion. Being yourself is proof you know nothing of responsibility or accountability or even common courtesy and basic humanity."

Instead of stonewalling her again, he just nodded impassively. "You're right. My old self was nothing to be proud of. But the past couple of years changed me, and the man I am today is capable of at least being fully responsible and accountable, and resolved to take on his duties."

"Good for 'him.' And as long as 'he' takes his resolutions away from my family, I wish 'him' the best of luck."

"The thing is, your family is also mine. The twins are the primary duty I'm determined to take on."

She fought harder against the screams gathering at the back of her throat. "That would have been a commendable sentiment if they needed anything from you. Which they don't. And they never will. You've done your part and can now feel proud of yourself when you leave and never come back."

His azure gaze remained unwavering. "I do understand your alarm and rejection. But even if the past was rife with pain, I'm certain everything happened for a reason. Why else would I have twin girls, and now be called on to take the mantle of responsibility in the land of the twin goddesses?"

This made zero sense to her, leaving her speechless again.

Realizing she had no ready comeback, he straightened even more, seeming to grow bigger, more rigid and imposing. "I won't push for this audience tonight. I'll give you some time. Not long but enough to let it all sink in."

And a croak finally escaped her. "Let what sink in?"

"The fact that I am back to stay. That nothing will stop me from claiming my throne, and my heirs."

Two

Kassandra's entranced gaze followed Leonid as he descended the stairs of her porch, then crossed her driveway in measured strides to his parked car, a gleaming black Jaguar that looked like an extension of him.

Without looking back, he got in and drove away slowly, almost soundlessly. After the car disappeared, she remained staring at the void it had left, her mind a debris field in the wake of the havoc he'd wreaked.

Had he really been here? Or had she conjured him after seeing him earlier in that news spot? Had it all been a dream, a nightmare?

But if it had been, why couldn't she wake up, as she always did whenever his phantasm came to suffocate her at night? As much as she would have preferred an actual breakdown to him being here, she knew. He had been here. And he would be back. His last words rang in her ears in an unending loop.

Nothing will stop me from claiming my throne, and my heirs.

Legs trembling with futile rage and incipient dread, she closed the door. But it was no use. She didn't feel she'd successfully shut him out, or that she was safe anymore inside her home.

As she shakily made her way inside, one thing he'd said buzzed into her brain like an electric drill.

Why else would I have twin girls, and now be called on to take the mantle of responsibility in the land of the twin goddesses?

What had *that* meant?

She had to find out. Her first priority was to understand the motive behind his sudden interest in Eva and Zoya. Knowledge would be her best weapon against his unexpected incursion.

Still unsteady, she got some water and headed to her home office. She sat down at her desk and opened her laptop. After staring at the search engine numbly for several moments, she typed in *Zorya.*

For hours, she read all there was to read about the mythology behind that name and the land that wielded it.

It turned out Zorya was a plural name, incorporating the two guardian goddesses, Zarya and Zvezda, who represented the morning and evening stars. According to Slavic mythology, they were charged through eternity with guarding the doomsday hound, Simargi, lest he consumed the constellation Ursa Minor. They were also responsible for opening and closing the gates for the sun. Zorya, the former—and soon to be again—kingdom was said to be the only place where both stars could be perpetually seen on all clear nights. Its coat of arms depicted the blonde and dark-haired goddesses holding up stars. Though the goddesses were twins, they were quite literally night and day.

Just like her girls.

Eva had taken after her, Zoya after Leonid.

So this was what he'd meant. He considered this a sign he was meant to have both the throne and the girls.

And she'd seen it in his eyes.

He would make it all come true.

After an oppressive night spent pondering every possible distressing outcome of Leonid's reappearance, Kassandra struggled to perform her morning rituals with the girls before leaving them with Kyria Despina and heading to work. Not that she expected to get any work done, but she needed to be away from them. She'd be damned if she'd let Leonid poison their moods, too.

In half an hour, she was in her personal office on the second floor of her company, looking out the window at downtown LA but only seeing the chaos inside her mind.

What disturbed her most was that she hadn't come up with a plan of action in case Leonid *did* pursue his objectives. Which she had no doubt he would.

"I'm sorry, Kass, I tried to…"

Even before her PA's cut-short exclamation, Kassandra's senses had gone haywire.

Swinging around, hoping she was wrong but certain she wasn't, the air was still knocked out of her at the sight of him. Leonid.

He filled her doorway, dwarfing her delicate PA. Mindy was looking up at him with a mixture of mortification and all-out awe.

Kassandra understood. How she did. A god walking the earth wouldn't have looked as imposing and over-powering.

Their gazes collided, almost making her stumble against the plate glass of her wall-to-wall window. It was him who relinquished their visual lock first to look down at Mindy, who resembled a tiny herbivore that found itself in the crosshairs of a great feline.

"I apologize for overriding you, Ms. Levine. Ms. Stavros will fully understand that there was nothing you could have done to stop me. You can rest assured she'll chastise me appropriately for such high-handed behavior."

Gathering what she could of her wits, Kassandra tore her gaze off him and focused on her assistant. "It's okay, Mindy." Mindy looked back as if in a trance. Kassandra sighed. "You can go now, thanks. I'll let you know if I decide to call security."

With a ghost of a smile, Leonid stepped aside to allow Mindy to stumble out. "She won't. You can drop the red alert."

The moment the door closed, Leonid turned his focus to her. It was a good thing she'd moved to her desk so she could mask her own unsteadiness and feign a con-frontational pose.

"Don't be so sure, Leonid. My private security isn't the police and won't care if you broke any laws. The one thing that will matter to them is that I don't want you here."

"How do you know you don't want me here before you hear what I have to say?"

"I already heard it, and I not only would rather you spare me an encore, but I also wish there was some cosmic erase button to have it unsaid. If that's all you're here to say, I will cut everything short and have you removed."

"You don't need to bother. I will remove myself once I've done what I've come to do. And it's not to reiterate what I said last night. I'm here to state my terms."

"This time I will spare myself the aggravation of reacting to your terminal audacity. The answer to anything you have to say is no anyway."

"If you remember anything about me, you should know I do not take no for an answer. Now, more than ever, I won't."

Every nerve jangled as he approached, as if to emphasize that there was no stopping his invasion of her life. With every step, she felt as if he was planting a foothold that she wouldn't be able to uproot.

"My terms are the following—I want to become Eva and Zoya's father, in name and in reality. You will give me full access to them, effective immediately. You won't try to do anything to put them off me, or to put off the procedure of declaring me as their father. I will have them bear my name before the coronation. It is in just over a month's time."

Feeling she'd taken a deep breath underwater, her protest came out a gurgle. "Now, look here…"

He continued as if she hadn't interrupted. "As their mother, you can and will of course dictate your own terms and I will meet every one."

She shook her head, as if to shake off a punch to the face. "My only term is that you get the hell out of my life. You stayed out of it for two years. And that is where I demand you stay."

His face remained as hard as stone. "That is not an option. Anything else is negotiable."

"Nothing else is worth negotiating. I won't let you walk into my life, making those insane demands and expecting me to fall in with your timetable."

"I'm not walking into your life, but my daughters'."

Knowing he was powerful enough to do whatever he wished, her mind burned rubber trying to latch on to an alternative to anger or defiance to hold him at bay. Those had gotten her nowhere. Continuing to challenge him head-on would only make him more intractable. If that was even possible.

Her only way out could be to negotiate a less-damaging deal. Something other than the takeover he was bent on.

"Listen, Leonid, let's take a time-out and rewind to the beginning. Let's say, for whatever reasons, you wish to acknowledge the girls as your daughters. I can, if necessary, live with that. We can come to an agreement where you can be...included. That doesn't mean you have to be in their lives. You haven't been since before they were born and they *are* totally fine without a father. I'm not saying this to be vindictive, or because of our personal history. It's just a fact. Also consider the effort and time commitment that goes into being a parent. You can't possibly want to be a father, especially now that you're on the verge of becoming a king. You literally have far better and more important things to do."

He waited until she finished her speech, then demolished it with that vacant look. "There's nothing better or more important than becoming the father my daughters deserve. And need. No matter how adequate you are as a single parent."

Her rage seethed again. "You know nothing of how

adequate I am as a single parent, or what my daughters need."

"Like you take exception to my opinion of your life, I would appreciate you not passing judgment on mine. Being a father is exactly what I now want to be. Becoming a king only makes it more imperative I claim all my responsibilities with the utmost commitment."

"Fine, I won't presume to know what you want. I'll keep to my side of things. I need no commitment from you."

"Then, I will change your mind about what you need."

The way he'd said that… The way his gaze dropped to envelop her body before returning stonily to hers…

Did…did he mean something personal? Intimate…?

Before her thoughts caught fire, he disabused her of any ridiculous notion this was in any way about her. "No matter how strong, resourceful and successful you are, and though you've been coping exceptionally well being both a mother and a businesswoman, you will experience a huge improvement in the quality of your and the twins' lives when you have me as a fully committed partner in raising them."

She shook her head, feeling punch-drunk. "You come here…and just dictate to me…about the quality of my—"

"I came here, your territory still, but a less personal one, after your reaction to my showing up on your doorstep last night, because I thought you might feel less cornered here. It's also why I didn't have you brought to me."

That made her locate her faltering verbal skills with a vengeance. "Oh, how considerate of you. I should be grateful you didn't have me dragged to your territory, and instead chose to invade my professional space, getting my whole company abuzz with speculation, launching a hundred rumors, undermining me and generally disrupting my life?"

"I figured whatever I did, it wouldn't meet with your approval, so I did what I thought least threatening to you."

"Great rationalization, but…"

He continued speaking as if he was playing back a recording. "Starting tomorrow, I expect to be allowed in to see my daughters without resistance or ill will. I would very much prefer, for their sake and yours, if we do this on the most amicable terms possible. I hope you won't force me to resort to more drastic measures."

Having finished the speech he'd come to deliver, he turned and walked away. She could only stare after him, feeling as if she were sinking in quicksand.

Before he stepped out the door, he paused, turned. "I'll come by your house a couple of hours before the twins' bedtime."

Kassandra waited until he closed the door after him, then collapsed on her chair like a demolished building.

As everything seeped into her mind and its full impact registered, she reeled harder. Not only with the disaster in progress she could see spiraling out of control, but with how much of a stranger he'd become.

Those first hellish months after he'd kicked her out of his life, she'd been anguished by how his feelings for her had withered, then reversed. But with him so distant and clinical now, she finally believed he'd never felt anything in the first place. She didn't count at all to him, neither in the past nor in the future he had so carefully planned for them all.

The future she couldn't let come to pass.

She couldn't let this automaton near her daughters. His new programming might dictate it, but if there was anyone Eva and Zoya were better off without it was him.

But she couldn't stop him. He had the legal and personal clout to do what he wanted. She didn't have a leg to stand on, let alone a weapon to fight him off with.

But…that wasn't true. She did have weapons.

At least her best friends did. Selene, Caliope and Naomi had access to three of the most lethal weapons in the world. Their husbands. Each man was at least as powerful as Leonid was, if not more. He'd have no chance against their combined might.

Fumbling for her cell phone, she called Selene. As soon as she answered, she told her she was adding another call to Caliope, then repeated the process with her, adding another to Naomi, too, merging the calls.

The three women, once they were part of a four-way conference call with her, chorused anxiously, "What's wrong?"

"Everything," she choked. "I need Aristedes. And Maksim. And Andreas."

Six hours later, Kassandra looked around her office, her cheeks burning.

Her friends hadn't even asked her why she'd needed their husbands. After making sure she wasn't in any immediate danger, they'd all hung up. She'd expected them to get their husbands to call. They'd actually sent them over in person.

And here they all were. Aside from Leonid, the three most imposing and hard-hitting men she'd ever seen.

According to Aristedes's concise explanation, as soon as their wives had told them to drop everything and fly to her side, they'd each jumped on their jets and crossed the continent from New York to her. And they didn't seem bothered in the least by being ordered around like that to do her bidding…or rather their wives'. If she didn't love her friends so completely, she would have envied them having such unique men wrapping themselves so lovingly around their every inch. Their fairytale relationships had always emphasized how abysmal her situation with Leonid was.

Loath to impose on them more than absolutely necessary, she rushed to recount her dilemma.

But as she talked, the men looked much like three souls who'd walked into the middle of a foreign movie, clearly lost.

"Hold on a minute." That was Aristedes, shipping magnate and Selene's, her oldest friend's, husband. It had been through Selene's marriage to him that all of them had become best friends. Caliope being Aristedes's sister and Maksim's wife, and Naomi, Selene's sister-in-law and Andreas's wife. He sat forward with a spectacular frown marring his impossibly handsome face. "You're talking about Leonid Voronov?"

She'd confided in her best friends about Leonid when she'd told them of her pregnancy. Since they told their husbands everything, she'd assumed they'd told them. But it was clear, if Aristedes's reaction was any indication, that her friends considered her secrets sacrosanct.

It meant this meeting just got more agonizingly embarrassing, as she had to explain everything from the start.

After she did, Maksim, the one who used to have a personal relationship with Leonid, stood up, rage distorting his equally impressive face. "You mean you told him you were pregnant, and he didn't only kick you out of his life, but implied he'd prefer you terminated your pregnancy?" As she nodded warily, he growled, "*I'm* dealing with that scum of the earth. He's a fellow Russian and it's on me you met him at all. I invited the louse to my wedding."

"Settle down, Maksim." That was Andreas, Aristedes's younger brother and the most dangerous of the lot. "If there's punishment to be doled out, we're all getting a piece of him." He swung his icy gaze to Kassandra, making her almost regret recruiting their help. Andreas had once been involved in organized crime, and remained as lethal, if not more so, now that he'd gone legit. "But this guy says he's back to atone for his mistakes. Any reason to believe he doesn't mean it?"

"Oh, I believe he means it," she groaned. "As much as I believe the road to hell for me and the girls is paved with his good intentions."

Aristedes pursed his lips, propping an elbow on a knee. "But if he's owning up to his responsibilities, perhaps you should give him some leeway, in a limited wait-and-see fashion, without making any promises or changes in your lives?" Aristedes looked first at Maksim and then Andreas. "I think I speak for all of us when I say we were all once in more or less his same position, and we would have given anything for a second chance with the women we love and the children we fathered, or in Andreas's case, the child he was named guardian of."

Maksim's dark fury ebbed as he considered his brother-in-law's point of view. "Now that you put it that way, I can't even think what would have become of me if Caliope hadn't given me a second chance. One I didn't think I deserved and she had every right not to give me at the time."

Heart contracting at the turn in conversation, she choked out, "None of your situations was anything like mine with him."

Maksim winced. "Now that I think of it, I almost did the same thing to Caliope. I, too, abandoned her when I knew she was pregnant."

"It's not the same at all," she protested. Maksim had had the best of reasons for walking away. His father had been abusive. He'd feared he'd inherited his proclivities and had been terrified of hurting his vulnerable loved ones. "You thought you were protecting her and your baby."

Maksim sat back down, gaze gentling. "Maybe he has a valid reason, too? At least one he believed to be valid?"

Feeling cornered, she realized she couldn't get them on board without telling them *everything*. What he'd said to her in the past, and in the present, that she'd never meant a thing to him, that he was only back now for his "heirs" because he believed it was his duty and destiny, now that he was going to be king of the land of the two goddesses.

By the time she'd finished, all three men's faces were closed with so much wrath, she felt anxious about the extreme measures they might take in dealing with Leonid. In spite of everything, she found herself worried for him.

As she tried to think of a way to mitigate their outrage and their consequent actions, Maksim heaved up to his feet again, clearly bringing this meeting to an end.

"Don't worry about Leonid anymore, Kassandra," Maksim said. "I'll deal with him."

Following him up, Andreas corrected, "*We'll* deal with him."

Troubled by the respectively murderous and predatory looks in the two men's eyes, she turned to Aristedes, her oldest acquaintance among them, and ironically, since he was generally known as the devil, the one who scared her the least.

Sensing her anxiety, Aristedes gave her shoulder a bolstering squeeze. "I'll keep those two in check, and resolve this situation with the least damage possible."

As they each gave her pecks on the cheek, she was torn between being alarmed she'd let loose those hounds of hell on Leonid, and being relieved she'd soon have this nightmare over with.

By the time she leaned back on the door, panting as if she'd run a mile, she decided she should be only relieved.

Leonid had only himself to blame for whatever they did to him. If he wanted to escape those men's punishment, he should have settled for being a king, away from her and the girls.

"Yes, I understand," Kassandra said to Maksim.

She'd said almost the same thing to Andreas and Aristedes before him, just to end the calls with them, too.

For she certainly didn't understand at all. How the three predators, who'd left her office out for blood yesterday, had each come back to her less than a day later, purring a totally different tune. That of urging her to give Leonid a chance.

How had he managed to get to them all? What had he said to have them so wholeheartedly on his side?

But why was she even wondering? Didn't she already know how irresistible he could be when he put his mind to it? He'd worked the three men over but good. It was clear that their initial thoughts about having once been in Leonid's shoes and in need of clemency were back in full force. Anything she said now would be her intolerant word against Leonid's penitent one.

Putting down her cell phone, she pressed her fingers against burning eyelids.

So. She was out of options. There was no way she could stop Leonid herself. All she could do now was make sure he didn't turn their lives upside down.

Suddenly, another bolt of agitation zapped her.

The bell. Leonid. He was here. *Exactly* two hours before Eva and Zoya's bedtime, as promised.

She wouldn't even wonder how he knew at what time she put them to bed. She had a sick feeling he knew everything about her life with the girls over the past two years. And that there was far more to this whole thing than he was letting on.

Yet she could do nothing but play along, and see what exactly he wanted, and where this would lead.

Crossing from her home office past the living room, she signaled to Kyria Despina that she'd get the door.

She took her time, but Leonid didn't ring again. Stopping at the door, she could almost feel him on the other side, silently telling her he'd wait out her reluctance and wear down her resistance.

She pressed her forehead against the cool mahogany, gathering her wits and stamina. Then she straightened, filled her lungs with much-needed air and opened the door.

As always, nothing prepared her for laying eyes on him. Every time she ever had, an invisible hand wrapped around her heart and squeezed. Her senses ignited at his nearness, each time more than the time before.

Standing like a monolith on her doorstep, he was swathed in a slate-gray coat, a suit of the same color and a shirt as vivid as his eyes, radiating that inescapable magnetism that had snared her even before she'd laid eyes on him. Blood rushed to her head before flooding her body in scalding torrents.

And she cursed him, and herself, all over again. For him to still have this choke hold over her senses, when he didn't even try, didn't even want to, was the epitome of unfairness. But life was exactly that. As was he. Both did what they wanted to her, her approval irrelevant, her will overruled.

So she'd let him take his invasion to the next level. She only hoped after getting a dose of domesticity, he'd retreat to a nominal position in the girls' lives, which she could deal with without too much damage to herself.

Certain she was opening the door to a new dimension of heartache, she said, "Come in, Leonid."

Three

Leonid crossed Kassandra's threshold.

For a second, before she retreated, he almost touched her. It was the last thing he wanted to do. The one thing he couldn't bear.

If he could have done any of this without seeing her at all, he would have jumped at the chance. But it was out of the question. If he wanted his daughters, she had to be involved. Closely. Suffocatingly.

Mercifully, she'd been averse, keeping him at the distance he needed to remain, in every way. But right now he'd miscalculated his movement, and she hadn't receded fast enough. A second after he'd advanced, their clothes had whispered off each other. Just being near her caused the slow burn in his every nerve to spark into a scalding sizzle.

Before he could judge if the fleeting contact had disturbed her, too, she turned and strode away, leaving him to follow in her wake, a path filled with her sense-warping warmth and scent.

The glance she threw at him over her shoulder spoke volumes, making it even harder to breathe. The surface layer was annoyance that he'd showed up at all, and at the exact time he'd said he would. Then there was resignation that she couldn't turn him away. Beneath that lay another sort of anger he couldn't fathom. And at the core of it all, there was…a threat.

They both knew he wielded power that would give him access to the twins no matter what she did. She'd tried to recruit allies to stop him. She'd picked them well. But after he'd neutralized their threat, she must have realized there was no point in prolonging a losing fight. Being the pragmatic businesswoman that she was, she'd wasted no more time coming to the best course of action. Let him have what he wanted. For now. Until she studied the situation further and decided if she could adjust her trajectory.

But he also knew she wouldn't use the twins in her struggle against him, not even for a cause as vital as keeping him out of their lives. She'd never do anything to disturb them. So her threat didn't have any real power behind it.

Still, he couldn't let her suspect how anxious he was, how uncertain of his ability to conduct himself in any acceptable manner. For what constituted acceptable with eighteen-month-old toddlers? He knew far more about astrophysics and the latest trends in nail polish than about interacting with children. And it was almost beyond him to keep his upheaval in check.

But he had to pretend equanimity as he followed her

deeper into her exquisite home, the oasis of color, gaiety and contentment she'd built for her—for *their*—daughters, taking him to meet them for the first time. After he'd spent every day since they'd been born obsessing over their every detail.

Then she turned a corner into a great room equipped with a short plastic fence, decorative and sturdy, and just enough to keep little feet from wandering without detracting from the wide-open, welcoming feel of what must be every child's dream wonderland. And it was empty.

"Darling…"

Kassandra's breathy endearment made him stop. Suspended him in time.

She used to call him darling. Not always, just when she'd been incoherent with pleasure, which had been very frequently. The last time she'd said it to him he'd swiped at her proverbial jugular and severed it.

For heart-thudding moments, he didn't understand why she'd said it now, once, then again. Then he realized.

From what turned out to be an elaborate playhouse blended into the periphery of the room, a gleaming dark head peeked out of a tiny doorway, followed by an equally shiny golden one. She held out her arms and squeaks of glee issued from both girls as they competed to crawl out first, struggling to their feet as soon as they cleared the entrance. Two young cats, reflecting the girls' colorings, a black Angora and a golden Abyssinian, slinked out after them.

His heart contracted painfully. They were fast. He knew from his surveillance of them that their toddling had been improving every day. They were now almost running to their mother.

Kassandra went down on her haunches, preparing to receive them in her arms. But her descent only exposed him fully, bringing him into their line of vision. Their eyes rounded and their momentum slowed, both stopping just short of throwing themselves into her arms.

Knowing she was now no longer the focus of her girls' attention, Kassandra slowly stood up and slid him a sideways glance. Among the messages there was a challenge. He might have gotten what he'd demanded, but now she'd evaluate his performance and decide her consequent actions.

If he'd had any words left in him, he would have asked her to allow him a grace period without passing judgment. He'd fail her every test right now. Being face-to-face with those two tiny entities at last felt like a hurricane was uprooting everything inside him.

Before he could find his next breath, the twins rushed to stand behind Kassandra as she turned to him, each clinging to one endless jeans-clad leg and peeking up at him from the safety of their mother's barricade.

In contrast to their caution, the cats approached him, sniffing the air. Seeming to decide he didn't smell of danger, they neared him in degrees until they brushed against legs that felt as if they had grown roots. His throat tightened more as he bent without conscious thought to stroke them and receive head butts and arched backs. Then, seeming to consider this enough welcome for now, they sauntered away and jumped on shelves by the wall to watch the developing scene and groom themselves.

Unfolding with difficulty to his full height again, he found Kassandra with the miniatures of both of them staring at him. Avoiding her eyes, he focused on the girls'. Emerald eyes like Kassandra's and azure ones like his dominated faces that had occupied his thoughts since they'd been born. Two tiny sets of dewy rose lips rounded in questioning suspense.

"Vy oba...ideal'no."

It was only when chubby arms wrapped around their mother's legs tighter and those sparkling eyes widened more that he realized he'd spoken. Saying the one thing that filled his being. They were both perfect.

He waited. For Kassandra to say something. To introduce him. But she was silent, continuing to add the weight of her watchful gaze to theirs.

His mind crowded with everything he'd longed to do since they'd taken their first breaths. To swoop down and scoop them up in his arms was foremost among those urges.

But he knew there was no way this would be welcomed by Eva and Zoya, who were hanging on his every breath, bracing for his every move. They probably hadn't scurried back into their hiding place only because their mother was showing no signs of alarm, calmly facing him as if he was no threat, or at least one she was capable of protecting them from. It was as if they'd never seen anyone like him. Which was strange. He knew for a fact that their world was filled with big and imposing-looking men. The three men Kassandra had sent after him, and Kassandra's male relatives.

So why did he feel such total surprise emanating from them? Could it be they instinctively felt the bond between them?

Unable to decide, he emptied his mind, let his instincts take over. He trusted them now far more than he trusted his messed-up emotions and stalled logic.

He moved away from the trio training all their senses on him, circumventing them in a wide circle that took him to the playhouse the girls had exited. His aching gaze took in the evidence of their play session and of Kassandra's doting care. The strewn toys, coloring books and crayons, the half-built castle, the half-eaten finger foods and half-finished smoothies.

He'd missed all that. Everything, from their first day. He hadn't held them or comforted them or cleaned or served them or played with them or put them to bed. Kassandra had been alone in doing all that. Would any of them ever accept him into their lives, let him into their routines? Or even let him in any way at all? When he didn't deserve to be let in?

Feeling all eyes in the room on him, he went down on his knees, one of the hardest moves for him now. As he felt their surprise spike, he started to gather the toys and books.

Without looking back, so he'd give the girls respite from his focus, give them a sense of control and security, he started to order everything they'd knocked off onto the lushly carpeted floor on the low, sturdy plastic table. Out of the corner of his eyes, he saw Kassandra moving toward the long couch that dominated the opposite side of the space, with both girls still flocking around her legs, their gazes clinging to him.

Sampling one of the thin pineapple spears that were laid out on a cartoon-character tray among other healthy and colorful foods, he said, "That's very tasty. Can I have some more? I haven't eaten all day."

In his peripheral vision he could see the girls exchanging a glance, as if they understood his words and knew they were meant for them. Then they both looked up to their mother, as if seeking her permission to react. He stole a glance at her, found her giving them an exquisite smile. A special one he'd never seen, no doubt reserved only for them. Then she nodded, and they simultaneously let go of her legs and advanced toward him tentatively.

As they approached, he sat down on the ground, another challenging move, putting himself more at their level. This appeared to reassure them even more as their steps picked up speed. He pointed at a blunt skewer of cheese, cucumbers and strawberries, making direct eye contact with one girl, then the other. "Can I have that?"

The girls stopped on the other side of the table, eyes full of questions and curiosity. Then after what seemed to be serious consideration, Eva, the mini-Kassandra, reached out and grabbed the skewer in her dimpled hand…and leaned over to give it to him. Zoya, who'd held back, clearly more reserved like he was, took her cue from her older-by-ten-minutes sister, and repeated her action.

Throat closing, Leonid looked down on those two skewers, offered by the girls he'd fathered and hadn't been there for, until this moment. They were his life's biggest reward. And responsibility.

With hands that almost trembled out of control, he reached out and took both offerings at the same time. "That's very kind of you to share your snacks with me. *Spasiba.*"

As if both recognized he'd just said a word in a language different from the one they'd been hearing and processing since birth, they looked at him questioningly.

"That is Russian. In English it means 'thank you.'" Then he repeated it a few times. "*Spasiba*…thank you."

Eyes gleaming at recognizing thank-you and clearly

making the connection between the two words, looking triumphant, Eva parroted him, "Patheba...thakyoo."

His heart thundered, its chambers just about melting at Eva's adorable lisp.

And that was before Zoya delivered the second punch of a one-two combo as she enthused, "Aseba...ankoo."

Before he could gather his wits, Eva picked up another skewer and proceeded to nibble at it, looking up at him, as if encouraging him to eat. Zoya at once did the same. When he didn't follow suit immediately, Zoya reached out and pushed his hand up, urging him to partake of their offering.

He raised the food to lips that had gone numb, unable to taste anything as he chewed. Swallowing was an even harder feat, pushing the food past the blockage in his throat. All the time he could feel Kassandra's gaze on him, scorching layers off his inflamed skin. It took what was left of his control not to turn to her, ask for her intervention.

But she didn't intervene. She didn't make a single move, as if she was trying to blend into the background to make them all forget she was there.

While that was what he'd asked her to do, now that he had the girls' full attention and interest, he would have given anything for her to dilute their focus. Which was pathetic, since this was the opportunity he'd badgered her for, what he'd been dreaming of for so long.

Inching closer now that they literally had him eating out of their hands, the two girls started handing him their favorite toys as more evidence of their acceptance, naming each one to show off their knowledge.

It became clear the second time they waited after naming something that they were waiting for him to provide the Russian equivalent. And so it started, a game of translation.

The Russian word they loved the most was the one for *doll*. They both kept giggling and reiterating, *"Kukla... kukla!"*

They then moved on to testing him. One of them presented a coloring book and the other the crayons. When he colored a pony in a color scheme that was different from all the examples in the colored pages, they got more excited, and tried to emulate him in other books. After a while, dissatisfied with their own results compared to his impeccable ones, they reverted to the name-and-translate game.

Suddenly Eva seemed to realize she'd forgotten a vital issue. Then she pointed at herself and said, with a great sense of importance, "Eva."

Not to be outdone, Zoya immediately pointed to herself and said, "Zoya."

Then they both pointed at him, demanding he reciprocated the introduction.

He struggled to make his voice sound as normal as possible. "Leonid."

Not expecting them to be able to say such an abrupt name, they both surprised him by repeating accurately. "Leonid."

Swallowing past the growing pain in his throat, he felt the urge to complete the introduction, even when he knew they wouldn't understand the significance. *"Ya tvoy Papa.* This is also in Russian. It means 'I'm your father.'"

Feeling terminally stupid for speaking in such long sentences, and in two languages, too, when they at most only knew a few dozen words in English and maybe also in Greek, he smiled shakily, waiting for their attempt at the word.

This time they almost gave him a heart attack.

Getting to the heart of what he'd said, they both pointed at him and chorused, "Papa."

By now, Kassandra had gotten used to her heart's erratic function. Since Leonid had appeared on her doorstep, it had been stopping periodically before it stampeded out of control in compensation.

From the moment the girls hadn't run to welcome him as they did anyone who entered their home with her, she'd known.

They'd at once realized he wasn't just a friend or an acquaintance, but someone on a totally different level from anyone they'd seen before. Far more important than even Kassandra's family. Someone on par in importance to them with Kassandra herself.

Kassandra had bated her breath, dreading that Leonid would botch this, knowing from their instant recognition of his significance to them that it would hurt them. But Leonid had proceeded to provide one shock after another, everything he'd done and said sensitive and inventive. He'd followed no known path with the girls, and soon had them so engrossed in his presence, they'd forgotten to include her.

What had at first rattled her with chagrin and jealousy had gradually become incredibly emotional, as she watched something she'd always dreamed of but never believed would come to pass. The girls with their father, the only other person who should love them as completely as she did, behaving as if they'd known him

all their lives. She couldn't have interacted with the trio
had they asked.

Hours could have passed since they'd become im-
mersed in one another. She'd lost track of self and time
as she'd watched them. She'd even lost sight of her memories of the past and everything that had led to this situation. All she could see was her girls delighting in their
father, and him appearing to delight in them back.

And then came their fervent proclamation that he was
their "papa." Just as her stalled heart sputtered into a
forced restart, Leonid stopped it again, saying so deeply
and gently, "Yes, you brilliant girls, I'm your papa."

Before she could draw a breath, before she passed
out and spoiled everything, the girls threw themselves
at Leonid.

A surprised laugh issued from him as he hugged tight
the small, robust bodies of her daughters. Kassandra
reeled, trying to make sense of this.

She could only think the girls had always realized
other kids had papas while they didn't. Then they had
seen Leonid and simply recognized him as their own
papa. Once they'd approved him through their own brand
of testing, and he'd validated their belief, they'd accepted
him in their own unique way.

No, they'd more than accepted him. They'd claimed
him.

It was funny she'd think of this specific term, what
he'd already used about them. But nothing else described
what was happening in front of her eyes. It was a claiming. Declared and accepted, on both sides.

Leonid, who'd been doing everything right to put the
girls at ease, from body language to expression to tone of
voice, now rumbled with unfettered laughter as the girls

attacked him with their zeal. But what he did next had her slumping back against the couch in a nerveless mass.

He sprawled flat on the ground, letting the girls prowl all over his great body. Thrilled by his action and the invitation it afforded them, they drowned him in hugs and kisses before launching into examining every inch of his very-different-to-hers body and clothes, acquainting themselves with the details of that new powerful entity they'd made their own.

Then she started to worry again. That this would still end badly, that Leonid would be appalled or fed up by their level of enthusiasm and attention. Would he decide he'd made a mistake coming near them and withdraw? Then she scolded herself for worrying. She should hope for that to happen so he'd leave, let them return to their contented status quo. As for the girls' psyches, they were young enough that if he disappeared now, no matter his impact on them, they'd soon forget him.

Just as she'd come to this conclusion and was pulling herself up to intervene, he looked up at her from his flat-on-his-back position on the floor, covered in toddler limbs and laughter, with a grin she'd never seen on his face before.

"Any help here?"

Okay, that didn't look like the face or attitude of a man who was regretting anything. His call for help seemed to be part of the game, maybe his way of including her in it.

Forcing her feet to function, she approached the merry mass on the ground made up of the beings who mattered most to her. Leonid once, and her girls forever.

She stopped over them, her lips quirking involuntarily at the infectious gaiety at her feet.

"What help does the unstoppable future king require?"

Eyes that had haunted her for the past five years flashed azure merriment up at her, the stiff stranger of the first two encounters gone. "I have no idea. But I can tell you that if you don't do something and they don't let me up, you may have to let me spend the night right here on the ground."

"Take heart. In a worst-case scenario, they'll keep you there until they fall asleep. Once they do, I can get them off you and you'll be free to get up."

Eva pulled his face toward her to show him another toy, a miniature lion. After he told her it was *lev* and she dutifully repeated her own version of the word, Zoya pointed to her cat Shadow, who'd come to join the fun with Goldie. After he told her both the word for *cat* and their breeds in Russian and she did the same, he swung his gaze back to Kassandra.

"Do they usually use you as a mattress or am I getting special treatment?"

"You're the one who made yourself one. But then, I'm nowhere as big and comfortable as you are."

She knew that from extensive experience. Going to sleep spread over him after long, depleting nights of excruciating pleasure.

Thankfully, he wasn't the man he'd been. That man would have latched on to that comment, teasing and provoking her. That man had been raging wildfire, while this new man was a bottomless ocean. His unexpected behavior with the girls was just another depth to him she hadn't thought could exist.

He broke eye contact when the quartet of girls and cats demanded his attention. Then one duo was climbing off him only for the other to climb on. With only the cats to contend with, he sat up, with them roaming his lap. Eva and Zoya called him to another part of their playroom, and he looked at her again, seeming to find some trouble rising to his feet.

Her heart gave a sick lurch. It appeared his injuries had never fully healed, as she'd once feared. He hid it well, but now that she was looking for evidence of it, she could see his gait wasn't normal. After sitting on the floor for so long, it was harder for him to conceal.

Not that she was about to feel bad for him. He'd never needed or even tolerated her empathy. The best she could be was civil, and it was only for the girls' sake.

After he followed the girls to their sandbox in the adjoining enclosed terrace, he looked back at her.

"So you enlisted The Savage Sarantoses and the Big Bad Russian Wolf's help to…deal with me."

Not knowing what to make of his attitude, if he was angry about her siccing them on him, or taunting her about her effort's failure, she arched an eyebrow. "Should've saved my breath. They turned out to be neither savage nor big and bad. You neutralized them as if by magic."

His lips twitched as he kneeled where the girls indicated at the edge of their sandbox, clearly unconcerned by the damages his handmade suit would certainly suffer.

With a shovel in hand, he slanted her another glance that set her insides quivering. "No spells were involved. But I applaud your effort. It was a very sound strategy. That it didn't work doesn't make it any less so."

Was he…entertained by her struggle against him? Teasing her about its futility? If he was, it was a more understated form of provocation than anything he'd ever exposed her to. And whether she was more susceptible now, or he was more potent, it was far more…unsettling.

"Join me in building a castle for our princesses?"

For several long seconds she could only stare at him. It had just dawned on her.

Eva and Zoya were actual princesses.

When one daunting eyebrow prodded a response from her, she made herself move. She came down on her knees far enough from him to keep her agitation at manageable levels, but close enough to work with him, if need be. The girls flitted between them, handing them tools, then climbing inside to make their own little molds as she and Leonid started collaborating on something intricate.

Trying to focus on what they were doing, she said, "I've never attempted anything elaborate, since their appreciation takes the form of destructive admiration. Then they're crestfallen when my creations crumble."

He shrugged those endless shoulders. "I'll try to make them realize how to preserve it, but if they level it or it's time to replace it, I'll make them understand I'll build them another. In time, I'll teach them how to build their own."

"You seem certain you can get all this across."

"I am. They're extremely intelligent and very receptive."

She almost blurted out that while they were indeed intelligent, she'd only seen this level of receptiveness directed at him. But she held her tongue. The admission would only complicate matters further.

From then on, there were stretches of silence between them as they worked, with Leonid taking the lead, creating a castle that looked like a miniature of a real one in every detail. Then, true to his conviction, he curbed the girls' appetite for destruction, encouraging them to expend their excitement in making flower and animal molds to surround it.

Then it was time for the girls' dinner, and he pounced on the chance to feed them, insisting on handling the soup part. He managed to complete the task with even less mess than she usually did. And he'd turned the whole thing into another game, pointing to kitchen articles with each spoonful, getting names in English, correcting and translating what the girls didn't know. The girls competed to provide answers, and get Papa's attention and appreciation.

An hour after dinner, two hours after their bedtime, the girls lost the fight to prolong their wakefulness to remain with Leonid. And they again did something unprecedented. Instead of turning to her, they went to him, arms raised, demanding to be picked up. At once complying, he gathered them in a secure hold, where they both promptly dozed off.

Without a word, she led him to the nursery, where he placed them, one after the other, in their cribs. She stood with bated breath, waiting to see what he'd do next as he remained standing over them, his eyes wells of mystery in the dimness.

At length, he bent and kissed them. Each girl gave a contented gurgle at his tender caress before assuming her favorite sleeping position.

Straightening, he led the way out of the room, then headed straight for the door. He didn't look her way until he'd opened it and stepped outside.

"Thank you for tonight."

With that, he turned and slowly walked down the steps. In a minute, he climbed into his car and drove away.

Closing the door, she automatically armed her security system, turned off the lights and headed to her room.

It was only after she'd gone through her nighttime routine and slipped into bed that she let it all crash on her. Everything he'd said and done all through the evening, everything about him.

Nothing made sense anymore.

For two years, the last thing she'd wanted was Leonid near again. Now, she was forced to face the truth.

She'd wanted him to come near tonight. So much that his pointed avoidance of her had felt like a knife in her gut. It still twisted there now.

She might have been able to handle it if she'd had any hope he would stay away from her altogether. But after this incredible first meeting between him and her...his... *their* daughters, she knew there was no hope for that.

Leonid would be in their lives. If everything she'd felt from him toward the girls tonight was real, and she couldn't doubt it was, she could no longer deny him, or them, that reality.

Which meant he would be in her life, too, maybe even forever.

The only man she'd ever wanted.

When he'd long stopped wanting her.

Four

A rewind button had yanked Kassandra back into her worst days—only with an even darker twist. For this time, it wasn't Leonid discarding her, leaving her desolate and then disappearing. He was now planning to stay around forever.

After she'd thought she'd been cured of any emotions she'd felt for him, she'd woken up today with her resolve to stay neutral pulverized. It had taken him exactly four hours last night to show her how self-deluding she'd been, how susceptible to his magic she remained. How pathetic she was.

If only he'd lived up to her expectations, had been the unfeeling entity he'd been with her, with the girls. It would have given her ammunition to stop him coming near them again. It would have saved her from stumbling back into the abyss of longing. But he'd been…perfect.

Worse, they'd *all* been perfect together. It had been like she'd watched scattered pieces of a vital whole finally clicking together. She of all people recognized and realized the significance of what she'd witnessed. Her very self had been built around a tight relationship with her father as much as her mother. She knew exactly how wonderful such a relationship could be, how essential a loving paternal influence was. And just by being wonderful with the girls, he'd snatched away her last weapon against him, that of his potential disruptiveness to the girls' psyches and lives. Now she had to let him be the girls' father, as she could no longer doubt he truly wanted to be. She had to let the girls have him as the other half of their world, while trying to preserve her sanity with him around. But now that she'd discovered her unilateral fixation with him had never weakened, she had no idea how she'd achieve that.

Dwelling on that terrible fate had to be postponed. Now she had work to do, far more than usual since she hadn't worked a lick since he'd reappeared. The summer line wouldn't approve itself and put itself into production.

Walking into her design house's new headquarters, she concentrated on being attentive and friendly with each and every one of her employees. She'd done it wholeheartedly so many times she could do it on autopilot now.

Reaching her office, she thought she'd escaped with her turmoil undetected, anxious to plunge into work, the only thing that would ameliorate it. But the moment she entered, she knew salvaging her schedule would have to wait. Right there in her sitting area were three of the people her staff knew to let into her private space without question.

Her best friends.

It should have been a shock to find them here, as dropping by her office on a whim was no longer something they did with her on the other side of the continent. It should have at least been a surprise. It was neither. Seemed Leonid had depleted her reserves for shock and surprise for the foreseeable future.

Bracing herself for what she knew would come, she plastered a smile back onto her face.

Selene was the first to rise to her feet, despite being the most heavily pregnant of them all. Yes, they were all pregnant. Again. Selene and Caliope were now on their third babies. Naomi, too, even if it was only her second biological one, with her first child being her late sister's.

After kissing and hugging her, Caliope and Naomi let Selene, as her oldest friend, lead the interrogation.

Selene shot her opening salvo, getting to the point at once. "What exactly is going on with Leonid?"

Kassandra's lips twisted. "You tell me. Your husbands are the ones who have answers."

Something that resembled annoyance tinged Selene's deep blue eyes. "They haven't been forthcoming, for the first time since the days they were closed-off icebergs. Each aggravating man only said it's for the best that you and Leonid work this out alone."

Kassandra flopped down on an armchair across from the couch where they sat facing her like a tribunal. "And you clearly disagree and that's why you're here."

"You scared the hell out of us when you called!" Caliope exclaimed. "We've never heard you so distressed. And when it comes to you, even our men's words aren't enough."

Naomi nodded, looking as concerned. "We had to get the final word from the source."

Kassandra huffed a mirthless chuckle. "And that's me?"

Selene's gaze softened and hardened at once. "You don't call for the big guns—who clearly didn't fire a shot—then answer our messages with more vagueness, and expect us to sit back and wait."

Kassandra squeezed her friend's hand fondly. "Vagueness is an achievement in my situation, since I'm as in the dark as any of you. Your men left this office promising me they'd leash Leonid away from me and the girls. Then each called me to cajole me into giving him a full and fair chance."

"A chance at what exactly?" Caliope sat forward, reaching for Kassandra's other hand, her smooth brow furrowing. "This is the part no one is clear on."

"At being the girls' father."

"Is that all he wants a chance at?" Naomi probed.

"Yes."

"You mean he didn't…?"

"Didn't ask for a second chance with me? No. According to him, he never wanted a first one."

"He said that?" Selene's gaze hardened to granite.

Knowing she was sealing Leonid's coffin where her friends were concerned, Kassandra sighed. "What amounted to that. When he was breaking it off, he made it clear he considered our liaison only sexual entertainment and he'd had enough long before he told me to get the hell away from him when I failed to take a hint."

Caliope, the softest heart among them, piped up. "He was at his worst when he said that. It could have been his frustration and anger at the whole world talking."

Exactly what Kassandra had thought at first. She

shrugged. "He disappeared for over two years. Too long to be at your worst."

"Maybe he realized the gravity of his mistake," Naomi offered, her newest bestie, the one clearly trying to keep emotions out of the equation. "But didn't know how to fix it."

"You mean he stayed away because he couldn't face me?" Kassandra huffed. "This is a man who has faced tens of thousands of people on the athletic field, the rest of the world when he was in the rabid spotlight of the media, not to mention the sharks of business he wrestled under the table on a regular basis. He squared off with *your* unstoppable predators and turned them into purring pussycats."

Selene exhaled heavily. "This last bit *is* something we're all beyond perplexed about. We thought only us and the kids could do this to our Triumvirate."

Kassandra gave a there-you-go gesture. "Since you know your endless power over your men, you can measure Leonid's."

Caliope's eyes shone. "Maybe *that's* your answer, since when it comes to us, our men's rules are inverted. Maybe it's the same with Leonid. The man who can make the world heel could be powerless when it comes to you."

That was the last straw. She had to put a stop to her friends' efforts to give her hope that her story could end as happily as theirs.

Sitting forward, she let any lightness she'd painted on drain from her face. "Okay, let me make one thing clear. My situation with Leonid is nothing like yours with your men. Those men were more than ninety percent in love with you when each left you or let you go or did whatever they did. Leonid never felt a thing for me, and he'd been itching to move on. He would have done so without the accident, but it gave him the opportunity to do it abruptly." And viciously. She'd never been able to bring herself to tell them just how viciously. "Now he's only back for the girls. He made this far more than clear."

Echoes of her hard tone and words rang in the silence that stretched afterward. A myriad of emotions streaked across the women's faces, each according to her character and relationship with Kassandra. What they shared seemed to be mortification, empathy…and fury.

Selene was first to gather her wits enough to ask another question. "Are you even considering giving him that chance?"

"Since I don't have a way of keeping him away, and since my reasons for wanting to do so no longer apply, I don't have the choice not to."

"So you're feeling forced into it." Naomi chewed her lip thoughtfully. "Would you have considered his return and his demand more favorably if he was back for you, too?"

"No." Kassandra paused, then had to add, "Not at first."

And *that* told them everything. That after everything he'd put her through, she still wanted him. That after her initial anger and rejection, her buried emotions had resurfaced, and she now wished he wanted her, too. Which he didn't.

Clearly realizing all that, anger set Selene's exquisite features on fire. "I don't care how he got Aris and the others on his side, I'll make them wipe him off the face of the earth. And if they don't, we three can still do a lot of damage on our own."

Caliope nodded. "You know we would do anything for you."

"Even if it means standing against your husbands?"

The three women's exclamations were simultaneous.

"Just say the word."

"Without hesitation."

"Hell, yeah."

Kassandra's eyes stung, a smile shaking her lips. "And I love you, too. But that won't be necessary. Everything changed, literally overnight. He came to visit the girls last night. And no matter what I feel, how he was with them, how they were with him, makes him deserve that full and fair chance he's convinced your men he should get."

"That man crushed your heart," Selene ground out. "And I have a feeling if he invades your life again to be with the girls, he'll hurt you again."

Kassandra sighed. "And I can't do anything about it. It's not his or the girls' fault he feels nothing for me."

Caliope threw her hands up in the air. "You should have moved on when you got the chance. *All* those chances. There were at least three men who could have been perfect for you! And they're all still waiting for your slightest signal."

"Could any of you have moved on when you were estranged from your own member of the Triumvirate?" The three women winced, lips twisting in concession. "Exactly. Same here."

"But if you know nothing would come out of it because you're feeling this way about the wrong man…"

"The problem is he isn't the wrong man," Kassandra said, interrupting Naomi. "Apart from his treatment of me and his lack of feelings for me, he remains everything I admire in a man. And though I hate it and wish it wasn't so, the fact remains that no one withstands the comparison to him in my eyes."

"But you can't just resign yourself to being miserable like this!" Selene exclaimed, her face reddening.

"As long as Eva and Zoya are happy, it's a price I have to pay. You would pay the same price and more for your kids."

"How do you know he'll make them happy?" Selene countered.

"Surely you can't tell from one meeting!" Calliope added.

Kassandra sighed. "Regretfully for me, and fortunately for them, I can. You have to see them together to understand."

Selene wouldn't give up that easily. "What if, once the novelty wears off, he becomes the son of a bitch he was with you with them?"

Kassandra set her teeth. "If he even breathes wrong around them, I'll rip out his jugular."

"That's our Kassandra!" Selene's approval was ferocious.

Caliope's face fell. "So the only thing that can make you hate him is if there's a hint of mistreatment or neglect toward Eva and Zoya. Which you don't seem to think would happen."

Naomi was as crestfallen. "*And* we can't even wish it."

"Can't we?" Selene growled protectively. "They wouldn't lose anything if he exited their lives as he entered it. They were perfectly fine without him after all."

"They were." Kassandra exhaled heavily. "But with him in their lives, they could be far more than fine. You really have to—"

"See them together to understand?" Caliope sighed. "Not really. If his effect on the girls is anything like Maksim's effect on our children, I know exactly what you're talking about."

Selene looked more horrified by the second. "So you're stuck with him? You have to suffer forever and we have to watch it and be unable to do anything about it?"

Wanting to alleviate her friend's distress on her behalf and end this debate once and for all, Kassandra decided to placate them. "Who knows? Maybe I'm just experiencing echoes of what I once felt for him, and being around him again will show me I've blown everything out of proportion, allowing me to move on at last. Maybe this will turn out to be a blessing in disguise after all."

The three women looked at her, then exchanged a look among themselves before finally nodding. It was evident they hoped so with all their hearts. But even though they let her change the subject, she knew they didn't believe this was even in the realm of possibility.

Not for a second.

At last, Selene rose to her feet, prompting the others to do so, too. As Kassandra followed suit, Selene waddled toward her, holding out both hands to pull her into a tight hug. At least as tight as her burgeoning belly allowed.

Drawing back, Selene's dark blue eyes were almost grim. "If you change your mind and you need help getting rid of him, I'll do anything."

"Ditto," the other two chorused.

Choking on a cry, Kassandra surged to envelop them in a group hug, thanking the fates for them.

Pulling back, she gave her friends a wobbly smile. "Next time I know who to run to when I need impenetrable barriers against unstoppable missiles. What was I thinking asking for your men's help when I have you?"

Selene's features relaxed into a mischievous smile. "As long as you've learned your mistake. Right, ladies?"

Caliope and Naomi expressed their enthusiastic agreement, and the meeting that had started out tense ended on a merry note.

As merry as a breather in the ongoing drama that had become her life could be.

After her friends left her office, Kassandra struggled to get any work done. But as all the lightheartedness and optimism their love and support had brought her started to dissipate, she was dragged back into the bottomless well of worries and what-ifs.

Though she'd planned to stay at work hours longer, and she'd only done a fraction of what she'd set out to do, she gave up. At least at home she wouldn't have to make decisions that had millions of dollars and hundreds of jobs riding on them. Decisions she was starting to doubt she'd be able to make again.

Half an hour later, as she entered her home, a shroud of premonition descended around her heart. Though there was no car parked outside, and there were no sounds coming from inside, all her senses rioted with certainty.

Leonid was in there. She could scent him in the air, sense his presence in her every cell.

Trying to curb her stampeding reactions, she leaned on the wall, only to feel it tilt beneath her. Struggling with the wave of dizziness, she shrugged out of her suddenly suffocating coat, was trying to hang it when Kyria

Despina came rushing toward her, her expression the very definition of awe.

"Kassandra, dearest, I'm so glad you're home early!" The woman's voice buzzed with excitement as she took Kassandra's coat and hung it in the foyer's closet. "Prince Voronov has been here for two hours."

So he was here. Seemed her extrasensory abilities where he was concerned remained infallible.

Dark brown eyes gleaming with curiosity and pleasure, Despina linked their arms as she hurried Kassandra to the living room. "He came thinking you'd be back home at your usual time. The girls were beside themselves with delight to see him."

Feeling her legs about to buckle as the quietly prattling Despina led her to him, her mind was a battlefield of suspense, aversion and resignation. Confusion soon took precedence over the absolute silence emanating from the living room.

Then they reached it and it all made sense.

At the end of the room, Leonid was propped up against the playhouse. The girls were asleep on top of him. The cats were also snoozing, one on his legs, the other against his thigh.

"He played with them nonstop, games I'm sure he invented just for them," Despina whispered. "The darlings laughed and bounced around like I've never seen them. Then about fifteen minutes before you arrived, they climbed on his lap and turned off. The dear man made them comfortable, even crooned what must be a Russian nursery rhyme."

They'd slept on top of him. They hadn't fallen asleep in her arms since they were six months old.

"He hasn't moved or made a sound since, even when

I assured him nothing would wake them up again. You should go save him before he cramps something." Despina patted her on the back. "Now, since you're home and he's here to help you put the girls to bed, I may yet catch a bit of the ladies' poker night I had to miss to stay late tonight."

As if from the depths of a dream, Kassandra thought she nodded her agreement. Then everything fell off her radar but the sight Leonid and the girls made, a majestic lion with his cubs curled in slumber over him, totally content and secure in their father's presence and protection.

His eyes remained closed, but she knew he wasn't asleep. She could sense it. He was savoring the texture of the new experience, soaking in the girls' feel and closeness and trust. She also knew he was aware of her standing there. Like her, he'd always had an uncanny ability to sense her presence. She'd once thought he'd been so attuned to her, he felt her before he had reason to think she was near. That had been before she'd realized she'd never been special or even worthwhile to him.

Swallowing the lump that seemed to have taken permanent residence in her throat, she approached the pile. He let her come within less than a foot of them before he opened his eyes, connecting with hers, and almost compromised her precarious balance. Then he lowered his gaze to the girls in his arms again.

Forcing air into her shut-down lungs, she attempted nonchalance. "You can flip the girls in the air and they still wouldn't wake. Not now anyway. They only wake up around an hour after I put them in bed."

"Did they wake up last night after I left?"

"No."

She'd told herself they hadn't because he'd kept them way beyond their bedtime. But apart from logic, another theory explained the unusual occurrence. She believed that they always woke up out of some sense of uncertainty. But after he'd appeared, and they'd sensed his intention of being here to stay, that anxiety that woke them up was gone.

She exhaled. "My point is, you can move if you want."

"I don't want. There's no place I'd rather be."

What felt like acid welled behind her eyes. "Well, though you do look as if you make them very comfortable, I don't think they should start considering you a substitute for their bed."

His lips twisted as he kept gazing at the shiny heads nestled into his chest. "Though I would fully welcome that, I can appreciate the repercussions of such a development."

Sighing as he secured them both, he sat up. She again almost winced at the difficulty he had in adjusting his position, of rising to his feet. It had nothing to do with the girls being in his arms, since their weight had to be negligible to him. That knot behind her sternum, the same one that had formed when she'd realized the extent of his injuries and their consequences, tightened to an ache again.

Taking her eyes off him, so she wouldn't focus on his stiff gait and the fact that he was looking everywhere but at her, she led the way to the nursery, her mind racing.

Though the competition circuits were certainly out, had it been possible for him to practice his sports on any level? Being extremely fit but bulkier than before, it was clear he maintained his fitness with exercise that didn't rely on the speed and agility of his former specialties. So how much did he resent being forced to relinquish what he'd considered the epitome of his personal achievement? How much did he miss what had once been the main pillar of his existence?

Giving herself the mental equivalent of a smack upside the head as they put the girls in the cribs, she reminded herself how pointless and pathetic it was to wonder. Whatever his trials to adjust his path, and whatever he'd suffered or now felt about it all was none of her concern. He'd made that clear in the past. He was making it clearer now. This was all about Eva and Zoya. Beyond what she represented to them, she, and anything she thought and felt, mattered nothing to him.

As they exited the room, he finally looked at her. "I hope it's not your habit to sleep as soon as they do. I have a few things I need to discuss with you."

She stifled the urge to hiss that she'd lost the habit of sleeping altogether since him, that she had to exhaust herself on a daily basis only so she could turn off and hope for the oppressive silence and darkness of dreamlessness.

Managing to reach her living room without blasting his thick hide off, she sat down carefully instead of flinging herself on the couch. She also refrained from hurling a remote at him as he remained towering over her.

"How would you like to go about declaring me the girls' father?"

Blinking, her mind emptied. Had she heard him right? He wasn't dictating a course of action, but asking her preference?

Suddenly her blood tumbled in a boil. "How about you spare me the pretense that you care about what I want?"

"I do care. As Eva's and Zoya's mother you are—"

"Entitled to dictate my own terms. Yeah, I heard it the first time. And I already told you, my only term is to have the life I built for myself and the girls. But since this isn't going to happen, just do what you wish, and don't bother pretending that my preferences matter."

Those winged eyebrows she'd once luxuriated in tracing with fingertips and lips knotted as he seemed to examine every fiber in her lush carpet. The way he kept avoiding making eye contact with her at crucial moments was driving her up the wall.

He finally exhaled, his gaze once again on her and maddening her with its opacity. "That first night I came, I had to drive it home that I wasn't taking *go away* for an answer. But ever since I met the twins, and we interacted as their parents, many things have changed. I do want this arrangement to work for you, not only for them."

She never thought he'd say those words—and he actually seemed to mean them. It made everything even worse. Anger was her only defense against him, her last shield. If he made her let that go, what would become of her?

But that was a consideration for another time. For the rest of her lifetime. Now she had to give him an answer.

The truth was the only thing she had. "I haven't given any thought to how I'll break the news about you being the girls' father. I suppose I'll just tell the people I care about. Anyone else doesn't matter. Even if I am a public figure, I'm not in the spotlight nearly as much as you and my importance to the media is nothing compared to yours. You're also the one with a kingdom to consider in your public statements from now on. I'll leave it up to you to announce this as you see fit."

"In that case, I'll move on to the major reason I came." Suddenly, she wished she hadn't resented his lack of eye contact as his gaze transfixed hers, paralyzing her with a bolt of blue lightning. And that was before he said, "I came to ask you to marry me."

Five

"Marry you?"

Kassandra wasn't even sure she'd said that out loud. From the way her voice sounded, as if issuing from beneath a ton of rubble, maybe it was in her head. All of it. Including what he'd just said, so earnestly, asking her to…

"*Marry* you?"

This time she was sure she'd said it, judging by the urgency that surged in his eyes.

"I'm only asking this for Eva and Zoya."

Of course. None of it was or had ever been for her.

"It's the only way to secure their legitimacy."

"Legitimacy…" She parroted him again, her shock deepening.

She hadn't even thought of this aspect of things before. But he had said he'd *claim* them, and she'd vaguely realized he meant giving them his name. Yet the significance of that, that it would make them "legitimate," had escaped her. Now, knowing the implications, it felt so...offensive.

Fury flooded her, drowning her shock. "Legitimacy is an outdated concept. My daughters aren't and won't ever be defined or even affected by it. In this day and age, it's not a stigma anymore to have children out of wedlock." Suddenly, the room spun, making her slouch back on the couch. "And will you quit looming over me like this?"

He sat down at once, still careful to keep her at arm's length. His eyes took on a hypnotic edge, as if trying to compel her to succumb to his demand.

"Legitimacy wouldn't have mattered to me if I was anyone else. I would have become their father in all ways that matter and left it up to you when or if you let them have my name on official papers. But as you just pointed out, with my future role, bowing to the social and political mores of my kingdom has become imperative. Eva and Zoya aren't only my daughters, they're my heirs. They have to carry my name."

"And marrying me is the only way to have them carry your name instead of mine?"

"Not instead, with yours. I want them to have both our family names. They would be Eva and Zoya Stavros Voronov."

Her heart kicked her ribs so hard she almost keeled over. Those names. They sounded so...right.

But still... "We can do that without getting—"

He shook his majestic head, cutting her off.

"Getting married is also an unquestionable necessity. Consider that not even in recent history has the president of a progressive country had children out of wedlock. It isn't even a possibility for a king in Zorya. Our marriage isn't only a must for social acceptance and political stability in this case, it's also the only guarantee of the twins' rights and privileges as my heirs."

"*And* the restrictions and responsibilities, maybe even dangers. Even if you prove to be a great father to them, and that would be in their best interests, being heirs to the precarious throne of such a stuck-in-time kingdom isn't."

The azure of his eyes darkened to cobalt. "While your worries are logical, I pledge I will protect them from anything in this world, starting with any drawbacks of their title and my position. It's part of the reason why I'm taking the crown in Zorya. To see to it that it retains its useful traditions, but discards any backward practices. It must fully join the modern world where it matters on every level, be it social or political or economical. I will make Zorya a land I would be proud to raise our daughters in."

His fervent convictions and assured intentions seeped into her thoughts, suppressing misgivings and painting an enchanted future she'd certainly want for Eva and Zoya. Then his last words sank in with a thud, jogging her out of the trance.

"You mean you expect us to move there?"

"It's the only way for me to be in the twins' lives constantly, but it's you who'll dictate how to divide your time between Zorya and the United States. Of course, it would be ideal if you move to Zorya now."

She gaped at him, feeling as if she was watching a movie playing so fast everything had ceased to make sense.

"If you fear being in Zorya would interrupt the normal flow of your life, don't. I'll have every resource constantly at your disposal. You'll be able to travel anywhere in the world at a moment's notice. And when you have to be somewhere for any length of time, or even return here for an extended period, of course the girls will be with you, and I'll arrange my affairs so that I may join you as much as possible."

His assurances again underlined the extent of his power and wealth. But only one thing kept screeching like a siren in her mind.

"You expect me—us—to live with you in Zorya, and when we're back here…?"

His hand rose in a placating gesture. "You'll have your own quarters in the royal palace with the twins. I will visit them there according to the schedule you set, or have them with me within the parameters you approve. When you return here for visits or for longer stretches and I join you, I will arrange my own accommodations. I'm ready to provide all of these terms and any others you specify in a legally binding format."

This nightmare was getting darker with his every word. Though he was insisting she'd retain control of all decisions that shaped the girls' daily lives and futures, his every promise made her more heartsick. It all reinforced the simple fact that they were adversaries forced to come to an understanding. He'd progressed from bulldozing her to drawing legal lines to protect her share of rights, and no doubt his own. The only interactions they would have would be with the girls and through them, with them playing the part of polite partners in their presence and in front of others. Or would he ask her to play the part of a loving bride in front of the latter…?

Then he answered her uncertainties. "You have nothing to worry about when it comes to my presence in your life. In front of the girls, you need only keep doing what you have. In front of others, it's accepted for royal couples to be reserved in public, so you don't need to worry about putting on a facade of intimacy. In both private and public, our relationship would remain as it is."

In other words, nonexistent.

"I expect you'll have your own demands and modifications and I intend to fully accommodate your every wish."

Feeling the quicksand dragging her down into its depths even harder, she choked out, "You're talking as if I've already accepted, as if the only thing to do now is vet out details."

He stilled. "Why wouldn't you accept?"

"Why?" She huffed in incredulity. "Are you for real? This is my *life* you're turning upside down."

"I gave you my pledge your life won't be affected in any adverse way, but only enhanced. You'd be a queen…"

The word *queen* went off like a gong inside her head.

She found herself on her feet, staring down at him, shaking from head to toe. "You think I care about that title or could even want it? I never wanted *anything* but to raise my daughters in privacy and peace, and with you in our lives, there will never be either of those things ever again!"

He rose slowly to his feet, and even in her distress her muscles contracted in empathy at the difficulty he found in rising from her too-low couch. As he straightened, his balance wavered, and for seconds, he came so close, heat flaring from his body, in his eyes, and she thought he'd reach for her...touch her. All her nerves tangled, firing in unison.

Then he regained his stability and stepped back, leaving a cold draft in his wake. The blaze in his eyes was gone, as if she'd imagined it. Perhaps she had.

Turning, he walked to the opposite armchair, picked up the coat he'd draped over its back and put it on in measured movements. Then he came back to her where she stood ramrod tense.

He stopped even farther away than usual, his expression as impassive as ever. "I know this is too much to take in, so I'll leave you to think. I didn't expect you to give me an answer right away."

Trying to suppress her tremors, she failed to stem the shaking in her voice. "Are you even expecting any answer but yes? Would you accept any other answer?"

The perfect mask that had replaced his previously animated face became even harder to read. "Any other answer would be no. So no, I can't accept that."

Her lips twisted in bitterness. "So why are you pretending you'd give me time to think? Think of what? How to say yes? Or to reach the conclusion that it's pointless to say anything at all from now on, since you'll always do what you want anyway, using the girls' and your kingdom's best interests to silence my protests and misgivings and make me fall in line with your plans?"

His eyes dimmed even more. And she realized.

What she'd thought was meticulous impassiveness was something else altogether. Bleakness.

This epiphany silenced the rest of the tirade that had been brewing inside her. His despondency dug into her chest, snatching at her heart.

Was he distraught because he had to tie himself to

her? Was he feeling as hopeless as she was, sacrificing his freedom and what remained of his ambitions of pursuing what fulfilled *him*, for the girls' and his kingdom's sakes? Would being near her, to have access to his daughters, be too harsh a sentence to bear?

When she couldn't say anything more, he exhaled. "I didn't expect you'd welcome my proposition, but I do want you to take some time to think. Contrary to what you believe, there's a lot to consider, practical details that you need to sort out, questions you need to ask, demands you will want to make. I regret this is unavoidable but I pledge I will comply with any measures you specify to make everything as painless as possible."

As painless as possible.

The words ricocheted in Kassandra's head until she felt they'd pulped her brain.

He didn't even realize he'd already done the most painful thing he could have. Proposing marriage, for everyone's and everything's sake but hers.

What made it all worse was admitting she would have jumped at his proposal if there'd been any hope they could have rekindled a fraction of what they'd once had. His offer would have even been somewhat acceptable, for all other considerations, if he wasn't as averse to her being a constant part of his life.

But with both of them feeling they'd be imprisoned for life, there was no way she could accept.

Forcing her focus back on him, now that she saw through his expressionlessness, it battered her heart to feel the gloom gripping his stance, the dejection that blasted from him.

She struggled not to sound as shredded as she felt. "Even if I believe you'd keep every word, and though I understand the need for this step, I *can't* say yes. But I have an alternative. We can tell everyone we are already married but estranged, and that we decided to get back together. I would play my part for as long as you need to 'claim' the girls to fulfill your kingdom's traditional requirements, solving all your problems without creating a bigger one...for both of us."

His gaze dropped to the ground he now seemed to find so fascinating. Then without even a nod, he turned away.

Feeling him recede, she stared into nothingness, struggling to stem the bottled-up misery he'd stirred up.

The moment she heard him closing the front door with the softest thud, she broke down, let the storm overtake her.

Each time he'd gone to Kassandra, Leonid had sent away his driver and bodyguards.

The latter, fellow patriotic Zoryans who'd volunteered for the job and considered guarding him a sacred duty and ultimate honor, had always objected. There was no doubt in their minds anymore he'd become king, and his safety was no longer his personal concern, but a matter of national security and what the future of their kingdom rested on.

He'd still been adamant. He hadn't wanted anyone to know about Kassandra and the girls until he'd resolved everything with her. As he'd gone to her tonight bent on doing.

He'd parked miles away. He still found it hard to walk, always ended up in varying levels of discomfort after being on his feet and moving for a considerable length of time. And that was exactly what he'd needed tonight.

He'd needed the pain of exertion to dissipate some of the storm frying his system, the bite of cold to chill a measure of the inferno that had been raging higher every time he'd seen her.

He'd arrived at her home earlier to find the girls with only their nanny. Kassandra had picked today to swerve from her unchanging timetable to catch up on the schedule he'd disrupted.

He'd been dismayed by her absence for about ten seconds. Then the girls had come running to meet him, making him glad instead that she wasn't there. He could have some time with them alone, savoring their unbridled eagerness for his presence without the searing upheaval of hers.

The nanny, who'd instantly recognized him from the constant media exposure he'd been suffering recently, had delightedly invited him in. Though it had been to his advantage, he'd at first been disturbed she had without consulting the lady of the house. However, his thorough research, which he subjected anyone who came near Kassandra and the twins to, had indicated she was impeccably trustworthy. Though in her case, Kassandra's implicit trust in her would have been enough to put his mind at ease.

But besides judging someone in his exalted position to be safe, the lady must have taken one look at him with Zoya and worked out with 100 percent certainty who he really was. Yet even if she'd let him in for all the right reasons, he still needed to have an aside with her about never assuming anything, always checking first with Kassandra. He had zero tolerance when it came to the security of this household.

Only one thing had made him lenient with her. The

girls' fervent welcome. He still couldn't believe its extent. It had been as if they'd been waiting for him all their lives. As he had been for them.

The only pursuit that had kept him sane had been monitoring their every breath, along with Kassandra's, in those endless months after his accident. He hadn't allowed himself to imagine, let alone hope, for anything like that. He hadn't even tried to extrapolate his own reactions to seeing and feeling them in the flesh.

To have them respond so…miraculously to him had been beyond belief. As for his own feelings, they were… beyond description. At times, beyond endurance. From that moment they'd so unbelievably given him their trust, he'd known. He wouldn't be able to live another day without either of them.

Tonight had been further proof the magic he'd experienced with them the night before hadn't been a fluke. By the time they'd climbed over him and fallen asleep in perfect synchronicity, as if they shared an off switch and had telepathically agreed to flip it simultaneously, he'd been beyond enchanted and overwhelmed. Then he'd felt Kassandra's approach. Long before he heard her garage door opening.

He'd been suddenly loath to face her, yet unable to do anything but clasp the girls and wait for her to initiate the confrontation. His heart now thundered in his chest like it had then. In tandem, his hip joint started to throb with a red-hot warning that he'd pay the price of these miles in shoes unfit for walking for days to come.

He would welcome the physical discomfort. If only it were potent enough to counter his emotional turmoil. But no amount of pain could do so.

He'd expected being near Kassandra again would be

hard. Horrible, even. It wasn't. It was unbearable. With every passing moment in her company, the corrosive longing he'd suffered since he'd pushed her out of his life had been escalating to all-consuming need.

After her initial rejection, she'd been evidently shocked at the twins' reaction to him, and at his handling of them. She'd surrendered to the necessity of putting up with him, for her—their—daughters' sake. But it was clear this was the extent of her concession. She wanted nothing more to do with him.

As she shouldn't. Even if she weren't so averse, he'd be the one to keep away. As he'd been exhausting himself trying to. Then he'd asked her to marry him.

He'd thought he'd braced himself for any response. But her horror had been so deep, so total, he'd scrambled to pledge every guarantee, offer every incentive to make the union worth her while. But it had only made things worse. Her desperation as she'd offered to lie to the whole world for as long as it took had made clear the depth of her abhorrence of him. Of anything that bound her to him, even a marriage in name only. Even if it made her a queen.

But how could he have expected any less? After the way he'd rejected and abandoned her? In the cruelest way, at the worst time?

And he'd only come back to add more injuries. He'd forced his way back into the life she'd struggled long and hard to make into an oasis of peace and stability for their daughters.

That moment she'd stepped back and told him to come into her home, into her life, he'd felt as if he'd been taken in after being out in the freezing cold forever. But that had only been an illusion. As it should be.

He didn't want her to take him back.

But though her extreme reaction to his proposal had proved she never would accept him, even for show, she hadn't moved on. She hadn't found another man to bless. She hadn't even let any near. During his painstaking surveillance, many, many men had approached her. Three had offered her everything a man could offer a woman, starting with their hearts. It pained him to admit it, but she wouldn't have gone wrong accepting any of them.

So why hadn't she?

Had she been so busy with work and the twins she'd had nothing left to offer, or want? Or was he responsible for her being unable to move on, for becoming defensive and distant, even with the people closest to her, when she'd been the most emotionally generous and approachable person he'd had the undeserved privilege to know?

Pushing her away after the accident, he'd known he'd hurt her. But he'd thought her pain would soon become anger, helping her get over it. Over him. He hadn't suspected she'd linger in perpetual purgatory. Like he had.

But if she couldn't move on, then he hadn't just hurt her. He'd crippled her. And this had only one explanation: her feelings for him had been much deeper than he'd suspected.

Now she'd distilled her entire existence to being the twins' mother. Even her business seemed to have become a means to financial independence for their sake. Success and achievement were by-products, not the goals they'd once been.

He couldn't bear to think he'd damaged her irrevocably. That just by being near her again, he'd cause her even more harm.

But…maybe he didn't have to. Maybe instead of being

a disruption to her peace and a threat to her psyche, he could instead be her support, her ally. Maybe in time, he could heal her. Enough so she could move on, find love and build a life for herself, as a woman, with another man.

Even if it would finish him off.

When Leonid arrived at Kassandra's office the next day, her PA didn't intercept him, only fumblingly gave her boss the heads-up she'd failed to give her at his first incursion.

This time Kassandra opened her office door herself, and stepped silently aside to let him in, making no eye contact.

As she turned to him, he began at once. "I know how inconvenient and unfair to you the whole situation is, and if it was up to me, I'd accept your alternative proposition without qualifications. I will, as soon as I make certain it would satisfy the twins' legal legitimacy requirements in my kingdom."

Pushing a swathe of hair that seemed to encompass a thousand golden hues behind her ear, her emerald gaze regarded him steadily. "Then, it's as good as accepted. I'm sure you can achieve anything."

He tried not to wince at the cold resentment in her eyes, and the hot pain in his hip. "If only that was true. But I'll need your help to authenticate our fictitious marriage."

Everything about her stilled. "What am I supposed to do?"

"You have to come to my homeland."

A dozen conflicting emotions raced across her face before she shrugged. "Once you 'legitimize' the girls and become king, if I have to sign or swear anything in front of kingdom officials, I'll come."

He shook his head in frustration at his inability to make this easier on her. "I need you there before the coronation."

That wary watchfulness gripped her again. "When is that?"

"If all goes well, in a month's time now."

Her lips fell open. "You mean you want me to go to Zorya in less than a month?"

"No, I don't mean that." Before she could relax her clenched muscles, he exhaled. "We have to leave tomorrow."

Six

By the time the limo stopped at the private airfield, Eva and Zoya were sound asleep. Kyria Despina had also nodded off. Kassandra's alertness and agitation had only intensified with every passing second.

They reached a screaming pitch when Leonid got out and came around to hand her out. His smile, more than the coldness of the night after the warmth of the limo, sprouted goose bumps all over her. Oblivious to his effect on her, he got busy releasing the girls' car seat harnesses, insisting on carrying both.

After gesturing for those awaiting them on the tarmac to take her and the groggy Despina's hand luggage and the cats' carriers, he led them up into the giant silver jet.

With many of her family and friends being billionaires, she'd been on private jets before. But she'd never been on one of Leonid's. That fact underlined the superficiality of their liaison. She'd been the one who'd made the fatal mistake of becoming deeply involved, breaking the rules they'd agreed on, as he'd accused her of.

But all the other jets were nothing compared to this one. It felt…royal. So was it Zorya's equivalent of Air Force One? That made sense. From the news, Zorya no longer considered Leonid a candidate, but the future king, the man who'd resurrect their kingdom and restore its grandeur. It was a fitting ride for a man of his stature and importance.

With his staff and the jet's crew hovering in the background, Leonid led them through many compartments to a spiral staircase to the upper deck. Once there, he walked them across an ultrachic foyer, then through an automatic door that he opened using a fingerprint recognition module. So no one was allowed past this point except him, and those he let in.

The door whirred shut behind them as he guided them to a bedroom with two double beds, two special cribs and a huge pet enclosure for the cats. He'd prepared the jet for them!

After she helped him secure the girls and cats, he showed Despina the suite's amenities and assured her she should settle down for a full night's sleep.

As he led Kassandra back outside, it dawned on her that, with the transcontinental flight, they'd be traveling all through the night. Alone together.

Even if she convinced him to sleep himself, so she'd be spared the turmoil of his company, she wouldn't be able to even close her eyes knowing he was so close by. But she doubted he'd sleep and leave her. Apart from that one time he'd been beyond observing decorum and had told her what he'd really felt, he'd always been terminally gallant. And since she'd agreed to go to Zorya, he'd been more courteous than ever. It was enough to make her want to scream.

Resigned to a night in the hell of his nearness, she sagged down on a cream leather couch. Forcing her attention off him, she looked around the grand lounge.

Dominated by Slavic designs, the room was drenched in golden lights and earth tones, embodying the serenity of sumptuousness and seclusion. At the far end of the space that occupied the breadth of the massive jet, a screen of complementing colors and designs obscured another area behind it.

"This—" he gestured to a door "—is the lavatory." Another gesture. "And those buttons access all functions and services in this compartment. Please order refreshments or whatever you wish for until I come back."

She almost blurted out that he *didn't* need to come back, that he should go tend to matters of state or something. But she remained silent as he paused at the lounge's door, his fathomless voice caressing every starved cell in her.

"I'll only be a few minutes."

Once he disappeared, she headed to the lavatory, just for something to do, and stayed inside for as long as she could bear.

Once she came out, she did a double take, and faltered, gulping air. He'd come back, and he'd taken off his...jacket!

Had he been naked, he probably wouldn't have affected her more. Okay, he would have, but it was bad enough now. And his clothes weren't even that fitted, just a loose and simple white shirt and black pants. If anything about him or what he provoked in her could be called simple.

He smiled that slow, searing smile he'd been bestowing on her again since yesterday. Unable to smile back, she approached him, her stamina tank running lower by the second.

He'd been supremely fit before, but the added bulk of his new lifestyle suited him endlessly. The breadth of his chest and shoulders that had never owed their perfection to tailoring felt magnified now that only a layer of finest silk covered them. They, and his arms, bulged with strength and symmetry. Yet his abdomen was as hard as ever, his waist and hips as narrow, making his upper body look even more formidable. She didn't dare pause on the area at the juncture of his powerful thighs.

And that was only his body. The body that had enslaved her every sense, owned her every response, had possessed and pleasured her for a whole year. The body whose essence had mingled with hers and created their twin miracles. Then came the rest. The regal shape of his head, the deep, dark gloss of his hair, the hewn sculpture of his face, the seductiveness of his lips, the hypnosis of his eyes.

If he'd been Hermes before, he was now Ares. If ever a man was born to lead, to be king, it was him.

He extended one of those perfect, powerful hands that had once treated her to unimaginable intimacies and ecstasies.

"Come sit down, Kassandra. We're about to take off."

She sat down where the tranquil sweep of his hand indicated. Before she collapsed. No longer the stiff stranger he'd been with her, the way he moved, sounded, smelled, breathed, the way he just *was*...

It was all too much.

Unaware that just being near, just being him, was causing her unbearable pain, he sat down on the seat opposite her couch. His descent was smoother than her flop, yet a frown shadowed his leonine brow. She could feel frustration radiating from him at his inability to move as effortlessly as before. After his previous pre-ternatural litheness, it must be indescribably disconcerting to him to no longer have total control over his every move, to orchestrate them in that symphony of grace that he used to.

Getting his irritation under control with obvious difficulty, he secured his seat belt and pressed a button in his armrest. The engines revved higher and the jet started moving.

To escape the gaze he pinned on her again, she fastened her seat belt and examined the panel in her own armrest. She didn't get most of the functions. But then, in her condition, she wouldn't have recognized a neon exit sign.

If only this situation came with one. It didn't, not for the foreseeable future. If one ever became available, it wouldn't be called an exit, but an escape, with whatever could be saved. If anything remained salvageable this time.

For now, she couldn't even figure out what had happened since Leonid had said they had to go to Zorya in a day's time.

That statement had been met with her finest snort. But he'd been as serious as a tidal wave, inundating her objections. And as she continued to discover, resistance with him was indeed futile.

After he'd left, she'd done what he'd made her agree

to, called every person, agency and organization she'd made prior plans, signed contracts or had delivery dates with, to request extensions. Not expecting to get any, she'd felt secure that these commitments would be her excuse not to comply with his timetable.

But they'd all come back to her within hours, *offering* her all the time she wanted. Sans penalty. Some with an increase in compensation for her "extra time and effort."

Not only was she burning to know how he'd done that, but she was getting more anxious about what he'd done to achieve these unbelievable results.

But now that she was sentenced to a night of sleepless torture in his company, she was bent on getting some answers. She wouldn't let him escape her questioning again as he had so far, on account of being too busy preparing their departure.

She raised her gaze to him, found him studying her with yet another inscrutable expression in his incredible eyes.

Suppressing tremors of longing, she cocked her head at him. "Now that you have nowhere to go for the next fourteen hours, you will tell me."

His eyes maintained that enigmatic cast. "Who says I have nowhere to go? This jet has a depressurizing compartment in the rear so I can make a dash for it in extreme emergencies."

"And you consider this one? You'd skydive from forty thousand feet, at six hundred miles an hour, into the big unknown below, to escape telling me how you got all those multibillion-dollar enterprises to postpone my multimillion-dollar deals with a smile and a bonus on top?"

His eyes crinkled, filling with what she thought she'd

never see there again. Bedevilment. "If you saw the look in your eyes, you'd categorize this as a jump-worthy situation."

Pursing her lips to suppress the moronic urge to grin at him, when for the past two years plus he'd certainly caused her nothing to grin about, she plastered her best attempt at severity on her face. "What did you do, Leonid?"

His lips mimicked hers in earnestness, but the smile kept attempting to escape. "What do you think I did?"

"I have theories, and fears. Not in your best interests to keep me in suspense with that combustible mix."

A revving chuckle erupted deep in his endless chest. "I did mean it when I said I'd tell you when I had the time and presence of mind. But now that I realize you have all those theories and fears, I must hear them first. So you tell me what you think I did, and if it's close, I'll tell you the exact details."

Was he…teasing her? What had gotten into him? Where was the automaton who'd stood on her doorstep playing back what had sounded like a recorded script and programmed responses?

Was he practicing the ease they'd display as newly reconciled husband and wife? He had said polite formality would be fine in public, but what if he'd decided it was more effective to give his adoring subjects a doting couple to moon over?

In other modern kingdoms, the alleged love stories between royal couples counted as a major asset for the monarchy, contributing to its political and social stability. It was also a huge source of economic prosperity via revenues for the media and tourism machines.

So now that she'd accommodated all his demands and

he was no longer anxious about his plans, was he relaxing and rehearsing in preparation for giving the public a convincing performance?

Or was it even worse? Had he decided to enslave the world by reverting to his previous self, the one she'd fallen fathoms deep for, and hadn't been able to kick her way to the surface since?

Unable to even think of the ramifications to herself if this was the case, she focused on his current challenge, knowing he wouldn't reveal anything if she didn't meet it.

"It's not what I think as much as what I hope you did. For the future of my business, I hope there was no coercion or intimidation on your part, but that as a former world champion, current mogul and future king, you have endless strings to pull, gently, and that you binged on using all the favors you could."

Those perfectly arched eyebrows shot up. "And leave myself in a favor deficit as I embark on ruling a historically contested land with a nascent independence amidst a turbulent sea of cranky killer-whale and bloodthirsty-shark nations?"

When he put it that way, her worries didn't even seem relevant.

Shoulders drooping, she flopped back on the couch. "So my business was too small a fry for you to spend favors on, huh?"

He unbuckled himself, rose and came down beside her, much closer than his usual very long arm's length. "Actually, your business is a huge enough fish I didn't need to."

Her wits scattering at his action, his nearness, she tried to focus on the meaning of his words. And failed.

Giving up, she croaked, "What's that supposed to mean?"

"It means the only good my calls did was explain the time-sensitive nature of your request, since you didn't."

"What exactly did you tell them?"

"The truth, but I requested their discretion until we made a public announcement. But they were already falling over themselves to adjust their plans to accommodate your needs. I just told them you needed their response ASAP for your peace of mind before our trip and subsequent major events. All I did was make them call you sooner with their acceptance."

When she could only gape at him in disbelief, his lips crooked with what very dangerously resembled indulgent pride.

"I already knew how respected and valued you are, but today I discovered your popularity is phenomenal. You've built such a massive reserve of goodwill, such need for your name, products and collaboration, everyone said and proved they'd do whatever they had to for the opportunity to keep on working with you."

Finding this revelation too much to accept, she shook her head. "They must have hoped it would be a big favor to you. Who wouldn't want to be in your good graces?"

His pout was all gentle chastisement. "You don't know your own influence on people at all, do you?"

I used to have a pretty good idea. Until you pulverized my belief in my own judgment and my self-esteem.

But it wasn't time now, or ever, to voice that grievance.

"Even if some were willing to accommodate me, you have to be exaggerating such a sweeping response. It had to be *your* influence. They must have calculated that a point with you would appreciate astronomically. No advantage gained by rejecting my request would be worth being in your bad books."

Without saying anything further, he got out his phone, dialed a number. In seconds, the line opened.

"Signor Bernatelli..." He paused for a second as an exclamation carried to her ears from the other side.

Sergio Bernatelli, the top Italian designer she was collaborating with in her biggest project to date, had recognized his voice, or saved his number. Probably both.

"...yes, it's indeed fortunate to be talking to you again. Yes, we are on our way to Zorya." Another pause as the man bubbled over on the other side. "That would be totally up to Kassandra. Why don't you ask her? And can you please also repeat to her what you said to me when I called you earlier? Thank you, Signor Bernatelli, and look for our invitation to the coronation in the mail in a couple of weeks."

After she numbly took the phone from him, she barely got a hello in before the flamboyant man submerged her in his excitement about her upgrade to royal status, and his hopes she would consider him for a creation designed for her to wear to the coronation, or any royal function at all. Before she could express her gratitude for such a gift—though it would mean huge publicity for him—he repeated everything Leonid had told her, in his far more over-the-top language, which he usually reserved for blistering complaints and demolishing critique.

After she ended the call, she kept staring at Leonid, tingling with the incredible praise Bernatelli had lavished on her. Not only where it pertained to him and his design empire, but to the whole field.

"I trust you believe me now?" Leonid smiled expectantly.

She started to nod, but stopped. "Maybe not. Maybe knowing I'd ask, you put him up to this so he'd back your story."

Incredulity widened his eyes. "Following that reasoning, shouldn't I have picked an accomplice you'd be more inclined to believe would have such a glowing opinion of you? Why pick that cantankerous scrooge when praises from him would be the most suspicious?"

"Maybe that's exactly why you chose him, because it would have been too obvious to pick someone agreeable, and such a famed grouch's vote would carry more weight and credibility."

Leonid threw his hands up in the air, "*Bozhe moy*, Kassandra! That's too convoluted for even me. My brain is now starting to ache trying to contort around that pretzeled piece of logic."

She opened her mouth to confront him with another suspicion, but closed it. That was real bewilderment in his eyes. Worse, the levity that had been present all day, that she'd delighted in in spite of herself, was gone. She'd weirded him out because of her attack of dogged insecurity.

At her prolonged silence, he exhaled. "Did you only run out of arguments, but still believe in my deceit?"

Grimacing at how unreasonable she must have sounded, she sighed. "No, I believe you. But even if your calls only made a difference in timing, that's still a big thing. I would have been beside myself with worry if we left without hearing back from them. And because of your calls I learned something I wouldn't have on my own. People find it hard to say their opinions to someone's face, even if it's glowing praise. Or especially when it is. It's good to know I'm in such universal favor."

A relieved smile dawned on his heartbreakingly handsome face. "Which isn't a favor at all, but your due." He sat up, eagerness entering his pose. "And now that you realize your power, I'll counsel you on how to exercise it more effectively, to your benefit and that of the whole industry."

Her first instinct was to decline his offer. Then her mind did a one-eighty.

Why refuse? What made more sense than for her to accept the advantages of his invaluable insight and enormous experience, when it would be for everyone's benefit?

Suddenly, what she'd thought would never come to pass happened. She exchanged a smile with him, devoid of tension and shadows. Then the door to the bedroom opened.

Tousled and half-asleep on her feet, Despina stood in the door, carrying a very awake Eva and Zoya.

Leonid pushed to his feet before she could, his delight at seeing the girls blatant and unreserved. Their equal glee at finding him again manifested in excited shrieks as both of them flung themselves into his open arms.

Resigned that she was the old news they'd forgo until Leonid's novelty wore off, Kassandra sighed. "Sorry, Kyria Despina. I really thought they'd sleep through the night since they haven't woken up the past few days. Wonder if they're back to their habit, or if it's only today's different pattern and strange cribs that roused them."

"Why do you think they wake up?" Leonid asked.

"They seemed to hate letting go of all the fun they

were having before they sleep, wanting a few more hugs or another song or anything they were enjoying before they turned off."

Squeezing the girls tighter into his chest until their squeals became piercing, he laughed...*laughed*. "And there's plenty more of all of those things for *moy zvezdochky*."

His starlets. This was his favorite endearment for them already. His morning and evening stars.

He used to have endearments for her, too. Mostly while in the throes of pleasure. *Moya dorogaya krasavista... moya zolotoya krasota... My beautiful darling...my golden beauty.*

She would never hear them from him again.

Now all his attention was diverted to the girls, and he looked as if he'd been given an unexpected second chance at something irreplaceable. Then he grimaced, turning his gaze to Despina.

"Kyria Despina, please go back to sleep. We'll keep them with us if they fall asleep again, so as not to disturb you."

Shaking off her dimming mood, Kassandra had to intervene. "Uh, I actually never let them wake up to find themselves outside their cribs. They're notorious for picking up bad habits once I break a pattern and it's a struggle going back to any sort of order."

Nodding his deference to her decree at once, he strode toward Despina. "Let me take you to another bedroom. I'm sorry to move you, but from now on your sleep will be uninterrupted when the twins wake up at night."

Despina rushed beside him, assuring him she didn't mind at all, her cheeks flushed by the pleasure of having a royal god like Leonid fussing over her.

Within moments, Leonid marched back with the girls, one straddling his shoulders, the other his waist. They babbled as he cooed to them. "Papa" was repeated profusely as both swamped him in hugs and kisses, with him looking utterly blissful as he reciprocated.

They looked agonizingly beautiful together.

But that agony dissipated as they joined her, and she was infected by their gaiety and pleasure at being together.

An hour later, long after they should have gone back to sleep, as they all sat playing in the sandbox that had been ingeniously hidden until Leonid had unveiled it, the toddlers started gnawing their fists and drooling.

Concern coated Leonid's magnificent face as they both rushed to clean the twins' hands, even if what passed for sand was totally safe. He looked at her. "They're in the molar eruption phase now, right?"

She was impressed. "Give the new daddy a star. You've done your homework, I see."

"Of course. But since they didn't display any of the usual signs of teething before, I almost forgot about it."

"Well, health-wise, the girls have been a dream. Even teething has been progressing without signs of discomfort."

"But they're almost gnawing their little hands off and drooling up a storm!"

She chuckled at his growing agitation, content to be the wise, experienced parent who kept a cool head. "Don't ask me why, but it's their current method of letting me know they're hungry. No, let me correct that. Starving."

His eyes lit up in relief. "Of course they are. I thought they ate so much less than usual during their dinner."

"They were too excited with all the preparations to eat."

"And it turned out to be the best thing they did. So they'd wake up and play with their papa, and let him feed them their first Zoryan meal. I'm ordering you a feast!"

His enthusiasm widened her grin as he reached for the panel in his chair. He'd explained he'd given that jet to Zorya, not the other way around, to be the monarch's jet, long before he knew it would be him.

Though she'd thought she wasn't hungry, by the time he opened the door to waiters holding trays high, her stomach rumbled. Loudly. The food aromas were distressingly delicious, and even the fussy girls were smacking their lips.

Grinning at their demonstration of hunger, he rose, held his hand down to her. She took it, but along with her own upward momentum, she ended up falling against him. For a moment, it felt as if a thousand-volt lash had flayed her where their bodies touched, from chest to hip.

It was he who pulled back first, almost anxiously, his eyes once more unfathomable. The moment passed as the girls scampered around, pulling at them to get on with feeding them.

Getting back into the flow of talking with Eva and Zoya with their system of English, Zoryan Russian and baby talk, he led them behind the screen she'd noticed before. Turned out there was a full dining area there, with gold-and-black silk-upholstered chairs. In the center stood an elaborate table decorated with Zorya's magnificently rendered and detailed emblem of the two goddesses.

As they sat down, Leonid explained to the girls that they were like those two goddesses, night and day twins. Zorya would consider them the symbol of its rebirth, just like the goddesses were responsible for its original birth. He enlisted Kassandra's help in simplifying the concept, and it all turned into a game as the girls caught on to the resemblance and imitated the goddesses' poses.

The food, which Leonid explained in detail, was beyond delicious. Even the usually picky girls devoured anything Leonid offered them. Kassandra insisted it had more to do with him doing the offering than the tastiness of the food itself.

Midmeal, the girls asked to sit in the place of the goddesses in the emblem. Getting her okay, Leonid improvised a new game, placing plates on the symbols surrounding the goddesses, offering them all forkfuls, and making Eva and Zoya laugh all the harder each time he theatrically dipped a fork in a plate and zoomed it toward a wide-open mouth, sometimes even Kassandra's.

She kept wondering how this had become the last thing she'd expected it to be—a delightful family trip. His new approachability and the girls' enthusiasm and spontaneity had dissolved the artifice and distance the past had imposed on them, revealing Leonid as he was now. He'd told the truth. He was no longer the man she'd loved, but far better, warmer, endlessly patient and accommodating, the perfect companion and the best father-in-training she could have imagined.

After they finished eating and the waiters had removed all signs of their meal, Leonid got the girls off the table and clapped. "How about some Zoryan music, *moy zvezdochky*?"

As if they understood, and maybe they truly did, the girls yelled in agreement. Once Leonid had the infectiously joyous music filling their cocoon of luxury, he started teaching the girls the steps of a Zoryan folk dance. Noticing how hard it was for him to execute even those simple steps, she studied them quickly and took over teaching them as best she could. Soon they were all dancing with Leonid watching them, keeping the tempo with powerful claps, singing along, his rich bass deepening the spell.

Whenever one song ended and another started, Leonid would urge them on. *"Tantsevat', moy prekrasnyye damy.* Dance!"

This time, he'd included her when he'd said "my beautiful ladies." At least she thought he'd included her.

But why should she doubt it? The whole day he'd gone above and beyond doting on both the girls and her. He'd given her the gift of showing her how important she was to her colleagues in her field. He'd been exemplary in recognizing her superior knowledge of the girls, had showed them in no uncertain terms that, though he was their papa who would do anything for them, it was mama who was the boss. He'd been plain magnificent to her.

When she said no more, he invited her down on the carpeted floor. They sat with their backs to the couch, with the girls climbing on and off them, bringing them toys and asking them to name them in their respective languages. Then she and Leonid quizzed them. To all their excitement, the girls remembered almost everything and said the words as accurately as possible in the three languages.

The games continued for hours. Then the girls suddenly lay down across his and her side-by-side bodies, making a bridge between them with theirs, and promptly fell asleep.

They remained sitting like this, sharing the connection their daughters had spontaneously created between them in serene silence for what could have been another hour, alternating caressing the girls' silky heads.

Suddenly, his black-velvet voice spread over her like a caress. *"Oni ideal'ny."*

She nodded, heart swelling with sudden, overwhelming gratitude. For them. And for him. "Yes. They are perfect." At length, she added, "Let's put them to bed."

Without objection, even when she could see he wanted to savor them for far longer, he gathered one girl after the other and rose with them in his arms.

On the way to their bedroom, she had to voice her wonder. "You'll have to show me how you keep them stuck to you like this when they're asleep. Either you're a literal babe magnet, or you three share some Voronov Vacuum quality."

A surprised huff of mirth escaped him before he suppressed it. Then he seemed to remember nothing could disturb them, and let it all out.

As they went back to the lounge, he was still chuckling as he put on a different kind of music, still Zoryan, but perfect for setting a soothing mood.

Sitting down on the couch, he suddenly guffawed again. "Voronov Vacuum. I should patent this."

She grinned her pleasure at his appreciation of her quip. "You should. That brand name is just meant to be."

He sighed, still smiling. "I wanted to ask you to let them sleep like that between us, as if laying claim to both of us. You know I lost my parents when I was not much older than they are, was raised by indulgent relatives. What you don't know is that I struggled to cultivate the discipline my parents would have instilled in me, had they lived. So I know how important it is to have structure in one's life, and I truly admire your ability to provide and maintain it. I will happily follow your lead and reinforce your methods." He signed even more exaggeratedly. "Even if the new papa in me wants to mindlessly indulge them to thorough and decadent rottenness."

She chuckled at his mock-mournful complaint. "You have a lifetime to indulge them, *and* discipline them, *and* the rest of the roller coaster of unimaginable ups and downs of parenthood to look forward to. Pace yourself. I'm trying to."

His eyes glittered with such poignancy, as if it was the first time he dared to let himself look forward that far. "I do have a lifetime, don't I? I am their father forever."

Throat sealing with emotion, she nodded. "If you want to be."

His azure eyes flared with such elation and entreaty. Then he only said a hoarse "Please."

The word rolled through her every cell like thunder. And everything inside her snapped.

Then she was pressing all she could of herself into what she could of him, lips blindly seeking every part of him she'd starved for, all her suppressed longing bursting out in a reiteration so ragged it was a prayer.

"Yes, Leonid, yes, please...*please*..."

Seven

Among the cacophony of her thundering heart and strident breathing, Kassandra heard a piece of music ending and a more evocative one starting. And she was pleading. Pleading. Pleading. For what, she didn't know.

But she *did* know. She was pleading for him. For them. For an explanation. A reconnection. A resurrection.

Just touching him again felt like coming back to life. If only he'd touch her back.

But he had frozen from the moment she'd obliterated the distance between them, had done what she'd been suffocating for since that moment she'd seen his crumpled car in the news. To touch him, feel him, reassure herself he was here and whole, that she hadn't lost him.

But she had lost him. He'd imposed his loss on her. But she now realized that through all the pain, there had remained the consolation that he still existed, that she hadn't lost him that way. In the depths of her soul, hidden from her pain and pride, there had always been the hope that maybe, one day, this meant she could have him back.

Now nothing mattered to her anymore but the fact that he was the only man she'd ever want, that he was her girls' father and he loved them. That he'd come back for them had shown her a glimpse of the perfection they could have.

Now all she wanted was for him to end her exile.

Her hands and lips roaming his solid vitality, singed by his heat, tapping into his life, she begged for his response.

Please. Please. Please.

Then he moved…away.

Her lips stilled on his chest, mortification welling inside her like lava. He was rejecting her again.

But…maybe not. With the debris of the past between them, he wouldn't presume to take what she was offering when he didn't know what it was, or how it would affect their sensitive situation and fragile new harmony.

But this wasn't the past. This was now. It could be their tomorrows. She had to risk new injury for the slightest possibility this new man he'd become had changed toward her, too, and might now want her as she wanted him. He had wanted her once, before he'd stopped. Maybe this time he wouldn't stop.

Pulling back to look up at him through eyes filling with tears, she found his face clenched as hard as the muscles that had turned to rock beneath her fingers, buzzed like live wires. He was shocked. And aroused as hell.

His hunger buffeted her, left her in no doubt. It wasn't lack of desire that made him pull back, but uncertainty.

Attempting to erase any doubts he had, she pressed against him, sobbed into his hot neck against his bounding pulse, "Take me, Leonid, just take me, *please*…"

"Kassandra…" His rumble of her name reverberated inside her as he heaved up, tugging her with him. In the past, he would have scooped her up, but she knew he couldn't now.

Her legs still almost gave out as he rushed her through compartments, past the dining area to another closed door. Behind it was a bedroom as big as the lounge, dominated by a king-size bed covered in gold-and-black satin. His bedroom.

Before she could use what was left of her coordination to stumble to the bed, he closed the door and pressed her against it, taking her face in both hands. In the pervasive golden light, his face was supernatural in beauty, reflecting the hurricane building up inside him. His blue-fire gaze was explicit with one question: Did she know what she'd be getting into when he let it break over her?

Feeling she'd crumble into ashes if it didn't, she cried out, "Leonid, I want it all with you…"

With a groan that sounded as if something had ripped inside him, his head swooped down and blocked out existence.

Then he was swallowing her moans of his name, giving her his breath, reanimating her as he growled hers inside her.

"Kassandra…"

It was like opening a floodgate. To the past. To that first kiss that had been exactly like that. A conquering; a claiming. Her breath fractured inside her chest as she drowned in his feel and scent and taste. As she had that first time, and for a whole year afterward. She'd only drowned in desolation, alone, after he'd cast her out.

But she *was* drowning again now. In kisses that tantalized her with only glimpses of the ferocity she needed from him. His hands added to her torment, gliding all over her, never pausing long enough to appease, until she writhed against him, whimpering for what she'd never and could never stop wanting. Everything with and from him.

But he wasn't giving her everything, as if still testing her, not sure how total her surrender was.

She dug her fingers into his shoulders. "Leonid... *please*, give me *everything* you've got."

His head rose for one suspended moment, long enough for her to see his shackles snapping, then at last, he clamped his lips down on hers, hard, hot branding. His tongue thrust deep, singeing her with pleasure, breaching her with need, draining her of moans and reason.

She took it all, too lost to pleasure him in turn. His absence had left a void that had been growing larger every day until she'd feared it would hollow her out, leaving only a shell. Now he was here again, filling the emptiness.

Pressure built in her eyes, chest and core. Her hands convulsed on his arms until he relented, pushed her blouse up and over her head, pulled her bra strap down, setting her swollen breasts free.

She keened with relief, with the spike in arousal. He had her exposed, vulnerable. Desperate with arousal. Shaking hands pressed her breasts together to mitigate their aching as everything inside her surged, gushed, needing anything he would do to her. His fingers and tongue and teeth exploiting her every secret, his body

all over hers, his manhood filling her core, thrusting her
to oblivion…reclaiming her from the void.

Tears flooded down her cheeks. "Don't go slow,
Leonid… I can't wait, I can't…"

Leonid had to be dreaming.

It had to be one of those tormenting figments that
had hunted him mercilessly every moment since he'd
watched her stumble out of his hospital room. Kassandra couldn't be pressing into him, all that glorious passion and flesh, sobbing for him to take her. He couldn't
be scenting her arousal, feeling it vibrating in his loins,
hearing it thundering in his cells.

She couldn't want him still, after what he'd done to
her.

Her teeth sank into his bottom lip, hard, breaking his
flesh. The taste of his blood mixing with her taste, inflamed his every nerve. Her distress felt so real.

It *was* real, a firebomb of madness detonating inside him, blowing away the last of his disbelief, and
his control.

He smashed his lips harder into hers, and her cry of
relief, of exultation tore through him. The need to ram
into her, ride her, spill himself inside her, with no finesse,
no restraint, drove him. Her flesh buzzed with her distress beneath his burning hands. Her incessant moans
filled his head.

She wanted an invasion. And he would deliver.

It had been so long without her…so agonizingly long.
He'd thought it would be for the rest of his miserable
life. But his banishment was suddenly over. She was
taking him back when he'd thought it an impossibility.

And he would take her as she needed him to, binge on her, perish inside her.

He swept her off her feet and she arched deep against the door, making a desperate offering of her core, her breasts, her hands behind his head sinking further into his sanity, speeding his descent into delirium.

He fell on her engorged breasts, starving, took what he could of her ripened femininity, where his daughters had suckled, insane with regret that he hadn't been there to witness it. Tearing her skirt farther up in rough, un-coordinated moves, he spread her thighs wide around his hips. She thrashed, clamped him with her legs and need, her sobs sharpening. His distress just as deep, he held her with one arm, reached between her legs, pushed aside her soaked panties, opened her folds and shud-dered, on the brink of release just gliding his fingers through her fluid heat.

Drawing harder on one nipple, then the other, he rubbed two fingers in shaking circles over the knot of flesh where her nerves converged. Once, twice, then he felt her stiffen, that soon. He gritted his teeth, anxious for the music of her release, even if he suffered perma-nent damage hearing it.

She came apart in his arms, magnificent, abandoned, her cries fueling his arousal to the point of agony. His hands shook out of control as he freed himself, the antici-pation so brutal his grip on consciousness was slipping.

Fighting to focus, he snatched her thighs back around him, groaned as her wet heat singed his erection, even as her heavy-lidded gaze scalded the rest of him. Growl-ing something not even he understood, driven, wild, his fingers dug into her buttocks. Her breasts swelled more at his roughness, her hardened nipples branding his raw flesh even through his clothes.

His vision distorted over lips swollen from his ferocity, quivering from a taut-with-need face. "Come inside me n—"

He drove up into her, roaring her name. But though molten for him, she was as tight as ever, her flesh resisting his invasion as he stretched her beyond her limits. But knowing their impossible fit only drove her beyond coherence with pleasure, he pulled out only to thrust back, again, then again, again, again, to the rhythm of her piercing screams as she consumed him in her velvet inferno, until he'd embedded himself inside her to the hilt.

Then he stilled in her depths, surrendered to her clenching hunger as it wrung him, razed him. At last. *At last.*

He rested his forehead against hers, overwhelmed, transported, listening to her delirium, to his. Her graceful back was a deep arch, granting him total freedom with her body.

Then it was no longer enough. The need to conquer her, finish her, end inside her rose like a tidal wave, as it always had, crashing and destroying everything, before building again as if it had never dissipated.

Blind, out of his mind, he lifted her, filled his mouth and hands with her flesh. He had to leave no fiber of her being unsaturated with pleasure. He withdrew all the way out of her then thrust back, harder, then harder still, until he was hammering inside her to the cadence he knew would overload her, until she convulsed in orgasm, her satin screams echoing his roars as he followed her into the abyss of pleasure.

Her convulsions spiked in intensity at the first splash of his seed against her womb, and he felt her heart spiraling out of control with his as a sustained seizure of release destroyed the world around them.

Then it was another life, where nothing existed except being merged with her, riding the aftershocks, savoring the plateau of ecstasy, sharing the descent.

It had been beyond control or description. Everything.

Yet it wasn't enough. Would anything with Kassandra ever be?

He knew the answer to that. Nothing ever would. He'd never had enough of her. He'd been hers alone since that first time he'd laid eyes on her. He would have remained hers even if he'd never had her again. Even if she'd hated him forever.

But defying comprehension, she didn't. Not only didn't she hate him, not only did she still want him, she seemed to have forgiven him. She'd given him her body again, her acceptance, her support with the twins, her ease. Her laughter. How was it even possible?

And he realized. *He'd* done that. When he hadn't meant to.

All he'd meant when he'd let go of the act of stiffness and distance had been to end her fears toward him, neutralize her hostility, for her own peace of mind. He hadn't dreamed she would not only relinquish her rightful hatred of him but seek his intimacy again, and with this unstoppable urgency.

And he realized something else. Even though she'd completed her descent from the peak of pleasure, she wasn't pulling away.

He withdrew a bit, keeping them merged as he looked down at her. She seemed disoriented, her eyes slumberous, fathomless as they gazed up at him. A goddess of temptation and fulfillment, something every man dreamed of but never really expected to find. And he'd found her, not only once, but against all odds, twice.

Unable to stop himself, his hands dug into her buttocks, gathering her tighter to him.

Her eyes scorched him to the bone with the amalgam of pleasure and pain that transfigured her amazing beauty as he expanded even more inside her. Her core, molten with their combined pleasure, contracted around him, making him thrust deeper into her, wrenching moans from both their depths. Then slowly, her lids slid down.

In seconds her breathing evened. She'd fallen asleep.

Overwhelming pride that he'd pleasured her so completely, as he'd used to, it had literally knocked her out, burgeoned inside him. He hardened even more, that first explosive encounter only serving to whet his appetite. As it always had, during their past extended sessions of delirium. Visions assailed him, of taking her to bed, making love to her again as she slept, until she woke up on another orgasm.

But he couldn't do that. He had to let her sleep.

Cursing his shoddy coordination, he gathered her in his arms and walked slowly with her precious weight. She'd left it all to his power in lax trust, testing his precarious balance. The trek to the bed felt endless. Placing her under the covers and adjusting her clothes, she stirred only to touch what she could of him with sleepy kisses and caresses, murmuring wonderful little incoherencies in appreciation of his caresses and coddling. He struggled up, heart thundering, brow covered in cold sweat. His control had one last notch before it slipped again.

One thing pulled him back from the temptation. The sheer regret and despair that pulverized the heart he'd thought had shriveled the day he'd pushed her away all over again.

This had been a terrible mistake.

For her sake, from now on, he had to leave her alone.

He couldn't succumb to her need, or his weakness, ever again.

Kassandra woke up from an inferno of eroticism, on fire.

Gasping as her dream about Leonid evaporated and with it the impending orgasm he'd been about to give her, it took her a disoriented minute to realize where she was. In Leonid's luxurious jet bedroom, fully clothed and tucked beneath covers that felt alive with silky touches and sighs.

Leonid had knocked her out with pleasure. As he'd always done. So even this hadn't changed.

Barely able to move, she turned her head to squint at the digital clock pinned down on the bedside table... and gasped. It was seven hours since she'd shut down in his arms. They must be about to land. And he must have had things to attend to. Which was a good thing. She didn't know how she would have faced him after what she'd done.

She'd almost attacked him in her arousal!

But once he'd made sure he knew what she'd been asking for, how far she'd wanted him to go, he'd...devastated her. She felt...ravished. Every inch of her felt fully exploited, delightfully sore and was screaming for an encore. Pushing away the covers that suddenly felt filled with hot thorns, she teetered barefoot to the adjoining bathroom.

It turned out to have a whirlpool tub, which she couldn't rush to fast enough, taking her clothes off to sink in.

As the warm currents bombarded her ultrasensitive flesh, her condition worsened as the memories of her encounter with Leonid boiled over in her blood. If he'd been here, she would have lost her mind all over again, and again.

When she couldn't take it anymore, she heaved out of the water and headed on trembling legs for the mirror, in front of which she shakily dried herself. She looked exactly like what she was. A woman who'd been possessed and pleasured within an inch of her sanity, and was now looking wild with her need for more.

But…would there be more? What would he say and do when she next saw…

"We are now approaching Zvaria, and will be landing in ten minutes. Please fasten your seat belts."

The pilot's announcement pulled her out of her feverish musings. But before she could head for the door, it opened. And she found herself face-to-face with Leonid.

Before her next heartbeat, he smiled, but it was detached, impersonal.

"Good, you're awake." Before she could respond, he opened the door wider. "Let's join the twins and share this historic event of landing in the Zoryan capital for the first time together."

As she approached him, he receded to let her pass. She tried to meet his eyes, read in them his response to what had happened between them, where he thought they'd go from there.

But he turned his gaze away in what seemed like a natural move as he invited her to lead the way.

Heart thudding to the rhythm of uncertainty and mortification, she walked ahead, her thoughts tangling.

Did he have too much on his mind, with the resolution of their situation and his looming responsibilities? Or was he just regretting what had happened?

Trying to project the ease she'd perfected for the girls' sake, she pinned a brittle smile on her face as they joined the others. As usual, Eva and Zoya demanded his attention, and hers to a lesser degree, leaving no room to focus on anything but them until they landed.

By the time they did, she'd decided she wouldn't torment herself with conjectures, that she'd let Leonid tell her what he thought and wanted when he had time for her alone again.

The moment she stepped out of the jet behind Leonid, who was carrying the girls, frosty air flayed her face and filled her lungs, so crisp and clean it made her gasp. The winter-wonderland vista beyond what was clearly another private airfield, with the imposing Carpathian Mountains in the distance, was so different from anywhere she'd ever lived, or even visited, that it reinforced again that she was a world away from her normal life in every sense.

She didn't have time to marvel at the awe-inspiring surroundings, or to linger over the realization that this rugged land must be responsible in part for Leonid's uncompromising distinctiveness. Her attention was drawn instead to the multitude of reporters and photographers who came literally out of left field to gather around the bottom of the stairs.

Her every hair stood on end as Leonid, who'd secured both girls in one arm, reached for her with the other one, posing for their first-ever family picture.

Then, as they resumed descending the stairs, the girls clung to him, burying their faces in his chest, eyeing the dozens of strangers calling out a cacophony of questions. Feeling his heat and power surrounding her, she found herself instinctively seeking his protection, too, dimly realizing what a sight they must make. The proud lion king, literally, with his pride of clinging females.

Leonid paused at the last step of the stairs and addressed the crowd. "Thank you for coming to meet my family, but you will understand that after the long flight, my only priority is their comfort. Each of you will get invitations to the press conference I will hold to answer all your questions as soon as my family is settled in their new home."

The reporters still tried to get him to say more, their voices rising with dozens of queries.

Leonid chose to answer one. "I do believe my daughters, Eva and Zoya, represent new life for our kingdom. They are literally that for me."

Brooking no further interruptions, he strode ahead and even the most dogged reporters parted before him as if unable to stand being in the path of his power.

Within minutes, they were seated inside a gleaming black stretch limo with the Zoryan flag flapping at the front.

She sat beside Leonid with the girls in their car seats facing them and Despina beside them. Leonid focused almost exclusively on the girls all the way to the palace, pointing out landmarks on the way and explaining their significance and history, with the girls appearing to take absolute interest in everything he brought to their attention and gleefully repeating the words he emphasized. Kassandra just kept telling herself to stick to her decision not to analyze his behavior, to stop thinking altogether.

Then they entered the palace complex grounds and all thought became impossible as she plunged ever deeper into the unreality of it all.

She'd been to the world's grandest palaces, as a tourist. Entering this place as a future resident, if things went according to Leonid's plan, was something else altogether. With the massive grounds populated by only those who worked there, it felt totally different from all the other palaces that had been crawling with visitors.

"This place was first laid out on the orders of Esfir the First, Zorya's founder and first queen." Her gaze swung to Leonid, and he gestured to her to look back at their surroundings as he continued narrating its history. "Her name, the Russian variant of Esther, also means *star*. This complex of palaces and gardens are sometimes referred to as the Zoryan Versailles. The central palace ensemble had been recognized as a UNESCO World Heritage Site since the fall of the Soviet Union and its return to the Zoryan state."

As she took in the information, he pointed toward another landmark. "The dominant natural feature is this sixteen-meter-high bluff lying less than a hundred meters from the shore of the Sea of Azov, which is part of the Black Sea. The Lower Gardens, or *Nizhny Sad*, encompassing over a square kilometer, are confined between this bluff and the shore. The majority of the complex's fountains are there, as are several small palaces and outbuildings. Atop the bluff, near the middle of the Lower Gardens, stands the Grand Palace, or *Bolshoi*

Dvorets, where the monarch historically resided…which I'm now repairing and renovating, so I hope you'll excuse any mess. Ah, here is one of my favorite features of the place…"

Kassandra's head swung to where he was pointing, the most glorious cascade and fountain she'd ever seen, situated right on the bluff's face below the body of a palace so grand it looked right out of a fairy tale.

"That's the Grand Cascade, or *Bolshoi Kaskad*, with the Grand Palace forming the centerpiece of the entire complex, and it's one of the most extensive waterworks of the Baroque period."

Leonid kept explaining and describing what they were passing through, with all of them, including the girls, hanging on his every word. Apart from realizing he was telling them important things he wanted them to learn, the girls, like every other living being, she suspected, just loved listening to his voice and were hypnotized by the way he spoke.

The hypnosis only deepened as Leonid took them inside what he kept referring to as their "new home."

In her jumbled state, Kassandra's mind couldn't assimilate the details her eyes were registering, just the major strokes. From beneath the scaffoldings of in-progress renovations clearly close to being finished, she could see an entrance, staggering in size and grandeur, under hundred-foot, painted dome ceilings, halls with soaring arches with dozens of paintings depicting naval battles, atmospheric landscapes and royal ancestry, and chambers displaying countless ethnic influences in their art and decor.

What made her focus sharpen were an inner garden and pool that, while they had elements of the rest of the place, were evidently new, and the most incredible parts of the palace to her. Somehow she had no doubt they were Leonid's idea and taste.

Throughout the tour, the girls, who'd never been in an edifice of that size, ran around squealing and pointing out their discoveries to interrogate Leonid about before another thing distracted them.

"And here are your quarters, for now."

They entered through white-painted, gold-paneled double doors to the most exquisite, expansive living area she'd ever seen. Though the dimensions and architecture echoed the rest of the palace, the furnishings and decor were more modern, comfort inducing and closely resembling the style and color scheme of her own living room in LA. And it was also outfitted and proofed for toddlers, clearly with Eva and Zoya in mind.

She wouldn't even ask how and when he'd had such personalized furnishings installed. He was powerful and rich enough he could have anything realized as soon as he thought of it.

But one thing didn't make sense. "For now?"

His smile didn't reach his eyes. "This is my effort at anticipating your needs and preferences. But you may decide you'd prefer some other place in the palace, or want something built on the grounds from scratch to your demands. So this will do until then."

"You can't seriously think I wouldn't find this perfect? It's actually…too much. This living *room* is as big as my whole place, which is big to start with. And I see glimpses of more tennis court–size rooms beyond."

He shrugged dismissively. "Everything is built on a grand scale in Zorya, even peasant's houses. You'll get used to it."

Will I? Will I also get used to you blowing searing then arctic, to never knowing where I really stand with you?

She only tossed her head toward Despina and the girls, who were rushing about exclaiming at all the delights he'd layered the place with. "Even if this magnificent place for some inexplicable reason didn't suit my taste, the girls and their nanny have given it their fervent seal of approval."

His lips twisted fondly before his eyes returned to hers earnestly. "I hope I thought of everything you might need, but you already met Fedor and Anya during our tour, my valet and his wife. Anya will be at your service for any domestic needs, and Fedor for anything else. Always call *me* first, with anything serious, even if I'm occupied with state emergencies. But Anya and Fedor are always ready for immediate and trivial matters." She nodded and he walked away. Midway to the door, he turned again. "You promise you *will* call me if you need anything?"

Heart expanding at his solicitude, shriveling at his withdrawal, she knew he'd wait until she said, "I promise."

Once he was gone, she rushed to the nearest bathroom and locked herself in. And let the tears flow. For she'd just promised she'd call him if she needed anything.

Anything but him. When he was all she needed.

Eight

Leonid stared at his reflection in the bathroom mirror.

He looked like hell. Much like he had in those days after he'd sent Kassandra away. He'd been keeping her away since they'd come to Zvaria three days ago. Every hour, every minute, every *second* had been sheer torture. Total chaos.

Every moment had been dedicated to concocting legitimate ways to escape being alone with her, so he wouldn't be forced to clarify his position. It had been getting progressively harder, with him perpetually on the precipice of doing something totally insane or irrevocably damaging. Or both. Like taking her against the nearest vertical surface, as he'd done back on the jet.

And he'd run out of excuses, could no longer run from a confrontation. Doing so could cause the very damage he'd been trying to avoid.

So he hadn't disappeared after they'd put the twins to bed. He was sure she would come after him. He could feel her drawing nearer, his every cell rioting with her proximity.

And he had no idea about what to say or do. None.

Severing the visual clash with his own bloodshot eyes, he stiffly moved away from the mirror, shuffled back to his reception area and sank down on an armchair facing the door. Counted down the heartbeats that would bring her to him with an infallible certainty. The soft knock on the door came as his countdown ran out. Though expected, it still juddered through him. His nerves were shot, his resistance depleted. At any point in this encounter, if she touched him, he would devour her.

Unable to rise again, he called out thickly, "Come in."

She'd realize he knew it was her. Who else would his guards allow to walk up to his quarters at this hour, or at all?

Bracing himself, his nerves still fired in unison when he saw her. That magnificent creature that had occupied his every waking and sleeping thought since he'd first laid eyes on her. In that deep burgundy floor-length dress she'd worn earlier tonight for dinner, which accentuated her complexion and curves. With her thousand-shade golden waterfall of silk and green-meadow eyes, she looked as magical as always. And as haggard as he did.

Without closing the door behind her, she approached, her gaze stripping away what was left of his tatters of control.

Thankfully, she didn't come close enough to test his nonexistent resolve. She started without preamble.

"I could pretend I didn't still want you when I was

angry with you, when I was afraid of you. But even before I quit being either, I admitted it to myself first, then to you on that jet. I do want you, more than ever."

He stared at her. He'd expected outrage, scolding, blame, anything but this confession.

She went on, "I know we agreed on a plan, and I haven't changed my mind about it. You tell everyone whatever would be best for you, the girls and your kingdom, and I'll back it up. I know you'd prefer to be together only for the girls, and I realize you haven't said a word about what happened between us on the jet because you're uncertain how to handle it. But I'm here to tell you that you don't need to overthink it or feel anxious about it. If your response to me wasn't just a random male one, if you want *me*, I am asking you not to hold back out of worry for your other considerations. Let's have this. Let's be together. No strings, no expectations. Just like in the past."

Then she fell silent, the brittle hope in her gaze shattering what remained of his sanity, and his heart. He struggled to force himself to remain still, expressionless, but inside him, a hurricane raged.

How was it possible she could offer him this? Not knowing his reasons for taking everything she had, in the past and recently, then throwing it in her face, she would be a masochist, a victim, to offer him a second, and now a third chance. Which she wasn't.

So did she want him so much that she was convincing herself his reasons were justifiable? Or was it even worse? Did she love him? In the past, and still now? Was she, after this magical trip to Zorya, and their explosive episode of passion, ready to expose herself to further injury for the chance of resurrecting something she shouldn't believe had ever been real?

It overwhelmed him, agonized him, that her feelings for him could be so fierce and profound they'd survived his humiliation, his desertion. When he had to let her down, again. And for the last time.

Even though it would leave him bloodied and extinguished.

But he was still unable to rebuff her, hurt her like that again. He had to try to soften the blow any way he could.

Feeling he'd be cutting off a vital part of himself with a jagged blade all over again, he started, "I doesn't matter what I want…"

Her stepping closer stopped him, and her tremulous objection twisted the knife hacking his guts. "It's all that matters. This isn't the past. Things have changed. You have. I have, too, along with things between us and everything else. We should be together for the sole reason that we want each other."

Feeling he was drowning, a breath away from heaving up and crushing her in his arms, begging for anything for as long as she would give it, come what may, he shook his head.

"You're right, this isn't the past. It's far worse. In the past, when I messed up, I hurt only you. Not that that was any less significant, or any more forgivable, but it remains a fact the damages I caused were limited to you. You've contained any repercussions for the twins so far with your strength and resourcefulness, aided by their young age. But now the situation is exceedingly more complicated. Personal considerations are the last thing to feature in my worries, and any damages would ripple out into widespread destruction."

Another urgent step brought her closer, her incredible beauty alight with passion. "That's what I meant by no expectations. There would be no repercussions to your kingdom or your relationship with the girls no matter what happens between us."

Destroyed by her offer of carte blanche, hating himself and the whole world even more for being forced to do this, her next words cleaved the remaining tatters keeping his heart in place.

"I've been thinking back to the time of your accident. Just before it happened, I was starting to feel restless. You were right when you thought I wanted to change the rules of our liaison. Though it wasn't premeditated, as you had believed. And contrary to what you thought, I wanted to negotiate, not for strings, but for more freedom. Our secrecy imposed too many barriers and limitations, and I wanted to be free of those, not to suggest different shackles. But when I saw your crumpled car, I knew then I only wanted you alive and well. That if I could only have you again, any way at all, I'd never want anything more. That feeling came back to me on the way here, made me face that I prefer the way it ended a million times to having it end…*that* way. And now I can't bear the possibility of missing out on being with you because I didn't let you know how I feel."

He looked away, unable to bear her baring everything inside her to him like that. He wasn't worthy of her courage and generosity, deserved none of her pure and magnificent emotions.

But escaping her gaze only brought her closer, until she touched him. Burned him to the marrow with one gentle, trembling caress on his shoulder.

"All that time, after you said you didn't want me anymore, what hurt most was the confusion, the disbelief. I couldn't imagine that what I felt from you, and so powerfully, didn't exist. Now everything inside me tells me what I felt from you back on the jet wasn't just sex. So please, Leonid…" Her cold, trembling hand cupped his jaw. It clenched so hard he was worried he'd grind his teeth to dust. "Tell me the truth. If you tell me you don't want me now, I'll walk away and this time I'll keep my distance and will never bring it up again. Just tell me, and I promise you, it won't change anything for you."

Tell her you don't want her. Set her free.

But he couldn't look at her and tell another such terrible lie. He couldn't watch the last embers go out in her eyes, and be replaced by the darkness of his final letdown.

Unable to breathe, praying he'd suffocate, cease to exist, he escaped the brutality of her gossamer touch, pitched forward, elbows crashing on his knees and head in his hands.

"Was this my mistake, then and now? Showing you how I feel? Was that what put you off?" And there they were. The tears she'd been holding at bay, soaking her voice as she entreated him one last time. "Leonid?"

He shook his head. Shook, period.

She made no sound, no gasp or whimper or sob. Even her steps were soundless. Yet her anguish as she silently left him was deafening, almost rupturing his head.

He'd hurt her irreparably and unforgivably again.

But now more than ever, now that he knew the sheer extent of her emotions, he knew he'd made the right decision. In the past and now. It was better to push her away, have her hate him, hurt her temporarily…than to do so permanently.

* * *

Kassandra walked through the majestic halls and corridors of the palace, afraid she'd scatter apart if she went any faster.

But she had to hold it together until she reached her quarters. Apart from the eyes that she felt were looking at her disapprovingly and pityingly from those lofty portraits, other hidden ones were monitoring her progress. Leonid's invisible security detail.

Not that they should be worried about him. Their future king was impervious. And lethal. As he should be, as he'd just explained he had to be, to be king.

The distance to her quarters seemed to have doubled. And they weren't her quarters. They were just the place Leonid had exiled her to across the massive palace. Now she knew beyond a doubt why. She had known since the first night he'd avoided her, but just had to make him stab any hope she'd been wrong to death.

Not that she could blame him this time. She'd taken a gamble that there was something between them, something old to resurrect or new to nurture, and she'd lost. She'd thought the slightest possibility she was right had been worth any price she'd have to pay if she turned out to be totally wrong. As she had been.

Leonid didn't want her. That incendiary encounter had been an unspecific response of an overendowed male to a female in heat. And he was clearly disgusted with himself for succumbing to a base urge he feared would jeopardize his priorities: his relationship with the girls, and his position as a king reestablishing a struggling monarchy.

And though it devastated her that she wasn't one of the things he cared about, she understood. He couldn't help how he felt, and how she felt wasn't his problem. He owed her nothing, but owed the girls and his kingdom everything.

So now she had to live up to her promises. Live close to him for her girls' sake, for his kingdom's, playing her expected role for the world, while showing him nothing but neutrality and pleasantness. Even as she withered with futile yearning for him forever. As she would.

In spite of everything, she'd never stopped loving him.

No. It was far worse that that.

Inexplicably, she loved him now more than ever.

"You were married all this time, let us suffer through the scandal of your pregnancy, and you want me to calm down?"

Kassandra winced. Her father's booming voice was loud enough it actually made the phone vibrate in her hand. Not to mention her brain shudder in her skull.

"Hush, Loukas, as if this is important anymore." That was her mother on the other line of a five-way video call.

It had taken Kassandra four days after her last confrontation with Leonid to call her family, who mainly lived in New York but for two exceptions, to explain the whole situation and invite them to the coronation in three weeks' time.

Only four out of the seven who made up her immediate family had been available. Her other two older brothers and another older sister texted to say they'd call as soon as they could. Now she was talking to her parents and two of her siblings.

"But Leonid Voronov… Now, *that's* the relevant thing here!" her mother exclaimed. "How were you even able to hide your relationship? Hide *him*?"

Kassandra sighed. Leave it to her parents to each fix-ate on what they considered the issue here. Her father felt she'd shamed him socially for nothing, and would now make him look like the oblivious father his daughter had ignored in choosing a husband, and her mother was questioning her gossiping network and her own secret-divining prowess.

"What's not making sense to me is that your breakup clearly happened after his accident." That was her old-est sister, Salome, married with four kids and living in Greece since her marriage. "The Kassandra we all know wouldn't have left the man she loved, at least loved enough to marry and submit to those convoluted cloak-and-dagger shenanigans to accommodate his desire for secrecy, when he'd just had a major accident."

"Can't you see you just answered your own ques-tion?" That was Aleksander, her year-younger brother, and almost her twin. "Voronov was the one who broke it off."

"But why, for God's sake?" Salome exclaimed as she rushed to stop her youngest, a four-year-old tornado by the name of Tomas, from dragging her laptop off the countertop. "At the time when he must have needed you most, when you needed to be with him…!" She put her son on the ground and focused back on her. "Say, it was around that time you discovered you were pregnant with the girls, wasn't it?"

She'd already resigned to spending this conversation answering questions, and sighing. As she was now. "I found out just before his accident."

"So he broke it off before you told him?" That was her father again, his voice like rumbling thunder. When she hesitated, he exploded. "He *knew* and still broke it off? And he's back now expecting you to forgive him and give him every right to the girls? I don't care who he is or who he's going to be, this man doesn't deserve to come near my daughter or granddaughters, and I'll see to it that he doesn't! I'll kill him first!"

"Baba…" Kassandra parroted her siblings' similar groans.

"Loukas!" her mother intervened. "You will calm down right this second. You're not going to kill anyone, starting with yourself. I forbid you to have another coronary!"

Kassandra's heart kicked. "Coronary! When was that?"

"See what you did, Rhea?" her father grumbled, looking like a petulant grizzly. "We agreed we wouldn't tell her. Now she'll worry herself silly when it was just a minor thing."

"Minor?" her mother huffed furiously. "You call multiple balloon catheters and stents minor? How about keeping me on my feet and dashing around for days as you whined and grouched and made impossible demands until I literally dropped? Still minor?"

"Don't mind them, Kass." Aleks chuckled, the mellowest male in their pureblood-Greek clan, and the one who'd been fully Americanized. Almost. "They're both back to peak condition, as you can see *and* hear, so don't even start asking what happened. Their tempers have been more hair-trigger than usual since that hospital stay and we won't be able to get them to stop if they start another episode in their Greek-tragedy love affair."

Aleks had always joked that their parents' dramatic fights were their way of spicing up a forty-plus-year marriage.

Looking positively murderous, her father glared at

his son, then turned to her. "I'm bringing your uncles and cousins, even those from your maternal side, to take care of this man."

"Whoa, you're deeming to enlist my brothers' and their progeny's help?" Her mother scoffed. "After forty-three years, they're finally good for something, in your opinion?"

Ignoring his wife, her father focused his wrath on Kassandra. "Russian king or billionaire or mobster or whatever that Voronov guy is…"

"He's actually Zoryan, not Russian," Aleks piped up.

"*Whatever* he is," their father shouted to drown out his youngest son's bedeviling, "we're teaching him a lesson about being a man, one he won't forget in this lifetime."

Kassandra's sigh was her deepest yet. "Congratulations, Baba. Now that you've detailed your plan to cause an international incident, you just made me revoke your invitation to the coronation."

Paternal thunder broke over her again, making everyone grimace and groan. "You're protecting him? He came back to you with puppy-dog eyes and all is forgiven? Not in my book. He needs to know the kind of consequences he faces when he messes with the Stavroses and their own."

"So you're drafting the Papagiannis in your war, but they don't even get mentioned in the credits?" Her mother snorted.

Salome raised her hand like a student seeking to be heard in a raucous class. "Didn't you notice the little detail that he came back with something more than a wagging tail? He's making your granddaughters princesses and your daughter a queen, for God's sake." She turned her eyes to Kassandra, the implication clearly just sink-ing in. "Oh, God, I can't wait to tell everyone here we're going to be European royalty!"

"Is Zorya a European kingdom, or is it counted as Asian?" Aleks mused the pragmatic curiosity on pur-pose, Kassandra was sure, to amplify her father's fury.

Ignoring him, Loukas Stavros leveled a glare at his firstborn, as if Salome had just called him a dirty name to his face. "I care nothing about what he offers. My granddaughters and daughter are already princesses and a queen without him."

Aleks chuckled. "As are all girls to their fathers, espe-cially Greek fossils. Lighten up, Baba, this is the twenty-first century and your daughter is a world-renowned celebrity and businesswoman. She can take care of herself."

"And I *don't* care what she is to the world. To me, she is and will remain my little girl and I'll take care of her as long as there's breath in my body."

"You won't have many of those left if you keep hol-lering like that," her mother grumbled.

Kassandra raised her hand. "I knew I'd regret tell-ing you anything, so thanks, everyone, for proving me right." She turned her gaze to her father. "If taking care of me means bringing the Stavros and Papagianni tes-tosterone mob to Zorya to ambush Leonid, I'll have im-migration revoke your visas at the airport and send you back on the first flight home."

Eyes widening at her threat, knowing she didn't make them lightly, her father pretended to laugh. "You're wor-ried we're going to rough him up or something, *nariy kyria*? Nah, we'll just take him aside and…convince him of the error of his ways. I'm sure he'll be a better husband and father after our talk. This is men's stuff, so leave it to the men."

"Fine." As her father's face started relaxing, macho triumph coating his ruggedly handsome face, Kassandra added, "I'll have them send you home with heavily armed escorts from the CIA and its Zoryan equivalent."

Before her father went off again, she raised her voice, looking at her mother and sister. "About the estrogen posse... I'll leave instructions that the authorities are to sift you from your male components and let you through. But *only* if you promise you won't ambush Leonid yourselves, if for other purposes."

Salome burst out laughing. "After seeing the latest footage of him on the news today? No promises."

Her mother chuckled in agreement. "Don't be stingy. Let the women have some crumbs of your fairy-tale king. You're going to have, *and* eat, his whole cake, forever."

After that overt innuendo, her parents left the conference call to continue their argument in private. Her siblings had dozens of questions for her, each according to his or her interests.

She detailed the hectic preparations for the coronation, and the sweeping changes Leonid was implementing as he transitioned Zorya back to a sovereign state and kingdom. But whenever Salome asked about their relationship, she steered the conversation to Leonid's blossoming relationship with the girls. She wasn't about to tell her sister she'd resigned herself to a lifetime of co-parenting the girls with Leonid as polite strangers.

Not that that was accurate. He wasn't one. She had no idea what he was, had been going insane, constantly exposed to the suppressed emotions and hunger that blasted out of him.

Either she was imagining it, or what she sensed was real. But even if it was, by now she knew he had made up his mind never to act on those feelings, had zero hope he ever would.

For now, she managed to end the call without letting her siblings suspect this whole thing was the furthest thing from a fairy tale, or even an actual reconciliation. Or that she'd never been more miserable, hopeless and confused in her life.

She'd resigned herself to being so for the rest of her life. For the girls, and for the larger-than-life destiny she by now believed was their birthright.

Later that night, after disappearing all day, Leonid materialized like clockwork to have dinner with her and the girls, and to share in all their nightly rituals.

After they put their daughters to bed, he headed out of the wing, saying little, seeming anxious to leave her, alone and unappeased on every level, for another endlessly bleak night.

As he reached the door, she cried out, "Leonid!"

He stiffened, as if her voice was an arrow that had hit him between the shoulder blades. Then he turned, his movement reluctant, his gaze apprehensive.

"I thought I could go on like this," she choked. "But I can't. You never gave me a straight answer and I have to have one. However terrible it is, it will be far better than never knowing for sure where we stand and why, and going nuts forever wondering."

In response, there it was again, that corrosive, devouring longing in his eyes.

"You can't keep looking at me like that! Not when you never let me know what it means!"

He only squeezed his eyes shut. But it was too late. She'd seen that look, could no longer doubt what it was.

Her voice rose to a shriek. "If you want your daughters to have a mother and not a wreck, you must put me out of my misery. Tell me what the *hell* is going on."

His gaze lowered, and she thought he'd escape her again, leaving her to go insane with speculation.

Then he raised his gaze and she saw it. The severe aversion to coming clean. And his intention to do it. At last.

Still saying nothing, he walked toward her. But instead of stopping, he bypassed her. Feeling like a marionette, she followed him until he reached the master bedroom.

After closing the door behind them, he half turned to her. "There's something I need to...show you."

Then he started to strip.

Her stupefaction wavered into deeper bewilderment when she realized he wasn't exactly stripping. Turning sideways, brow knotted, face darkened with pain-laced consternation, he left his shirt on, took off his shoes, his belt, undid his zipper, let his pants drop before kicking them away.

Straightening, he finally turned to face her.

But long before he had, with each inch he exposed, her confusion had turned to shock, then to horror.

One of his legs was a map of livid, hideous scars, where massive tissue had been lost, where fractured bones had torn through muscles and shredded skin, and surgeries had put it all back in a horribly disfigured whole.

His other leg was...gone.

Nine

His leg.

Leonid had lost his leg.

In its place, there was a midthigh prosthesis with a facade that resembled his previously normal leg, looking even more macabre than his remaining, mutilated one for it.

All the instances she'd noticed his difficulties in moving, his discomfort, his pain, came crashing back, burying her in an avalanche of details. Then the wheel of memory was yanked to a stop before spooling back at a dizzying speed to that time in his hospital room. New explanations to his every word and glance, making such perfect sense now with hindsight, thudded into place, decimating everything she'd thought she'd known, until she felt everything in her brain falling in a domino effect.

The wheel shot forward through time again, to

the moment he'd reappeared in her life. The way he'd avoided coming near. Stepped away every time she had. Their time on the jet, undoing his clothes only enough to release himself. Not lying down with her, so she wouldn't find out.

But she should have.

Nausea welled, the bile of recriminations filling her up to her eyes. That she hadn't even suspected the significance of what she'd noticed, what she'd felt from him, that she'd been so disconnected from him, so wrapped up in her own suffering and loss, she hadn't felt his.

Every thought and feeling she'd had, toward him, about him, built on that obliviousness, came back to lodge in her brain like an ax, shame hacking at her.

But it wasn't only because he'd lost a limb. Leonid's loss cut so much deeper than that. His legs, both of them, had been more than a vital part of his body. He'd used them like so few on the planet ever had, turning them through discipline and persistence into supreme instruments, catapulting himself to an almost superhuman level of physical prowess and achievement.

But—oh, God—he hadn't only lost his supremacy, he'd lost the ability to walk and run like any other average human being.

And she hadn't been there for him. He'd been alone through the loss and the struggle back to his feet. Such as they were.

Now he was reversing the painfully stilted process of exposing his loss to her, putting his pants and shoes back on, the difficulty with which he found something so simple shredding her heart to smaller pieces. And that was when she was still shell-shocked. When it all sank in, it would tear her apart.

Not that what she felt mattered. Only he did.

Numb with agony, mind and soul in an uproar, she watched him as he walked to the room's sitting area, his every step now taking on a whole new meaning and dimension. Reaching the couch by the balcony with her favorite view of the grounds and the sea, he sank down as if he could no longer stand.

When he finally raised his eyes to her, they were totally empty, like they'd been when he'd first come back.

"That's your answer, Kassandra. From the look on your face, it's even more terrible than anything you've imagined."

Fighting the muteness to contradict his catastrophically inaccurate analysis, she choked, "It's…not…not…"

"Not terrible?" His subdued voice cut across her failed efforts to put what raged inside her into words. "There's no need to placate me, Kassandra. I know exactly how my legs…my *leg*…and the prosthesis look. They're both right out of a horror movie, one from a Frankenstein-like one, the other a Terminator-like one. It's perfectly normal you're appalled."

Objections burst out of her, her anguish at the way he perceived his injuries, her indignation that he thought the way they looked was what horrified her. But they only sounded in her mind. Out loud, she couldn't say one word.

Keeping his dejected gaze fixed on her no doubt stricken one, he exhaled as he heaved up again. "Now you've had your answer, I hope everything is settled."

Her muteness shattered. "Settled? Settled how? You think showing me this answered anything?"

His teeth made a terrible sound. He said nothing.

More realizations bombarded her. "Was that why?

Why you broke it off with me in the past, why you didn't take me up on my offer now? For God's sake, Leonid, why?"

"What do you mean, why? I just showed you."

"I see no answers here. Absolutely none. What do your injuries and loss have to do with anything between us?"

He looked away, as if to hide his response to her feverish response. She teetered up to her feet, approached him. Her heart broke into tinier pieces as he pulled farther away, as if unable to bear her proximity, guarding against her possible touch.

She stopped advancing, stood trembling from head to toe. "If you think you've given me an answer, *the* answer, all you've done is give me more maddening questions. So just tell me, Leonid. Everything since the accident. *Please.*"

He appeared about to evade her again, then she sensed something crumbling inside him. That...dread of laying everything inside him bare before her.

Heading back to the couch, he sat down heavily. Wincing, supersensitive to his every move more than ever, she followed him, sat far enough away to give him the space he needed.

Then he talked. "Everything started *before* the accident. While I was training, I realized our arrangement had only been satisfactory because we were together almost every day. Being apart from you made me realize I wanted to be with you, all the time, all my life. I wasn't sure if you felt the same, but I was going to risk it. I was going to propose."

She'd thought she was now prepared for anything he'd say, would hold it together no matter what he threw at her. But this confession made her collapse back on the couch in a nerveless heap.

His expression blipping momentarily at her reaction, he went on. "Even if you'd said no, I'd have waited until you one day wanted me enough or trusted me enough, if that was the issue, to change your mind. But before I could, the accident happened. Then you came to me.

"I'd just been told my legs were beyond salvaging. I also had a spinal injury, and they thought I'd suffer severe erectile dysfunction or even total impotence."

Falling deeper into shock, every second brought her more proof the past two years had been built on misconceptions and ignorance. She'd known nothing of the life-uprooting blows he'd suffered, and he had chosen to suffer alone.

Oh, God, Leonid.

"I was agonized I'd never be a competitive athlete again, would at best rehabilitate enough to walk with a minimum of pain. But what devastated me most was knowing I'd never be the man you'd wanted so fiercely, and had taken such pleasure in."

Before she could cry out that she would want him whatever happened, his next words made her see how he would have never believed it, how he'd convinced himself of the opposite.

"But I knew you were noble, and if you knew, even when it repulsed and horrified you, you wouldn't leave me. I couldn't have you stay with me out of pity. I couldn't saddle you with an impotent cripple. I would have been worse than useless to you, a constant source of unhappiness. I knew even if I was selfish and terrified enough that I clung to you, I'd lose you anyway, when the reality of my situation drove you away in disgust or crushed you in despair.

"I decided to drive you away, without letting you even doubt my prognosis, thought it better to do it at once, rather than in a slow and far more mutilating ordeal. But I didn't expect you to make it that hard. You forced me to push you away as viciously as it took for you to leave me, to save yourself.

"Just as I thought I succeeded in setting you free, you told me you were pregnant. I asked if you'd keep the baby, vaguely wishing your pregnancy wouldn't continue somehow, or that you'd maybe consider giving the baby up for adoption, so you'd sever every tie you had to me, so you could restart your life unburdened again."

This. This was it. What she'd gone insane for, the explanation for his sudden cruelty and coldness, what she'd felt had to exist, but had to accept didn't, to her deepening heartache. But it existed. It explained everything and rewrote history. He'd forced himself to hurt her, fearing he'd destroy her if he didn't. He'd loved her so much, he couldn't let her share the bleak fate he'd thought awaited him.

His gaze swept downward, as if he was looking into his darkest days. "The next months were a worse hell than even I'd imagined they would be. The least of it was the anxiety over my impending physical losses. The memory of hurting you became more suffocating as time went by. My sanity became more compromised as I lived in dread that what I'd hoped for you, that you'd move on, would come to pass, and *then* feeling even worse when it didn't, when you had Eva and Zoya and confined your whole life to them.

"After many setbacks, they managed to save one of

my legs, if in the condition you saw. My spinal injury healed without any neurological deficit, and they hoped I wouldn't be impotent. Not that I could test that. All I could do was struggle to heal, physically and psychologically, and cope with my new, severe limitations. And all that time, I watched you and the twins obsessively from afar as you went through everything I should have been there for, alone.

"Then I was back on my feet, real and prosthetic, just in time for Zorya to call me to duty. And though I never dreamed of having anything with you again, I was no longer going to let anything keep me from being there for you, and from serving the family you gave me, the family I never had, and my country.

"But the moment I saw you again, I knew. My potency was more than intact, and the separation and suffering had only left me perpetually, ferociously starving for you. Yet I had to stay away. You deserve better than the disfigured wreck I am now. I…I would have rather had my remaining leg cut off than let you see me this way, and see that look of horror in your eyes. But your anguish and confusion cornered me into showing you. Now you can at least understand, if not forgive, everything I did."

He fell silent, breathing strident, eyes reddened, face clenched as if with fighting against unbearable pain.

She stared at him, paralyzed.

The enormity of what he'd suffered and lost overwhelmed her. And through it all, he'd selflessly, if mistakenly, thought only of her needs, and not his own.

But his last words had been the worst. Along with his irrevocable losses, his self-worth had been shattered.

The tears finally came, pouring out of her very soul as if under pressure.

Grimacing as if she'd stabbed him, he groaned. "*Bozhe moy*, Kassandra, I can't bear your pain, or your pity."

"Pity? *Pity?*"

Finding nothing that could express her outrage at how totally he'd misconstrued her reaction, she charged him, knocking him back on the couch and climbing all over him, trembling hands groping every inch of him, real and replacement. Inert with shock, he lay beneath her as she smothered him in hugs and kisses and drowned him in tears.

"How dare you... How *dare* you think anything you suffered could have burdened me or put me off? How *could* you make that decision for me, deprive me of being there for you through your ordeal? Didn't you realize I would have given anything to be with you at all, let alone in your darkest time? Didn't you realize that whatever you lost only makes every inch of you even more precious to me? If I could give you a limb to restore yours, I wouldn't think twice."

Looking dazed by her fervor, this last bit made him shudder. "Don't say that, *Bozhe moy*, Kassandra, don't..."

"I'll say it because it's true. Because I love you. You are the only man I loved or would ever love."

He looked even more flabbergasted. "How can you love me after what I put you through, no matter the reasons?"

She grabbed his face, forced him to look at her, as if to drive her conviction into his mind. "I now know I must have always felt what's in your heart, never believed what you said in mine. It was what agonized me most, that what I felt and what I thought I knew were such opposites. Your reasons would have been more than enough to forgive you if you'd done much worse that just pushed me away, and thinking it was for my own good."

His breathing, which usually never quickened due to his supreme fitness, came in rapid, ragged wheezes beneath her burning chest. "Kassandra, you don't know what you're saying, you're shocked by what you saw and heard, feeling sorry for me…"

"Oh, my beloved Leo, I do feel sorry, but not only for you, for me, for us. I am crushed with regret, because I wasn't there for you through it all, because you deprived me of you, throwing us both in hell apart. I feel as if my heart is splintering because you deprived yourself of me and my love and support, of our daughters, missed out on having them bless your life and heal your heart during your darkest time, as they would have even before they were born. But I'm not letting you deprive us of each other anymore. Marry me, Leonid, my love, my only love, for real and forever."

His eyes had been reddening more with her every word. But with her last words, his face contorted and air rushed into his chest, as if he'd been drowning and was drawing a lifesaving breath after breaking the surface.

His eyes glittered, but not with the tears she rained over his face. With what she'd thought she'd never see. *His* tears.

"Don't decide anything now, take time to think, wait…"

Her trembling lips silenced his working ones. "You've been making me wait since I first laid eyes on you. Before you let us be together, while we were together, since you pushed me away and since you came back. And I can't wait anymore. I won't, ever again. I will never waste another moment waiting or worrying or doing anything but loving you and being with you."

And his tears flowed. His body shook beneath hers as she cried out, moved beyond endurance, sobs rocking her.

Straining over him, as if she wanted to slip beneath his skin, to hide him under hers, she moaned into his gasping lips, "Stop thinking, stop assuming what's best for me. You are what's best for me. You are everything I ever wanted for myself. Will you give me everything I want? Will you give me yourself?"

His tears flowing faster, his body beneath hers easing toward impending surrender, he said, "But I'm not the man you once loved anymore…"

She pulled back, let him see himself in her eyes, willing everything she felt for him to restore his faith in himself. "You're not. You're better. Far better. Your ordeals have tempered you into the purest, strongest, best form of yourself. I loved the man you were, but when forced to, I could live without him. I can't live without the man you are now."

"It was the inferno of yearning for you." She gazed in confusion down at him and he elaborated. "What tempered me."

"Then, say yes, Leonid. Marry me, be with me, love me and never leave me alone again."

Tears froze in his eyes as his gaze deepened, as if trying to probe her soul, filling with so much vulnerability, disbelief and hesitation she felt she'd burst with it all.

Slowly, conviction seeped in, followed by dawning elation. Then it was as if he was letting her see into *his* soul for the first time, and all she saw there was…love.

God, *so* much love. Adoration.

"Kassandra, *moya lyubov*, my love, if you'll have me, if you'll let me love you for the rest of my life…yes. Yes to anything and everything you want or will ever want."

Flinging herself at him with all her strength, she bombarded him with tear-drenched kisses, reiterating her supplication. "You. You're all I ever wanted or will ever want."

"And you are everything," he pledged as he surrendered to her fervor, his voice as deep as the sea, and as turbulent with fathoms-deep emotion, mirroring what his eyes detailed. "From the moment I first saw you, I was always yours. Even when I believed you'd never be mine again, I remained yours. I would have remained yours forever."

Suddenly everything inside her exploded into a devastating blaze of lust. After this beyond-belief declaration, she felt she'd crumble if he didn't merge them in every way, right now, hard and long and completely.

Shuddering with need, she scrambled off him, tugging him up with her. He followed her silently as she stumbled to bed, stood watching her as she flung herself onto it, searing her with his hunger.

"Love me, Leonid." Her voice was a husky tremolo that fractured with the desperation of her passion. "Now that I know you love me, *show* me."

Groaning, he came down over her, filled her arms, his hands trembling all over her, as if afraid she wasn't real. Her hands shook in turn over his stubble-covered jawline, up the chiseled planes of his divine face until they dipped into his raven-hued hair. Pulling him closer, her desperate lips clamped over his, her tongue restlessly searching their seam. A pained rumble escaped him as his tongue lashed out to snare hers, duel with it.

His rumbles deepened, filling her, shaking her apart; his hands owned her every inch, setting it ablaze. Reaching her buttocks, he squeezed hard, as if trying to bring himself under control.

Needing him to unleash everything inside him, devastate her with it, her thighs fell apart for him, begging his invasion. "Since you took me again, needing you has become agony. Please, do everything to me again."

Groaning, he nodded, snatching her clothes off her burning body. But as she undid his pants, tried to push them down, his teeth clenched, like his hands over hers.

"Don't. I don't want you to see me like that."

She freed her hands from his convulsive grip, grabbed his face, needing him to believe her once and for all. "I already saw you, and it did horrify me, but only to realize the extent of your injury, what you lost, what you're suffering. But for me, the scars and prosthesis are now part of you, and I love and crave all of you. I'll forever feel thankful whenever I look at them and see a reminder that I still have you, that fate didn't take you from me and granted me the miracle of being able to love you and share our daughters and everything I am with you."

Groaning as if in searing pain, he buried kisses in her palms mixed with tears and a litany of her name and *lyublyu tebya*. It was the first time he'd said it. *I love you.*

She drowned him with her reciprocation.

Getting rid of her last shred of clothes, he freed himself and brought her to his daunting hardness. Shaking with the need to impale herself on it, she threw herself over his chest, pushing his jacket off, teeth undoing his shirt, needing his flesh on hers. But he stopped her again.

"Let me pleasure you like that. I did on the jet, didn't I?"

He meant without exposing himself, at all. He didn't want her to see any part of him, probably was concealing other scars.

He was teetering on the edge of control between her thighs, everything about him promising her the explosive pleasure he'd given her before. She only had to say yes and his hot, throbbing girth and length would slam inside her, in that rough, frenzied tempo that had made her orgasm around him repeatedly on the jet before he'd made her come one last time as he'd climaxed deep inside her.

But… "I want you to *love* me this time. With all of you. I want to make love to all of you."

He held her gaze for one last second before capitulating.

Laying her back on the bed, he rose on his knees, started to take off his clothes. She whimpered as each button, each shrug revealed more to her starving eyes.

She'd been wrong. He hadn't just been upgraded; he'd metamorphosed. This was what the next step of evolution had to look like. And there *were* more scars, crisscrossing his chest, running down his arms and abdomen, interrupting the dark, silky patterns adorning his magnificence. And to her, they looked like arcane patterns, bestowed by destiny, marking him as chosen for glory and uniqueness, and were as beautiful and arousing as everything else about him.

Surging up, she traced the scars with worshiping hands and lips, making him shudder harder with every touch and nip. Delighted to discover they were even more sensitive than the rest of him, would amplify his pleasure, she got bolder.

"Kassandra, you're driving me past insanity."

"Just like you do to me. Stop tormenting me and let me see all of you. Now, Leonid."

Naked from the waist up, eyes averted, he stood up and exposed the rest, his movements so reluctant it squeezed her heart with anguish. He hated doing this, was sick with self-consciousness, still unable to believe she wouldn't cringe at his physical damage and deficit. It would have been easier to let him hide from her. But she couldn't. It would only become a barrier.

She was done letting anything come between them.

She lay back, spread herself, gaze devouring him. "Look at me, my love. See how much more arousing I find you now. Every inch of you is stamped with maturity and power, more than ever. The marks of your suffering tell me incredible stories of endurance and persistence. They're like brands of triumph and they only make you more unique to me. Give me everything you are, my darling Leonid."

Exhaling raggedly, he nodded, growled something ferocious at the sight of her spread in surrender before him. Coming down on the bed, he prowled over her like a ravenous tiger, fully exposed, dauntingly engorged. His hands sought her secrets, her triggers. He took her mouth in a rough kiss before he withdrew, his eyes flaring and subsiding like blue infernos.

"Every single inch of you, every word you say, every breath and look—you are an aphrodisiac I could dilute and dispense to the world and cure all sexual dysfunction. Had I suffered from any, you would have cured me."

Unable to hold back anymore, she writhed beneath him, twisted over him. Realizing what she wanted, he reversed their positions, spread himself for her, letting her have his mind-blowing potency where she craved it, in her watering mouth. He let her do everything she wanted to him, explore him with darting tongue and trembling hands, growling his enjoyment of her homage.

"Own me, *moya dorogaya*, take what's always been yours."

Unable to bear the joy of knowing it had been the same for him, that it had to be her and only her, she took it all, roaming his leg, his prosthesis, his potency, all of him.

She wanted to ask him to take his prosthesis off, let her touch what remained of his leg without barriers. But he'd already crossed too many lines to accommodate her need. That had to wait until he had no lingering doubts of how she'd react, or discomforts in exposing the rest of his vulnerabilities to her.

She was lapping his arousal, more rushes of molten agony flooding her core as she wondered how she would accommodate that much demand, when his hands on her shoulders stopped her. She cried out in frustration, only to find herself on her back again. She held out her arms, hurrying him, hands flailing over whatever she could reach of him. Chuckling his gratification at her urgency, he drowned her in a luxurious, tongue-mating embrace, before he suddenly started extricating himself from her clinging limbs. She whimpered, tried to drag him back, but he restrained her hands.

"Patience. This time, I'm doing this right."

She tried to drag him back with her legs. "You did it right the first time and every time. Just do it again."

He bit into one of the thighs clinging to him. "I will do it, again and again. But I want to do something first."

Getting off the bed, he strode out of sight, then suddenly the chamber was plunged in total darkness.

Her heart thudded. Was he still loath to make love to her while she saw all of him? Or maybe now that he *had* let her see all of him, he needed the respite of darkness?

Suddenly silver light engulfed the whole bed. It took her several stunned heartbeats to realize he'd thrown the drapes and inner shutters of the enclosed balcony open to the night sky. The full moon was framed in the middle of the paneled windows. The moonlight was so intense, she could see nothing outside its domain, didn't know where Leonid was now.

"This is how you should be showcased…" She lurched at his bass rasp as he seemed to materialize before her moonstruck eyes, a colossal shadow detaching from the darkness, made of mystery and magic. "A goddess of wanton desires, of rampant pleasures, waiting for worshippers to come pay homage, glowing, ripe, voracious, spellbinding."

She was all that?

She could only murmur, "Look who's talking."

He came into the moon's spotlight, the stark illumination casting harsh shadows over the noble sculpture of his face, turning it from regal to supernatural. His skin and hair glimmered with highlights as he pushed her back on the bed, loomed over her, the full moon blazing at his back, turning him into a magnificent silhouette. Only his eyes caught its silver beams, glowing like incandescent sapphires. She went limp beneath him with the power of it all, the sheer brutal beauty of him, of these moments.

Her chest tightened one last time over the jagged pieces of the past, the terrible memories, before it let them go, then swelled with the new and uncontainable hopes and expectations. Those of having him again. This time, forever.

Crying out, her desperation shattered the last shackle holding him back. He lunged between her eagerly spreading thighs, letting her feel his dominance for a fraught moment.

"Moya boginya..." Gazing into her streaming eyes, calling her his goddess, he plunged inside her with one long, hard thrust.

Her body jerked beneath him as the hot, vital glide of his thick, rigid shaft in her core drove her into profound sensual shock. She clamped her legs around him, high over his back, giving him full surrender, delirious with witnessing the pleasure of possessing her seizing his face. He ground deeper into her until his whole length was buried inside her, filling her beyond capacity. Sensation sharpened, shattering her. She cried out again, tears flowing faster.

He started moving, severing eye contact only to run fevered appreciation over her body, watching her every quake and grimace of pleasure, all the while growling driven, tormenting things.

"How could there be wanting like this...pleasure like *this*?"

She keened as he accentuated every word with a harder thrust. He devoured the explicit sounds, his tongue invading her mouth, mimicking his body's movements inside her.

Her sanity burned with the friction and fullness of his flesh in hers, the fusion, the totality of it, now that she knew it was indeed total, and would never end.

Her cries grew louder as his plunges grew longer,

until she clawed at him for the jarring rhythm that would finish her. Only then did he build to it, his eyes burning, his face taut, savage with need, sublime in beauty. She fought back her own ecstasy, greedy for the moment his seized him.

Realizing she was holding back, he growled, "Come for me, *moya koroleva*, let me see what I do to you."

Her body almost erupted hearing him call her *my queen*.

But she held on, thrashed her head. "Come with me…"

Roaring, he thrust deeper, destroying her restraint. Release buffeted her, razing her body in convulsions. Those peaked to agony when he succumbed to her demand, gave her what she always craved. Him, at the mercy of the ecstasy of union with her, pleasure racking him, his seed filling her in hard jets. She felt it all, and shattered.

Time and space vanished as he melted into her, grounded the magic into reality, eased her back into her body.

Everything came back into jarring focus when he tried to move off her. She caught him. His weight should have been crushing, but it had always been only anchoring, necessary. Like he was.

But he'd never let her have his weight as long as she wished, insisting it burdened her. He now rose on outstretched arms, his eyes gleaming satisfaction over her ravished state.

"Koroleva moyey zhizhni." He trailed a gently abrasive hand over her, eyes worshipping. "Queen of my life."

A vast thankfulness expanded inside her so hard,

she could barely speak. "How do you say 'king of my world'?"

His whole face blazed with pleasure and pride, his drawl painfully sexy and harsh with emotion. *"Korol' moy mir."*

"Korol' moy mir."

Whispering the pledge against his lips, she could say no more as perfect peace, for the first time in her life, dragged her into a well of contentment where nothing else existed...

Live classic Zoryan music woke Kassandra from a delicious dream filled with Leonid.

The royal band was rehearsing in the seafront gardens again for the coming ceremonies.

Though the drapes were securely drawn, and the chamber was dark, she just knew. The sun was shining today.

It had been shining the past two weeks. Everyone she met insisted it was the blessing of the new king and his twin stars. Kassandra was ready to believe it. If happiness like this was possible, then maybe it bent the very laws of nature to itself, too.

It had changed *her* on a fundamental level. Her heart beat to a different rhythm, her skin had a richer texture, colors had magical hues and life tasted and smelled of him.

Leonid.

Even if she was back in her quarters, and he hadn't been sleeping beside her this past week, practically had no time for her at all in his consuming preoccupation with preparations, she felt him all around her.

And as if he hadn't been insanely busy enough, he

was now preparing living quarters for *them*, not his or the ones she was currently staying in, but something totally new and theirs, now that their marriage would be real.

She'd refused to even see where it would be, wanted him to surprise her. Even as a designer, her imagination could never match what his love would bestow on her.

Now he was running against time so it would be ready on the day of the combined rituals: his coronation, and their wedding.

God…their wedding!

She still couldn't believe any of this was happening.

When she'd asked him to marry her, she'd thought they'd elope, since they'd told everyone they were already married. But Zorya's newly reformed royal council wouldn't sanction an undocumented marriage as proof of the twins' legitimacy. Leonid had said if she hadn't proposed that night, he would have the next morning. Zorya was demanding a wedding to fix their lack of documentation. And from what she was seeing, it was going to be the royal wedding of the century. Her family, who would come two days before the rituals, were all beside themselves with excitement. Yes, even her father.

Everything felt like a fantasy. Far better than one. She constantly found herself wondering if she was having a ridiculously extravagant wish-fulfillment dream and would wake up to the bleak reality of two weeks ago.

Could everything really be this perfect?

Suddenly, her heart contracted with foreboding.

Pausing until the spasm passed, she wondered at the far stronger than usual attack. Seemed the approaching ceremonies and the superstitious bent of this land had her spooked.

Pushing the ridiculous and unfounded anxieties away, she rose and rushed through getting ready.

Hurrying to the girls first, her mood soared again as they concluded their morning rituals. Afterward, she left them with Despina and Anya and went in search of Leonid. Though she'd been leaving him alone to take care of his endless details, she had to see him today. Just touch and kiss him, before leaving him to his urgent affairs.

As she reached his stateroom, Fedor informed her that Leonid had a surprise visit from an important royal family member.

Before she told Fedor to ask Leonid to touch base with her when he could as she didn't want to call and disturb him, the door opened, and what she thought a Valkyrie would look like walked out. And it was clear she was not happy.

Suddenly, Leonid appeared after the woman, and the expression on his face froze her heart. He looked... pained.

The woman turned to him and they shared a charged moment. She was clearly angry. He appeared to be doing all he could to placate her.

Refusing his efforts, the mystery statuesque blonde turned away, leaving him looking more distressed. In a minute she passed Kassandra as she stood in the shadows. Surprise flickered in the woman's eyes before she impaled her on a glance of hostility and walked away.

Leonid just then noticed her and rushed to her, his expression trying to warm, and failing.

Heart thudding, she asked, "Anything wrong?"

He waved. "A trivial dispute. Olga already doesn't approve of my policy making. She'll come around."

Then, kissing her, he promised he'd be there for dinner as usual, excused himself and rushed away.

After watching him until he disappeared, she walked back slowly, wrestling with tremors all the way back to her quarters. It had to be that time of the month making her morose, making her find normal things distressing.

But…if this was normal, why had Leonid lied?

For she had no doubt that he had.

Was there anything else he could have lied about? Like the reason he hadn't been sleeping with her since they'd announced their coming wedding ten days ago?

Had her intuition that nothing could be this perfect been right?

As the girls received her with their usual fanfare, she tried to shake those insidious, malignant doubts.

But they'd already taken root.

Ten

"I so hope Princess Olga will get over her disappointment soon."

Kassandra's hands froze over the gold-and-black costumes she'd designed for Eva and Zoya for the ceremonies.

Anya's words brought images of the incredibly beautiful and regal Olga assailing her. Standing toe-to-toe with Leonid, looking like his female counterpart, every line in her majestic body taut with emotion.

Did Olga's disappointment have to do with Leonid's impending wedding to her? Was that why she'd shot her that antagonistic look? Was she what stood between Olga and the man she wanted?

Forcing herself to sound normal, she asked, "Disappointment over what?"

"That she won't be queen."

That was the first time she'd heard that. No one around here, including Leonid, had told her the details of what had led to him being announced the future king. Even in the news, when other candidates were said to exist, they were never named, since Leonid was the only one who mattered, the one with the global fame and clout.

"So she was one of the candidates for the throne?"

Anya, who Leonid had appointed as her lady-in-waiting, nodded. "She was actually the preferred one. Not only has Zorya always preferred female monarchs, since its birth at the hands of a queen and under the mantle of two goddesses, but Olga is the spitting image of Esfir, Zorya's founder and first queen. Many believe she's her reincarnation."

Kassandra's heart started to thud. "So what happened?"

Oblivious to her condition, Anya handed her another needle threaded with the last color Kassandra needed to finish embroidering Zorya's emblem on Eva's skirt.

"Prince Leonid was always the better candidate, logically speaking, outstripping Olga, and anyone in Zorya for that matter, in wealth and influence by light years. But everyone in Zorya would have overlooked all that because of Olga answering Zorya's specific criteria better. We are a land steeped in tradition and legend, and our beliefs in what makes us Zoryan rule supreme. Olga was an omen, representing our founding queen, a return to the glory days, a rebirth. But *then* Prince Leonid produced something even better. Nonidentical twin daughters, the very personification of our patron goddesses. That made the scale crash in his favor. The representatives of the people and the new royal council were unanimous that it was a sign from the fates. You, my lady, naming them both names meaning *life*, heralding a new life for the kingdom, was, as you Americans say, the cherry on top."

Kassandra tried not to stare at Anya as if she'd just shot her. But the woman's next words felt like more bullets.

"Before Prince Leonid announced the existence of the royal twins and his marriage to you, Princess Olga's supporters advised her to marry him, so Zorya would have him and his power as the queen's consort. So you can understand her disappointment that she not only won't have the title, but won't have the best man on earth as a husband. I only hope she gets over her displeasure and starts collaborating with Prince Leonid. Zorya needs them both."

Three hours and endless details later, Anya left her only when the girls' costumes were done.

Still in an uproar over the revelations, which Leonid hadn't once hinted at, Kassandra continued her efforts to distract herself, now having the girls try on the costumes they'd just finished.

Looking at her daughters in the ornate dresses she'd designed to reflect their new home's history, their new roles as the kingdom's icons, she couldn't help but believe they were born to wear them, to be princesses, with a legacy rooted in tradition and legend.

No wonder the people whose beliefs were based on the lore of the two goddesses thought them a sign from the fates.

But those same people bowed to tradition so much, they'd still refused to sanction such signs' legitimacy based on an undocumented marriage, and had demanded a new wedding. That had been what Kassandra wanted most in life. To marry her beloved Leonid on the same day he became king.

At least, it was what she'd wanted until a few hours ago.

But now…now…she didn't know what to think.

Actually, she did know. And it was…terrible.

If Leonid had needed Eva and Zoya to win the race for the crown, if this is why he'd come for them, it changed everything.

It meant he hadn't come back for them as his daughters. He'd only needed them as his ace, which would trump anyone else's claim, even the preferred heir. But what about her?

Had everything that had happened between them been second to attaining his goal? Was he now marrying her because it was the one way to seal the deal? Or was it far worse than that?

Could it be Olga had always been his preferred choice, but he wouldn't accept anything less than being king himself, with her by his side as his queen consort? Could Kassandra be simply the more convenient choice, a means to make the best of a terrible situation, since he adamantly believed that he and the girls were what was best for the kingdom?

Could he be that driven to become king, over anybody's hearts and lives, including his own? Could it be all that passion, all those emotions, all the things he'd told her, had all been him doing whatever it took to fulfill his duty, to claim his destiny?

From then on her projections grew even more morbid. Maybe he was biding his time until after the coronation and the wedding, when his need for her would end, so he could leave her for the woman he wanted for real.

If so, was what he'd told her that day in his hospital room the truth after all? That he'd never cared for her, hated her clinging and couldn't wait to be rid of her?

It all made sense in a macabre way. For if it didn't, why had he come back for the girls, and according to him for her, too, only when Zorya had announced its secession and its revival of the monarchy? Why hadn't he told her anything about Olga or his need for the girls to secure the throne before? Was he really as preoccupied as he appeared, or was he only unable to feign desire for her anymore?

If *any* of that was real, how could she go through with the wedding? How could she give him every right to the girls?

If any of those horrible suspicions were true, it made him a monster.

"Yes, sir, I understand."

This statement, or variations of it, had been all that Leonid got to say for the past half hour, as Kassandra's father gave him a winded lecture, liberally peppered with ill-veiled threats, about manhood, marriage and family life.

At least it seemed his total submission to the man's badgering and his unqualified acceptance of his menacing directives appeased the proud and forceful Greek man. Now Leonid decided to put his mind to rest completely.

"I assure you, Kyrie Stavros, I left Kassandra only because I thought my life was over after the accident, and I believed it was for the best not to tie her life, and the twins', to someone as damaged as I was. But I've since been restored more than I dreamed possible, and Kassandra, and Eva and Zoya, have completed my healing. Kassandra is my heart, my everything, and I'd give my life without a second thought to never hurt her again. I *will* give my life to make her happy."

Loukas Stavros's eyes had widened with every word, seemingly impressed by Leonid's impassioned declaration, which he clearly hadn't expected.

Reeling back his surprise, Stavros tried to pin austerity back on his face. "As long as we understand each other."

Fiercely glad that Kassandra, and the twins, had such a man, such a family to love and protect them so fiercely, Leonid's lips spread in a grin. "We certainly do. And thanks for your restraint. If it was me talking to the man who left either Eva or Zoya pregnant and heartbroken, I would have taken him apart first, *then* given him the lecture."

The man flung his arms at him in a see-what-I-mean gesture. "I told her that! But she threatened she'd ban me from ever entering Zorya if I didn't give my word to take it easy on you!"

Leonid laughed, his gaze seeking Kassandra. His golden goddess was fierce in her protectiveness of him.

Finding her nowhere, he turned his attention to Stavros. "That sounds very much like our indomitable Kassandra. I'm only glad you complied so you can attend the wedding, and give her away as is your, and her, right. But if you want to discipline me afterward, I'm at your service."

The man gave him an excited wolflike grin. "It seems you and me are going to get along, boy."

Leonid grinned back at him as widely. "I have no doubt we will. I would get along with the devil if he loved and cherished Kassandra. But as my father-in-law, and my daughters' grandfather, you automatically commanded privileges few in this world do. Now after meeting you, you've just moved to the top of my list."

Stavros laughed. "The list of devils?"

Leonid winked at him. "I do have a weakness for my kind."

Stavros guffawed louder and thumped him on the back so hard he almost knocked him off his unsteady feet.

By the time Stavros moved on, the demonstrative man had inundated him with enough physical gestures to tell him he was already family to him.

Relieved that he'd won over the most important man in Kassandra's life, Leonid turned to the other people who sought his attention at the reception, all the while seeking Kassandra, to no avail.

The coronation, and more important, the wedding, was tomorrow, and her whole family, all two-hundred-plus members of it, had arrived in Zorya the day before. She'd been lost in their sea ever since. Not that she'd been easily found before that. In the two weeks after they'd come together, he'd almost killed himself to wrap a million things up so he could rush back into her arms. But once he could, there had always been something stopping her from taking him there. For the past week she'd either been busy, sleeping, out or just unavailable when he'd sought her.

Even when he did see her, he couldn't help but notice she'd...changed. She was subdued, as if all her fire had gone out. She'd only told him she had her period, and it was a particularly distressing one, what with all the preceding events.

But when he'd thought they'd go to meet her arriving family members together, and she'd gone alone, all his past doubts had crashed back on him.

For what if, after the first rush of sympathy for what had happened to him, it had all sunk in, that she'd be tying herself to a man who wasn't only damaged, and who in spite of her protestations, she found revolting, but who would be the king of a country passing through turbulent times for the foreseeable future? What if she dreaded all the tension and trouble he would bring into her own life by association?

But though it agonized him to think any of that could be true, he dreaded saying anything to her even more, in case she validated his suspicions. So he'd chosen to convince himself she'd been having wedding jitters, that whatever it was, it was a passing thing that had nothing to do with him, or their impending marriage.

But when the reception ended, and she'd reappeared only to entertain her guests while keeping dozens of feet and people between them, he could no longer fool himself.

Something was wrong. Horribly wrong.

Three hours before the coronation and wedding ceremonies, Leonid stood before the full-length mirror in the quarters he'd relinquish forever tonight to move with Kassandra to the ones he'd slaved over realizing for her, her perfect wonderland.

His traditional Zoryan regal costume fit him perfectly. And weighed down on him absolutely. But he realized it wasn't the lifelong responsibility it represented that was getting him down, but the hovering dread that he wouldn't be bearing its burdens with a happy Kassandra by his side.

Then, as if he'd summoned her with his anxiety, Kassandra entered his quarters.

Just one look into her extinguished eyes told him.

His worst fears were about to be realized.

Forcing himself to ignore his trepidations, he rushed to take her in his arms. His heart almost ruptured when the woman who'd dissolved with passion in his arms a couple of weeks ago turned to stone there now. When she was supposed to walk down the aisle with him to a lifetime together in mere hours.

Before he could choke out his anguish, she whispered, "In spite of everything that happened, and how you came back into our lives, I believe you now love our daughters."

Confused beyond words at hers, he again tried to reach for her. "Kassandra, *moya lyubov'*…"

Her hand rose, a feeble move without any energy. It still stopped him in his tracks. "I also do believe you'd make Zorya the best king. So for our daughters and for your kingdom, I'll walk out there in three hours and marry you, Leonid. But for myself, I want things to go back to what you intended before. A marriage in name only, with separate lives."

Feeling his world coming to an end, he couldn't even breathe for long moments until he thought he might suffocate.

It was finally uncontainable agony that forced the choking question from his lips. "What changed?"

"Nothing changed. Things only became clear."

He squeezed his eyes, his whole left side going numb.

Things were clear to her now. When he'd been trying to cling to the hope that she'd never come to her senses.

"It's too much for you, isn't it?" he rasped. "You tried to pretend my mutilation doesn't appall you, but it does, doesn't it? You can't face a lifetime of curbing your revulsion at the sight of my stump, to the feel of my scars, can you?"

Her gaze deadened even more. "You can pick whatever reason you want. I'll back up any story you decide on."

"Story?"

"If you ever need grounds for divorce."

With that, she turned and walked out, looking like an automaton.

But somewhere in the tornado that was uprooting everything inside him, he knew. She was now going to put on her wedding dress, then she'd walk with him to the altar, pledge to be his wife and queen, and instead of love and joy, he'd see in her eyes that she no longer wanted him. But out of duty to her daughters and their kingdom, she would still walk into the prison of being with him forever.

He couldn't let her do this to herself.

He had to set her free, forever this time.

Shattered by her brief yet annihilating confrontation with Leonid, Kassandra had gone back to her quarters, where all the women of her family had gathered. In a fugue, she surrendered to their fussing as they dressed her in the fairy-tale dress Signor Bernatelli had designed for her. She thought she'd talked, smiled, even laughed, putting on a show for her family's sake, for Eva's and Zoya's, for Zorya's.

After her suspicions about Leonid's intentions had

erupted, wiping out her sanity, they'd receded enough to make her see the facts. That Leonid did love Eva and Zoya, with everything in him, and they loved him back. He was everything they could have hoped for in a father. Also undeniable was the fact that he was a formidable force for good, and as Zorya's king, he would not only save the kingdom, but he'd stabilize the whole region.

As for his feelings for her, whatever he'd felt before, she now believed he was trying sincerely to be as attentive and loving as he could be. In the past week, he'd resumed seeking her, yet it had been as if it hurt him to do so.

Whatever it was, it wasn't as sinister as she'd thought in that first wave of insanity. He was trying to do his best for all of them. It was she who was too greedy, too damaged. She couldn't take what he was offering, when it was far more than what most women could dream of. Because it wasn't everything. She'd either have all of him, or none of him at all.

In keeping with tradition, everyone left her for one last hour of solitude before the wedding. As the minutes counted down to zero, she waited to be called when the ceremonies began.

Then Anya walked in, looking stricken.

"My lady, it's terrible. An absolute shock!"

Kassandra shot to her feet, her blood not following her up, making her sway. "What happened?"

"Prince Leonid has left the palace. After calling Princess Olga and relinquishing the crown to her!"

Among the total mayhem Leonid's departure had caused, Kassandra clung to one thing.

The letter he'd left her.

Not that she'd even tried to read it. His actions had spoken far louder than anything he could ever say. That she'd catastrophically and unforgivably misjudged his feelings and misread his intentions. Again.

She'd exploded from the palace in search of him five hours ago. She'd taken Fedor and he'd driven her to every single place he could think of where Leonid might be. Leonid had turned off his phone, hadn't been anywhere they'd searched. There'd been no sighting of him anywhere. Yet there was no evidence that he'd left the kingdom.

After the last failed attempt, she broke down and wept until she felt she'd come apart. But she got out his letter, hoping it would give her a clue where he'd gone.

Shaking so hard, eyes so swollen, it was almost impossible to read it. But she kept trying.

And every word killed her all over again.

Kassandra,

I will never be able to beg your forgiveness enough or atone enough for everything I cost you, every heartache I caused you, but I'll make sure you never again sacrifice your well-being and desires for anything, starting with me. I will always love you, and our daughters. You will all, always, have everything that I have. But I only want you to be free and happy. While I will always be infinitely grateful for all the happiness and blessings you've given me, I only wish I could take back the suffering I've inflicted on you. But since I can't, I can only cause you no more.

The letter ended, no signature, no closing, just this ominous pledge. The whole message sounded like... like a...

No. No. *No.*

Then it erupted in her mind. A memory. A realization. Of the only place he could be. *Had* to be. One with significance only to him, where he'd taken her and the girls, saying it had been his favorite spot when he'd been a child. The one memory he had of his parents, where they'd taken him right before they died.

Crying out for Fedor to find it, knowing just a name and a description, it felt like forever before Fedor found out where it was. All that time terror hacked at her, that she might have pushed him into doing something drastic.

Then they were there...and...so was Leonid.

He stood in the distance, looking over the frozen lake where his parents had taken him skating for the first, and last, time. A colossus among the snow, looking desolate, defeated.

"Leonid!"

He jerked so hard at her shriek. He must have been so lost in thought that he hadn't heard the car's approach. He almost lost his balance as he swung around. Then he gaped.

She knew how she must look to him. Maniacal, her elaborate wedding gown tearing in places, hair falling all over out of its chignon, eyes reddened and bleeding mascara, the rest of her makeup streaked down her swollen face.

She only cared that she'd found him. That she'd give her life to make it up to him, that she still had the chance to.

When she was a few dozen feet away, he started talking, voice hoarse and even deeper than usual with bleakness. "You shouldn't have come, Kassandra. I meant every word, that only your happiness and peace of mind matter to me."

She would have closed those final feet between them in a flying leap that landed her against him. The old Leonid would have caught her midair as easily as a pro basketball player caught a ball. But as it was, she could knock him off his feet or even injure him. She'd done enough of that, and she'd die before she hurt him again.

"I don't want you to feel bad," he choked. "It's not your fault..."

And she wrapped her arms around as much of his bulk as she could, squeezed him until she felt her arms would break off.

Stiffening as if with insupportable pain in her arms, he groaned in protest again. "Don't, Kassandra. Don't let your tender heart overrule your best interests again. I don't matter..."

"Only you *ever* mattered." She shut him up when he attempted to protest, surging for his precious lips, taking them in wrenching kisses, pouring her love and agony into him. Then she told him what she'd learned that day from Anya, and how it had set off the chain reaction of uncertainty.

"I've lived with the demons of doubt tormenting me for so long," she sobbed in between desperate kisses. "And they overwhelmed my reason. I was terrified you couldn't possibly love me as totally as I love you, that I couldn't be your one and only choice, and that you were only struggling to accommodate my emotions to make the best of a less-than-ideal situation for all involved. And once I thought that, I couldn't do this to you, couldn't bear having you on those terms." Tears poured thicker, sobs coming harder as she mashed her lips against his. "Please forgive me, my love, forgive me for letting malignant insecurity drive me insane enough to commit the unforgivable crime of doubting you again."

As he started to push away, to get a word in, she clung harder, sobs dismantling her soul as she rushed on to confess her original sin.

"I should have *never* walked away when you asked me to. I *knew* you were at your lowest, *knew* you couldn't be in your right mind. Your decision to push me away for my own good was wrong. But the blame for everything that happened is mine, for not insisting on staying, taking anything from you, until you realized I'd a million times rather be miserable with you than at peace without you. I'm the one who made us all suffer."

"Now, wait a minute here…"

She cut across his protest. "No more waiting. And no more doubts or distance of any sort, ever again. I'm never leaving your side again. And I'm *not* letting you relinquish the crown."

"Kassandra, listen to me…"

"No, you listen. I'm not letting you even think of abandoning something this enormous and imperative, your duty to the land only you can rule."

"If you'll just let me get a word in here…"

"What word would that be? If it's not yes to everything I've just said, don't bother. Zorya needs you as much as I and the girls do." She stopped, grimaced. Every cell hurt with loving him so much, finding him so damned beautiful. "Okay, so that's not true. Anyone else, even the girls, can live without you. I can't. And I never will. I need you to believe this, my love, and understand it as a fundamental fact of my being. For the girls, my family and work, I can exist, appear to be functioning, for a lifetime if need be. But to *live*, to know joy and ecstasy and peace, I need you. Only you."

Anguish and insecurity evaporating slowly in his eyes under the flames of her fervor, he caressed her face with trembling hands, the love in his gaze so fierce it seared her to her soul, the raggedness in his deep, velvet voice heart wrenching.

"It was so easy to fall prey to my own demons as soon as I felt your withdrawal. They convinced me I repelled you, and the kingdom's duties and dangers oppressed you. And I would rather die a thousand deaths than inflict a moment's unhappiness on you. But without you fueling my will to be, nothing else mattered. Leaving everything behind became the only thing I could do, and my one desire."

Before she could lament a protest, his lips shook in a smile of reassurance. "But Olga will make a fine queen. And with you by my side again, I can again function, can serve Zorya as her advisor, as a businessman and politician. But it is better for our family that I step down now."

"If you're referring to those moronic fears I had at the start, please forget I ever said anything so stupid. Whatever hardships will be involved in reestablishing the monarchy, this is your *destiny*. I will eagerly and proudly share in all its tests and burdens, and be the happiest woman on earth, because I will do it all with you, and will have the honor and delight of being your succor and support through it all."

And she felt it, the exact moment he let go of the last traces of reluctance and doubt and hesitation. Then she was in the only home she ever wanted, his embrace, crushed and cherished and contained.

"You've got one thing wrong, *dorogaya*. The crown isn't my destiny. You are. You and our girls." Suddenly he groaned. "But how can I now go back and demand to be crowned? After I left the whole kingdom in the lurch?"

Caressing his chiseled cheek dreamily, she sighed. "Don't you worry. Everything about you is the stuff of fairy tales, and when I'm finished playing the media, the whole world will be raving about the king who started his rule with a romantic gesture for the ages. Bet you will go down history as a legend to rival that of the goddesses or even Cinderella and Prince Charming."

His breathtaking smile singed her to her toes. "You mean *we* will. Even though the roles were embarrassingly reversed here, and it was the big, lethal hero who ran away."

A laugh bubbled from her depths. "Leaving me a priceless letter instead of a glass slipper."

His eyes glowed with so much love it caused a literal pain in her gut. "And you didn't send people to look for me, but cast out your love like a net to find me."

Suddenly a storm of honking erupted, jogging them out of their complete absorption with one another.

Swinging around in shock, they found their whole wedding party, six-hundred-plus strong, descending from a fleet of limos. Fedor must have reported their position. Or her testosterone tribe had followed her GPS signal. Or her friends had had their Triumvirate comb the planet for them.

Whatever had really happened, they'd found them and were advancing on them en masse. In the first line of the approaching army were her parents, each with a girl yelling for Kassandra and Leonid in their arms.

Before they reached them, she looked up at Leonid, her soul in human form, the source of every towering emotion she'd ever experienced and the fuel for every ambition and passion and delight for the rest of her life. He was looking back at her, so hungrily, so adoringly, she again wondered how she could have ever doubted his feelings. But never again.

Heart soaring with all the endless possibilities and promises of a lifetime with him, she suddenly grinned at him.

"How about you demonstrate one of your unique abilities to the good people who came trudging through the snow after us?"

His eyes filled with the mischief that had started appearing in his eyes in those short days of bliss, the bliss that would now be their status quo.

"The Voronov Vacuum Maneuver?"

Devouring his lips once again, she caressed his chiseled cheek. "Right the first time."

Laughing, the most delightful sound in heaven or on earth, he opened his arms wide.

The girls launched themselves there, and stuck.

As she explained the property he and the girls, the pieces of her soul, shared, everyone laughed. Then their interrupted wedding guests inundated them with a hundred questions about what was going on.

As they tried to escape answering any, her friends, their Triumvirate and her siblings came to their rescue.

Selene, hooking her arm around her own Greek god, grinned. "You people just have to get used to having a very unconventional, unpredictable king and queen. Don't bother trying to figure them out."

Aristedes grinned adoringly at his wife and corroborated her words. "There's no doubt that under Leonid and Kassandra's rule Zorya will rise to unprecedented prosperity, but it won't be in any way you people would expect. So just sit back and enjoy their reign."

Maksim nodded, grinning, too, as he hugged Caliope to his side. "Now you'll add a new legend to your impressive arsenal, that of The King Who Ran."

Caliope smiled from ear to ear. "And The Queen Who Brought Him Back."

Naomi chuckled. "With yours being a femalecentric culture, that gender-reversal twist on Cinderella and Prince Charming is right up your alley."

Andreas kissed the top of Naomi's head, clearly loving the wit of his wife's remark. "One thing is certain. With those two and their twin stars, I assure you, you'll be forever entertained."

Aleks chuckled. "Indeed. I have a feeling those two will treat us all to lifelong episodes of an epic Greek *and* Slavic–in-one drama. I, for one, can't wait to watch it unfold."

As everyone laughed, Kassandra's eldest brother, Dimitri, who'd spent last night's reception wrapped around Olga, cleared his throat importantly.

"And now I interrupt today's episode with a news bulletin. A message for you, Leonid, from HRH Princess Olga."

As everyone turned to Dimitri, all ears, he smirked.

"The lady is telling you, quote, she'll be your spare heir, until your real ones grow up, but that would be it. You have to get back where you belong, that lofty palace you spent bazillions renovating, put that crown on your head and take the weight of this messed-up kingdom on your endless shoulders. And if you think every time she pinches your ear over some state policy you can flounce away and say you're not playing, you have another think coming, unquote."

Dimitri turned his bedeviling gaze to Kassandra. "*And* she thought you were the reason Leonid was being so uncharacteristically lenient as to approve that policy that made her blast him. But I assured her you're a shark, and that as soon as you knew he didn't use his many rows of teeth when he should have, you'll straighten him, and those teeth, out. And that if she ever needs anything at all done to him, including twisting him into a pretzel, you're the girl to call." He winked broadly at her. "She thinks you'll be her new best friend."

Leonid again laughed along with everyone, unable to believe what a difference an hour made. A minute. A word. Even a breath from Kassandra turned his world upside down, then right side up again.

And she'd given him everything he'd never dared dream of having, dissipating the darkness of despair and insecurity and guilt forever. She'd given him certainty, stability, permanence. She'd taken him and would keep him, no matter what—scars, fake parts, burdens and obsessions and all.

And he finally knew what happiness felt like. And boundless hope. What he'd been scared to even wish for since he'd lost her that first time.

She'd given him everything. And more.

As everyone's voices rose in side conversations and questions and proddings, he was unable to go on another second without another kiss.

Everyone hooted and said they should have brought the minister with them and completed the wedding right here.

Whispering to Kassandra, she just nodded delight-edly and said, "Anything you want, always."

He addressed the crowd. "I apologize for the drama I caused, though it seems you all enjoyed the mystery and the exercise. But my queen and bride has decreed we go back and resume the interrupted ceremonies, even if by now they'll be concluded long after the sun of the new day rises. I hope you're all game."

As everyone's voices rose in approval, he squeezed his little princesses, who were beside themselves with the excitement of the unusual circumstances.

"And now it's time your papa took you back to your new home, where you will always be the earthbound Zoryan stars that will guide me with their bright light, and the blessing of our kingdom."

As everyone walked back to the limos, Kassandra, whose tears of joy had been flowing freely, reached for his lips, her voice thick with emotion, sultry with hunger.

"I've got news for you, my liege. After all the odds you've beaten, how you've survived and become far more than you've been, how you've come back for us, how you love us and how you make our lives far better than any dream, the real blessing is you."

He hugged the twins tighter, hugged his Kassandra until he felt her under his skin, inside his heart, cours-ing through his veins and pledged, "And I am all yours totally, irrevocably…and forever."

* * * * *

LET'S TALK
Romance

For exclusive extracts, competitions
and special offers, find us online:

f facebook.com/millsandboon

  @MillsandBoon

  @MillsandBoonUK

Get in touch on 01413 063232

For all the latest titles coming soon, visit
millsandboon.co.uk/nextmonth